REUNION
in Time

RAY HANLEY

outskirts
press

Reunion in Time
All Rights Reserved.
Copyright © 2017 Ray Hanley
v5.0

This is a work of fiction. The events and characters described herein are imaginary and are not intended to refer to specific places or living persons. The opinions expressed in this manuscript are solely the opinions of the author and do not represent the opinions or thoughts of the publisher. The author has represented and warranted full ownership and/or legal right to publish all the materials in this book.

This book may not be reproduced, transmitted, or stored in whole or in part by any means, including graphic, electronic, or mechanical without the express written consent of the publisher except in the case of brief quotations embodied in critical articles and reviews.

Outskirts Press, Inc.
http://www.outskirtspress.com

ISBN: 978-1-4787-8469-2

Cover Photo © 2017 Ray Hanley. All rights reserved - used with permission.

Outskirts Press and the "OP" logo are trademarks belonging to Outskirts Press, Inc.

PRINTED IN THE UNITED STATES OF AMERICA

Author's Introduction

This book has been years in the making and comes from my long-time interest in both Arkansas history and the genre of time travel science fiction. I've sought to blend a fictional time-travel story with a very real, but little studied, chapter in Arkansas history: three days in May of 1911 when the Capital City of Little Rock hosted the annual meeting of the United Confederate Veterans or UCV. At that time, the city's population was 45,000, about a fourth of what it is today. During those three days, however, the population reportedly swelled to 150,000, a crowd that would be unsurpassed until the night in 1992 when Arkansas Governor Bill Clinton was elected President.

The book was written over a period of about five years while I was working for Electronic Data Systems (EDS), the computer services firm founded by Texas billionaire Ross Perot. I would fly some two million miles during this period and started this book early in that segment of my career, usually writing a page or two during each flight on my laptop. Thus the story was written almost entirely at 35,000 feet.

Just as the historical event of the UCV annual meeting in Little Rock is real, so as well are many of the characters the fictitious Dr. Kernick meets while traveling through time – ranging from governors to congressmen to Confederate veterans like General Shaver or the old veteran trying to find the owner of a bible picked up on a bloody battlefield a half century earlier. Newspaper archives from 1911 document that these real-life characters actually said many of the things attributed to them in this book. I've previously authored or co-authored 20 Arkansas history books, but this is my first venture into historical fiction. Special thanks to my friend Gloria Gordon of North Little Rock for reading and editing more than one draft of this manuscript. I hope you enjoy the story.

Ray Hanley
Little Rock, Arkansas 2016

Chapter 1

Year of 2026

"JACK, PLEASE COME quickly. I need you," was the plea coming from my old friend Charlie Rawlins as I lifted the phone. Brief words, poured out in short seconds, but words that opened a tale so incredible I hesitate to put it to paper lest I be taken for mad and committed to an asylum. Yet, compelled I am to write this all down while it's still real to me. For those under whose eyes it will fall, you can believe or not. It doesn't matter, for I know what actually happened 15 years ago, or in a real sense most of it happened 115 years ago.

I stood, in the spring of 2011, looking out the rain-streaked window of my overpriced condominium on Little Rock's President Clinton Avenue, listening to the frightened pleading in my old friend's voice as he said, "It's Dave, I know what happened to him. He was murdered, but I think you can save him. I know it sounds crazy, but……."

"Charlie, slow down. What? Murdered, Dave? How? Who?....I'll call the police" was all I could say in a failed attempt to slow the cascade of frantic words from my friend of many years.

"No, no!!! They can't help. It's too crazy. You have to come today and give me a chance to show you. I need you. Dave needs you."

"Charlie, I don't understand. Murdered?... But I can save him?... What are you talking about?"

"Just come, please Jack." In the resounding silence that followed, all I could say was, "I'll be there by 3:00 this afternoon. Charlie's parting words rattled me further: "It could be…uh…a long trip I will ask you to take, but thank you my friend."

I dropped down into my chair and leaned back to collect my troubled thoughts in an office crammed full of books. My cat Henry took advantage of the opportunity to leap into my lap, blissfully unaware of my state of mind, as images of my friend Charlie flooded my mind as I remembered many shared life-changing events. Charlie – small, wiry, with snow white hair and beard – was a retired college physics professor who lived in the deep woods near the hamlet of Little Italy, some 40 miles west of Little Rock. His wife, Rosie, had died a decade ago, leaving him and a son, Dave

Dave, last I saw him closing in on his 30th birthday, was born late in life to his devoted mother and eccentric but adoring father. Dave was the light of his aging father's life and had traveled the world as a journalist and sometimes explorer/adventurer, sending frequent letters, photographs and emails from around the world. When he was in Little Rock, the two of us would often dine with his father, sometimes poking good-natured fun at Charlie's current theories, which ranged from how the human race would go extinct to time travel. He talked about his varied inventions that always seemed to be "in progress" but unfinished that were housed in the laboratory located in the massive barn behind Charlie's old farmhouse. Little did I know as I sat stroking Henry and staring out into the rain that one of Charlie's inventions would soon propel me on a journey beyond even my wildest imagination.

"It may be a long trip," had been Charlie's parting words. With that thought in mind, I retrieved a shoulder bag from my closet and tossed together some clothes, my blood pressure medication, and a first aid kit. As an afterthought, I packed my Colt 45 pistol. Then, thinking better of it, I unpacked the gun and put it away. Surely any trip to help Charlie wouldn't require a gun. Not a standard part of a physician's luggage, but then – while I was a doctor – I probably fit few people's images of the healing arts.

I had semi-retired from the practice of medicine after profiting handsomely by investing early on a few years ago in the drug company that invented Viagra. I'd grown weary of dealing with too many people with more aches and pains than my own and a system choked in paperwork and lawyers. I'd chosen to spend my days toying at writing books and walking in the Arkansas woods with a camera and my imagination about what I wanted to do with the rest of my life....something that – at the age of 50 – perhaps I was overdue to decide. I'd acquired a permit for the gun as a part of my training and part-time work with the Little Rock Police SWAT team, which provided me some interesting adventures that I may one day choose to tell. If I could only have known what lay in store..........

Racing to meet with Charlie, I left Henry in the care of my elderly, pleasantly nosy neighbor, Mrs. Longinotti, and I exited my building into a rainy, raw day, surely to be soaked before reaching my truck parked down the street. As I raced for the truck, a voice I knew better than any other echoed from half a block away, "Dad, Dad.... wait for me." Turning, I saw my 21-year-old daughter, Lydia, leaping puddles, her broken umbrella doing little to keep the cold rain off her blonde head.

While I was normally delighted by the often unannounced visits of my tall, gorgeous and ever perplexing daughter, given the urgency of my summons from Charlie, I was taken a bit off guard.

Hunkered back under the overhang of my building, I watched Lydia wrestle with her broken umbrella, a mischievous smile on her rain-washed face, saying, "Gee Dad, why the glum look? Aren't you glad to see your loving daughter?" A recent college graduate, still sorting through career and boyfriend options, she had a way of drawing everyone's attention, whether entering a crowded room or standing on a rainy sidewalk.

"I've been over in the Stephens building for an interview. What kind of stock broker do you think I'd make?" Considering her degree in pre-med, this question should have made me laugh, as I could anticipate her following up with, "What, me become a doctor? Look what it did to you Pop?" – an oft-repeated remark that was designed to make me crazy. "Where are you headed in this monsoon? Buy your favorite girl lunch?" As was her pattern since she learned to talk, she fired more questions without pausing for answers. "Running away from home?" she jested upon noting the stuffed bag looped over my shoulder.

I quickly related the urgent, strange call from Charlie, leaving out the part about Dave's "murder" for now, along with the part about how I was supposed to "save him." Not surprising, Lydia announced she was coming with me, perhaps for the pleasure of my company but also, I suspected, because she had long been attracted to Dave, with his rugged good looks and globe-hopping lifestyle. She had also grown up with a "favorite uncle" affection for Charlie Rawlins, who doted upon her on frequent visits over the years.

On the drive out of the city, the rain-soaked pavement narrowed, with housing tracts giving way to forest, and Lydia prodded me for details of Charlie's plea for help. "Dad, I didn't know doctors still made house calls. What's the whacky old coot into now? Don't hold back on me." I described Charlie's rattled message, including the part that Dave had been murdered but that I could still "save him." Lydia's breath caught in her throat at that part, and she sobbed aloud. The sobs gave way to a forced, somewhat successful effort at composure....a part of a daughters failed attempt to hide her feelings for a young man from her father – an age-old pattern repeated through centuries, I expect, of father-daughter relationships.

We drove the rest of the way mostly in silence, with Lydia staring out the window, lost in a jumbled maze of thoughts and remembrances of the beloved Dave. We turned off the county road onto Charlie's farm and Lydia left the truck in the rain to open the gate, ignoring the "beware of dogs" sign that she knew full well applied to Charlie's only remaining geriatric golden retriever. A quarter mile down the mud hole-filled path that passed for a driveway, we pulled into Charlie's front yard behind his motor home that was parked under a shed that once almost killed me. I had been part of group of friends trying to add a foot's height to the shelter to accommodate a newer, taller behemoth on wheels when bracing jacks slipped and the entire structure fell over. Only a well-placed tree stopped the falling shed short of mashing me into my eternal reward. Things just happen when you are around Charlie. Now some sixth sense was telling me what I'd been summoned for would make the falling shed near-death experience pale by comparison.

When Charlie didn't answer our knock on the front door, we made our way around the corner of the house in a yard littered with cast-off machinery parts interspersed with pink plastic flamingos. I briefly pondered the ridiculous image of the tropical bird replicas decorating the wooded retreat of my eccentric friend and wondered if I was equally as out of place and ill-suited to respond to his call for help. I said a silent prayer for my friend that I could at least ease his pain.

As we started down the graveled path to the enlarged 19th century barn that served as Charlie's workshop, we were greeted by the fiercely barking Pharaoh, his grizzled old golden retriever. The threatening barks quickly turned to tail-wagging recognition, as he turned about to lead us through the side door of the workshop into Charlie's office. Despite Pharaoh's best efforts, Charlie seemed unaware of our presence, as we were greeted by the back of his snowy head bent over a work table littered with papers. With Pharaoh tugging at his sleeve, Charlie stood up and saw us for the first time, a mixture of anguish and relief flooding his tired, craggy face.

Only then, when Charlie straightened up and turned in the light of the lamp on his work table, did I see the coat and clothing he was wearing. I stared in open-mouthed astonishment, speechless, when I realized he was wearing what almost certainly was a confederate soldier's gray uniform, with a sergeant's rank on the faded sleeves.

Lydia moved quickly and wrapped her arms around Charlie's neck, concern evident in the tone of her voice, "Charlie, hope you don't mind my tagging along with Dad here, but maybe I can help both of you." Charlie leaned around her and clenched my hand in the grip of a much younger man. "Thank you Jack for coming. This is so, so…. hard and confusing." A tear rolled down his lined face. Stepping back, Lydia looked Charlie up and down, taking in the confederate uniform for the first time and said not a word.

Trying only partly successfully to pull himself together, Charlie directed us to "Sit down, please. I've got coffee on, or maybe something stronger. You may need it to bear with me through explaining this nightmare I've created." We sat down at the table and took the coffee, sensing it might well need to be something stronger soon, as we watched Charlie pace the room. He finally stopped to stare out the window, his back to us and hands clenched behind his back.

"Charlie…please tell me what happened to Dave", I begged. "There's been nothing in the papers. The news on the radio says nothing about any murder. Please, tell us what happened? Lord knows, you have been under some awful strain, and that uniform? We want to help. Just tell us what has happened."

Across the table from me, Lydia fought back tears, struggling with what to say but uncharacteristically at a loss for words. Charlie turned slowly away from the window, collapsed in the chair at the head of the table and said, "Dave is dead, has been for 100 years." Knowing we must think he'd lost his mind, he added, "He was murdered on the dome of the State Capitol the night of May 18, 1911."

Chapter 2

THE STUNNED SILENCE blanketing the room with my friend's pronouncement that his son had been dead longer than any of the three of us had been alive was finally broken by Lydia: "Charlie, you're not well. You have to come back to town with us. Let Dad get you some help, the hospital maybe…" She rose from her chair and started around the table to him, with a look in her eyes that silently asked, "What do we do now, Pop?"

Before I could come up with something to say, Charlie said, "Please, I know you think I've lost my mind, and maybe I have or else I would never have created the machine that caused the death of my son. But as guilty as I am, I'm not mad. Dave did indeed die in 1911. Please bear with me and you will believe me shortly."

Lydia dropped back into a chair on my side of the paper-strewn work table while Charlie shuffled through what were obviously copies of old newspapers and handed us a folded photocopy of the Arkansas Gazette. I saw from the dated banner heading across the top page that it was the edition of May 19, 1911. The headlines were all about the previous day's parade that closed out the reunion of The United Confederate Veterans that apparently had drawn tens of thousands of spectators. I still had no clue what this had to do with Dave's disappearance. Reaching the crease in the fold, I turned over the paper to see the bottom half of the front page. Lydia, standing behind me to read over my shoulder, solved the riddle before my older tired eyes that were focused on the photo. "Dad, Dad….it's Dave! It is him….isn't it?"

In a hushed silence, Lydia and I read the story that appeared under a photo of a man who certainly appeared to be Dave with a heading, "Do you know this man? Unidentified Man Shot, plunges off dome of New Capitol Building".

It continued, "Amidst the celebrated glories of our heroes in gray that gave Little Rock its greatest crowds in history is a stunning mystery that led to the death of a night watchman at the new State Capitol and the shocking death of the unidentified man seen in today's paper."

"The photo was taken earlier this week by one of the studio photographers working overtime during this week's reunion. We know this because the photographer, Jon LeMay, was at St. Vincent's Infirmary when the Little Rock Police carried the battered body into the side entrance to the hospital located only three blocks from the Capitol. Mr. Lemay recognized the deceased from a visit he had made to the photographer's studio, apparently a day or two earlier. What happened between the time of the studio pose and the man's death is capturing much of the attention of the police today."

Sitting back in my chair, I could only look from the newspaper copy to Charlie, and say, "This is a bizarre nightmare, Charlie. Its .... it's just not possible. Somebody is surely playing some cruel hoax on you."

As Charlie turned back to the window with an admonition to "keep reading", I joined Lydia in following the rest of the article

"The account given by Police Chief Tom Robinson early today leaves many questions unanswered, not only the man's identity, but why a lone night watchman at the still uncompleted new Capitol building was found shot dead on the marble floor of the rotunda, why the man pictured here was on the ledge around the outside of the building's dome, and who shot him before he plunged to the ground near the front steps."

The Police Chief declined to confirm or deny rumors, but speculation is that the shocking events may be related to violent crimes that occurred during the course of this past week when our fair city was almost overwhelmed with an estimated 100,000 visitors."

The story told of violent robberies over the preceding days. Two banks had been robbed at gunpoint, with the wounding of one teller. A third robbery, getting by far the larger headlines, dealt with the late night assault on Cave's Jewelry. A number of loose diamonds and gold watches were taken when a safe was broken open, but that was not the loot that generated the bold headline. Whether or not the robberies had been committed by the same people seemed undetermined.

Charlie handed me a printout of another 1911 newspaper with a glaring headline, "GENERAL LEE' SWORD TAKEN IN A DARING ROBBERY. In the latest of an embarrassing string of violent crimes assaulting our fair city, a shocking late night robbery has resulted in the injury of an elderly night watchman and, to the great anger of the gathered heroes of the noble south, the loss of the sword of General Robert E. Lee."

"The sacred sword of the Confederacy's leader, the surrender of which Gen. U.S. Grant refused to accept at Appomattox, was on loan from the state of Virginia for the duration of the reunion. On display in the Main Street window of Cave's Jewelry store, the sword and the store were under the guard of night watchman, Julius Jenkins. The old gentleman, himself a Civil War veteran, was wearing his Confederate uniform while on duty in honor of the reunion this week."

"Mr. Jenkins remains in guarded condition this morning at St. Vincent's Infirmary, to where he was removed last night after being found sprawled in the broken glass on the floor of the looted jewelry store. Though suffering a head wound, the elderly gentleman was able to tell the police that he was in the backroom of the store at around 11:00 last night when the store's back door leading from the alley was broken open. He was quickly set upon by two large men wearing white pillowcase-like masks over their heads. When Mr. Jenkins regained consciousness sometime later, bleeding from about the head, he discovered the store's jewelry cases broken and looted. Stumbling out onto Main Street, Mr. Jenkins summoned a passing patrolman…and only then. to his horror did he discover the bandits had also taken General Lee's sword from the store's front window."

"An award has already been offered for the return of General Lee's sword, with the first contribution coming from Worthen Bank, and quickly matched by the editor of Arkansas Gazette, William Heiskell."

I dropped the paper on the table and got up to pace the room, my mind filled with images created by the century-old newspaper account of a truly bizarre affair. "Charlie, guess you need to start at the beginning with all of this…We'll just be quiet and listen. Then we can decide what to do."

Chapter 3

CHARLIE, EERILY NOBLE in the faded Confederate uniform with his snow white hair, leaned over the table and said as calmly as a sane man would mention the weather, "I invented a machine that makes time travel possible. It has caused the death of my son, and I think likely Cabot and Sexton committed at least some of the other crimes you read about in the 1911 newspaper stories." Clearly the look on our faces suggested we thought him quite mentally ill, but we were both at a loss for words in light of what we had seen and read over the preceding half hour.

"It may be easier to show you while I try to explain," and with that, he asked us to follow him through the door into his laboratory. When we entered the large adjoining room, the automatic sensors turned on a bright bank of overhead lights, drawing our attention immediately to an elevated platform, perhaps six feet square. A tarp-draped shape was sitting in the center of the platform, tilted toward the ceiling, looking surprisingly reminiscent of the scud missile batteries I'd seen in the 1990 Gulf War. Charlie pulled the tarp away with the flick of a wrist to reveal an elongated machine, equipped with two seats, a built-in computer bank, and what appeared to be twin lasers on the front of the machine. It reminded me of a scaled down fighter jet complete with a plexi-glass cover over the two-seated compartment, but lacking wings and a tail fin.

"I built this machine and an identical one over a period of the last three years with the help of two men who later betrayed me. As crazy as I know you must think me, you must believe me that Dave journeyed back to 1911 in one of these machines where he was murdered, as you have just read. I'm almost certain my two associates also went back in time and are responsible for the violence and murders described in the old newspaper accounts." "Charlie, this is…." I started to express my raging doubts, but Charlie stopped me in mid-sentence. "No, Jack…please, please just sit down. Give me some time. Listen and then afterwards you will believe me, help me, or just declare me insane…for if I can't make this right, then insane I may be."

Totally confused at this point, Lydia and I sat on a work bench and watched Charlie pull around a chalk board covered with a maze of equations and notes. For an instant, I had a flashback to the old Disney movie with Fred MacMurry – something about an absent-minded professor who created science defying inventions. A few hours later, I would have traded the role in which I'd been cast with any Disney movie – any movie for that matter I'd ever seen.

"Jack, don't you recall the many conversations we had about the science of time travel?" "Sure," I said, "but it was only after about the fourth beer that I was able to even begin to imagine the idea."

"Well, it is possible. It has been done," said Charlie, "and I of all people wish to hell it had remained in the realm of science fiction."

"The idea of time travel has been around for at least a century," Charlie told us, gathering his thoughts and assuming a semblance of his old professor's stance in front of the board. "Isaac Newton espoused the theory that the universe was divided into four dimensions, three of space and one of time. In 1916 young Albert Einstein went further to promote the possibility of time travel with his general theory of relativity." Charlie, by this point, knew Lydia and I were not going to benefit by an in-depth lesson in theoretical physics. "Let me cut to the chase of how this is possible."

"You know that I was doing classified work for the Department of Defense up until four years ago," he said to jog my memory. It came back to me, something about the Nuclear Regulatory Commission, along with weapons research. "Yes Charlie, I recall part of this, but you were always pretty vague about what you were doing, by necessity I guess."

"Yes, yes, lots of secrets." Charlie's voice trailed off, perhaps lost in memories and regret. "The project was halted abruptly, rather than submit to a Senate Oversight Committee's push to audit the project's budget. The commanding General overseeing the project also dropped dead… uh… in the company of a woman who was, well…other than his wife, shall we say. But I digress… sorry. Let me get to the point and tell you what I must ask you to do for me and for Dave."

"When the project in Colorado ended abruptly I watched in horror, along with my fellow scientists, as a group of soldiers swept through the facility, collecting our notebooks and work papers 'for security reasons' they said, but one told me all records of the project were to be destroyed."

Charlie paused to let us collect our confused thoughts and then continued, "I had anticipated the possibility of this – having monitored government agencies for much of my life, and was appalled at the waste of the science, the potential…though even I had doubts at the time that time travel could be achieved. I handed over my notebooks, and the soldiers secured my computer. But what they didn't know is I'd downloaded the work onto six flash drives that were tucked away in my pants pocket.

"When I came back to Arkansas to resume teaching at the University in Conway, I told myself I'd try to forget about the project. Maybe I could have left it alone, but late one night on TV, I saw the Senate Oversight Committee hearing where some bird Colonel was being grilled about what the money spent in Colorado had been used for. The son of a bitch…uh, sorry Lydia, said we were doing work on a missile defense technology…..lying SOB. It made me furious."

Putting aside the contempt for military bureaucracy common to academics, Charlie tried again to explain to us in layman's terms how time travel was indeed possible.

"Again, it goes back – at least in part – to the thinking of Einstein, that treats the world as one that is four dimensional, that is three of space and one of time." Ignoring our blank looks, he rambled on in a rapidly rising pitch, to conclude with, "the machine blasts the body's electrons with a positive charge to drive one back in time, or a negative charge to move forward in, and software in the actual machine binds it to the body for the trip. "Blast?" I had to interject at this point. "That sounds, uh, painful, even fatal." "How do you know this really works? Are you certain these newspaper articles about Dave are not some sort of elaborate hoax?"

Lydia stood up and begin pacing the floor, joining in the cascade of doubt and confusion. "And even if...just if...it is possible to travel in time how can you control where you end up? How do you know you won't end up in front of some hungry dinosaur, or at Custer's last stand? Or in the middle of War World II somewhere?"

Charlie, ever the patient professor, looked up at us, not at all offended by our doubts, and said, "I know it works. Surely you do as well after reading those newspapers." Not allowing for interruption, he continued, "the geographical location will match the one from which a traveler left, or an alternative location if so programmed, thanks to the machine's onboard GPS device that gets the location fix before it leaves the present time, but the year is a bit trickier. It's essential to set the machine to propel you to the desired place on the time stream by controlling the level of the negative neutron charge."

"But how do you know?" was all I could say, still unable to grasp what was becoming all too real, that the machine sitting in a building in the rainy Arkansas woods could indeed send a human back in time. "Charlie, I just don't believe it. It's..... it's just too crazy...."

Undeterred, Charlie continued, "It was a process of trial and error. First I sent a camera, set on a timer, back in forth, pointed up at the sky. Each time I brought the camera back from the past, I cross-referenced the location of the stars in the photos taken against a computer program that shows where those stars would have been positioned at any point over the past couple hundred years." Taking our silence for slowly emerging understanding, he continued, "At first nothing matched up. I assumed I'd applied too much of an electrical charge, which sent the camera further back in time than the ability of computers to track the locations of stars. Science has only mapped the solar system with any degree of accuracy back to around the year 1100 AD."

"But how? I think I understand, you know, where the camera went, but how in the world did you even get it back?" I asked.

"Easy," he said. "It was sent inside a box that had an opening for a wide angled lens. The box contained software programmed to reverse the electric charge to positive, which pushed it back in the time stream an identical distance to which it had earlier been sent. The GPS returned it to this room once it entered our time and got a fix on the satellites that control the GPS."

Picking up where I'd interrupted, Charlie continued, "By trial and error, and a lot of long nights of CPU time on the college mainframe in Conway, I got the process down to where I knew the exact electron charge it took to hit a time period within a window of three days, that was as close as I could get. My next test was, while a camera would withstand the trip process, what would be the effect on living tissue. Fortunately, I had a friend.... good old Pharaoh." Hearing his name, the old dog jumped up to place his feet on Charlie's lap, seemingly proud of his contribution to science.

"Six months ago I sent Pharaoh back to May 10, 1900 to land in the clearing that would have been in front of my old barn at that time. He wore a timed camera around his neck, and a programmed laptop computer in a pouch on his side. It was a close call, I found out later when I printed the pictures.....Oh, here they are." The stack of grainy, jerky photos he handed me showed the back end of a deer darting back and forth as I flipped through the photos. "Old Pharaoh apparently hit the ground and immediately eyed a deer he just had to chase. He's just lucky he didn't lose the computer in the brush before the program recalled him back to the lab here. He was on a retractable harness, I guess its pull at the end of the cord brought him up short and he returned to the platform back in the lab. He and I trained for three days in a row before I sent him back in time."

"I ran lab work and did a CAT scan on the dog at the college lab. I was thrilled to find Pharaoh was as healthy after the trip as before time-traveling back a century – no molecular change in his cells or DNA, or damage to his organs, and no changes to his cognitive memory. At least, he could sure find his food bowl in the kitchen."

Staring at the dog, who seemed pleased to be the center of attention, I battled through my maze of doubts with a growing acknowledgement that my old friend was not deranged and that the time travel saga really had occurred. All I could say to Charlie was, "I truly don't know what to say or do. But please, tell us the rest – how Dave ended up murdered in 1911, who you think did it, and why on earth you think I can help...while I ponder the wisdom of my recent decision to give up drinking." Lydia, who'd been silent for the past few minutes, piped up, "Dad, I think I'm taking up drinking myself after this."

Charlie resumed his tale, "When I decided to continue the time travel project on my own, I had to have help, which is where Gabriel Sexton came into the picture. Gabe and I had worked together in Colorado. He was a gifted, but troubled, physicist who I felt was both brilliant and loyal. Sadly, my trust was misplaced. He came back to Arkansas with me, bringing a friend he vouched for, Henry Cabot, who had the engineering skills we needed for the final design and assembly of the machines." Pausing to collect his troubled thoughts, Charlie continued, "See, what I didn't know was Gabe Sexton was the subject of an FBI investigation for trying to sell some blue prints for a missile system he was working on after he and I left the Colorado time-travel project. He knew they were closing in on him, and he took advantage of my naiveté to escape where the FBI could not pursue him– into the year 1911."

"Wait a minute – machines?" Lydia interrupted Charlie's tale of his partner gone bad.... "Why did you build two of them?" Charlie took a deep breath before resuming his tale. "In science one builds backups to safeguard against what more often than not goes wrong the first time, or when something complex is attempted. It took more work, testing, and a lot of trial and error to get all the bugs out."

"So where are Gabe and Henry?" I asked. Lydia's 30 year's younger brain leaped to the conclusion before Charlie could reply.

"They went back to 1911, committed the reported crimes, and had a role in Dave's death I'm sure." Her quivering voice trailing off with the mental image of the young man who populated her adolescent fantasies plunging to his death from atop the capitol dome. "And Dave, he followed them using the second machine, didn't he?"

"Yes, sadly it is so." Charlie picked up the bizarre story once more. "Once we proved that the machines really worked by bringing Pharaoh back safely, my intention was to contact a friend in Washington – perhaps Senator Pryor – arrange to announce our success, and work ways to use the technology to solve some of the world's most pressing problems. Just think – going back in time to stop the rise of Hitler, preventing Oswald from shooting JFK, averting the war in Vietnam. What a better world we might have today!"

Prevent the war in Vietnam? Lydia and I locked eyes at that, likely both mindful that an older cousin of mine had died in a hail of machine gun fire on the Mekong River in 1969. Abruptly my thoughts came back to what I'd remembered from reading science fiction since the age of 12. "Charlie, even if time travel were…uh, is possible, you can't change the future… because, I thought, well…. oh, yeah, I remember the term… 'Paradox.' You can't change the future that was destined to be without creating a time paradox."

"Jack, forget all the science fiction novels, the twilight zone, or whatever else you're thinking of now. That's fiction. What I've done, Lord forgive me, is real – fact and science, not science fiction. By going back to the past, you can indeed change the future….which is why Dave died in 1911, seventy years before he was born. Now I need your help to undo what I've done."

Sensing the need to calm Charlie and get the thread of the ever more incredible tale back on course, Lydia interrupted, "Ok…..I believe you Charlie. We want to help you, though Lord knows I don't know how. Please tell us the rest of what happened and then let's figure out what to do."

"Right, sorry, there really isn't time…..Time? Well that's the root of the problem, isn't it….but….where was I? Oh, yes….Gabe and I disagreed, had a screaming argument here one night about my plans to turn the machine over to the government to use for the good of mankind. He was convinced that this would not end well...for the invention we created, or for us, but I sensed that his main concern was that we would lose an opportunity to do very well for ourselves financially. The money, of course, meant nothing to me. I've earned more in patents from my work than I, or even Dave, could spend.., if Dave were... It took a moment for Charlie to regain his composure to continue."

"I thought finally Gabe was convinced. He dropped the argument and I'd planned to make the call to Senator Pryor the next week, after I finished transcribing all my notes into a draft for publication and doing one last review of my calculations. I came out here one night a couple weeks back to see what Pharaoh was barking at and found the lights on here in the shop. When I opened the door, Gabe was seated in one of the transport machines, clearly preparing to enter the time stream...... I yelled at him, and started forward, only to be clobbered in the back of the head. As I was falling, I caught a glimpse of Henry Cabot, with a 2x4 in hand....and then all went black."

"When I came to hours later with Pharaoh licking my face, it was well past sunrise ....and both Henry and Gabe were gone, as was one of the machines. I was sitting here – still in a daze – when Dave arrived, unannounced as usual. A quick check of the computer showed us that the two bastards had traveled to May of 1911. After I explained what had happened, he immediately wanted to go after Gabe and Henry. He has always had an impulsive nature and a short fuse. Amazingly, he never questioned what I told him had happened. He just believed my story that the two men had cold-cocked me and fled back in time."

"Charlie,...you didn't let Dave do it?" Now I joined Lydia pacing the floor, my brain again swirling between total disbelief and the burgeoning realization that the tale I was hearing was really true. "We argued for hours," said Charlie, "talking about their potential to do harm – what might they do to change the time stream, to change history. We knew where in time they had gone. That information was captured by the computer over there." He pointed a bony finger at the bank of computer equipment against one wall.

"We went on line to read the newspapers for the week they went back to – May 1911....and of course, whatever they had done, or not, it was now history. We found accounts of the robberies in Little Rock that week, the violence, and the theft of General Lee's sword."... "But of course, what wasn't in the stories was anything about Dave's murder at the Capitol because it didn't happen...or rather it had not happened in the time stream in which we sat, reading online archives of the Arkansas Democrat. While we could not know that Gabe and Henry had anything to do with the reported violent crimes, our gut instinct just told us it was them. They would have arrived in 1911 without money or resources, so robbing a store was a likely solution to remedy that handicap. Regardless, however, allowing them to remain in 1911, with their knowledge of the future and their ability to alter historical events, big or small, wasn't something we could allow."

"But Uncle Charlie, if they did this...what else did they do? How can you know?" A very good question, I silently echoed...and watched Charlie gather his thoughts. "We can't know, can't even guess...because while we had the dates captured in the computer to show where they originally went, there was no way to know what they did in subsequent years to change events, commit crimes, or hurt people. Lord help me, Jack, because anything they did, anyone they harmed, any crimes they committed...it was my creation of these machines that made it all possible."

"Dave and I were struck with the responsibility for what I had done. My scientific breakthrough, with all its promise, had instead cast two men back into the past to hurt people and surely – in small, and perhaps very large ways – to change the course of history, in part because they know the course of future events for a century of time. Charlie hung his head, burdened with his guilt, while Lydia and I tried to control our conflicting emotions and deal with the situation we found ourselves in that rainy day in the Arkansas forest. Charlie brought us back to reality when he resumed his story with, "We both knew something had to be done."

Chapter 4

"AFTER HOURS OF debate, I was exhausted" Charlie said, collapsing into a worn, swivel chair. "Had I not been, I would have realized there were reasons Dave asked detailed questions about the time machines, how they were programmed, why he studied the manual made from my notes, and so forth."

"We agreed to get a good night's sleep and then revisit our options the following morning, for – as Dave pointed out – whatever the men had done, it was long over and both had surely been dead for years, as they were both in their 40s when they journeyed back to 1911.

Doing the math, Lydia said, almost to herself, "Yep, if the two old farts were still around, they would have to be about 140 years old…..You are right, Uncle Charlie. They have gone to meet their maker and account for whatever they did. It's history now. Why worry about it? What can you do anyway?" The words were no more out of her mouth when it dawned on her that the major burden on Charlie's troubled heart was Dave. "But, of course, there is Dave. I'm sorry, Uncle Charlie…..But what can we do?"

Charlie, clearly compelled to get the entire story out for us, rushed on, "when I woke up the next morning, Dave was nowhere to be found, and first I thought he'd taken a walk……..but then I knew. The computer log showed he too had left during the night, headed for the first week of May, 1911 with coordinates to arrive near the river on the edge of downtown Little Rock."

He used the remaining machine, but had returned it to the lab when he reached his destination, as best I could determine. The coordinates on the computer showed he had indeed arrived on the bank of the Arkansas River, on the edge of down town during the night."

"But how do you know he……?" But Charlie quickly cut Lydia off with irrefutable logic, "You read the newspaper archives. He surely succeeded in reaching 1911, and only to be murdered in the mystery that I don't think was ever solved…not in any subsequent papers I've read."

"Lydia, though in so many ways you have always been like a daughter to me, Dave is, or was, my only child, my one flesh-and-blood link to humanity, and I can't accept that he is lost forever because of the abuse of technology I created. Aside from refusing to accept that there is no way to rescue Dave, I can't escape responsibility for the death and havoc I showed you in the 1911 newspapers…. nor for whatever changes those two men made in the time stream between 1911 and their eventual deaths."

"Charlie," I chimed in. "What can we do? Are you sure it's still possible for you, or me, or any of us…to go from this old barn, standing here in 2011, back a century to 1911? Tell me. I know we have read the old newspapers but it's still very hard to believe. Show us. Help us understand…..How do you know it's possible since you haven't done it yourself?"

Charlie calmly replied, "Oh, but I have made the trip." With more than a little satisfaction that his out-of-the-blue statement had left us both speechless, Charlie continued. "I waited half a day to see if Dave would come back before I went out on the Internet once again to read the newspapers for May of 1911………and that's, that's when I found stories different than what Dave and I had read before. The report of his murder had been added to the coverage of the robberies and of General Lee's missing sword."

"I didn't think really, didn't take time to grieve….I was totally consumed by guilt and the need to time-travel back to 1911 myself to prevent Dave's murder. I went straight to the lab, programmed the machine, and with little preparation beyond grabbing a jacket and strapping on the laptop programmed to return me to the present, I commenced my journey through time." Charlie paused to make sure we were following him, and at last believed he was telling us the truth in hopes we could...we would help him correct the chaos his genius had wrought.

"The room faded away into a blur, as if I were on a train pulling slowly at first and then rapidly away from a station that faded into the distance....and then for a time – maybe seconds, maybe minutes – blackness. It occurred to me that perhaps I'd died, that the strain on my heart had simply killed me. But then, then.......my vision cleared and I found myself in the clearing beside this old barn, where the lab's concrete floor is today. It was pouring down rain and dark as the inside of a grave."

Charlie paused his increasingly bizarre and frightening tale, prompting me to ask "What happened?"

"I realized what a damn fool I'd been," Charlie explained in a matter-of-fact tone. "I was an old man, unarmed, poorly equipped, not dressed for the era, without any money – of the 1911 vintage or otherwise...and beyond that, at a total loss for what to do. How I would travel the 30 miles into Little Rock, and what would I do if I ever made it that far? I crawled out of the machine and went into the old barn, which seemed to have been long abandoned but that's when I realized I was not prepared to stay." Hanging his head in shame, Charlie plaintively added, "I got back in the machine and returned to the present."

"You did the right thing, Uncle Charlie," offered Lydia in a consoling voice that she had to have acquired from her mother, for on my tongue was little more than, "You crazy old coot, what in the hell were you thinking?" But saved perhaps by Lydia's more compassionate nature, I could only shake my head.

"This happened three days ago" Charlie continued, after giving Lydia's hand a grateful squeeze. "I spent the larger part of the last three nights sitting on the front porch, doing what I've done little of in years, praying to the almighty for help and talking to Pharaoh a lot. I guess the good Lord must have been listening, at least as well as that old dog. By this morning, I knew the only thing I could do, the only person I could call who could help was you Jack."

"So you want me to go after Dave then, don't you?" Like I hadn't known this since the reality of this crazy tale first cracked my thick skull. "You think I can go back to 1911 to intervene in the events we read about in the newspaper archives and change the course of history. You want me to find Henry and Gabe and stop them from committing crimes and from, we presume, murdering Dave. Does that about sum it up?"

"Uh, yes Jack, that's the only way I can see to set this awful nightmare right. I don't have anyone else to turn to, nobody else who knows or cares about Dave and me. You can do this." Charlie's pleas broke my heart. I would have sooner walked barefoot through the fires of hell than look into those sad old eyes and say, "No, I won't do it."

I looked at Lydia, at least halfway hoping she would tell me not to pursue what must surely sound like an insane quest. Instead, before I could pull myself together to say "yes," she said, "Dad, you need to go – and you have to take me with you. Two of us can find the two bastards and find Dave quicker than you can alone. I want to go with you."

"No way, your mother would kill me. This is dangerous enough for me as it is. I won't put your life and future at risk." This was the firmest, fatherly retort I could come up with. Lydia, though gritting her teeth, seemed to accept what she surely had known would be my reply. However, the temptation to retort got the best of her when she came back with, "If Mom didn't kill you while you two were married I think you're safe, Dad."

A belated thought occurred to me. "Charlie, of all the possibilities on years to travel to what made Gabe and Henry choose May of 1911?"

Charlie shoved aside some papers and came up with a book which he handed me entitled *Remembering Arkansas' Confederates and the United Confederate Veterans Reunion of 1911*. "This book has lain around here for a couple of years since the authors gave it to me at a university event over in Conway. Gabe used to read it in down times and talked a lot about the old rebels, how different Little Rock was a hundred years ago.

"Charlie, before I change my mind, let's get on with it. What do I need to do to get ready for this trip? And please tell me you really can bring me back." An image of being stuck in time a century ago, dying – even at a ripe old age – before my daughter's birth, settled in my imagination like a lead weight.

"Thank you Jack. Yes, I went and came back, so I'm confident we can get you back as well. We need to do a much better job equipping and preparing you Jack." Charlie picked up a cardboard box that was in the corner of the room and placed it on the table. "I took the liberty of putting together clothing that will allow you to blend in and other things you will need to accomplish the job."

Always the methodical old professor, Charlie laid out the contents of the box. The more items he produced, the more real in my mind became the whole idea of traveling back to 1911.

Charlie started with my wardrobe. "I went into town yesterday, while I was still struggling with the idea of calling you for help, all while knowing I had nowhere else to turn…. but, I digress, sorry. First you need clothes….and these worn, but very serviceable cotton shirts and wool slacks will fit in pretty well in May of 1911. The leather belt here will work. Shoes are a bit harder."

"These should fit in for a 1911 look or, if you like" Charlie added, with a flicker of a smile, "you could wear one of the broken in Confederate re-enactors uniforms I borrowed when I thought I might try to return to 1911." The look on my face put an end to that idea, so Charlie proceeded to lay out the rest of his 1911 survival kit.

"What, I can't wear my Nike's," was my wiseass retort. "Maybe my Rockports? OK, guess not. What about my size 14 feet?" Lydia stifled a laugh.

"Well, I got the clothes at the Goodwill, and these," he said while lifting out some battered boots, "I got at the shoe repair shop over on 7th street. They are size 14. Hope they fit. The guy found them for me in the back of his shop. I told him I was researching a movie script and wanted to be able to describe a century-old pair of shoes. He added leather laces, and put what look like hobnails into the heels."

"You'll need some money. Your American Express and ATM cards won't exactly be accepted," Charlie proceeded, showing he had indeed thought about this crazy thing before calling me earlier in the day. "The price was considerably over the face value, but the Coin & Stamp Shop on Main Street was able to pull together these bills and coins dated 1911 or earlier." He added an obviously antique compass and a bar of soap wrapped in wax paper to the pile. All I could think, looking at the wardrobe and props that would accompany me 100 years back in time was, "At least I don't have to wear one of those old confederate uniforms."

"OK, I've got the right clothes and money. I'll arrive after dark but I'll be 30 miles from Little Rock. How do I get into the city?" "And why can't you just send me to Little Rock of 1911 and save time?"

"Well" Charlie said in an almost inaudible voice, "actually you will be more like 40 miles from the city. Keep in mind the city limits were much more compact in 1911 before the western expansion and growth of the suburbs. I also have a map for you, one of Little Rock as it was in 1911." Remembering the rest of my question he added, He handed me a rumpled, but apparently genuine, vintage map. "Here's another one of the state of Arkansas. Look how few roads road there are, mainly railroads."

I smoothed out the map and was taken back to a time before Little Rock became a modern sprawling city surrounded by suburbs and interstate highways. The boundaries of Little Rock in 1911 extended little further than Main Street and Broadway. The city seemed to end at a western boundary marked by the state capitol. In contrast, modern-day Little Rock extends miles to the west beyond the capitol into a sea of suburban neighborhoods and upscale housing developments.

Looking up from the maps, I couldn't help but exclaim, "Oh great! Forty miles to travel and no truck…and likely not much road.

How do I get out of the woods and into town, Charlie? And again, why can't the machine just put me down in Little Rock? Dave was able to program in coordinates that placed him right in town. Why can't I do the same thing?"

Charlie was ready for that question. "Jack, we could do that but the chances of being discovered are great and we would run the risk of losing the time machine. There just isn't any way to be sure who would be around to witness your arrival in a crowded city. Dave took an enormous chance when he went back. And another thing, I have determined the odds of hitting the exact date you want to arrive at are improved if you plan to land on the same spot from which you left in the future. I'm not sure why yet, but that seems to be the case."

"OK Charlie, I go to Bigelow from the barn here in Little Italy which should be a two or three hour walk. Then how do I get from there to Little Rock?", which seemed a pretty important question to me.

I think by train, Jack… yes, by train. There isn't much of a road, as you see on the maps of the time, just a narrow muddy rut from Little Italy almost to Little Rock. However, it should be just a little over a six-mile walk to Bigelow and, according the records and photos I've researched, there's a train depot with at least twice-a-day passenger service into Little Rock. A ticket to Little Rock should only cost a dollar or so." It seemed he had all the answers to my obvious questions…though, as I would find out all too soon, the law of unforeseen consequences would render a good part of such planning moot.

"Once you get on the train, it will be less than an hour's ride into Union Station in Little Rock, which, as you know, still stands at the bottom of Victory Street and is now used by Amtrak. You are going to have to get a place to stay, to base yourself from, and you need a plan for how you're going to search the city for Dave and the other two, Gabe and Henry.

"Yes, Union Station is still there. of course, and is used by Amtrak. I've visited it several times, Charlie. Once I get to the depot, what should be my first steps?"

"Well Jack beyond finding a place to stay it will come down to finding the best way to search the city, perhaps in some logical grid around the hotels that will likely be full. I wish we could reserve you a hotel room but well, …."

Chapter 5

IN OUR OWN collective common sense, we knew there was no urgency in launching this bizarre mission back to 1911. After all, the events that had happened occurred a century ago. Nevertheless, we all felt an urgency to get it done and over with, regardless of the outcome. Charlie desperately needed to heal the agony in his soul for what he had done to destroy his son. I wanted to get my adventure started before I came to my senses and changed my mind. I could not even guess why Lydia, seemingly reconciled to a supporting role, had dived into the preparations for my trip across time.

Lydia and I decided to spend the night at Charlie's house, and that I would "travel" the next afternoon. Late into the night, stopping only at Lydia's demand that I eat dinner, I studied the most "current" versions of the 1911 newspapers Charlie had downloaded.

For a time, I lost myself, almost like reading an historical novel, suspending a conscious image that I might soon be walking the crowded streets of Little Rock, Arkansas in a year in which William Howard Taft was President and world wars were yet to be numbered. The Reunion of the United Confederate Veterans, was previously held in Macon, Georgia. It was moved to Little Rock in 1911 when city officials, prompted by the ceaseless urging of the business community, bid to host the event they believed would bring thousands of visitors, money and exposure to their city, which was just beginning to respond to the awakening promise of the 20th century.

Little Rock, in its drive to win the right to host the reunion, had promised to house and feed an expected 6,000 elderly Confederate veterans at no charge. The city boosters were mindful of the fact that the average old soldier from a war in which the first shot had been fired 50 years before, would be in their eighties. An attendance projection of 6,000 was deemed manageable and the business community set about to raise the necessary funds through donations months in advance.

An impatient Attorney General Norwood , leading the fund raising effort, felt that many local saloon owners were not anteing up their fair share and threatened to close their businesses for the 3-day reunion. However, the specter of all the revenue lost from the flood of visitors was not enough to open their purse strings. Apparently Mr. Norwood didn't follow through on closing the saloons.

"Is it real to you?" Lydia asked, reading over my shoulder. Her question brought me back to the 21st century, sitting before the fireplace in Charlie's den.

Real?" I posed the question to myself as much as to my daughter. "Yes, in the sense that it's a fascinating story that I've never read, but which dominated daily newspaper pages in 1911. The news accounts make the story as real as George Washington or Abraham Lincoln..... until..... until I read about people in these articles and know that they and the reporter who wrote about them and the photographers who took their pictures have all been dead for decades. I'm slammed with the knowledge that before the week is out, I'll likely be walking among them." As an afterthought, looking perhaps for sanity, I added, "That's, of course, unless Charlie has not just completely gone around the bend and none of this is possible." But the accounts of Dave's death in 1911 and his familiar eyes staring at us from the front page of the 100 year old newspaper were all too real.

Sobered by my reality check, Lydia folded her long legs beneath her in front of the fireplace and silently joined me reading the newspaper accounts of the 1911 week I seemed fated to step into before another sunset.

According to both newspaper accounts and an historical journal article Charlie had found, the 1911 population of the Little Rock I would visit was about 45,000. During the 3-day UCV Reunion event, the number of people in the city would swell to 150,000, considerably complicating my efforts to find Dave and Charlie's former associates who we assumed were responsible for his death in time to prevent the murder.

The newspaper files offered a fascinating view of the popular mindset of the day toward the rapidly aging, dwindling numbers of Confederate veterans and the cause for which they had fought. The event in May 1911 unfolded only 50 years after the first shots had been fired at Fort Sumter, South Carolina. Thus, to the people of Little Rock in 1911, the Civil War was less in the past than is WW II to modern-day Little Rock residents. Certainly some of the adults – those over 60 who had lived in Little Rock during the war – would have had personal memories of the secession and subsequent occupation of the city by Union troops.

A significant part of the Little Rock businesses' sales pitch to win the host-city role for the reunion was a promise to house, feed and entertain the aging rebels at no charge. The attendance of some 12,000 old soldiers, twice the expected number – would challenge that pledge, one of the many things I learned while reading into the night.

I was struck by one local newspaper account in advance of the event which concluded with, *"Fifty years ago these veterans, now gathering, in the buoyancy of youth, were marching throughout this land. Then they were boys. Now the burden of the years is on them. Time, who is ever old but never grows weak, may crush their bodies back into the earth from whence they came, but their knightly souls will never die and the record they made time will never efface from the scrolls of Fame Impermeable."* My last thoughts before nodding off in front of the fireplace was that this would be an interesting trip. Interesting? Little did I know.......

Chapter 6

I WAS ON the battlefield at Gettysburg, charging across the field toward the Yankee lines with other screaming and some dying rebels in what, somehow I knew, was the ill-fated "Pickett's charge." The bullet that would kill me had slowed to a crawl, hanging in space as it headed for my heart. With a start, I awoke in a cold sweat to Lydia's grip on my shoulder and the smell of coffee brewing in Charlie's kitchen, for a time without a sense of where I was and why. "Dad, it's morning. You spent the night in that chair. Breakfast is ready." Shaking off the fog of my troubled sleep and death by a Yankee bullet at the battle of Gettysburg, reality hit me almost with the force of that fatal bullet. I needed to face up to what I was to do on this day.

An even more bleary-eyed Charlie was seated at the table in the kitchen, staring out the window into the rain, his untouched plate of bacon and eggs getting colder by the minute. "Good morning Charlie. I think it was a long night for both of us, my friend." He forced a smile that couldn't erase the worry lines and strain from his face.

"Charlie, I'm still ready. Just tell me it's really possible? If it is, if this is not a crazy dream, let's get on with it. We will get Dave back… get me back as well……uh, right?"

With a frail voice and trembling hands, looking older than I could ever recall, Charlie replied, "Thank you, you were my only hope, Dave's only hope….and yes, the technology really works. I proved that, even to my own satisfaction. We can….. no, we will bring you back… even… even if you can't find Dave. If I thought otherwise, I'd never let you do this Jack."

"OK, but I'm going to eat all the eggs and bacon Lydia fixed that I can hold. I may not like the 1911 grub all that well." I did just that, with an appetite I could not remember having in months. This seemed to animate Charlie at the same time, and he began to lay out a rapid stream of advice.

"You will be strapped in the machine, of course, and the electron bombardment process will start. You will likely black out, or come close to it, feeling a spinning motion like you've never felt." Charlie began a combination instruction and pep talk session. Lydia, I noticed, was taking notes on a tablet, perhaps a habit from having been much closer to a classroom than I had for many years.

"It will take – as near I as can determine from my brief round trip – about 10 minutes from departure until you arrive in front of the barn ….which will be abandoned and have a dirt floor. The space you will find yourself and the machine sitting, based on the exact GPS numbers loaded in the computer, will be right where you left from but, of course, this lab will not yet exist. Once you have your wits about you, unbuckle and drag the machine into the barn. Conceal it as best you can." Seeing my pinched brow and worried expression, Charlie paused to ask, as if back in the class room again, "any questions."

"Questions? Charlie, probably enough that if asked all of them, I'd be three days getting on with this. Just bear with me a few minutes and I'll tell you how I think I'm going to do this." My old friend nodded, while Lydia poised to take notes. Why? I didn't ask, a regret that would come back on me soon.

After further discussion we decided that leaving the time machine concealed in the barn while I went into Little Rock was too much a risk that it would be discovered. As scary as it was to me, like abandoning a life boat at sea, we decided I would send both the machine I went in and the one we reasoned might be hidden in the barn by Sexton and Cabot back to the present. How I'd get home again was a puzzle at first, but we decided I should place a classified ad in the Arkansas Gazette reading something like "Lydia, I'm ready to come home. Please wire fare to ──────," which would be the location in the city or country side where I would need the time machine to materialize. It seemed a chancy plan, but I was reconciled to the fact that it was the soundest option.

"When I arrive, it needs to be after dark, which should minimize my chance of meeting people – a random squirrel hunter or some kids on the prowl – so let's wait until 9:00 this evening. I'll hope it's not pouring down rain in 1911, as it is here today." Charlie, not surprisingly, had thought of this as well. "I can tell you it's likely to be a cool evening upon arrival, but if you hit the May 12th date we are programming into the computer, the weather will be dry. I checked the weather report for that day in the newspaper microfilm file. You are right though. You need to arrive after dark."

With that, I continued to outline my "battle plan." "I'm taking a flashlight…I'll have to bury it in the barn, since it won't fit my 1911 look but I may need it to pull myself together upon arrival. I've got a change of clothes in an old canvas satchel I found in your workshop, Charlie. I've got the money you pulled together, my Barlow knife, but no gun….I'd feel a lot better landing in the dark woods with a gun."

"I think I've got that covered Jack," and with those words, Charlie slid a cloth-wrapped object across the table. Inside I found an obviously old, but polished US Army revolver, but I wondered if it would raise questions if someone saw it in 1911. Charlie anticipated that concern, "It belonged to my father, it was his service revolver in the Philippines during the Spanish American War in 1898. He won a Congressional Medal of Honor, and a few more awards for holding off a charging group of Moro warrior's intent on beheading him and his patrol of wounded comrades. He never shared the details and I only learned the full story after he died by reading the citations I found in his law office."

"Jack, I have to be completely honest with you." Charlie shifted his focus away from his prep drill and offered almost apologetically, "I know I've said I can bring you back and I really believe that. However, if something goes wrong, coming after you may be impossible. The circuits, some of the other materials we built the two machines with, were, uh, sorta classified. I brought them with me when I left the Colorado lab. That's why I think both machines will be safer here than left to the elements and possible discovery back in 1911."

"There are only two machines," Charlie said, telling us of course what we already knew. "Dave used the one in the lab here and returned it, and the other one is still in 1911 where Gabe and Henry took it. The computers here show they aimed to land by the barn as well. I doubt they would have destroyed the second machine, or left it in the elements. All the more likely, they concealed it in the old barn, which, of course, should be your target landing. The real estate abstract records and county histories I've accessed show this old farm to have been abandoned for several years on either side of 1911." Seeing that we were following his train of thought, Charlie continued.

"Here, I've drawn instructions. Put them in your jacket. They show you how to program the machine Gabe and Henry used – if you can find it – so you can send it back to us here in the lab. If the machine comes back and you don't, I'll be able to join you in 1911 to help....well, help as best I can."

Lydia could not contain herself. "Charlie, you went back once, and told us you were not equipped to deal with the obstacles you faced. Let me do it this time. Just show me how."

"NO, NO, Charlie!" I exclaimed. "Promise me no matter what happens, if I never come back, you don't let her near that machine. If I can't accomplish this... this trip into the damned Twilight Zone, sending her back in time to join me won't make anything better. Promise me now Charlie."

"He's right Lydia, it wouldn't work." Charlie's word seemed to settle the issue for Lydia, but I knew her stubborn nature too well to have complete confidence. Still, it was about all the reassurance I could get that my hardheaded daughter would sit this one out. Regardless of who might or might not use the other machine, I couldn't help but find a bit of comfort in the idea it could be sent back here to 2011 like a kind "last resort" lifeboat – a lifeboat I hoped and prayed would not be needed.

I guessed I was feeling the way astronauts feel when they walk to the launch pad, or the way the explorers of old felt boarding a ship in an era when many thought the world was flat. But, as the three of us walked back to the shop and Charlie's time machine, I dismissed that analogy, for while the ancient explorers had left their world to face the unknown, they were confident that, at least, the world they left was still within the same realm of time on the planet and would be there when they returned. I realized that, unless this was a dream or that Charlie had lost his mind, I'd shortly be a century back in time, before my own mother had been born. It occurred to that my father had been born in a small town near Little Rock in 1909, two years before the UCV Reunion.

After a hug from Lydia that I dared not drag out, I hoisted myself into the seat of the machine, stowed my frayed canvas bag with the gun and clothes behind the seat, and looked down at Charlie and Lydia. At that moment, the reality of what we were doing struck Lydia and she began to cry. "Dad….. Don't go. I want to… oh God, this is hard!"

"Lydia, don't worry. I'll be back almost before you know I'm gone…and with that rascal Dave in tow." I tried to say it with far more conviction than I felt, like all fathers going off to war and other dangers have for centuries assured wives, sons and daughters they would return no matter the odds, praying as I said it that it would be so.

Charlie programmed the computer in front of me, marking date, time and the coordinates of where I needed to land in 1911. At the same time, he walked me through the process I'd need to follow to reverse the trip for my return home after hopefully accomplishing the mission. With a handshake and the sign of the cross – which I hastily matched – Charlie walked to the monitoring computers against the wall and looked back at me as if to say, "Are you sure?"

"Fire away Charlie," and with that I pulled down the Plexiglas bubble, flipped the switch and waited, halfway expecting or hoping that nothing would happen and it would turn out to be a nutty hoax. One minute I was looking at Charlie and Lydia, and the next Lydia gasped, her hand flying to her face in shock. Then, nothing.... The world faded in front of my eyes. I guess I blacked out, or maybe there just was nothing to see but the void of space and time. Maybe this was what it was like to die, and it crossed my mind that indeed I had died and would soon face Saint Peter to answer for my sometimes-less-than saintly life.

Chapter 7

CONSCIOUSNESS RETURNED ABRUPTLY, with the light –or at least what light existed in the dead of night, as rain pelted down on the bubble over my head. Either I'd landed badly off course, or Charlie's check of the weather in the May 1911 newspaper archives had missed the mark. Satisfied that my bones and internal organs were intact, I took a deep breath and pulled back the Plexiglas dome to let the pounding rain fall on my face, a refreshing reminder that I was still alive.

I climbed out of the machine, pulled the cover closed, and looked around. My first hesitant steps in the mud landed me on my backside in a puddle deep enough to drown in, had I been less than sober. My aggravation over my wet, muddy condition faded immediately when I recognized the old barn that was, in my time, attached to Charlie's workshop. Almost certainly, the muddy yard in which I sat would one day be the concrete floor of his laboratory. For the first time since all this started, the preponderance of my logic said time travel was, indeed, possible.

Pulling myself out of the mud, I ran through the downpour to the old barn and pulled open one of the double doors against groaning resistance. The small flashlight I carried in my vest pocket revealed what I had been led to expect – a dusty, long-abandoned barn, with an overwhelming smell of old hay and damp. In the back corner of the barn, I found a large pile of hay that appeared to sit in an unnatural shape. Pulling aside a few armfuls of hay revealed a canvas tarp, which, once removed, revealed a time machine that was an exact match to the one I'd climbed into seemingly only minutes before in Charlie's workshop. I then realized that, while I was perceiving time in minutes in one sense, I had indeed traveled back a century.

Plotting my course of action in my head, I went back out into the rain to pull my time machine into the barn next to the one Charlie's traitorous assistants had used only days – or almost a century – ago, depending on your perception about the passage of time. In my case, with my present altered sense of time, it was surely just days ago, a conclusion supported by the fact that the machine they used was still shiny new and lacked even the faintest trace of dust.

Following Charlie's instructions, I programmed both the stolen machine that minutes ago rested under the tarp and the machine I'd arrived in moments ago. After flipping the switches, the doubting Thomas in me stepped back, expecting little to happen despite the adventure that brought me to this dusty barn. If I remained in need of any convincing, it came within seconds as the machines vibrated, took on a misty glow and then…. simply vanished before my eyes. I could only trust that both machines would materialize shortly thereafter in front of Charlie and Lydia.

I next opened the bag of supplies I brought with me, cleaned off my muddy clothes using the soap I had brought and rainwater captured in an old bucket I found in the barn, and changed into the clean set of "period" clothes Charlie had packed for me. The woolen pants and cotton shirt actually fit well, and put me in a better frame of mind to consider my next steps. Clearly I'd ended up in the right geographical location, but the question of the date in time remained uncertain. I could only await the dawn to seek some verification of this essential piece of information. If I'd missed by more than a few days, I could arrive in Little Rock too late to help Dave. It had to be May 12th, or no more than two or three days later for, as the news accounts conveyed, Dave would be murdered on the Capitol dome the night of May 18. Somehow I had to get to Little Rock, some 40 miles or so from where I stood before the 18th and I could only do that if I could indeed catch a train in Bigelow.

My jumbled thoughts and questions about my location in time were interrupted by growling pangs of hunger, sending me into the bag I'd brought in search of the food Lydia packed. I found two ham sandwiches in plastic wrap in a brown paper bag, and I was struck by the fact that polyvinyl chloride plastic wrap would not be invented until years into the future. I built a small fire in the center of the barn to ward off the chill that enveloped me as I munched on the food, wondering where and with whom I might be dining in the days to come. I was little closer to a plan for the coming dawn when I drifted off to sleep on a bed of hay, a deep but troubled rest in which vivid images drifted through my mind of the shattered, bleeding bodies of men in blue and gray littering a bloody battle field at dawn.

In my dream, I was alone, the day just starting to break, with a mist rising from the dew soaking the bloody grass. My eyes were drawn to one body in Confederate gray, face down, his hand wrapped tightly around the handle of a sword that had run through the breast of a young Union Captain. His sightless eyes seemed to somehow peer into mine like I'd awoke him from the dead. As I started to turn away I noticed a tintype photo protruding from the dead Confederate's bloodstained tunic. Staring back at me was the sepia-toned image of a young woman and, I said almost aloud, "You look like my daughter Lydia." I reached down and turned the dead man over to face the breaking of a day he would not see. If one can hear their own screams in a dream, mine reverberated across the silent field, for the dead Confederate soldier was me.

I awoke with a start, the image of lying dead on the battlefield fading slowly as I shook myself awake. In a rambling inventory of my thoughts, I wondered how such a dream could seem so real, and I was overwhelmed with compassion for those who actually lived through the horrors of the Civil War. Then it slowly downed on me that thousands of such men were alive and massing in the city of Little Rock in the year of 1911, and perhaps I'd have the chance soon to hear the stories of these survivors in their own words.

First, however, I had to find a way to travel the 40 miles into Little Rock, hoping against hope that I had arrived in time to save Dave and set right the course of history. According to the plan formed back in 2011 that meant first getting to Bigelow.

With a silent prayer for those 'back home,' as I had come to think of my own time, I set off down the rutted, overgrown road toward the village of Bigelow, which was the closest place I might find a train to take me into Little Rock, following the compass that Charlie had included in my equipment. I was mindful that all my worldly possessions in this year of 1911 were the clothes I was wearing and the contents of the knapsack on my back. The materialism of the 21st century, from which I'd come only the day before, seemed bizarrely otherworldly. Although it was my life only hours before, in my present reality, it was a century span away.

I had gone but a mile or two at most, losing the path more than once, when I came out onto a more traveled road heading towards Bigelow according to my compass. As I rounded a turn in the road, I was startled to hear, "Well, looka here Clyde, we got us a trespasser on our road." In a small clearing on my left, I confronted Clyde, a slumped over fat man sitting astride a mule. His companion, tall and lankly was seated against the trunk of a huge pine tree, pausing to drink from a fruit jar of clear liquid I knew could not have been water. "Oh Lord," I thought, "Why do the first two people I meet in 1911 have to look like they just stepped off the movie set of Deliverance?"

As I stopped to assess my situation, it was clear to me that I hadn't been greeted by Welcome Wagon neighborhood volunteers or the Bigelow Chamber of Commerce. The man seated on the ground, clearly well lubricated by the contents of the fruit jar, lurched to his feet, cursing as he spilled his drink onto his filthy, ragged pants.

As I sorted out my options in silence, looking from one man to the other, and I was jarred out of my deliberations by a woman's scream to my right, "Help me mister. They robbed the bank in Bigelow. They have guns and they killed a man." The voice belonged to a woman with fiery, curly red hair, who was tied to a large pine tree with several loops of rope. A few feet beyond the woman was a horse tied to a tree, seemingly oblivious to the drama playing out.

The fat man, who I now knew as Clyde, called to his staggering friend, "OK, Billy, think we should shoot him now or see how much money he has in that sack on his back?"

Billy – apparently not the brighter of the two – had to gather his thoughts a bit to reply, "Well, since you dropped most of the bank's money when the guy from the hardware store shot at us, I think we need whatever this here gentleman is carrying. Yep, lets lighten his load. Then maybe we shoot him or just run his sorry ass out into the woods."

Clyde, taking charge, bellowed, "Open the pack up now mister," as he struggled to pull a pistol out of the holster on his belt past the heavy gut hanging over his strained waistband.

Stalling, I said, "OK, no need to hurt anybody. You can have what little I have." I was mindful that the aged cash Charlie put together for me in the century I'd just left was likely essential to my getting to Little Rock in time to save Dave. When I put my hand into the canvas pack, it closed around the gun carried into battle by Charlie's father. A ridiculous thought flitted through my mind. OK, maybe I'd seen this in a movie. How would Indiana Jones have played this?

Clyde looked down at his belt, as if a visual assist would help him pry his pistol from beneath his ample gut. When he looked up again, he found my gun pointed at his chest, which from my vantage point seemed to be 10 feet above my head. "Don't move, either of you. Nobody has to get hurt." As I trained the gun first on one man and then the other, the woman tied to the tree shouted words of encouragement. "Those scum shot the Sheriff in Bigelow and kidnapped me, so if you have to shoot both of them, it's no loss mister."

Perhaps afraid I'd take the screaming woman's advice, Clyde pulled up his gun with one hand, while pulling up on the reins of the mule. He fired wildly, sending a bullet 20 feet above my head. I returned his fire, striking the unfortunate mule square in the forehead.

Clyde's mule collapsed onto its side, pinning his ample girth to the ground, one leg caught beneath maybe 1,000 pounds of stone dead mule. Clyde's gun sailed off into the woods, leaving his only offensive weapon a bellowed string of pain-laced expletives.

Out of the corner of my eye, I saw Billy was pointing a shotgun at me to send me into the hereafter to join the departed mule. He very likely would have succeeded if not for a blow across the back of the head with a heavy tree branch delivered by the redheaded lady, who had somehow freed herself from the ropes around the tree. The distraction of my arrival had apparently been all she needed to wriggle free of the ropes and she might well have caved in the man's head once he was on the ground had I not stayed her hand.

"That son of bitch! World's better off with him dead as that mule you shot." While I restrained myself from commenting on her unladylike language, she added, "pretty poor shot, by the way. Assume you were shooting at the disgusting piece of trash riding the mule, not the poor dumb animal?" Despite the torn dress, sweat-streaked face, and eyes sparking anger, she was a very pretty woman – even with the club in her hand. The year 1911 was certainly proving to be interesting.

"Yes Mam, I guess my aim was a little off, but better the mule than the man there, who by the way, doesn't seem in any shape to do you harm." This was no exaggeration, as old Clyde could do no more than cry and curse in pain with what likely was a broken leg.

"Well, you can't shoot worth a tinker's damn, but you saved my honor and probably my life. Thank you," she said. "My name is Sarah Murphy. Who might you be, and where in tarnation did you come from?" Not quite sure how to respond to that, considering that she would think me a raging lunatic and whack me with that limb if I told her the truth, it seemed the better part of valor to tell her only part of the truth. "Jack Kernick, my name is Jack Kernick and I'm trying to get to Little Rock for the Confederate Reunion."

I watched her collect her thoughts to ask more questions I would not want to answer, so instead I asked her, "Where are you from, and how did you end up with these two?" Before she could answer, Billy, on the ground, interrupted, "Bitch, you busted my head. I'll kill…." Whatever he was going to say was cut off in mid-sentence when Ms. Murphy applied her laced-up shoe to the side of his head.

"I run a boarding house on the outskirts of Bigelow, about halfway between town and the sawmill," she said. "I was in my garden, across the road from the house, when I heard shots coming from town. Then in a few minutes, these two came riding up, both of them on the back of that poor mule."

"They grabbed, me and stole my horse out of the pasture. It's tied up over there by those big rocks. I soon learned they had robbed the Bank of Bigelow, but the idiots let their horses run off when they came out of the bank shooting. They stole that poor mule and then dropped most of the money they stole. They planned to use me as a hostage or a shield if the law chased them."

Since the threat of imminent danger had passed, I thought I'd get back to the mission at hand and get some important information from my lovely companion. "Tell me a couple of things. I've been, uh, traveling a while. What day is today?" Sarah replied, "It's May 13th, of course." Relief flooded over me when I realized that I'd arrive in 1911 in the right time frame required. "May 13, 1911?" I exclaimed, concerned that I might have missed the year.

"Of course it's 1911 mister, what'd you think it was? And yes, there are two trains a day passing through Bigelow on the way too Little Rock, a question I bet you was fixin' to ask next." Alas, this lady was going to be a challenge for me to keep my story straight and sound reasonable. I had to keep my wits about me.

"How far is it to Bigelow? Yes, I do need to catch a train into Little Rock from there." Rather than answer, she bombarded me with questions of her own. "Is Jack Kernick really your name?" Before I could assure her that was indeed my Christian name, she continued, "Where did you come from and how did you get out here in the woods?"

"It's long story. Just know I've come a long way. I got lost. Let's save getting better acquainted until we figure out what we're going to do with these two?" At this point, I had the pistol more or less pointed at the still dazed Billy on the ground, and Clyde was still safely secured under the dead mule. I figured the humane thing was to get him out from under the beast, but first I asked Sarah...."You said they killed someone in the robbery?"

"I don't know. That's what they said, that they shot the Sheriff when they made their escape on the stolen mule. Bigelow only has two lawmen that normally only have to deal with drunken loggers and mill workers. It's only about 6 miles back into town. We can find out when we get there."

Sarah kept Billy's shotgun pointed at the two men while I looped the rope that had previously been used to tie her to the tree around the dead mule's neck and tossed the other end over a nearby tree limb. I tugged on the rope to raise the mule's head and shoulders up enough for Clyde to pull himself out, whining in pain. A quick examination told me his leg was indeed broken, a very ugly compound fracture.

"OK, here's what we should do. I'll tie up Billy here. Clyde isn't going anywhere with this leg, and the lawman in Bigelow can come out with a wagon to pick them up." Fifteen minutes later Ms. Murphy and I were riding away on her reclaimed horse, leaving a cursing pair of outlaws who had clearly chosen the wrong line of work.

Chapter 8

RIDING ON A shared horse with my attractive and very curious companion holding onto my waist, I knew we would not be far down the road before the questions would start again. "How did you happen to wind up back there? That road comes from nowhere, just an old abandoned homestead, nothing there but a barn."

"Well, I was just sorta lost in the woods," was the best I could marshal. "I was coming from Russellville," which was the closest town I could remember to the west, and I lost my horse. "I was walking in the woods, following my compass toward Bigelow."

"Lost your horse?" she exclaimed, "and you were heading to Little Rock for the old rebels meeting? You look mighty young to have fought with General Lee, or maybe General Grant if you are a Yankee. I hope not. That's a real sore point with folks around here still."

"Nope, I'm not a Yankee. I came originally from Texas," thinking that naming a large enough state would help quell the woman's curiosity. But then, the question of occupation was inevitable. "How do you support yourself and your wife and younguns? I know you're not a lawman, considering what a terrible shot you are."

Should I tell the truth? Well my mother always said, "Tell the truth and you won't have to remember what you said later," and this seemed to be my best option with this woman sharing a horse with me. "I'm a physician, and I don't have a wife. I have one grown daughter and another in college."

"A doctor? Well, that's right impressive. We don't have but one in Bigelow, and he's not often sober. You might consider opening up an office – lots of doctoring work with the loggers and Mr. Bigelow's lumber mill. Bigelow's not a bad little town, only an hour's train ride to Little Rock. Now that's a huge city. Hear they claim to have 45,000 people living there now." Almost as an afterthought, she added, "I wish Bigelow did have a decent doctor. If it did, I might not be a widow woman today. My husband, John, was hurt bad at the mill almost two years ago. He died later the same day. The worthless drunkard we have for a doctor couldn't help him."

"Uh, thanks, but I'm really just here for the reunion, and to hook up with a friend who is supposed to be there. Then I need to go back to Texas. My patients need me."

By this time the muddy road had widened, opening into a vista of tree stumps where the slash-and-burn logging practices had leveled hundreds of acres of hills. The smoke stacks from the lumber mill dominated the horizon, and I could not help but notice the giant pines and oaks at the edge of the woods that would be long gone before my time a century into the future.

We rode on in silence until the quite was shattered by the distant whistle of a locomotive in the distance. "The mill runs around the clock. It only closes on Sunday," Ms. Murphy volunteered, taking on a tour-guide role. "There are over 300 men working in that mill, and lots more cutting the trees in the woods. The foreman, and some of the office clerks rent rooms in my boarding house. Many of the rest live in the shacks the lumber company provides."

Coming to a junction in the road, we had to ride around an oxen-drawn wagon laden with four large pine logs. The wheels were sunk in the mud to the wheel hubs, and the massive pair of oxen seemed to have tired of trying to pull the wagon out. A man on the wagon seat whipped and cursed the poor beasts, while two others, knee-deep behind the logs, made a half-hearted effort to push. Yes, I could see a lot of work for physicians in 1911 Arkansas.

As we passed the sprawling sawmill, I was reminded of the history I'd read in a book on turn-of-the-century Arkansas, which emphasized clear-cut timber harvests followed by conversion of much of the land to grow crops. The sea of logs floating in the holding pond we rode around would be sawed into pine lumber and shipped across the nation to build homes the men working in the mill would never be able to afford. Pondering such economic injustice wasn't helping me though, and I cleared my head to focus on the mission that brought me here but…if not for the urgency of finding Dave, this would be one heck of tour.

Not long after, we passed the mill and crested a ridge to find the road improved without logging traffic to mire our passage. Looking down into the valley below, Sarah pointed a shapely finger, "There in the clearing, where the road makes a bend, that's my place."

Soon we pulled up in front of the boarding house – a well-maintained two-story frame house, painted yellow, with a wrap-around porch. As I dismounted, trying to ignore my aching backside, and was trying to help Sarah off the horse, an almost hysterical black woman came tearing down the steps. "Ms. Sarah, Ms. Sarah, what happened to you? Who is this man? Did he hurt you? I'll wop him with this here skillet?" I found myself reflexes working as I was ducking as the woman swung a large iron skillet at my head. I hoped her aim wouldn't improve with another pass of the skillet.

"It's OK, Mattie" Sarah said, too casually from my defensive point of view. "He rescued me from the sorry trash that snatched me out of my garden and now he's brought me home." Mattie, still breathing hard, lowered the skillet that would have stove in the head of a buffalo, but continued to eye me with undisguised suspicion.

Before I could figure out how to get in Mattie's good graces, a red-haired boy of about eleven or twelve came tearing around the corner of the house, whooping, "Mama, Mama, what happened? Mattie said the robbers had taken you. I wanted to go after you, but she wouldn't let me have one of the guns." With an angry lady with a skillet swinging at my head and now a small boy exploding onto the scene, I had to wonder what was coming next.

"I'm OK Sam," Sarah reassured the boy, whose arms were now wrapped around her waist. A tremble in her voice belied the relief she felt, mixed with the thought she might not have come home to her son had I not appeared out of the blue. At least, no matter whether or not I was able to rescue Dave, I could tell Charlie Rawlins that something good came of my trip to 1911. Only later in the day would it hit me that I'd changed history for a mother and child in saving the boarding house owner on a lonely road in the woods.

Suddenly our attention was drawn by the dusty clatter of two rapidly approaching horses. The first rider jumped off his winded mount and paused to spit tobacco from beneath his handlebar moustache. He wore a badge, so I assumed he was the local deputy.

"Sarah, thank God you are OK," the deputy eyed Ms. Murphy in a way that suggested she was more of an interest to him than just any rescued citizen.

Focusing somewhat bloodshot eyes on me for the first time, Deputy Dwag..... well, Deputy Wooster, as it turned out, asked, "Who are you and what are you doing here?" His hand rested on his holstered pistol while he glared at me suspiciously. Sarah spoke on my behalf with a spark of Irish anger in her voice. "Bill, back off, for crying out loud. I wouldn't be standing here if not for him. He saved me from that trash that robbed the bank and tied me to a tree. Don't worry about him and go arrest that sorry pair we left back on the old Roland Pike. They can't have gone far; one has a broken leg."

"Broken leg, uh, what'd you do Buster? Didn't shoot him did you? Looks like a city slicker to me. Likely don't even own a gun." Clearly Deputy Wooster and I were not going to bond here in Ms. Murphy's yard. "I shot his mule out from under him, and it fell on him." I didn't have any intention of telling the deputy, who clearly was suspicious of me, that I'd actually been aiming at the mounted man and felt sorry for the mule I'd killed instead.

"Where you from Bub? I keep a close eye on strangers around here – part of my job. I'm also keeping an eye on Sarah's place here. You're just passing through, right? Not staying here, are you mister?"

"Bill, damn it, and excuse my language. Leave the man alone and go pick up the bank robbers that would likely have killed me, or worse, if it wasn't for Dr. Kernick here. And yes, he is staying. I've got a vacant room, if he wants it." Sarah clearly was a woman to speak her mind.

Wanting to have the last word, Wooster leaned into my face, giving me the full impact of his bad breath, and said, "Yeah, a spare room... hear her cooking killed the last guy who had that room." Sarah clenched her fists, preparing to let him have it, when the deputy pulled his horse between her and his body as he mounted up. "I'll be checking on you fella" was his parting shot.

"You're welcome to the room – at no charge of course. I can't put a price on what I owe you, Jack. Jack...is that really your name?" The woman had a way of making a statement that left little room for debate.

"Uh...I think maybe just for tonight. I really need to get to Little Rock. I have to locate a friend I'm supposed to meet there. How long does it take to drive into...no... I mean, when can I catch a train to Little Rock?" Drive, geeze, I was going to have to be more careful with my sense of place and forget that, in the time from which I came, a broad paved Highway #10 and my truck would have taken me to Little Rock in less than an hour.

Young Sam jumped back into the conversation with, "Mom, I'll take him to his room – the one old Mr. Jenkins had, right? See, he died mister...died dead, right there on the front porch in that rocking chair... just died. Had Zeke, Zeke's my dog, a howling up a storm. But don't worry. He didn't die or anything in your room."

I followed the copper-haired boy, who would have made a good Opie on the Andy Griffith show of my era, through a parlor with Victorian furnishings and up two flights of stairs. The thought occurred to me that perhaps old Mr. Jenkins wouldn't have keeled over on the porch, had he not had the strain of hiking up these steps every day. Finally, at the end of hallway, Sam opened the door to my room, in which I found a bed and a washstand in front of a window overlooking the garden.

"Hope you like the room, Mister. I think Mom changed the sheets Mr. Jenkins used. He was kinda nasty, always dipping snuff. Mamma caught him drinking moonshine which he got at a still over near the mill. Thought she was gonna kick him out then. See Mamma don't allow no drinking in her boarding house. You don't drink, do you Mister?

If you smoke, Mamma says gotta go out to the porch. Don't want the house catching fire, she says." Lord, this boy could talk! But it was impossible not to like him. He was a refreshing change from the television-bred kids of my own time.

"Sam, uh, where's the bathroom?" I asked, feeling the call of nature.

Bathroom?? Uh, well the tub is on the back porch."Comprehension sinking in, the boy said, "oh, you mean the outhouse, I think. It's out there," he said, pointing out the window. Following his stubby finger, I saw a classic, but oddly painted yellow, outhouse between two large oak trees not far from the garden. Sensing my surprise that it was so far from the house, Sam reassured me, "but, let me show you. There's a thunder mug under the bed here." He lifted the colorful quilt and pulled out a ceramic bowl, complete with handle and cover. "This is sure nice in the middle of the night when it's raining or cold enough to freeze your…uh…when its freezing. Just don't do what old Mr. Jenkins did. Mama didn't like that at all – no sir! You know, he would just empty his slop jar there out that window sometimes, right on Mama's roses. Dang near killed some of them, she says." I promised Sam his mother's roses would be safe from me during my stay.

After Sam left, his feet bounding down the stairs, I looked around the simple, but clean wallpapered room, noting the absence of electric lights and outlets. The kerosene lamp on the washstand was the only thing that would hold off the dark of a night in 1911. I closed my eyes for a second, visualizing a modern hotel room like the hundreds I'd slept in when traveling for business or pleasure – the bedside lamps, cable TV, alarm clocks, and fully equipped private bathrooms. Though only a century removed from my own time, I felt in some ways I'd been hurled into the wild west.

I was returning from the outhouse, with two dogs in tow I'd not seen before, when I met Sarah coming out of the garden with a basket of lettuce under her arm. "I hope Sam got you settled OK. I told him to draw you up a bath on the back porch. Figured you would want to get rid of the mud and grime from the woods before dinner."

Before I could find the bath tub on my own, Sam met me on the back steps, and showed me a curtained-off room with steam rising above the curtain rod. He pulled it back for me, and pointed with some pride to a tin, high-backed bath tub full of steaming water. "Heated the water on the stove in the kitchen for you. Took eight buckets. We gets our water out of that well out back... pretty good water too." Next to the tub was a chair draped with clothing I didn't recognize.

"Mama noticed you was traveling a little light. These are some of my daddy's old clothes. She thought you and he was about the same size. He was a pretty big man – real strong too ...lots of muscles from working up at the mill." The boy's voice trailed off, a sadness coming through as he talked about his father.

After Sam drew the curtain and left me, I removed my dirty clothes and settled slowly into the steamy water. A bar of what must have been lye soap and a washcloth were on the chair next to the tub. I wondered idly how often the departed Mr. Jenkins had bathed here and how such a system worked in the dead of a short, but often cold, Arkansas winter.

Sitting neck deep in the soapy water, I nodded off to sleep. The dream came again like a slippery fog, except this time it was a red-haired woman walking the smoky, death-strewn battlefield I somehow knew was Gettysburg. She seemed to be looking for something or someone among the scattered dead, whose shot- and shell-shattered bodies littered the bloody grass like grotesque puppets. As the woman turned in profile, she seemed very familiar, but her identity was hidden inside the fog of my brain.

"Oh Lord, oh Lord," the woman moaned as she found the body she sought. She looked down, her hands gripping a scarf, and the tears started to flow as she bent to close the staring dead eyes of the blue-clad officer. In a flash, I knew the fallen soldier was me. When she turned her head, as if toward the camera of my mind, I saw the woman was Sarah Murphy.

"Mister, Mister, you ain't done died in there, has you? I gotta come in there if you don't answer me Mister." I woke with a start to almost cold water and the booming voice of Mattie standing outside the curtain.

"No, no, I'm fine Mattie. Just give me a minute, and I'll be out," I said as I toweled off while struggling to clear the battlefield dream from my mind. I found Sarah's deceased husband's red plaid shirt and cotton pants to be an acceptable fit, although the chest-to-knee-length underwear were decidedly not my style. Mattie told me to leave my dirty clothes on the chair so she could wash them. I first examined the outfit carefully to make sure nothing like zippers would be out of place for the era. With snaps on the pants I decided the wardrobe would pass Mattie's inspection.

As I walked by the kitchen on my way to the dining room in the front of the sprawling house, my sense of gloom faded with the aromas coming from the stove. At least some things had not changed when I traveled back in time. I was suddenly ravenous and looking forward to a good meal.

Chapter 9

THAT I WAS holding up dinner was apparent on the faces of the eight other boarding-house patrons. As I entered the dining room, one skinny little man felt obliged to mutter, "Well, it's about time. I pay four bits a day for food here. Ought not to have it get cold waiting on lollygagging new folks."

Sarah entered the room, with a bustling Mattie in tow with serving dishes in both hands. Without question, dinner had been delayed while I was nodding off in the tub. The aroma of steaming chicken and dumplings, fresh bread, and purple hull peas wafted the length of the table, filling my senses. As I started to reach for the bowl Mattie had set in the center of the table, the mood was broken a bit by the skinny little man, "Mister, be careful, that chicken and dumplings will hurt your eyes. Not bothering to wait on my response, the little man laughed and said, "cause will sure hurt your eyes trying to find the chicken." Apparently this tired joke was tried out on all new guests. Nonetheless, it was greeted with appreciative laughter by the other guests. It flashed back to me then that author Charles Portis had used that very line in his acclaimed novel, True Grit.

Sarah, long used to corny jokes from her regular guests, responded, "Now Mr. Jones I don't expect we will see you pushing back from the table without your fill, now will we?" "Well no," responded the jokester. You know one reason we all stay here is the grub is the best in town." The somewhat embarrassed little man then felt compelled to introduce himself and he reached across the table to shake my hand. "My name's Homer Jones. I'm a lumber buyer from Chicago and I visit the mill here in Bigelow about every three months...always stay here at Ms. Sarah's place."

Seeing, as well as feeling, all eyes on me, I politely returned Homer's greeting, nodding to the other men at the table. "Thanks, I'm sorry for holding up dinner. It's been, uh...well, a rough day. I'm Jack Kernick by the way, here from Texas to take in the reunion. Sarah saw fit to add, "Gentlemen, you should know that our new guest is also a physician and I hope you will make Dr. Kernick feel welcome."

A flood of questions followed from around the table as well as compliments on my bravery in rescuing their inn keeper from two inept bandits who – with repeated telling, I was sure – would soon sound like nothing short of the James gang. My lack of interest in rehashing my exploits soon steered the conversation to other topics.

"Not to worry, Doc, ...you is a doctor, a pheesician, Miss Sarah tells us?" I nodded, "Well, yes, Homer, I'm a doctor, though it has been a while since I practiced my trade." Somehow this funny little man brought an image of the comedian Jack Benny to my mind – an odd flash-back... or perhaps "flash-forward" would be a better term.

"Well Doctor... uh, Doctor Kernick, is it?" asked a bearded man, with an ample stomach straining his buttoned up vest coat. "I'm Reverend Elias Pickle. I'm staying here for two weeks to preach the revival down at the Brush Creek Baptist Church...which you are certainly welcome to attend after dinner. You are a church-going man, are you not Doctor?"

The entire table awaited my response, so I replied, "well, of course, I go to Mass almost every Sunday... uh...back home in Texas." The shock on the Reverends' three-chinned face was worth having replied to what would have been considered a rude question to a stranger in my own time.

"A Papist? You have to come to my revival, Dr. Kernick. Hell is a waiting on you for sure. You can't pay your allegiance to Rome and expect to go to heaven. You gotta accept Jesus. We will have an alter call tonight. You gotta..." At that point in my mind, the Reverend became as obnoxious as the worst TV preacher I could recall from my own time. He was drowned out by first Sarah and then a tall man in a coat and tie who cut her off with "Reverend, shut up for crying out loud. I don't want to listen to your sermon – not at the church and certainly not over my dinner. The man can go to any church he wants. He rescued Sarah today, which is a sight more good than I expect you did today." Rendered what I expected was uncharacteristically speechless, the Rev. Pickle shrank back into his chair.

"Let me apologize for the reverend's rudeness, Dr. Kernick. I'm Eugene Karp of St. Louis, an attorney for the mill owners," and with that the well-groomed man extended his hand. I took his outstretched hand, thinking there was no better put down for a loud-mouthed holier-than-thou preacher. I expected from his name and being from up north that Mr. Karp was Jewish.

"Thank you Mr. Karp. No harm done. It's a big world with room for lots of opinions," which I hoped would put an end to this part of the dinner conversation.

"We heard from Sarah here that you are in Arkansas to go to the old rebel's reunion in Little Rock. I'd sort of planned on going into the city to see some of it myself, though my family fought on the other side – the winning side of course." Seeing the reactions around the table to Karp's insensitive remark, I could almost hear my grandfather commenting, "Son, them is fighting words."

The Reverend Pickle, temporarily deflected from the need to save my soul, was reignited with this "shot" fired some 50 years after the start of the Civil War. "Mr. Karp, speaking for myself and most of the rest of us, you have raised an ugly issue, and I'd urge you to remember the honor we all impart to the heroes of the sacred South that answered General Lee's call to strike back at the Northern oppressors who did not respect the heritage and culture of our people in the states of the old confederacy."

"Honor? Honor you say, preacher? Where was the honor in enslaving a race of people, or in trying to wreck the unity of the nation? My grandfather lost a leg at Gettysburg. His brother died at Shiloh...." Looking from one man to the other, along with other guests who seemed poised to join the "battle," I envisioned the Jewish lawyer from St. Louis and the Baptist preacher from Arkansas starting up the Civil War anew.

"Gentlemen, that's QUITE ENOUGH," Sarah's surprisingly stern voice echoed around the room from where she stood in the kitchen door. "I won't have a war refought in my house, at my table." The silence that followed soon supported that the only shot that needed to be fired to end this renewed conflict had come from an Irish boarding house owner who none of the diners, regardless of their allegiance, was going to challenge.

"Right, right, it's all in the history books now, and of course it's an historic occasion for Arkansas to host this reunion," said a man in a vest and bowtie who introduced himself as Ed Raines, a traveling salesman for a hardware company. "Most of us are going to try to see it. I hear Little Rock is going to see a record crowd of folks."

Ed, eager to change the topic of conversation, addressed me in a loud voice "So, you came all the way from Texas to see the reunion, didja Doc? Being from San Antonio, I'd think the Alamo was more your war. Visited there once when the train laid over. Just couldn't believe old Davy Crockett and Jim Bowie got whipped by a bunch of greasers. But, I digress. Did you have kin folks in the war of northern aggression Doc?"

Processing his term for the Civil War, I was reminded anew that it was still a sore point in the south when people of all ages had family members, or at least knew people, who had fought in the war. It occurred to me that I could tell the truth, that my great grandmother had actually had three husbands during the Civil War. The first two died in the Union Army and the third, my great grandfather, was both a rebel and a ne'er-do-well alcoholic. I was tiring of this line of questioning though. "No, no, my family was mostly still in Ireland at the time of the Civil War. I've always been a history buff, and I have a friend attending the reunion I want to meet up with." This was only partly untrue, but I hoped it would do.

The Civil War conversation, although thankfully shifted away from my lineage, was picked by up by the Rev. Pickle. "Historic occasion it is for sure, and such a chance to honor our heroes. Let me read to you what a fellow man of the cloth has to say here in the newspaper about the sacredness of the occasion." Not waiting for permission, the Rev. Pickle proceeded loudly, *"Moral reforms should not be attempted by fanatical appeals to passion, nor by deceit, nor force. Fire eating abolitionist, attempted raids and the underground Rail Road were responsible for all the horror and suffering of the Civil War...Again though the Confederacy lost, yet it is victorious in this, that until the thrilling record is forgotten no section of the country will attempt to dominate another portion—the price paid by the North was to great...Every man ought to thank God that we are united and cemented stronger together than could have been had with the War.*" The smug-faced Reverend, placing the paper beneath his chair, said, "Shall we all say Amen to that?"

Electing to have the final word, Eugene Karp put a period on the discussion with, "I say the North won. Shut up Reverend and let's eat."

The dinner wound down, with generous slices of apple pie Mattie brought out from the kitchen, and the diners adjourned to the front porch where they could light up cigars. I passed on the invitation. The idea of sitting amid a half dozen fogging cigars was something I'd have avoided in any time period.

Instead I excused myself and told my fellow dinners I would take a walk, perhaps into Bigelow, which appeared to be only a couple of hundred yards down the rutted dirt road in front of the house. In retrospect I would have been better off on the porch with the cigars.

Downtown Bigelow...on impulse I bought this postcard at the drugstore soda fountain off a display rack for .5 cents.
The store, as it turned out, was just across the street from the town's jail.

Chapter 10

AFTER LEAVING THE boarding house, I passed by what I assumed was the church where Rev. Pickle was to preach that evening. The choir was already tuning up and "Shall we gather at the River" echoed out the open windows over the adjoining graveyard. I was actually tempted to stop in and listen to the hymns, but the idea of Rev. Pickle showing up and mistakenly thinking he had enticed a sinner like me into his web persuaded me otherwise and I continued on into town.

Bigelow, in my day a century later, was a small cluster of homes, small stores, and a post office less than an hour from Little Rock – a sleepy place where little happened, but a convenient commute down paved Highway #10 for folks with jobs in the capital city. However, in 1911 the timber boom was on and the nearby mill was the major source of employment. A handful of mostly wood-framed shops lined the rutted dirt street, with no automobiles in evidence. Horses and wagons were moving up and down the street, with others tied to hitching posts. It could have easily been a set from the TV show, "Gun Smoke" although I noticed nobody was wearing holstered six guns.

Most of the shops were still open at 6:00 p.m., hoping to sell something to the mill workers ending their shift – those that didn't make do from Mr. Bigelow's company store. Noticing a drug store, one of the few brick buildings in town, my professional curiosity drew me to step inside. The pharmacy counter, such as it was, occupied the back of the store. The front of the business was dominated by a long soda fountain on one side and rows of glass cabinets on the other holding cigars, pipe tobacco and rolling papers. Spittoons lined the path leading back to the pharmacy counter, behind which were an array of jars and bottles. It occurred to me that in 1911 the drug choice was limited, and that the white shirted pharmacist nodding to me would have compounded most of his medicines himself.

A young man washing glasses behind the soda fountain said, "Yes sir, what can I get you?" I settled for a chocolate milk shake in a tall glass, which set me back five cents. I gave the boy a dime and told him to keep the change. His smile and thank you suggested he didn't get a lot of tipping customers. I purchased a three-day-old copy of the Arkansas Gazette for 3 cents and took my milk shake out onto the porch where a bench beneath the window offered a place to read and observe the world of 1911 a bit.

The UCV Reunion dominated the newspaper, and I felt drawn to study it, perhaps in the hope of getting some idea where I would begin my search for Dave once I arrived in Little Rock. Some of the coverage I'd seen in the blurry copies pulled from a computer Charlie gave me to read in 2011, but sitting here while the news was fresh, the ink rubbing off on my hands, brought the news to life. An editorial in the paper summed up a lot of the feelings engendered by the occasion. *"Most of the men who camped with Lee and Forrest and fought with them in the dark days of civil strife have already camped on the other side, and the few who remain are but awaiting the bugle signal to come up higher. Comrades of the past, men who fought battles of the world, will clasp hands and march together in Little Rock for the last time. It is unlike any other reunion or convention ever entertained by Little Rock, because of the fact that many of those who come here will join the great reunion above before the muster roll is called for another reunion here."*

The Civil war had ended only 46 years before the night I sat on the porch, with wagons passing on the muddy street. It occurred to me that the Civil War had been over for a period considerably shorter than WWII in my own time. I could not help but remember that the Arkansas Gazette, extolling the defeated Confederacy for readers in 1911, would win worldwide acclaim for its support of civil rights and public school integration by nine black students into Little Rock's Central High School in 1957. It was all such a jumble in my head of what was happening on this night in 1911 and what had not yet happened, what would not happen for decades to come. Knowing the future was more of a burden that I had expected.

Reading on into the editorial, I continued to marvel at the elegance of the writer. *"Of course, there is a business side to it, too, and the people of Little Rock will benefit from a successful reunion. But first and foremost and above all else is the perfect entertainment of those old soldiers who are packing their knapsacks for the last, tedious journey to the undiscovered country."* Quietly, I whispered, "Amen."

As I was finishing the story extolling the glories of the defeated, but most valiant Confederate fighting men, an unpleasant voice interrupted my private thoughts. "Well mister, see you are still here in my town. Not sure I like that." I took longer than necessary to look up into the expected face of the still unpleasant deputy Wooster.

"Well deputy, I'm not sure I really give a damn whether or not you like much of anything, truth be told," I said – words I could have chosen more wisely I reflected later in the evening. Not stopping to let him draw a less-than-snappy reply , I continued, "I trust you now have the bank robbers I waylaid in the woods locked up in your jail?"

"Well, funny you should bring that up mister," and I somehow knew I wasn't going to like the answer. "All we found on that road was a dead mule, a bullet through its head. The two outlaws – if they were there at all – was long gone."

"Gone? Hell, then why didn't you track them down?" I was starting to get angry at this dimwit, not the wisest response to a man with a badge and gun, whether in 1911 or the 2011 in which my world revolved less than 36 hours earlier. "One of them had a badly broken leg. The other was drunk. They could not have gotten far."

"Yeah, that's right, if you was telling the truth, but you know, I'm a trained lawman. I have a very good bullshit smeller, know when someone is telling me the truth, and boy…I think you are a lying." Before I could reply, my recently downed chocolate milk shake turned even colder in my stomach as Deputy Wooster pulled his gun and leveled it at me.

"I think those fellas that robbed the bank and shot the sheriff had a partner, someone to help them plan the robbery. You are the only stranger in town. I think it could have been you, so I'm locking you up in my jail while I investigate. You know we sent Sheriff Jenkins into Little Rock on a stretcher on the 5:00 pm train. He has a bullet in his gut somewhere. The doctors at the big city hospital may be able to save him, maybe not, but I'm in charge for now and I'm going to find out what's what. First off, I want to know who the hell you really are?"

"You already know. I'm Jack Kernick. I'm a physician – that's a doctor to you – from San Antonio, Texas," a rebuttal I tried to offer as strongly as I could while being mindful of the pistol pointed at me.

"A doc from San Antone, you say? Well, funny thing about that. I used the telephone up at the lumber mill to call the Judge over in Little Rock. Seems he has a good judge friend down in San Antone who he called up for me. The Judge in San Antone talked to the hospital there in the city, not sure who else, and he says nobody down there ever heared tell of you before. So I think you're lying about who you are and maybe lying about not being connected to them bank robbers that kidnapped Sarah."

The old Laurel and Hardy catch phrase – "another fine mess you've got me into" – passed unbidden through my mind. "Well I haven't practiced medicine since I came to San Antonio, not since I was out in California," was about the only lie I could think of, while I felt myself sinking deeper into trouble. "Well, I don't believe you. I think that's horse shit you're shoveling on me, and I'm locking you up in the jail. The Judge will be out from Little Rock next week. We'll just see what he thinks. Meanwhile, with you safely locked up and not laid up at Sarah's place, I'll do me some more investigating." With that he motioned me off the porch with his pistol toward the jail a half block down the dirt street.

Seeing little alternative, other than risk being shot, I got up and let Wooster lead me toward the jail. Once inside, the deputy wasted no time opening up a cell and shoving me inside, after which he loudly clanged the iron door shut and twisted the large key in the lock. Our abrupt arrival woke up an old man seated at a desk, causing him to spill cold coffee in his lap.

"Hank, we got us a prisoner here and I need to you to guard him close. Shoot him if he makes any fuss." Deputy Wooster's orders seemed to confuse the grizzled old man who had to be in his 70s

"Now Hank, I'm heading home to my dinner. You keep an eye on the good doctor here and I'll spell you in the morning." Wooster's orders seemed to confuse the old man further who could only reply with, "uh, Bill, what's he done, ain't he the doctor that saved Sarah from the robbers? Why we locking him up?" Judging by Hank's plaid shirt and lopsided badge hanging on the pocket, it appeared the poor man must have been called to duty only after the Sheriff was shot earlier in the day.

"Don't know for sure, but I think the doc – if he really is a doc – may have been in cohoots with them robbers. We gonna keep him locked up till Judge Wilson comes from Little Rock next week." Deputy Wooster clearly didn't like me, which normally would not have given me a second thought had I not been a century back in time and locked in a cell. The prospect of remaining caged in Bigelow, while the events of the Confederate Reunion transpired 50 miles away – complete with the death of Dave Rawlins a few days hence – sat on my mind like a millstone.

As Deputy Wooster left, slamming the heavy door, my elderly jailor shuffled over to the cell. "Mister, don't know who you ere. Don't know what you did. Don't care, truth be told, but you don't give me no trouble and we will be OK." With that, he returned to his desk and resumed reading what looked to be an old copy of the *Police Gazette*.

I'd never been in jail, never expected to be, and the more or less 10 foot by10 foot cage flashed back memories of a restless, pathetic

REUNION IN TIME

lion I'd once seen in the Little Rock zoo. Pacing didn't seem to help a lot. I told myself I needed a plan but was clueless as to what it could be. I was sitting on the sagging cot, trying to get comfortable, when the front door opened.

Sarah, wearing an almost floor-length dress and wrap around her shoulders blew through the door with a flourish, startling poor Hank, who dropped the tobacco he was trying to roll into a cigarette in his lap. Something told me the striking red-haired lady wasn't out to just inspect jail conditions.

"Uh, Sarah, what you doing here? It's after 10:00…drunks out. You gotta leave. Bill left me in charge. You can't just…" The poor old man was out of his league.

"Hank, please be quiet. I just stopped to talk to Jack a minute. This is crazy. I'd be dead in the woods if not for him. Now please, just forget I'm here. Go back to your smoke." Hank seemed at a loss for any more argument and remained seated behind the desk while Sarah pulled up a battered wooden chair in front of my cell.

"Jack, I'm sorry. This is nuts. I heard from one of the men at the mill what that fool Bill Wooster had done. I even stopped by his pig sty of a house on the edge of town before I came here. I told him he was a damn fool. You saved my life, and he has to know you had nothing to do with those trashy robbers, other than getting me away from them."

"Well, I'm glad you at least believe that. I just don't understand why he doesn't." As I said it, I could not help but notice a bit of confusion and coming questions behind those attractive green eyes.

"As nutty as it is, and I really don't believe he is serious about his theory you were mixed up with the robbers, the fact is that nobody in San Antonio seemed to know who you were. That town's not all that much bigger than Little Rock where every doctor in the city – even the county – is well known. If you could explain that, it would help. I could talk to one of the bosses at the mill, get them to use their telephone….." Sarah was transparently working me for answers to some of her own questions.

"Well, I'm not sure I can do much about that, sitting here in this lockup, but I'd tell them it's likely because I have not actually practiced medicine in a good while." I knew this wasn't going to pass muster with the attractive woman sitting in front of my barred cell. Anticipating more questions and hoping to minimize the lies that would only get me in deeper, I added, "I've supported myself with investments in others business and in stocks".

Silent for the moment, while casting a sideways glance at Deputy Hank, Sarah handed me a folded note through the bars. It had been a long time since I'd gotten a note from an attractive woman, or from any woman for that matter. Opening the note, I read, "the first train to Little Rock in the morning leaves at 6:00 am. I'll get you out in time, but not much before, and help you get on it." How she planned to do that, I had not a clue, but I silently mouthed "thank you."

Sarah said her farewells, made some idle pleasantries with the still-confused Deputy Hank, and left a paper bag on his desk. Then she left me alone with my jailer, who muttered under his breath to her departing back, "Women, God knows, never understood 'em." Under the circumstances, I'd have been hard pressed to disagree.

"But she did leave me a nice gift here," and with that, he extracted a flask-shaped bottle of what was obviously whisky from the bag Sarah left. "Sarah, she don't allow no drinking at her place. Said she found this bottle in the room of that old man that died up there a while back. Sure don't want it to go to waste." And with that, Hank took a healthy belt from the bottle, clearly headed for a bender. Something told me Sarah had not given the gift out of kindness toward the old jailer.

Sometime after midnight, I finally lapsed into a troubled sleep on the lumpy cot in the cell, while a rain starting to fall outside the barred back window. I was awakened by a tug on my pants leg at the end of the cot. Shaking myself awake, in the room lit only by a light near the front door, I made out Sarah standing in front of the bars.

Before I could even extract myself from the sagging cot, she had opened the door with a key affixed to a clanking iron ring. "What the …?." But she cut off my surprised reaction in mid utterance with a hand pressed against my mouth and an index finger against her lips, telling me to be quiet.

Standing up, my second or third thought was Deputy Hank, who I could hear, better than see – face down on his desk and snoring loud enough to almost rattle the bars on the cell block. "He's out. Don't worry about him, but we have to get you out of here quickly before someone else shows up to relieve him."

"Uh, what happened to the deputy?" I whispered, visions of Sarah having brained him with a pistol barrel or something equally hard flashing through my mind.

"Oh, the old coot will be fine. The flask I left him last night… The whisky had an additive the drug store had given me. I told them I had a boarder who was having trouble sleeping, keeping other folks up."

She had my knapsack with her, containing my clothes and money. Picking this up off the floor, she pulled me by the arm toward the back of the jail where the back door opened into a muddy, rather foul smelling alley. She reached into my bag and pulled out a battered black cloth hat, telling me, "this will disguise you a bit." I assumed it had also come from her late husband's things. "This way, follow me. I think we can make it almost to the depot by following the alley," Sarah advised while pulling me along.

I almost fell face down in the muddy alley and narrowly, I'm sure, avoided a heart attack when a large hog darted out from under the back porch of a building in front of me, disappearing into the brush on the other side of the alley. At another point, Sarah pulled me back when a second-floor door opened and a man emptied the contents of his slop jar over the railing, passed gas loudly, and disappeared back to bed, I hoped.

We stopped when we reached what appeared to be the end of the alley, with the dawn's light starting to break. Looking around the corner of what proved to be the general store, I could see the train station with several men milling around the passenger and freight docks. Before I could ponder what we were to do next, I heard the short whistle of a locomotive and, a minute later, a plume of smoke puffed over the trees just up the track.

"Let's go. Unless Bill Wooster shows up, or someone has found your cell empty, nobody should notice us. I bought you a ticket to Little Rock last night. The train should pull out in about 30 minutes. We need you aboard." Sarah was clearly in charge of my escape from Bigelow. "You also need a place to stay in Little Rock" and with that, she handed me what appeared to be a postcard of a large house. "This is the Remmel mansion. He's my cousin and they live in this huge rambling house. I've written a note on the back telling him you are a friend in need of a room for a few days. Take him that and I'm sure he will put you up."

Sarah started to cross the street to the depot, but I pulled her back around the corner of the building. "No, I think you need to stay out of sight. People at the depot know you. You don't need to be seen with me Sarah. At this point nobody knows it was you that got me out of the jail. I'd like to leave it that way….no matter how this works out." Not waiting on a reply, I strode across the street hopefully like a man just heading to Little Rock and not one just broken out of jail.

When I reached the plank walk at the end of the depot, I looked back to where I'd left Sarah but she had vanished, thankfully taking my advice. The thought crossed my mind that I'd likely not see her again, but I tried to shake off any regret and remind myself I was an escaped prisoner fleeing town.

I quickly walked past the ticket window and the line of a dozen people that had formed out of the darkness to purchase tickets. I could not help but hear one old man, leaning on a cane, "Wish I could still shoot me some Yankees like I done up at Pea Ridge back in '62." I was already handing my ticket to the conductor standing at the door to the closest passenger car when it struck me, the old guy meant 1862. Pea Ridge, I recalled from my history, had been the largest Civil War battle fought on Arkansas soil and had permanently ended the Confederacy's hope of pushing into Missouri. Putting the war out of my mind, it occurred to me that I'd not been on board a train since I was a child. Little did I know that the smoking locomotive five cars ahead of me was the least strange part of this journey that I sensed was beginning a new leg.

Chapter 11

LIKE WITH THE hundreds of airplanes I'd boarded in my time, I turned into the passenger railcar looking down at my ticket for a seat number, which it lacked. It appeared to be "open seating," as the Southwest Airlines of my day would have labeled it. When I looked up to find an open seat, the faces staring back at me formed a startling image like a scene from a movie. In almost every seat sat an elderly man, many wearing Confederate gray uniforms and most with white beards.

A number of the old men were accompanied by women, most of whom were much younger. A few of the old soldiers sat with younger men. From my reading about the reunion and from studying Civil War history, I knew many Confederate veterans married much younger women in their later years. The women would draw Confederate pensions paid by the state, some living into the 1960s. I took a seat across from an old man whose remote eyes stared at me out of a wrinkled face. I guessed that the young blonde woman seated with him could be little older than 25. She smiled at me, while gripping the old man's hand.

Seated beside me was an equally aged veteran in gray, who had pulled the window down and was having an animated conversation with someone on the depot platform. "Hell yes, we coulda won the war. You damn Yankees were just lucky to win. If we'd had a smarter General at Gettysburg, you'd be singing Dixie up there is St. Louis." Apparently he had been drawn into an argument with a railroad employee who didn't share his allegiance with Confederacy's lost cause.

Pulling the window closed, the old man noticed me for the first time. Still pumped up from his debate out the window, he put out his hand and said, "Hello young man. I'm Jude Glenn, late of General Lee's army where I served as a sergeant...fought at Vicksburg and Chattanooga, and am proud to make your acquaintance. Who might you be?" His long bony-fingered hand had the texture of ancient parchment, but the grip was strong.

"Jack Kernick from Texas, sir. It's a pleasure to meet you," I responded, feeling a genuineness from somewhere inside me. The good feeling vanished in an instant as I caught an image through the window of Deputy Wooster standing on the train platform.

I slumped a bit lower in the seat, pulling down the battered hat Sarah had given me, but maintaining a continued line of sight to Wooster. He didn't appear to be searching, just walking a bit and exchanging a casual greeting or two with men passing by. I breathed a sigh of relief as he turned away to walk down the street. In the instant it registered on my briefly relieved brain that he was likely headed for the jail, the train began to move out of the station.

"Are you all right son? You look as startled and worried as I felt the morning the yanks starting shelling my breastworks at Vicksburg back in '63 – danged near crapped my drawers, I did." Sergeant Glenn's interest in my well being brought me back to focus, and I replied, "Oh yes, I'm fine – just a bit lost in thought. You must be headed for the reunion?" As the words left my mouth, I thought a more stupid question likely had not been asked so far in 1911, this to an old man in a frayed Confederate uniform on board a train bound for the city hosting the gathering.

"Well yes, I've been looking forward to this reunion since the one last year in Macon...That's in Georgia, you know. Haven't missed a single reunion since the UCV started having them back in '90. Though I tell you son, it's getting harder every year. You know, I'm 83 years old, and still carrying a musket ball in my leg. There are so few of us left, though. I know most of us old soldiers are passing on soon. I just want to make at least one more reunion." The old man's voice trailed off, and a tear run down his lined face, disappearing into the wrinkles but emerging to leave a poignant wet stain on the collar of his gray coat.

Regaining his composure, as the train picked up speed in the gathering daylight striking the trees along the track, the old reb continued in a strong voice. "I've outlived two wives, and three of my nine children, Jack. My second wife – she died before the reunion in Macon last year, died in childbirth she did – was only 24 years-old. Lost the baby as well… right near broke my heart. You know, when she married me, I guess to just get off that dirt-poor farm, she joked about doing it so she could draw my Confederate pension someday when she was an old grandma. Son, just none of us know what the good Lord has in store in this life." "Oh Sergeant Glenn," I almost shouted, "you have no idea how true that is… no idea."

"Oh, I know what a young feller like you might be thinking. What was a 24-year-old girl doing having my baby?" said the old man, scanning my face for confirmation of my thoughts. That question was on the tip of my tongue, not that I'd have asked it. He was used to it, though, and felt obligated to continue.

"Edna was one of 14 kids – the oldest – up on a farm in the Ozarks a few miles outside of Jasper, looking forward only to backbreaking work taking care of that brood of kids her worthless, moonshining excuse for a pappy had brought into the world before his poor wife up and died one day. My farm was not too far away, just across the Buffalo River, but it was a sight more prosperous, mostly cause I worked it hard with my mules. We always had enough to eat anyway."

The old gentleman was silent then, and I heard him begin to snore softly. His head dropped down on his gray-clad chest and he slept in a world of peaceful dreams, I hoped…dreams where bloody battles were no more and young mothers to be didn't die before seeing the new life they bore.

The rhythmic noise from the train moving over the tracks would have lulled me to sleep as well, perhaps making up for my less than restful night in the Bigelow jail. However, sleep didn't come. I had to think through what I should do when the train arrived in Little

Rock in an hour or so. As the tall pine trees raced by the window, a worried thought struck me, one that should have been on my radar the instant I saw Deputy Wooster on the Bigelow depot siding.

Surely Wooster would find my cell empty this morning. Very likely, he already had. Certainly odds were high my escape would be noticed before the train pulled into Little Rock's Union Station. Surely he would call or telegraph the police force in Little Rock that I'd likely be embarking from the train arriving from Bigelow. Getting out of the capital city's jail would surely be harder than it was to escape from the one in Bigelow... likely impossible.

Racking my brain for a solution, I looked up as the conductor came down the aisle, chatting with the old soldiers. "Yep, my pappy was at Gettysburg, maybe even ran alongside you in Pickett's charge," was part of the conversation he was having with the passenger seated in front of me. The elderly rebel replied, "Maybe so. Maybe so. There were so many of our soldiers in General Pickett's regiment that day that never saw another sunrise. I always felt blessed that all I lost was this arm," he said, raising an empty sleeve as if to salute the long-dead comrades who died in Pennsylvania in 1863.

The uniformed conductor, moving his attention to me, spoke from under a massive handlebar mustache in a heavy Irish brogue, "Well sir, you look a might too young to have fought the Yankees. Would that be your pappy there you are traveling with to the reunion?"

"Uh, no sir... just, by chance, a seatmate, though I did enjoy meeting him. He seems to have drifted off." Since he remained standing there, it was apparent the friendly conductor was interested in knowing more about me, and I felt obligated to oblige him. "I'm just going to the reunion to see the doings and try to meet a friend."

"Well you enjoy yourself. I'm planning on at least going to the big parade on the last day myself. My old daddy, he never quit talking about the war... been gone neigh on to 15 years now...survived Pea Ridge and then worked for the railroad for 20 years." As the conductor started to move on, it occurred to me to ask, "Oh, wonder if you could tell me, does the train stop anywhere before it gets to the station in Little Rock?"

"Well, let's see? There isn't any depot stops, but we do stop for a bit just before we cross the Baring Cross bridge on the north side of the river. Normally we go into Little Rock on the west side of town, but the tracks are being worked on over by the new state capitol. We will go through Argenta and come into the Choctaw Station east of the main part of Little Rock, instead of the Iron Mountain station. We'll take on water and coal just before we take the Baring Cross bridge over the river. Can't get it at the depot. Likely will take us 20 minutes or so – time to stretch a little, if you need to." Argenta, I knew, had been the name of what later became North Little Rock.

"Bearing Cross? Sounds like a church," was a question that popped out of my head. "Ha, ha, not quite. It's BARING cross. I guess it means the bridges bare the load of this old train." The kindly conductor seemed pleased to educate me on the bridge.

He leaned down, pulled his fobbed pocket watch out to check the time, and looked out the window. "As a matter of fact, we should be coming to…." The train's shuddering as it slowed down made it unnecessary for him to finish the sentence. "Pulling close to the bridge right now – water stop coming up." Pocketing his heavy watch, he excused himself, "Well, I've got work to do. You enjoy the rest of the ride and maybe I'll see you at the reunion doings."

Indeed, while I'd been talking with the conductor, the train had pulled within sight of a massive iron bridge high above the Arkansas River, which to my vantage point seemed as wide as an ocean.

The train came to a shuddering stop beyond the northern end of the bridge, somewhere near what would be part of the city of North Little Rock in my own time. From my reading in advance of leaving 2011, I knew the community was still called Argenta in 1911. My view out the car window revealed trees, rocks and a platform for taking on water and coal, with no city in sight.

I walked to the front of the car and stepped out onto the outside small platform. By leaning out a little, I could see the wide, free-flowing river passing below the massive iron Baring Cross railroad bridge. I didn't expect the train would be stopped long and, as far as I could tell, this would be the last stop before arriving at the Little Rock depot. I had to move quickly, but how?

When I stepped back into the car, I noticed all the passengers were awake and milling around, looking out the windows, some wondering why the train was stopped, or looking for the Little Rock depot perhaps, not having had the advance information I possessed from the conductor. I retrieved my knapsack from beneath the seat, and started back toward the exit door. "Whoa fella, this isn't the station, just a stop for water," one of the old soldiers said, tugging at my sleeve. "Uh, oh I know that sir. I just have to, uh, take a leak while we're stopped." His puzzled expression suggested that perhaps that term in 1911 might refer to the train, rather than a function of my bladder.

I looked carefully up and down the tracks before I stepped down onto the crushed rock supporting the crossties near where a switch in the tracks would swing the train toward the iron bridge. I could see the smoking engine's tank being filled with water several cars up. None of the men so occupied appeared to notice me and I was able to make my way back onto the high river bank on the north side of the bridge. I slipped between a cleft in the large rock formations lining the track to get out of sight of the train. Although I was sure some passengers had observed my actions, it couldn't be helped. I could not afford to be on the train when it rolled into the Little Rock station.

I found a clump of brush and rocks in an elevated spot perhaps 30 yards from the idling train and settled down to wait and think about what I was to do next. About 10 minutes later, the trains whistle sounded and the engine began to pull the train away. Somehow I was going to have to cross that river again, without the train ride – how I didn't have a clue.

As I had so often found in my life, if I would just take the time to look around me, to assess my options, a plan would present itself for whatever problem was staring me in the face. In this case, such inspiration came from tilting my head back in thought to find myself looking straight up into the massive oak tree upon which I rested my back.

It took me at least 20 minutes, but finally I climbed to a lofty viewing perch some 30 feet up in the tree. Looking east down the river, a possible route into Little Rock revealed itself. In the distance I could clearly see at least two bridges spanning the river between what I'd known in 2011 as North Little Rock and the larger city of Little Rock. The vantage point also allowed me to discard the idea of walking over the Baring Cross bridge, which had some sort of gatehouse at the Little Rock end that might well be manned. Aside from that fact, the idea of walking over the bridge, while praying a train would not come along, was enough incentive alone to look for other options.

It seemed likely I could walk from the north bank of the river into downtown Little Rock provided I could transverse the five miles or so of rugged riverbank to reach one of the distant bridges. Surely if I kept the river in sight, eventually I'd reach one of the bridges I could see downstream that would surely accommodate foot traffic. I could not help but notice the state Capitol dome in the distance above some trees across the river.

It soon became apparent it would not be an easy walk to reach a bridge to Little Rock. Trying at first to stay near the river, as ever higher rocks seemed to rise on my left, I came within an hour to an impossible tangle of brush and rocks that seemed to terminate between the cliff to my left and the river to my right. I was going to have to backtrack and look for a way to climb the bluff, a daunting task. After resting for a while against a rock, and taking a drink from what I hoped was a clean spring coming from a seep in the cliff wall, I reversed my course. It occurred to me that in 2011, a paved bike and jogging path would run along the river between the Baring Cross bridge site and the downtown bridges I needed to reach.

Eventually I came to an accessible point where the rock wall dipped down toward the river, and gained a purchase. There I found a footpath, one that seemed well worn. For more than a half hour, I struggled up the path using a limb for a walking stick, while listening to man-made sounds somewhere above the bluff, though I couldn't be sure of their nature. It didn't matter. I only had one direction to go, and that was wherever this path would lead.

As I stepped around a large rock jutting into the rough path, I saw a blur of motion and felt a jarring impact on my right ankle. A large rattle snake was affixed to my boot. Breaking out of my trance-like fear, I hit the snake with my hiking stick, knocking it loose and into the brush. I heard it thrashing away and collapsed on the ground, wondering if I was going to die from a snakebite on this dusty rock pile.

However, I breathed a sigh of relief that could probably be heard across the river when I unlaced the rough old boot Charlie gave me to see there were no puncture marks on my ankle.

As I marveled at my good luck and intact ankle, my feeling of relief gave way to one almost of despair. In the two days since arriving in 1911, I'd been beset by outlaws, tossed into jail, and now attacked by a snake. What could happen next? Somehow I'd survived. My guardian angel was on duty, and a small prayer of thanksgiving was certainly in order. That obligation taken care of, I pulled myself up and started for the cliff summit. Not so far away now, the sounds of human activity grew louder. With anticipation laced with fatigue, I wondered what lay just out of sight over the edge of the cliff.

Chapter 12

FINALLY I REACHED the top of the cliff and, when I pulled my tired body around the last rock, the scene that opened up before me was both amazing and revealing as to my location. I was staring across the parade ground of what I knew to be Fort Logan Roots, then an active post of the US Army. In my own time, the facility – with many of its historic Calvary era buildings standing just as I saw them in 1911 – was a VA hospital campus.

The parade ground was bustling with troops doing close order drill, the soldiers in their khaki-colored uniforms moving back and forth to the shouts of a drill sergeant. It struck me, as I dropped down on a cliff-side rock to rest, I was watching the US Army in training for a world at peace in 1911. The men wearing the uniforms were blessed to not yet know the horrors of two world wars. I pondered again, as I had in random thought since arriving in the time machine, the burden of knowing much of the future – both the good and the horrors that were coming.

Very conscious that I was on an Army post, I worried that I might be challenged as I skirted the perimeter of the parade ground and the drilling troops, coming finally to a dirt road. I looked down the lane and saw a long line of mule-drawn wagons. There must have been dozens, with men loading freight of some sort.

Since most of the men didn't appear to be soldiers, I thought my chances of not being questioned seemed better if I approached the forming wagon train, rather than staying beside the parade ground with all its uniformed soldiers. A grizzled, stocky man – obviously a civilian – was seated atop a rail fence where the wagons were lining up, and it was he who first noticed me standing there watching the activity. "Hey fella, you looking for work?" he barked at me with a gravelly voice that spoke of a life time of hand-rolled cigarettes.

With little hesitation, thankful at least that I wasn't be arrested again, I replied, "Well, likely I would. What kind of job is it?"

"Well, we have been hired to help the army boys take 1,300 of these big, heavy canvas tents over too Little Rock. The city folks over there say they got thousands more of the old rebel soldiers coming than they planned on. They guaranteed to give them a free place to eat and sleep, but the hotels are all full. The plan is to set up a camp in the city park with these tents. Pay you, uh, say $3 to help load the tents here, and unload them in Little Rock. The soldier boys are supposed to set them up. You interested?"

While it seemed a hard way to earn $3, the good fortune falling into my lap was going to be a ride into Little Rock as part of a large group in which there was little likelihood of my being noticed. I would just be one of dozens of men on wagons delivering the tents. "Yes sir, that sounds fine. When do I start?" I'd been in 1911 for two days and I was already employed.

I spent the next four hours stacking heavy, oblong folded canvas tents and bundles of ropes and poles onto wagons. It was backbreaking work. Getting my foot stepped on by one mule and my shoulder bitten by another were hazards of employment that would not have occurred to me back in 2011.

Working beside me for much of the afternoon was a broad-shouldered black man who, as time passed, started to open up a bit. On a break to drink some water from a wooden bucket, it surprised me briefly that the white laborers took their water from one bucket, the few black men took theirs from a separate bucket at the end of the lane, having to walk further for a drink. Seated against a tree with my cup, looking up at the large man, I said, "Sir, why don't you take a load off your feet before we have to starting hoisting those damn tents again?"

Laughing, the man dropped down onto the grass beside me, asking "Mister, where you come from? You work hard but look at your hands, cracked and bleeding. You don't do a lot of hard work I'd guess? I'm wondering where you comes from to getcha here? Saw you walking down the road, and knowed you wasn't here earlier. Don't mean to pry, mind you. Know folks sometimes got to do stuff to make a dollar. And we's not making much more than that." He shook his head, adding, "Lordy, Lordy, what would my papa say, me taking a bunch of old rebels tents to sleep in."

In response to his headshaking comments, I extended my hand. "Sir, my name is Kernick. A pleasure to meet you." After a short hesitation, he took the proffered hand. "Well, thank you. I be Jim Jefferson. Folks mostly just calls me Jim though." I replied with the obvious, "This is hard work, isn't it? So what would your father say about you working to help shelter the rebels at the reunion?" I watched his face break into a broad grin at the question.

"Well Mr. Kernick, see it was this way. My daddy, he was a slave on a plantation down near Lake Village. Was as best I know about 30 years old when the war broke out, working in the cotton fields. I was born there in the shack his owner provided in 1862. Guess that made me a slave too, leastways till the Yankees come through a telling us we was free, but course I can't remember that as I was I guess only bout three years old. My daddy, he used to like telling the story though."

"No sir, what I was a laughing about, is what my old pap would say if he was still living and knew I was trying to earn a couple dollars hauling tents to put over the heads of old rebels that used to think he and his family was just something to be owned and worked hard, like these damned mules pulling these wagons." He paused a few seconds in thought and then added, "My Pappy, he would say don't matter son, you do what you gotta do to put food on the table." With that, Jim just laughed a bit more as he pulled himself back up to return to loading the tents. As I rose to help with the loading, I could only write in the journal of my mind that Jim Jefferson was one of the memorable people I'd never forget meeting in the year 1911.

It was no more than an hour from sunset when the last of the long line of wagons pulled up in the distance behind us, the last tent having been loaded. The gruff man who had offered me the work was seated on the front of the last wagon, the mule team reins in his hands. "Fella, you can ride up on the seat with me. The niggra there, he can ride in the back on top of the tents."

It crossed my mind to rebuke the offensive term by saying that I also would ride on the back with my new friend, but standing behind me, Jim seemed to sense what I was going to do. "Just hush up and get on the seat. Don't make me no mind. He don't mean nothing by it, just way folks are, but don't bother me none, so don't let it bother you."

Taking his advice, I climbed up onto the wagon seat, only to be handed the reins by the man, saying "you drive." Not having a clue what to do with the reins and recalling only the way I'd seen it done in movie westerns, I raised both hands, shook the reins, and ventured, "gettyup!" The mules ignored me. Our wagon sat still while those in front had begun to move.

"Shit, fella, you can't make mules move like that." He took the reins and pulled a long stiff whip from the floorboard, cracking the mules on the backside while shaking the reins. With this, the mules jumped forward, causing me to almost fall off the wagon. I grabbed a hold of the seat just in time.

We left the buildings of Fort Roots behind and the parade of wagons soon passed under a gated entrance to the post, dipping down on a dirt road with a sharp "S" curve. I remembered then having driven up this road, when it was paved in the future, while doing a part of my residency years ago at what had become the Fort Roots VA Hospital. The sun was starting to set in the west over my shoulder. It would certainly be dark before this wagon train arrived at the City Park in Little Rock. I silently told myself the after-dark arrival was a good thing, considering my assumed status as an escapee from the Bigelow jail.

As the slow string of wagons moved along a sprawling rail yard on the edge of Argenta, my seatmate and employer for the day started a conversation. "Don't think I've seen you around before fella. What'd you say your name was? Mine is Gus Wells. Got me a livery stable and own several of these here wagons."

"Kernick is my name, Jack Kernick. Good to meet you Gus. I appreciate the chance to earn a little money. I'm actually from Texas, just passing through, wanting to see the reunion," words that I could almost start to believe with enough repetition.

This seemed enough information to satisfy Gus's curiosity about me, and he continued to ramble while we stopped and started. I realized that a wagon train of mules moves little better than vehicles in a 2011 traffic jam. "I'm going to see me a lot of the reunion myself. Hear tell, there may be 100,000 people coming to town to see the old soldiers. You know, my old daddy, he was in the war, but hate to tell folks that around here fer he fought in Union blue. He was from Michigan – was living on a farm when the war started, just 18 years old."

"Daddy enlisted not long after Bull Run where Stonewall Jackson kicked the Yankees' butts up in Virginia. By the end of the war, he had lost a hand and was a prisoner at Andersonville, that rebel hellhole of a prison in Georgia. Lost the hand at Shiloh. Told me it was blown off by a cannon shell when he was carrying the American flag and charging the rebs who were dug in around a peach orchard. Said he would never have lived except there was a surgeon in the camp. Some of his buddies carried him back to him after the retreat."

"That's some story. I know you must be proud of him. I hope he is still well," I replied. "No, my daddy's been gone 20 years…died from tuberculosis, he did, back on the farm in Michigan. I joined the Army not long after that. Matter a fact, I fought in Cuba back in '98 when Teddy Roosevelt whipped the Spanish. After the war, I ended up back at Fort Roots here and mustered out. Found I liked it down here…a lot warmer winters than back in Michigan. Used my mustering out pay to get into the livery business. Married me a good woman and got me six kids now."

While looking out at a sea of trains and rails, I found myself – first impressions aside –actually, liking this gruff man I'd found myself sharing a wagon ride with. It occurred to me that the first automobiles would have begun to appear on the rough streets and roads of 1911. The age of the automobile would soon put a lot of livery businesses like Gus's into the history books. Maybe he saw that coming, but certainly not the revolution that the automobile would bring. I consigned this thought back to the future reality that I knew all too well and that the people of 1911 could never envision.

As the wagon started to move again, I looked back at my other new friend, Jim, who was asleep on the stack of canvas tents. In a sense, like Rosa Parks who would help start the civil rights movement by refusing to give up her bus seat to a white man in the 1950s, Jim was an oppressed, much wiser man than he would be given credit for in his lifetime. How much I would have liked for this man born into slavery, with his warm smile and kind eyes, to have seen the world of 2011 that, while far from perfect, at least would not have consigned him to the back of the wagon.

Soon we were moving onto Argenta's brick-lined Main Street, the darkness that had since set in broken by the yellow glow of the gas street lights. The wagons ahead were starting to move onto a bridge that I gathered would take us into Little Rock. Seeing me craning my neck for a better look over the wagons at the bridge, Gus turned tour guide for my benefit.

"This here is called the "free bridge"...leads onto Main Street over in Little Rock. Used to be a toll bridge here, but they built this one a few years back. Don't charge folks to ride horses or wagons or walk over it like they used to with that damn toll bridge. That's the government though, charge you to breathe the air if they could figure out how." I chuckled to myself with the knowledge Gus would have fit in well with some of my conservative friends in 2011 who blamed many ills on the government.

The wagon stopped for a few minutes in the center of the plank-lined bridge, allowing enough space for the heavy wagons not to have too many at a time on the bridge high over the river. I had my first view of 1911 Little Rock from this vantage point. Lights were everywhere. Main street ahead of us was bustling with people and activity. To my right, I saw the clock tower of the Pulaski County

Courthouse – little changed from my day. Noticeably absent, however, were the tall buildings that formed the skyline of 2011.

My friend Gus, sensing my excitement as that of a country boy's trip to the big city. resumed a tour-guide role that would have likely embarrassed the 2011 Chamber of Commerce, "Over there to the right – that tall building all lit up. That's the Marion Hotel, maybe finest in town, though the Capitol Hotel in front of it is right elegant as well. I hear tell that during the reunion, some of them hotel rooms, the really nice ones, are going for upwards of $10 a night. Who the hell would pay that much money just for a bed to sleep in? Speaking of which, you got anywhere to stay? My house over in Argenta is a bit small, with all my younguns, but we might find you a place to bed down."

Though the offer was tempting, I knew I needed to be on the Little Rock side of the river, so I replied, "uh, that's real generous Gus, but I've got a friend here whose expecting me as soon as we get these wagons unloaded." Besides, the prospect of a battery of questions from six kids gave me pause about accepting his kind invitation.

The Little Rock end of the bridge led down a small incline onto the head of Main Street, where we turned left, passing a building on the corner with a sign reading "US Army recruiting". The irony of all the old Confederate soldiers who would pass by the same building crossed my mind as the wagon moved on down what I realized would be called President Clinton Avenue in my own day. The street was lined with a few small shops and then mostly warehouses and livery stables. I could approximate the block I thought my condominium building would one day be built. The ample supplies of horse manure, now churned up anew by the parade of mule-drawn wagons was more than evident to the senses as the aroma drifted upward off the brick pavement.

"This is called East Markham Street," Gus told me, resuming his narrative, "though damned if I know who Markham was. We are going to make us a right handed turn up ahead.......Yep, see those first wagons are already turning onto Sherman Street. Ain't that a hoot? Not sure, but guess it's named for General Sherman who burned down Atlanta." I heard Jim's appreciative chuckle from atop the stacked tents in the back of the freight wagon, and surely so did Gus.

Looking east down Markham Street, I realized with a start what was missing from the familiar view I had seen daily when stepping out of my condo – the glaring absence of the Interstate 30 overpass. The street continued past more warehouses and what were probably small factories. "Where does this street lead, if we kept going straight, Gus?" I thought I might need a bit of orientation while I had a willing guide.

Gus was glad to oblige. "Well, see those lights in the distance, even smoke coming from one of the locomotives? That's the old Choctaw depot. All the trains coming into town used it last couple days. They had the Iron Mountain tracks closed up by the new capitol building, though I think they will be opened up tomorrow."

In 2011, a few blocks up from my condo, I had walked many times under the interstate overpass to the Choctaw station, which by then was a century old. As I recalled, the grand building had housed a spaghetti restaurant for a time which went under, then sat idle for years. At some point after the library opened, the depot I knew would be connected to the Clinton Presidential Library. It occurred to me that if I had not bailed off the train at the Baring Cross bridge, I would have arrived at the Choctaw depot, and perhaps been arrested. I think I preferred the wagon ride and conversation with two people I would likely always remember.

As Gus did his magic with the reins, the mules turned onto Sherman Street and the character of the street departed greatly from the Markham Street warehouse district. It was lined with large Victorian era homes with wrap-around porches. A number of residents had come out into the warm May evening to watch the caravan of mule-drawn wagons clatter down the brick-paved streets. Several homes prominently displayed the Confederate flag. My mind was flooded with images, comparing how different this residential street would be in my own time. These people had no air conditioning or televisions, although some of these upscale homes already appeared to have electric lights. I knew these people must spend a lot of quiet evenings on their porches looking out onto this peaceful, tree-lined street.

"Nine blocks of Sherman Street fore we come to Ninth street and the entrance to the City Park," Gus's dialogue brought me back to 1911. About this time our wagon stopped, while some unseen cause up the line delayed the parade. To my left, in what looked to be the 700 block of Sherman Street, was a somewhat familiar brick building, but with a most unfamiliar turret towering above it. Seated on the steps, leaning out the lighted windows, and shouting words of greeting to the passing wagons, were a dozen or more elderly, gray-clad Confederate veterans. My attention was drawn to two of them making a difficult passage down the stone steps; one missing an arm was assisting another missing a leg and relying on a single crutch.

Sensing my curiosity, Gus filled me in. "That building is the Kramer School. It was built as best I recall in '95 (1895) – pretty handsome place it is for sure. Kramer, and several of the other schools in town are being used to house some of the old rebels. The idiots down at City Hall promised to give all the old rebs who came to Little Rock a free place to eat and sleep. It never occurred to them that 12,000 would come, which is what the reunion organizers are now expecting."

As we sat on the still-idled wagon, one of the old men, with a grey beard reaching to his belt, limped over to the curb to shake both our hands. "Thank you gentlemen for what you are doing to help out some old soldiers. A few of us get to bed down in this nice school building here, but most of the old fellers who won't be getting in until tomorrow or the next day will be in Camp Shaver where you're taking these tents. Truth be told, that's where I want to be myself... be a little more like it was when I served with General Jackson in Virginia." The stooped-shouldered old gentleman was still talking when our wagon began to pull away, as I heard him say, "Yes sir, I was there the night Stonewall was shot... shot by one of our own men........."

Kramer School as I saw it in 1911. It still stood in my time a century later, but minus the soaring tower. It was being used to house old Confederate soldiers for the reunion.

I looked back over my shoulder at the red brick school building, thinking to myself that the building still stood in 2011, minus the spire-like tower. It had been restored into some sort of artist colony apartments. I knew that approximately on the spot where the old veteran of Stonewall Jackson's army was standing was, in 2011, some God-awful ugly modern sculpture that I never could make heads or tails out of as many times as I'd been by the former Kramer School.

Looking ahead, it became apparent why the line of wagons had taken so long to traverse the nine blocks of Sherman Street. Ninth Street, which stood between us and the City Park, was busy with street car traffic and even horse-drawn buggies, despite the late hour. Each wagon had to wait its turn to cross the wide street with its trolley car tracks.

As our wagon pulled to a halt at the intersection, I looked across Ninth to what in my day would be called MacArthur Park, but in 1911 was known only as the City Park. I could make out, in the glow of electric lights strung among the trees, the familiar red brick arsenal building. I had visited that building often in 2011, for it housed the Museum of Arkansas Military History for which I'd provided collected artifacts for its exhibits. It was in this building, which indeed had been a military arsenal building from about 1840 until about 1890 as best I could recall, that Douglas MacArthur had been born sometime in the 1880s. Of course, in 1911 nobody had heard of the future General of World War II, nor even had World War I darkened the pages of history.

Out of the corner of my eye, I noticed Gus make the sign of the cross when we stopped before another familiar building I had known well in 2011. It was St. Edwards Catholic Church, where I had often attended Mass, the church being only a short walk from my home on President Clinton Avenue. At that moment, one of the heavy wooden doors of the church swung open and a priest, clad in a long robe, came walking out beside an ancient Confederate Veteran carrying a battered gray hat in his hand. "Thank you, father, for hearing my confession. It's been far too long", the surprisingly strong voice faded off at the end.

RAY HANLEY

The Priest lifted a hand of greeting to Gus and me as our wagon pulled out onto Ninth Street. I was left wondering what I could never know – what sins had the old soldier brought before the Father. Somehow I expect they would differ little from the multitude of sins in my own time, the nature of the human condition changing so little across centuries.

The first really familiar structure in the Little Rock of 1911 rose out of the night fog as the wagon upon which I was seated rolled by St. Edwards Catholic Church, remarkably unchanged from a century in the future.

Our wagon turned into the park entrance, following the curved driveway around the arsenal building. Beside and behind the building, stretching into what was obviously a very large park. were uniformed soldiers from Fort Roots, working alongside civilian men in rough work clothes to unload the tents and other equipment from the wagons.

With Jim coming to life and pitching in, it took perhaps 30 minutes to unload our wagon and stack the tents in a spot pointed out to us by an Army Sergeant. Gus slapped me on the back. "Thank you, son, for the help. I'm sure glad to get my ass off that wagon seat for a while. Might go get me a beer 'fore I head home, if you want to join me." While I was equally glad to be off the hard wagon seat, I felt the urge to go somewhere alone and regroup my thoughts about what I was to do next, now that I was safely in Little Rock. "Thanks, Gus. That's mighty tempting, but I think I'm expected at my friend's house and already late."

With that, Gus handed me three crumpled dollar bills, and then paid Jim as well, though I couldn't tell if it was the same $3 dollars I'd earned, but I hoped so. "Maybe I'll see you during the reunion Jack... maybe at the big parade? My house is the yellow one on Ash Street over in Argenta. My livery stable is on Washington Avenue. You need any help, you come see me." With the farewells said, Gus hoisted his stocky body back onto the wagon and pulled away, heading back toward the north side of the river. When I looked around after watching Gus depart, I was surprised that Jim had vanished. I didn't even know where the man lived or if he had a family. The regretful thought left me a little sad.

What was I going to do immediately though? I didn't even have a place to sleep, and clearly it was too late to try to find the Remmel house, even though I had the address and the postcard picture of it Sarah had given me before I left Bigelow. It seemed apparent the work in the park was ending for the night. The erection of what Gus had said would be 1,300 tents would wait at least until day light. I could bed down among the stacks of tents but I saw that there would be at least a few soldiers on guard patrol for the night, and at least one policeman, walking one of the park's paths twirling his nightstick. It clearly wouldn't be a good idea to be found asleep in the park during the late night hours, even if I were not an escapee from the Bigelow jail.

What should I do with my weary body on what was only my second night in the year of our Lord, 1911? I'd spent the first night in jail. Standing in the darkened park, I told myself surely I could do better than that tonight. Then my eyes were drawn to St. Edward's church across Ninth street, and soon my feet followed toward the church.

Chapter 13

I STOOD IN front of the church, and it was apparent the building was locked up for the night. A fog had settled in, nestling around the top of the Gothic revival building. I knew from reading the historical plaque that would one day be placed on the building that it had been built in 1900 to serve the Catholic German immigrants who had come to America seeking a better life.

Seeing nobody on the street and noting on Charlie's pocket watch that it was almost midnight, I leaned on a massive tree that overhung the street and considered my few options. I decided to see what was behind the church, which I thought would have been a gas station in my own time, but really could not recall for sure. Instead of a gas station, I found a small garden plot and some sort of stable or carriage house.

Nothing was locked. Apparently folks were a lot more trusting in 1911 than in my own time. I found a horse drawn carriage parked inside, and standing asleep in a stall, the horse that must draw the carriage. I supposed the church's Padre used the vehicle to make his appointed rounds. He would never believe the way 2011 Priests drive cars on the freeways and use pagers and cell phones that weren't science fiction from the pen of Edgar Rice Burroughs. The creator of Tarzan and science fiction tales about travel to Mars was the only writer I could recall that might have been writing in the genre in 1911.

I found a stall in the back of the barn filled with straw, which provided a better bed than the iron cot I'd had the night before in the Bigelow jail cell. If I could deal with the growing hunger pangs that were setting in, I might indeed be comfortable for the night. I had money, and could surely buy breakfast with the coming of daylight. I did take a chance and had a long drink of water from a bucket set beneath a pump near the door of the barn, a bucket the horse might well have drank from.

I settled down against the back wall of the stall, and just as I was getting comfortable, I apparently dislodged what turned out to be a thankfully unlit kerosene lantern that had been hanging on the wall. The glass globe of the lantern hit a bare part of the stone floor, making a din that sounded like the breaking of an entire glass house. The next thing I heard as I held my breath over the shattered night silence was the clucking of what must have been an army of chickens behind the wall I'd settled down against. This night was going from bad to worse.

The chickens next door settled down in a few minutes and I tried to do the same, saying a silent prayer, "Lord, just get me through the night please." As my continued unexpected twists of fate would have it, I would make it through the night, but not in the stable.

A kind, but strong voice came to me out of the darkness from the door of the stable, "You are either a fox desiring a chicken dinner or a pilgrim seeking to sleep beside my horse. The Lord would be hard pressed to forgive me if I shot you for the former and you turned out to be the latter."

"It's not a fox, sir, so it would please both the Lord and myself if you would hold your fire." I responded to the disembodied voice I would soon know as the Priest of St. Edwards, speaking from the darkness like God addressing Moses.

A match was struck, and soon the Priest was standing before the stall with a lantern in his hand. He was dressed in overalls, but complete with his white clerical collar. "Yes, my son, you are indeed not the fox that sometimes comes in the night from its lair down by the river, seeking to steal my chickens. No respecter of the commandment 'thou shall not steal,', that wily fox." The man with the kindly voice, who didn't appear to have a gun in evidence, introduced himself, "I'm Father Schultz, the pastor of St. Edwards here, and the owner of the chickens you seem to have awakened."

I pulled myself to my feet, brushed off the straw, and offered my hand, "Thank you Father, I'm Jack Kernick from San Antonio, in town to see the reunion. I, uh, got here too late tonight to try to find the friends who will put me up. I came from the park across the street. I was enlisted to help deliver the tents to the park for the old soldiers to sleep in."

"Ah yes, I recognize you now. You were on the wagon with Gus. I saw you earlier tonight when the wagon train passed by the church. It was a busy night for me, more old Catholics, lapsed and not, among these old rebels than one might have expected," Father Schultz almost laughed at his own joke.

"Well Mr. Kernick, the hotels are all full in the city, pretty much every bed, but you are welcome to spend the night in the rectory with me. I have what may be the only spare bed this city will see for the next few days. I might even scare you up something to eat from what my housekeeper left in the kitchen tonight." With that, the priest, who I estimated to be at least 70 years-old, pivoted briskly and started across the church yard, lantern swinging. I quickly followed, almost running to catch up.

The elderly Priest took me through the back door of a white frame building that served as the rectory, and which I was sure had been long gone by my time. As best I could recall, the St. Edwards school building would one day sit where this modest cottage welcomed me late in the night.

The lights were on in the back of the cottage, and the priest pointed to a chair in a small bay-shaped room just off the kitchen. "Have a seat, son. You look like you've had a rough day." I resisted replying, "Father, you wouldn't believe it if I told you." Instead I simply agreed, "Yes, Father, it has indeed been a long, hard day."

"Let me see, what did Mrs. Merkel leave us here?" asked the Father, opening up a small refrigerator, which I noted was cooled with a large block of ice on a lower shelf. "We have a bit of fried chicken here, and some biscuits are still on the stove… and, let's see….yes, even some of her fabulous apple pie. How's that sound, Mr. Kernick?"

With that, the kindly priest placed a plate of cold fried chicken in front of me, with biscuits, apple pie and even a cup of hot coffee he warmed on the stove, a stove that looked like it burned coal. I tried not to gorge myself like a man who hadn't eaten all day.

The wise Father seemed to sense I was a puzzle – a hungry one – that he would like to know more about, but he was patient while I finished my meal. However, by the time he was serving coffee, his curiosity pushed him to seek some answers from the ragged stranger who had clumsily disturbed his chickens and came as a surprise guest to his table. "You know, it would not have surprised me to have found one of those old rebels sleeping in my stable, but you clearly are too young to have fought against my side in that most uncivil war." My puzzled expression drew what he assumed was a needed clarification.

"Yes, it's a bit of irony. I was here tonight hearing the confessions of these old Confederates, but I actually fought wearing Union blue. I was 18 years old, living on my family farm outside Milwaukee in 1861. That's the year the war started, as you may remember."

I, of course, did know the Civil War started in 1861, but Father Schultz would certainly have doubted the sanity of his table guest had I told him I was born in 1961, 50 years into the future and 100 years after he had gone to war. "Yes Father I've studied a lot of history, especially about the Civil War."

The priest picked up his tale again, "I was actually preparing to go to Chicago to the seminary, having known since I was ten years-old I was meant to be a priest. The sense of injustice, the way I knew the negro slaves were being treated here in the south, and the outrage of the rebels firing on US troops at Fort Sumter, it was all enough to give me pause, to cause me to enlist with other young men in the area. I missed the major battles of the war, but finally ended up with the troops that marched from Helena, over on the Mississippi River to occupy Little Rock in 1863. I actually spent several weeks in a tent on the arsenal grounds across the street in that park where you delivered the tents. As to the awful war, I certainly fired shots in battle but, truth be told, I'm not sure I ever hit anyone. I have prayed often that I did not."

"This is somehow, I gather, connected to why you minister in Arkansas today instead of back up north," I suggested, thinking that as long as the father was talking about himself, he wouldn't be asking me questions I couldn't answer.

"The ways of the Lord, my son, the ways of the Lord. I made it back north after the war as far as St. Louis where I finished the seminary, and then the Bishop of Little Rock down here needed a German speaking priest for St. Edwards....You know, some of these immigrants arrived here not able to speak English. Besides, I like the south – sight warmer winters, friendly people."

"But Mr. Kernick, enough about me. You will forgive me for wondering how you came to be in my stable so late at night. I sense there is more to your story than you have shared." Before I could decide how to reply to his question, he added, "but I know you are weary. Perhaps we can talk some more in the morning. I have to be up in time for the 7:00 a.m. Mass, so I expect we both need to turn in."

The kindly old man couldn't quite let his curiosity go for the evening. "You seem an educated man, Mr. Kernick. Might I inquire as to your profession?" It seemed a fair question that shouldn't reveal too much of a story he could not be prepared to believe. "Father Shultz, I'm actually a physician, although one who seldom sees patients anymore." This seemed to satisfy the priest. As we both rose from the table, he added, "Thank you Doctor Kernick, it seems we are both in the healing professions, though mine is in the spiritual realm."

Father Shultz led me through the house to a small guest room with a cot-like bed. "I trust you will be comfortable here. There's a wash basin in the corner. The toilet is down the hall… actually have it indoors now. I'll see you in the morning, perhaps at breakfast. I'll leave Mrs. Merkel a note in the kitchen to put you some breakfast on the table. I hope you rest well."

Resting well seemed unlikely, at least until I removed my clothes and washed up as best I could at the marble-topped wash stand in the corner. Once I laid down on the cot, I nodded off quickly, a large picture of the Virgin Mary looking down from its perch on the wall at the end of my bed.

The crowing of a rooster below my window woke me up. A glance at my pocket watch I'd laid on the wash stand told me it was almost 7:00 AM. I'd slept for close to 7 hours in my third night in the year 1911. What day three would bring, I could only imagine, but a good night's rest filled me with renewed confidence.

After visiting the bathroom down the hall, complete with a pull-chain toilet, I made my way to the kitchen, from which aromas of bacon and coffee were wafting down the hall. I could get used to living in a rectory I thought, as I walked into the kitchen.

"Well good morning. You must be Dr. Kernick that Father Schultz told me about" said the stout, rosy-faced Mrs. Merkel. "He already ate earlier…Has the Mass over at the church, you know. Such a wonderful man, Father is. Take a seat. I'll have your bacon and eggs in no time. Help yourself to that fruit on the table. Those peaches come right out of Father's garden out back."

Finding the fresh peaches quite alluring, I quickly sat down to breakfast. I looked for something to peel a peach, and not finding a knife on the table, I took the ancient buck knife from my pocket that I'd brought from 2011, knowing it had certainly been purchased by my grandfather before 1911. As I opened the knife a shiny dime that had been stuck between the blades popped out and rolled across the table and onto the floor. Mrs. Merkel watched the dime roll across the floor and stop between her laced high top shoes. She bent down and picked up the shiny coin, holding it up to the light from the bare bulb on the ceiling. "My, my, this must be one of them foreign coins. Ain't ever seen one like this. My husband, he collects coins, disabled since that railroad accident." I sensed her next question would be could she keep the coin.

"Yes, I'm sure it's one I must have gotten in Europe. It's, uh, sort of a lucky piece a friend gave me. I have to keep that one, but I may have some others. I'll check for you." – a bumbling response I hoped would win the return of the coin.

Thankfully the woman handed me back the coin in one hand and a plate of bacon and eggs in the other. "I'd appreciate that. Calvin doesn't seem to take a lot of pleasure in much since he lost his leg under the train in the Argenta switching yard. He does like to fool with those coins, though – pays more attention to them than he does me some days."

As Mrs. Merkel turned back to the stove, I glanced down at the dime. The date on the coin was 1999, some 88 years ahead of the time in which I sat. I slid the coin into my pocket, making a mental note to drop it in the river the first chance I got. How, I wondered, could I have ever explained that one?

I was just finishing up my breakfast when Father Schultz came in from Mass. "Well, how is our guest this morning Mrs. Merkel? Hope he had a good appetite and did right by your tasty cooking."

"Father, I'm not sure where your friend is from, but he does have a healthy appetite. Unless you need anything else, I'm going to do the marketing before these old rebs flooding into town eat up everything that's not nailed down." Finding nothing needed of her, the kindly lady took her basket out of a corner and left the Father and me to our coffee. I could not help but liken her to the "Aunt Bea" from the Andy Griffith TV show of the 1960s, albeit with a German accent.

"Well Dr. Kernick, what are your plans?" asked the priest, looking over his coffee cup at me. Clearly I owed him some explanation, given the unquestioning hospitality he had shown a stranger who trespassed in his barn late at night. I found it, for reasons buried deeper than I'd looked in a long while, harder to lie to this man than I had so casually done to others.

"Father, it has been a long time since I've done this…too long. I do believe that anything you hear in confession is sealed and not disclosed," I said, struggling with the decision forming in my mind.

"Of course, my son. The seal on the confession is irrevocable. It is among the most sacred parts of my vows. Anything said remains between the Lord, the Priest and the confessor. May I assume you have a reason for this question?"

"Yes father, I'd like for you to hear my confession. It has been a long time…far too long."

Chapter 14

"FATHER, FORGIVE ME for I have sinned……." As I began the familiar litany of the confession, I thought it had been far too long since I'd availed myself of this sacrament of the church. As Father Schultz made the sign of the cross, saying "Bless you my son," I felt a sense of peace, feeling that I was actually making a divinely inspired decision.

"Father, my past sins, I'm sure, are many, but I'm equally concerned today about those I may be forced by circumstances to commit over the next few days. In order to save a life, it's possible I may have to take one or more lives." The priest, cupping his hands in a prayerful position, showed no outward emotion. I knew there was very little he had not heard in his line of work. I was, however, going to change that as I finalized some decisions in my troubled mind. Clearly I needed not only absolution, but also an ally.

"Father, as incredible as it will be for you to believe, I traveled here two days ago…" As I paused to weigh my next words, the priest got ahead of me, "Yes, I knew of course you were from out of town. You arrived by train?" An obvious question and I struggled to prepare a suitable answer. I breathed a silent prayer that the kind man did not have a bad heart.

"No, father, not by train… well, I guess, by train from Bigelow… but well, not here, here exactly. I came here from the year 2011. I traveled back in time."

The silence that followed was deep, the upturned wrinkled brow of the priest even deeper. "My son, please pardon me. I'm an old man. My hearing is not as good as it once was. You did say you came from the year 2011? Which is, if I can do the math, about... yes, would be 100 years from now." He ran his hand through his thick white hair, pursed his lips, and with a twinkling hint of humor next said, "I trust that both you and the Lord will forgive me for saying that is a very hard story to take on faith from a man I found sleeping next to my horse in the dead of night."

"Yes father." As I said it, my thoughts flashed back an hour to the housekeeper holding up my shiny FDR dime. I fished the coin out of my pocket and slid it across the kitchen table in front of the priest. He looked down at the coin for a moment, then back to me, finally picking it up in his long fingers. He reached into a pocket for his bent, thick-lensed pair of glasses.

"Well, well, this is certainly interesting, my son. The date on the coin is 1999 and it bears the likeness of a man I do not recognize. Who might he be?" The casual tone of the query suggested that, while he might not believe me, he at least didn't think me a raving lunatic.

"Father, his name is Franklin Roosevelt. He was, or rather will be, elected President of the United States."

"Roosevelt, you say, my son. Would he, I wonder, be related to Teddy Roosevelt?" asked the Priest. "He was, you know, recently the president of the these United States, and a fine President he was, I thought."

"I believe Franklin Roosevelt was, uh, is a cousin to President Theodore Roosevelt. I don't know if anyone has heard of Franklin today. I do know he is alive...I think, in New York. He will be elected President of the United States in 1932 and will lead the country out of a great depression and most of World War II."

The question from Father Shultz came quickly behind the frown, "World War II? But there has never been a world war, and I pray to God there never is. One war fought in this country 50 years ago is one to many." Then the logical reality struck. "Oh, my, but if you are not just delusional and really are from almost a century ahead...then you are telling me there will be not one, but two world wars." With that, the priest made the sign of the cross and breathed a silent prayer between himself and the Lord.

"Father, believe me. The future holds much that is tragic, just as does the past, but also much that is amazing and wonderful. I believe, though, that these are things you really don't want to know, as it is a burden to be avoided, I think. I will tell you, however, that in the year 2011, St. Edwards remains strong, in the same building, and with an attached school. I live only a few blocks away on what is now East Markham Street. I attend Mass here often." His only reply was a slight, bewildered nod of what I took to be assent, and I continued on into what I knew to be the strangest confession the Father would ever hear.

I started at the beginning, with the call for help from Charlie, and why I had come back to 1911 to try to save Dave and stop the two men, Gabe and Henry, from causing grief in the weeks and years to come. I laid out all the events that had occurred since arriving in 1911, including my arrest and escape in Bigelow.

Feeling both the need to keep my part of the exchange in a confession mode and a sincere need for absolution, I more or less opened up to lay out sins I had not yet committed. "Father, my very presence here has the potential to do harm, to impact the future. Just as I inadvertently burdened you with the knowledge of world wars yet to come, even seemingly minor things I do or say can change what would otherwise be. Does this make any sense?"

"My son, yes. I certainly see your concern. However, you were right before, I really don't want to know what the future holds. I've lived a long, most interesting, and very rewarding life. I trust totally in the Lord for whatever my future holds. I want to instead concentrate on your problems and how we might together help you find the peace you seek."

"Father, the men who stole the first time machine – Gabe Sexton and Henry Cabot...They are here in 1911. I believe they will commit the violent robberies I told you about, and murder at least two men, the night watchman at the Capitol and my friend Dave Rawlins. I will, if necessary, kill them to prevent their crimes." "I must also stop them because of the changes they may cause in the future, things that – given their criminal bent – seem unlikely to be helpful to anybody but themselves. For this challenge I face, I would ask for your prayers and for absolution of my sins."

With the sign of the cross Father Shultz granted me absolution, instructing me to say the rosary faithfully once a day.

"Now, my son, though we are no longer in confession, I hope we can continue to discuss your challenges. Let me see if I might be able to help you. Can you trust me, Dr. Kernick?" The response from me could not have been otherwise, for I had no allies to call upon, and I truly believed I could rely on the word of this man. "Yes, Father. I need help and yes, I do trust you…completely."

The elderly Priest started by trying to make sure he actually believed that I'd come from the future and wasn't delusional. "Dr. Kernick, help me understand how you could be from a century in the future, how it's possible." As patiently as I could, I explained about Charlie and his time machines. At the end of the effort, Father Shultz looked first at the ceiling, rubbed his head, and then looked straight at me and said, "I think I believe you, as farfetched as it sounds. I believe you. Well, at least I want to believe you, but it is a great leap of logic isn't it?"

"I do have one question, Dr. Kernick. You spoke of changes that these two men may cause in events of the future. Do you have any idea what these might be – either bad, good or indifferent to the events of history?"

"Father, there is no way to know. I could reasonably be sure the men committed the robberies that occurred, or rather will occur, later in the week. The same is true of the murders I told you will occur. I could track these because I knew the time frame in which to read the old papers for this week, and because my friend Charlie had read the papers before and after his son traveled ahead of me back to 1911."

"Yes, I think I understand that part, Dr. Kernick. In the first reading, Dave was present with his father. In the later reading, the paper contained his photo and the story of his murder, which had not yet occurred until he traveled back to 1911. Am I understanding this correctly?"

"Yes Father, that strikes to the heart of the matter. As to what other changes the two men will cause – other crimes they will commit – I have no way to research this, even if I were back in 2011. I simply don't know what dates to look for within the 100-year time span, nor any way to know what changes they caused because it would have, by then, just become a part of history, an altered history though it would be. I just would not know what was altered. I have to stop the men here, this week."

Father Shultz turned in silent profile, drumming his fingers on the table, seemingly lost in thought as he looked out into his garden. Turning back to me, he said, "I understand and I believe you are correct. The men must be stopped and you must save your friend Dave. I really believe I can help and I pray we can do so without violence or harm to anyone. Regardless, you need a place to stay and it can be here in the rectory."

The idea of basing myself in a church rectory at first seemed almost laughable, but upon a quick mental review, it made a lot of sense. Certainly, if the Bigelow deputy had sent some alert to Little Rock on my escape, the last place any police would be looking for me would be in the rectory of St. Edwards. Beyond that, the rectory was only a few blocks from Main Street and just across the street from Camp Shaver, the center of activities for the reunion. It was in these areas I must look for Dave and for the men who would murder him later in the week, if I could not change events.

"Thank you Father. That is most kind. I will accept at least the offer of a roof over my head for the week. I do feel the need somehow to let Sarah Murphy, the woman in Bigelow who aided me, know that I am OK. She had arranged for me to stay at the home of a Mr. Remmel." Reaching into my back pocket, I pulled out a postcard of the Remmel's 'almost mansion' upon the back of which Sarah had written a note to the family for me.

Taking the postcard, Father Shultz said, "Yes, one of the finest homes in the city for sure… a lot more elegant than our humble rectory here."

"Let me do this. I'll send a telegram to Bigelow, to Ms. Murphy, to say… to say…What should it say?" Thinking a bit more, he got up and came back with a tablet and pencil and began to write. When done, he handed the tablet to me, saying, "I rather like this – cryptic, but I think it conveys that you are well."

The note read, "Dear Sarah: I wanted to thank you for your hospitality during my recent visit to Bigelow. I'm only sorry it was so very brief. My travels concluded safely and this finds me well. Sincerely, Father Shultz."

Looking up at the Priest, my obvious questions were, "Have you ever been to Bigelow or do you know Sarah?"

"No, I've been through Bigelow on the train a couple of times when I went to Fort Smith. A friend of mine from the seminary is the Pastor at Immaculate Conception over there. But I never got off the train and I don't know your friend Sarah. However, based on what you have told me, I gather she is an intelligent, resourceful woman. She will read between the lines and know the telegram conveys you are safely in Little Rock."

"Yes Father, I do believe that will work. If other eyes, even the Bigelow deputy, should see the telegram, it should not raise any suspicion. Thank you very much."

"I shall send the telegram when I go out this morning. I have to visit some parishioners who are patients at St. Vincent's. That's the hospital over on Cross Street. The Western Union office is just over on Main Street." He paused for a moment, and then asked, "What's our next move?"

"Let me see your pad and pencil." I said. I work best with a written plan." Picking up the pencil, I continued, "First, I think we need a time line for the next few days, what I know is supposed to happen and when. Today is May 15th. The UCV reunion actually begins on the 16th, tomorrow. Every train coming in will be filled with old soldiers and visitors. We know the city will be packed."

Next, I listed the start of the trouble I felt Gabe Sexton and Henry Cabot would cause, based on my memory from the old newspaper articles Charlie had laid out back in 2011. "We know that

Caves Jewelry Store will be robbed in the late hours of May 16th, with injuries to the night watchman. I believe this was, or rather will be, a crime committed by Sexton and Cabot."

"Caves Jewelry…why yes," said the priest. "That's the store that has Robert E. Lee's sword on display in the window. I went to see it yesterday – all shiny and polished, though there are a few nicks in the blade. This store will be robbed, you say? Lots of diamonds and gold in that store, just about the largest in town. Guess a lot of this will be stolen, right?"

"Yes Father, and not just the gold and diamonds, but also General Lee's sword. Ironic I guess, General Grant refused to accept the sword at Appomattox, and here almost 50 years later it will be stolen by two robbers from Arkansas, albeit from the year 2011."

"Then that's the plan, Dr. Kernick. Since we know the men will rob the store and when, we just tip off the police and have them arrested. That should wrap it up. They can't rob the jewelry store nor kill your friend and the watchman at the Capitol the night of the 18th, if they are in jail."

"It's not that simple, Father, for several reasons. First, we don't know what time the robbery will occur, although it was apparently in the early morning hours. The newspaper article was not specific, only that the security guard stumbled out into the street to summon a patrolman upon coming to from a blow to the head."

"Aside from that fact, the police may not believe an anonymous tip that a robbery is planned, and we certainly can't tell them why we know it will occur. They will never believe us. Sexton and Cabot are surely armed by now, so more policemen could be wounded or killed, further altering the course of history. Children to be fathered and born might never be and so on…..And lastly, Father, I have to make certain any future threat from these two men is ended before I hopefully return to 2011. How I can do that? Short of killing both, I don't know. Allowing them to be arrested, and held for who knows how long, is just too uncertain a proposition. Maybe I could somehow return them to 2011 and then… well, I just don't know. But I hope you see my point."

"Yes, as much as I want to avoid violence and harm to all, I believe I see the nature of the dilemma you describe. We shall just have to work hard to find the best solution." I prayed the father would bring more wisdom toward that goal than I now possessed.

Slowly, though, a semblance of a plan began to form in my mind, and I shared it with my confessor. "I can stake out a position near the back of the jewelry store tomorrow night, the 16th, beginning perhaps shortly after 10:00 p.m. I've studied photos of Sexton and Cabot, so I should recognize them. I actually have met Gabe Sexton at least once while visiting Charlie's farm."

"I don't know what I'll do when they arrive, but with the element of surprise, I'll try to get the drop on them, disarm them and then… then I'll just see what happens next. A lot of it will be up to them." The priest said nothing, but his pensive look suggested he lacked full faith in my idea. My next question didn't help. "Father, I'm sure these men will be armed and thus I need to be prepared. I did bring a gun, but in checking my bag this morning, I realized that I'd put up the gun back at Sarah's boarding house to be sure it remained out of her young son's reach. She had not known this when she brought my otherwise-loaded bag to the jail the morning she abetted my escape.

"No, no, I'm afraid a gun has never been called for in my line of work, at least not since I marched on Little Rock with the Union army back in '63. If you think you must have a gun… and I really hope you will consider some alternative, even alerting the police… you can easily purchase one at Bracy's hardware store on Main Street. Do you have money…I mean, other than that shiny dime with Teddy Roosevelt's cousin on it?"

"Yes Father, I came prepared. I do have currency dated 1911 or before, which was not easy to obtain and sold well above face value at a coin shop in 2011. I hope though, I have enough. What would a gun…I guess a pistol, sell for?"

"Well, as a rule, that's not something I'd know, Dr. Kernick. But, let's see, where'd I leave that catalog?" He headed for the living room and soon returned with a thick catalog from a local hardware dealer. He flipped through the pages, past pictures of farm implements and other tools, and soon found what he was looking for. "Here, on page 134, are enough guns to outfit an army."

I saw I could buy a pistol for as little as $12 and a box of ammunition for as little as $1. "Would a store sell me a gun?" I wondered, and then almost laughed out loud, realizing that the Brady bill, waiting periods, and background checks for the sale of guns were laws that would not be imagined for decades to come.

"Father, I'd like to walk about town a bit this morning. I'll think on the gun question, and who knows? Maybe I'll bump into Dave on the street and we can figure out a peaceful resolution to this mess." As I said it, I realized my words conveyed more hope than did the tone of my voice. My confessor departed to carry out his pastoral duties and I collected my thoughts, preparing to leave shortly to walk the streets of Little Rock, Arkansas in May, 1911.

Chapter 15

I LEFT THE rectory with a higher degree of confidence than I'd felt since arriving at the abandoned barn some two days earlier. Perhaps it was finally having a confidant in the elderly Priest, or perhaps even because my confidant was a Priest. The excitement of where I was started to take over as I pushed aside the challenges I'd overcome in the past two days. I would certainly face any number of unforeseen obstacles in the days to come, but somehow, standing in the yard of St. Edwards Catholic Church, I felt prepared.

I walked to the corner of Sherman and Ninth Street, taking in the view of the City Park across the street. The soldiers were already hard at work. I could see several swinging sledge hammers, driving in stakes to hold up the rows of canvas tents rising among the trees. My silent observations were broken by an argument between two men who had walked up behind me. They were, I soon determined, city employees concerned with the town's sewer system.

"Mr. Levinson, I just don't know if we can enforce this rule or not. Old man Tucker over on Rock Street already told me he'd throw anything he pleased into his sewer. It wasn't any of my business," said the younger man to a well-dressed man who had to be his boss.

"Jordan, rules is rules. We have run a sewer line into that camp over there for God only knows how many old men, and we may have 100,000 people in this town yanking toilet chains. If the sewer backs up on those old rebels, the Mayor will fire me, and I'll fire you. Now you keep your crew handing out those notices on every block." Before the men moved on down the street the young man silently handed me a flyer, I guess to lighten his load.

"CAUTION ALL HOMEOWNERS: INSTRUCT YOUR COOKS AND ALL FAMILY MEMBERS, DO NOT ALLOW SLOPS, VEGETABLE PEELINGS, OR OLD BREAD TO GET INTO THE CITY SANITARY SEWER SYSTEM THIS WEEK. WE ARE EXPECTED THOUSANDS OF VISITORS, AND OUR SEWER SYSTEM WILL BE OVERTAXED." As the men moved away, I heard the one named Levinson start up again, "Damn it Jordan…the report from yesterday…one of our crews had to clear out the sewer at Izard and Chester. It was full of tin cans, cabbage leaves, and you wouldn't believe what else. Get those notices out!"

Watching the men in the distance, Levinson's arms still waving, I thought with amusement about my friend Don Hamilton back in 2011 who was the attorney for the Little Rock Water Department, how he would have enjoyed the tirade I'd just witnessed. Don was also the most avid Civil War buff I'd ever met, having led the drive to produce a brochure and historic markers on the battle of Little Rock that occurred in 1863.

I considered catching a passing street car for the ride down to Main Street, but I knew the intersection was only a few blocks away and elected instead to walk instead. In the first block, I was struck anew – more so because I had arrived after dark the night before – at how different the Little Rock of 1911 was from my time. The trees lining the street were huge, and block after block-as I looked from right to left down the cross streets I could see many large Victorian homes. By 2011, this would be called the Quapaw section of the city and many of the homes would be gone, with many others converted to apartments and offices.

Reaching the intersection of 9th and Scott Streets, I paused a bit to get orientated. In my day, Scott Street was one way, with a stop light in every block to channel busy traffic toward the River Market section in which I lived. To my left would have been where Interstate 630 passed under the street. But in 1911 the street, lined with massive trees, just stretched into the distance, an unbroken line of fine homes. I watched well-dressed men and women on the sidewalks, some arm-in-arm, out to take in the hustle and bustle the Confederate reunion was bringing to their city.

REUNION IN TIME

Looking down the street to the north, I noticed a building on the corner of what I thought was 7th Street. Recalling the hundreds of times, I'd driven down Scott Street, I well knew what spanned that entire block in my time – the Masonic Temple. The block looked much different to me now in 1911, and I detoured in that direction, sidetracked for a moment from my search for Bracy's Hardware store on Main Street.

The Albert Pike Masonic Lodge occupied the corner even then it seemed. I could recognize the end of the building facing 7th Street, but little else. The building, with its striking curved portal on the front, took up a short part of the block and faced Scott Street. Apparently, over the next century the building would be enlarged and expanded the length of the block. Still, although smaller in 1911, it seemed as busy as on days I'd driven my car past, wondering about the mysterious rites performed.

Evidently a lot of the visiting Confederate veterans were Masons and, as I leaned on a lamp post on the corner, I watched a number going and coming from the building. My study of the Masonic foot traffic was interrupted by a female voice behind me, "Don't you wonder what those old men do in that place?"

Turning to see the source of the question, I found myself looking at a tall woman clad in a dress that almost reached the sidewalk, as seemed the fashion of the era. She was swinging a closed umbrella from side to side, carried I gathered if needed to keep the sun off on this May day that promised to be hot. "As a matter of fact, I have often wondered about that on the many occasions I've driven down this street." The words were barely out of my mouth when I realized "driven down the street" was a concept from my 2011 life.

"Well, I don't know where you parked your wagon today, but I'm tired of walking out here in the sun. My father wanted to come to this reunion, and I wouldn't let him come alone, so I volunteered to come with him. Oh, sorry, pardon my manners. My name is Rachel LeMay. My father and I are from Dallas." I took her offered hand. "Nice to meet you, Ms. LeMay. My name is Jack Kernick. I'm also from Texas, but from San Antonio."

"Why didn't you go inside with your father?" seemed a natural question, but having said it, I realized the likely answer.

RAY HANLEY

"Well, you know all this secret lodge stuff. He says they wouldn't let me in, that I'm a woman anyway. Stuff I'm not supposed to know or understand goes on in there, I guess...secret chants or something. I really don't understand this Masonic stuff. I should have left him here and just rode one of the streetcars around town."

"Your father is a Civil War veteran?" I asked.

"He certainly is, and it's surely the highlight of his life. Daddy is 88 years old this year. I was born when he was 60 years-old. He enlisted in the Confederate army in 1862 when he was already 38 years-old. He was clerking in a feed store in Huntsville, Texas. He was also one of the last to surrender...went to Mexico at the end of the war with General Shelby, that fool who thought he could continue to fight after General Lee gave up." The young woman stopped for a moment, hands on hips, blowing like a horse cooling off. I guess it was a combination of the heat and having to wait on the sidewalk outside a lodge into which no woman could enter. I tried not to laugh, but could not contain a smile.

When I stopped before this somewhat familiar landmark from 2011 to watch Confederate soldiers pouring out the door, it would result in my meeting a Congressman and making a hurried trip to the hospital.

REUNION IN TIME

"Well, I'm glad you are amused... not sure you would be if you'd spent your whole life listening to war stories and how the rebs could have won the war, or should have won the war if just this or just that had happened differently. I swear, if I wasn't a lady, it would have drove me to a cussing and a drinking." Before I could reply, she interrupted my thoughts, "Oh look, there comes Daddy out of that damn, oh, sh.... beg your pardon, Mr. Kernick. Daddy, over here!" She yelled unnecessarily loud I thought, in that we were only some 15 feet away from the steps of the building.

The elderly man creeping down the short steps with a cane wore his Confederate uniform and was carrying a bible under his arm. He raised his head, a breeze lifting up his long beard, smiled and waved. What happened next occurred in split seconds, but seemed to me to be in slow motion. Two other equally elderly uniformed men had come out of the building just behind Mr. LeMay, and it was immediately apparent they were locked in a deep argument. "Osborne, you are a damned liar and a disgrace to that uniform. How can you say General Lee made us lose the war? You should have joined the Yankees. Shoot, maybe if you had, the Union would have lost the war." These were serious fighting words.

It wasn't clear from my vantage point which of the men pushed the other, but their forward momentum carried both of them into the unsuspecting Mr. LeMay, who tumbled off the steps of the Masonic building, twisting as he fell and landing on his left side at the bottom of the step. In the blink of an eye, the other two men fell over on top of him, a pile of grey arms and legs angled in all directions.

Rachel bolted forward to reach the tangled pile before I did, but I was not far behind to help. When she pulled up first one old reb and then the other from atop Mr. LeMay, it was apparent that neither was injured badly. Rachel's elderly father had apparently cushioned the fall of the other two men. The pain in his face made it clear that Mr. LeMay had not fared as well.

"Daddy, Daddy, are you hurt? Tell me where? Can you get up?" Without breaking stride in the rapid-fire questions, she swung an arm at one of the other old men who was bending over her father on the steps. "Get away from him you old coot. You have done enough damage. Just get away from here!" The man and his companion took her advice, retreating a dozen feet away to resume the argument that had caused the mishap to start with.

"Let me check him over Rachel, I'm a doctor," I told her as I knelt next to the poor old man, who was clearly in pain. "Where does it hurt sir? Just tell me and I'll try to help you." Since he grabbed at his left sleeve with his right hand, yelling out in pain, I knew where to look first. I pulled back his sleeve gently to see that his wrist was broken, likely in more than one place.

"Rachel, he has to go to the hospital. This wrist is going to have to be set in a cast." Given the proper equipment, I could have set his arm, but certainly not on a street corner. Meanwhile I realized we were being surrounded by a crowd – a mix of elderly veterans and business men from inside the Masonic building, as well as a few more women who had materialized from somewhere in the area – what would have been called "rubber necking" in 2011.

"Step aside, step aside!" was followed by a shrill whistle. "I said STEP ASIDE and let me see what's going on here!" As the crowd parted, I looked up from my knelling position into the ruddy face of a city policeman. My heart sank, remembering in a flash my last encounter with the law in Bigelow and the possibility of my being a wanted man here in Little Rock. "Well, an old reb is down I see. Tell me old feller, was you shot by a Yankee?" The policemen laughed briefly at his own joke, but stifled it when he realized nobody else was laughing and that, indeed, the poor old man was hurt.

I turned my attention, and my potentially wanted face, back to the fallen man, rolling up the sleeve on his tattered gray uniform to better examine his wrist. The poor man's faced was flushed and he cursed the fellow vets who had fallen atop him on the sidewalk. "Is it broken? It's broken isn't it? Oh, Daddy, now I know it hurts, but this man is a doctor. Just lay still." If the policeman was looking for a doctor on the lam, Rachel had blown my cover.

"A Doc you are?" "Kin you fix him up doc? Or do we need to get him over to the hospital?"

"His wrist is broken, at least in one place and maybe two. I can't help him here. He's going to have to go to the hospital. He needs an X-Ray and a cast on his wrist." No more had the words left my mouth when I realized I'd likely blown it, using the term 'X-Ray,' which surely didn't exist yet. I was surprised when the policeman replied, however, "We'll get the old gent over to St. Vincent's, we will then. They got one of them new-fangled X-Ray machines. Let's see if I can get him a lift…could call an ambulance, but…" With that, the beefy patrolman stepped out into a street crammed full of a crowd of gawkers, and looked up and down Scott Street. I heard him shout, "You there, Mister Robinson, in the fine automobile. I'll be needing your help for this injured man, if you please. We need to get him over to St. Vincent's. Doc here says he has a busted arm."

The crowd parted and I watched a large, open-topped automobile pull up to the curb, the first I'd seen in the city. The driver, wearing goggles pushed up on his forehead, stepped from the car with measured hast. "Glad to be of assistance, officer," he said.

The policeman laughed. "This is a lucky reb, getting a ride to the hospital with a U.S. Congressman. I thank you Mr. Robinson."

I easily recognized the man then, whose name in my own time was attached to an auditorium in Little Rock. Joe T. Robinson, now a congressman, would later be elected Governor, become a powerful US Senator and be nominated as the Democratic Vice Presidential candidate in – as best I could recall – 1928. The ticket would lose to Herbert Hoover.

The policeman took charge, bending down to lift the fallen rebel up into a standing position. "Damn it, I can get up… was worse than this when I got shot by Yankees at Chickamauga, aw Lord, my arm hurts…." Mr. Lemay allowed Congressman Robinson to ease him into the back seat of the car.

While I was contemplating an exit from the scene, Rachel grabbed my arm, pulling me toward the car as well. "Please come with us, doctor. We may need your help." Looking at the policeman overseeing the loading, baton on his hip, I decided leaving with the patient might be the best of my options. I climbed into the front passenger seat. The Congressman quickly joined me, slipping behind the large steering wheel.

My first morning in the Little Rock of 1911 got stranger when the broken arm of an old rebel soldier put me into the automobile of Congressman Joe T. Robinson for a hurried trip to the hospital.

"Move out of the way! Move now, let the auto through," shouted the policeman, waving his baton to clear a path through a now much larger crowd. The massive automobile moved up Scott Street, Congressman Robinson at the wheel. "How do you like my automobile, doc? Just picked it up last week...came in on the train. It's a Locomobile."

I almost responded that I'd seen a lot of things that were "loco," but instead replied, "Congressman, it's a fine piece of machinery" and indeed it was. I looked through the windshield at the hood, which seemed to stretch out six feet or more. The seats were leather, the steering wheel made of some fine wood. The gear shift, worked expertly by the Congressman, moved flawlessly.

Behind me in the back seat of the open car, Rachel held her father's unbroken wrist, and the old man seemed, at least temporarily, to forget his pain while enjoying the ride. "He's never been in an automobile before. Oh but I have. I rode in one in New York City just last year." Nevertheless, Rachel's excited voice and windblown face suggested that the rushed trip down the brick street was also an experience she would long remember.

Congressman Robinson blew the car horn repeatedly at the traffic, which was mostly horse drawn. It parted quickly as the Locomobile rounded the corner of Main Street, coming far too close to a passing streetcar to suit my nerves. As I held tight to the car door, I could have testified to the benefits of seatbelts, yet to be invented.

While we sat briefly idle at the corner of Main and 12th, waiting on a streetcar to clear the intersection, the Congressman asked, "Doc, you live here or just visiting for the reunion? I thought I had met most of the doctors in Little Rock."

"I'm just visiting, sir. I'm from Texas...just in town to meet a friend and take in the reunion." Before he could think of another question, I was shoved back into the seat as the Congressman floored the gas pedal and whipped the car around the corner heading down 12th street.

My attention was drawn in brief glimpses to people on the street and on porches, many of whom waved and starred at the passing vehicle and waving Congressman. They had to wonder, I was sure, where this popular man was going in such a hurry.

Within minutes, the Congressman parked the car by the side entrance of an imposing red brick building, which I assumed had to be St. Vincent's Infirmary. His blowing horn brought two white-clad nurses down the stone steps, not welcoming the noisy arrival. "OK, hold your horses. Stop blowing the horn on this ugly thing. We got sick people in here. Who do you think you….." At that point the ruddy faced nurse recognized her Congressman. "Oh Congressman Robinson, I didn't see it was you driving this here contraption. You hurt?"

"Help me, Mildred…here in the back…got me a wounded rebel. Doc here says he has a broken wrist. I just saved your ambulance a trip across town." Turning back to me, he muttered under his breath, "and I bet the old heifer didn't even vote for me."

The two nurses took over at that point, and I stepped aside, pulling Rachel with me. Her father, a nurse on either side, was assisted up the short steps into the hospital. I was composing a suitable 'good bye,' but before I could tell Rachel I was leaving and wish her well, she grabbed my arm and pulled me toward the hospital door as well. I went, why I wasn't sure. As the door closed, I waved to the smiling Congressman Robinson. I wished for some reason I could tell him about the nationwide fame he would achieve before his death.

Rachel, still pulling my arm, rushed down the hallway following her father and the nurses. Finally, we came to an examination room, off what appeared to be the nurse's station somewhere in the center of the building. The nurses convinced Mr. Lemay to lay down on a gurney which was pulled behind a curtain. The large nurse introduced herself as Nurse Jacobi and took charge of trying to find a physician in the hospital, which I soon learned was crowded with patients.

Shortly a harried young doctor came down the hall, blowing by me and muttering under his breath, "General Grant didn't shoot enough of them…driving me nuts." But he couldn't get by the formidable Nurse Jacobi. "Doctor, please come in here, we got a poor old man with a broken arm, in a lot of pain he is."

My first hospital visit in almost a hundred years occurred at the Victorian era
St. Vincent's infirmary on a hot May morning in 1911, helping care for an old
reb with a broken arm. The arrival at the hospital in the massive vehicle of
a man who would be the second most famous politician in Arkansas history
would be forever ingrained in my memory. The building would be long gone by
my time of 2011, a century removed, replaced by a sprawling modern facility.

The young doctor knew he had to follow the nurse's lead and was soon beside the gurney, confirming the diagnosis. "Yes, it's broken, I can't tell how bad. Let's send him over for an X-ray...I'm not sure how long a wait. We are overrun here. There must be an extra 40,000 people in this town. We have had broken arms, legs, drunks fighting, two old men hit by an automobile...." At that point, the nurse said, "well maybe I can get you some help." When I heard her say that from my position in the hall, I should have exited the hospital and resumed my mission, but she was quicker than I.

"Dr. Ferguson, this here man is a doctor. He came in Congressman Robinson's auto when Mr. Lemay was brought in. I'm sorry though doctor, I didn't get your name. This here is Dr. Ferguson." The young man held out his hand, "Glad to meet you, Doctor?"

"Jack Kernick, Doctor Ferguson, I really need to be going. I was just on the sidewalk outside the Masonic temple when Mr. Lemay fell. I'm sure his wrist is broken, but know you can take care of it."

"Dr. Kernick, you can't imagine what I've got waiting on me all over this hospital. This reunion crowd has overtaxed the hospital staff. We can get his Xray, but it may be two or three hours before a doctor can set his arm. Could you do it for him?" Before I could make up an excuse, if I could at all, Rachel listening behind us joined the conversation.

"Dr. Kernick, please, please, won't you fix Daddy's arm? He is in pain. He's a poor old man. Won't you help him please?" In my mind, she seemed to have taken on a Scarlet O'Hara tone of pleading, in a southern accent that sounded more like it belonged in Mississippi than in Dallas. But how could I refuse. "Yes, yes, I'll try to set his arm once I can see the X-rays."

A large burly nurse, whom I'd not noticed standing behind me during the conversation, stepped up to say, "Miss, your daddy has gone upstairs for his X-ray. We should have him and the picture of his arm back down here in shortly." Turning to the nurse, whose girth reminded me of a cartoon get-well card from some distant memory, I asked, "How long have you had an X-Ray machine in the hospital? So many of our hospitals in, uh, Texas, don't have them yet."

Well, Dr.? Dr. Kernick, is it? St. Vincent's was the first hospital in Arkansas to have an X-Ray machine, I'll have you know. You must be from out of town Doctor."

"Why yes, Nurse, I'm from Texas, and I think you have a first rate hospital here," a declaration that seemed to satisfy her. "I'm just glad I can help out a bit with Mr. LeMay."

While resigning myself to postponing my exit, I heard the familiar voice of my one ally, "Well, Dr. Kernick, it is an unexpected pleasure to meet you again, but I hope you are not ill, finding you here in the hospital as I do?" Turning I found myself face-to-face with Father Schultz, a knowing twinkle in his eyes.

"No, no Father, nothing like that. It's just that, well I'm trying to help out a little...." But before I could finish piecing together the tale of my day since I left the rectory, Rachel leaped into the conversation, "Father, Dr. Kernick has been wonderful. He's going to fix daddy's arm. He was just walking by when Daddy fell, or rather when those two old farts... uh, other old soldiers fell on him on the Masonic steps, an act of the Lord for sure that he was there."

"Oh, Lord," I breathed a prayer, "just help me through this thing... all these well-meaning people. Just help me," and in looking back at Father Schultz, I somehow felt a prayer answered. Somehow this was going to work out.

"Dr. Kernick, you do seem to have been at the right place at the right time. I was here visiting two of my parishioners who are patients. Mr. Dickman, he is doing well, but sadly, Mrs. Irby...they say she may not live the day... so sad, those little children at home." Looking back at Rachel, he added, "I'm sorry, I know, young lady, you have burdens and don't need mine. Is there anything I might do for your father?"

"No, Reverend, uh Father, I think all is in hand with Dr. Kernick's help here. See, Daddy he ain't no Catholic, him being a Mason and all, he has always been a Methodist, though sometimes he goes to the First Baptist Church in Dallas. That's where we live, in Dallas, but I surely do appreciate your offer. Maybe you can just pray for him. That would be real nice."

"That I will, my child. I shall pray he has a quick recovery." Turning back to me, the Priest said, "I shall leave you, Dr. Kernick. I have business to attend to elsewhere. I hope to see you again soon." With those parting words, I watched the back of the snow-white head as the man moved on down the hallway, shaking hands with nurses, stopping to speak to one patient seated in a chair. A remarkable man I almost said aloud.

"Dr. Kernick, here are Mr. Lemay's X-Rays,", nurse's voice brought me back to my task at hand. Turning, she handed me the films, set between a folded piece of white paper. Looking around, I wondered where the light box to read them might be.

Seeing my confusion, the nurse added, "I'm sorry Dr. Kernick, I forgot you're not used to our hospital. She took the X-Rays back and stepped into a side room where a lamp sat in a corner on a pole. Holding the film up in front of the bare bulb, she asked, "What do you think, looks broke to me?"

A glance at the X-Rays, with the silhouette of the light bulb showing through, showed that the old man's wrist was broken about where a wrist watch would have been worn, if such were in use in the day. It appeared also that the bone was at least cracked two inches above the clear break. "Yes, it certainly does, the break is quite clear. We need to get a cast on his arm."

"We have Mr. Lemay next door, and I've already got Horace mixing up the plaster for you, Dr. Kernick." The nurse had clearly taken charge and I was determined to just do my job and get out of her hospital.

Next door I found my old patient on his gurney, sweat running down his face, his sunken, eyes reflecting the pain he felt. "Mr. Lemay, I'm Dr. Kernick, I was there when you fell, Rachel and I brought you here in Congressman Robinson's car. I'm going to set your arm and put a cast on it." My words seemed to calm the old man, and he tried to relax.

The nurse brought in the X-Ray, along with the lamp, which was on wheels, and placed it at the head of the gurney. The hospital aide, whom the nurse had called Horace, came in with a bowl of wet plaster and a roll of cheesecloth. After setting the break, the work of casting the arm went quickly. A shot of pain medicine would have been a great comfort to Mr. Lemay, but I knew not to ask. Pain medications were decades away in the time stream.

Then I tried to make my exit, with Rachel clinging to my hand to thank me for my service far longer than was warranted. "Rachel, he is going to be in some pain, but the wrist is set, it will take a couple of hours for the cast to harden, so you will need to keep him here until this afternoon." With that I started toward the exit I could see at the end of the long hallway. Thankfully she decided to stay with her father and I soon escaped to the front steps of the hospital. Looking to my right, I could see the dome of the state capitol gleaming in the hot May sun above the spring green trees.

What to do next, I wondered, while praying for no more unexpected detours in my search for Dave. I longed to deal with Gabe and Henry quickly and take Dave home but as I should have known it would prove far more complicated.

Chapter 16

TO GET MY bearings, I decided to walk over to the Capitol building, which appeared to be at most three blocks away. A short walk later, I was crossing a dirt path running by the south side of the building that I knew would one day be 7th Street. There were no trees on the lawn yet, and the building, although seemingly complete on the outside, was clearly still under construction, with workman coming and going.

Approaching from the front, I found myself looking at a familiar, but out of place, statue centered in the front of the building. A confederate soldier, flag waving, a bronze angel standing over him, almost pushing him ahead. Looking around the still raw lawn I knew that in my time the statue would still be present, but relocated down in the northeast corner of the lawn. In 1911 it shone in the sun, the new marble base almost still warm from the sculptor's hands.

"Pretty impressive, ain't it? Shame of it is there was two of them angels." The voice coming from behind me turned out to belong to a workman in overalls, speaking from beneath the bushiest mustached I think I'd ever seen. He appeared to be the foreman; his clothes were cleaner. With his hands on his hips, he seemed to be taking in the breadth of his work.

"Yes, it is most impressive," came my truthful reply, "but where is the companion one to it?" I looked around the expansive grounds, but saw no matching angel.

"Busted and bent beyond repair, sad to say," came the reply. "See there were two of these angels delivered here last year, not the rebel soldier mind you, just two of the bronze angels. The plan was to put them on top of the front of the Capitol building here," he pointed toward the top of the handsome building. "But when the jackass block and tackle crew was raising the second one up, they let the rope slip. The angel came crashing down…just missed landing on me by about two feet, and it shattered."

I had walked by this statue often, though a century in the future. By 2011 it had long been relocated from the prominent location directly in front of the Capitol. The last I'd seen the towering homage to the lost cause it stood on a far corner of the Capitol lawn. I had to travel back a century in time to learn the angel had a fallen twin and had been destined for the roof of the Capitol.

Obviously reading my thoughts – as I looked first at the angel towering over me and then at the top of the building – the man continued. "It looked real bad, just the one angel up there, not one on either side like the drawings showed was supposed to be there. So the Governor, I think… someone important anyway, decided to haul her down and put her behind the soldier's statue…stand her out here on the lawn."

Staring up into the face of the surviving angel, I was jolted with the mental image of young Dave Rawlins plunging to his death from atop the perch the shattered marble angel had once been intended to hold, three days hence unless I could alter the future events. My morbid thoughts were cut short by a conversation behind me.

Two Confederate vets had come up behind me and were taking in the marble soldier and his guardian angel. "Zeb, I swear, they surely used a picture of me to mold this soldier. Just look at that handsome face, the grip on the stars and bars staff. It's the spitting image of me for shure."

His companion wasn't buying it, however. "Your eyes are worse that I thought you old coot. Don't look a thing like you. Now, on the other hand, that there angel sure does favor my likeness, don't it.?"

The exchange had lightened my dark mood, at least for a while. I left the two old soldiers laughing at their own jokes, intending at first to walk down the hill and follow what I would one day know as Capitol Avenue toward Main Street in the distance. Instead I felt drawn to turn back and look at the Capitol dome. I decided I wanted to see the view from as near the top as I could get, to see where Dave Rawlins was fated to die three nights hence…unless I could rewrite history.

Once deciding on a direction, I moved briskly up the steps toward the second floor where I opened the large bronze doors opened easily. I was struck by a host of voices – workman, but also as it soon became apparent, politicians in coat and tie. The building was already in use.

I walked to the center of the building and looked down at the polished marble floor in the rotunda below. I heard the argument even

REUNION IN TIME

before the two men moved into view down below, "Mr. Christian, you are undoubtedly the biggest fool ever to win political office.... and I dare say this will be your last office. What in the bloody hell were you thinking to even write that bill, let alone introduce it?" The man's companion answered firmly, though in a less strident tone, "Nick, I just believe in a little bit of fairness. Those men fought and died as well, and you damned well know all I wanted was a tiny piece of lawn... wouldn't cost a dime....." I lost the rest of the conversation as the men moved on down a hallway.

My curiosity was satisfied, however, with a voice from a few feet to my left. Turning I faced a portly man, sweating in a coat and tie. "Jeff Davis is my name, I'm pleased to meet you sir. You likely know I used to be the Governor of this fine state." Actually I didn't and was at a bit of a loss for words that Arkansas had elected a Governor sharing the name of the President of the Confederacy. "Yes sir, I was," he continued, "but that was before George Donaghey – that windbag, – got the public's money to build this place." I slowed him down long enough to say that I was a visitor from Texas and not up on Arkansas politics.

"I'm a United States Senator from the great state of Arkansas... came over here today just to see if this place Donaghey spent so much money on has fallen down yet." The more I listened to him, the more I wanted to be elsewhere.

"Texas, you say. I serve in the United States Senate today with some fine men from your state." Pausing for a brief moment, the robust man continued. "Expect you might enjoy knowing what those two fine statesmen were ranting on down below just now?" Since I was truly interested, my reply was, "Yes I would. The one man seemed so angry and the other so composed in his rebuttal. I'd really like to know the rest of the story."

My new friend was happy to oblige me. "Rep. Christian, the calmer fellow...He is from up in the north Ozarks – poor, poor region, during the war, and still is for that matter. Arkansas, as I'm sure you know, was a part of the Confederacy. What most people forget today, except I expect for the veterans...those old guys never forget, there were about 2,000 men from Arkansas who chose to fight for the Union."

This was a surprise to me, and I acknowledged as much to the senator as he paused to wipe his sweaty brown with a crumpled handkerchief pulled from his back pocket.

Continuing, he said, "You likely saw the Confederate soldier statute standing out front, the one with the guardian angel? Couldn't hardly miss it I guess." I acknowledged I'd indeed seen it. "I also got the story of what happened to the other angel."

Laughing, he resumed the civics lesson. "See, the legislature paid for that rebel statue out there and it was pretty costly. Rep. Christian, he was bothered by the fact that there was no monument to honor those 2,000 Arkansas men who fought for the Union and against the Confederacy. So, last week he introduced a bill, asking that the state set aside a patch of ground on the lawn outside to hold a monument honoring the Arkansas Union troops."

My sense of justice blinded my sense of political logic. Forgetting for a moment the time in which I stood, I said, "That seems fair to me. Was the bill passed?"

The portly senator started to laugh. Then he laughed louder, slapping his knee, the exertion making him quite red in the face. Glancing below I saw people passing looking up to see the source of the loud mirth.

"Son, I know you're from out of town, but you might be from another world. This town is filling up with what's left of the Confederate Army, and even the newspapers are acting like they actually may have won the war. And I'll tell you something even funnier. See Rep. Christian, he didn't even ask for the money to build the monument, just for a patch of grass out front to put it on. He said states up north would send the money to erect the monument. He just wanted the spot to put it on."

"And he couldn't get even that. Why, why that's....." It wasn't fair of course, but I guessed I already knew the answer.

"Son, the only vote he got for that bill was his own. Some of the legislators here are Confederate vets themselves, you know. They said, and I'll just leave out some of the cuss words, that the damn

Yankee states would build a monument that was taller than the dome on this here new Capitol building if we gave them a piece of ground. Dumbest politician I ever did see. Introducing the bill was stupid enough. Doing it in the week before the UCV reunion, well old Christian is lucky he didn't get hauled down the road to the Insane Asylum."

Insane? I felt a rush of irrational anger flush my face. The man should more likely be given a chapter in JFK's "Profiles in Courage" in my opinion. With thoughts of a martyred President, my mind flipped out the fact that Kennedy would not even be born until 1917, some 6 years hence.

Senator Jeff Davis was an egotistical windbag upon our chance meeting at the Capitol. I learned he had been elected Governor in 1900 carrying 74 of 75 counties running a campaign with the slogan "The war is on, knife to knife, hilt to hilt, foot to foot." In 1902 Little Rock's Second Baptist Church accusing him of public drunkenness, and generally immoral behavior expelled him from membership in the church. Somehow his career survived and he was in the United States Senate when he died of a stroke in 1913, having one of the largest funerals in Little Rock history.

"I'm sorry sir, I do have to leave you here. I've got voters to meet today. I believe there's a resolution honoring the old rebs who are coming to town. My constituents would surely notice if I didn't get some words of praise in the newspapers on this one." With that, the man who reminded me of the Dog Patch politician named Foghorn turned and hurried away.

I'd visited the Capitol building on several occasions, recalling the highest up in the building I'd been was the gallery overlooking the House chamber. We had come one night to watch the swearing in of a new governor who had replaced the former one when he had to resign after a conviction very loosely related to the "Whitewater" scandal involving President Clinton, also a former Arkansas Governor, a conviction he didn't deserve in my view. I thought this might be the best direction to head.

I guessed correctly and a turn down the hall to the right brought me to the bottom of a marble staircase. A look up the grand steps gave me a view of a doorway labeled "House". Inspired for reasons I couldn't have explained, I moved up the steps briskly, taking them two at a time…too briskly as it turned out. Reaching the top of the steps in my haste, my foot caught the top of the final step and I fell flat on my face on the surprisingly cold marble floor directly in front of the House of Representatives chamber down below the gallery.

Before I could fully pull myself back to me feet, I felt a strong hand on my upper arm and a voice of concern, "Sir, are you all right? These marble floors are hard but built to last for ages, I do hope."

Regaining my clumsy feet, I found myself addressing a balding man of perhaps 60 years of age, a look of both concern and mild amusement in his eyes. "Yes, thank you sir. I believe I'm fine, just got in a bit of hurry coming up those steps," a reassurance I hoped to confirm as I surveyed myself from head to foot and decided that nothing was broken.

"Good, good, I'm glad of that. I'm George Donaghey. I don't believe we've met before. Would you be a new House member?"

"No sir. I'm, uh, only visiting for the reunion. I'm Jack Kernick from Texas." I said, accepting his handshake. At the same time a bit of my Arkansas history flashed across my mind. "Mr. Donaghey? Well you are the Governor then, aren't you sir?"

My improbable who's who encounters with prominent Arkansans continued when I met Governor George Donaghey in the building he had pushed to be built. I found him to be an impressive, humble man. The fact that I knew that late in life he would endow many good works with his wealth may have influenced that impression.

"Yes, sir. I'm proud to tell you I am the Governor of this great state and pleased that you are here to visit this wonderful building. I'm afraid perhaps my drive to build this place may have made me a few too many political enemies," and as he said it. he swept one arm around in an arc to take in the grandeur of the truly magnificent building. "I like to walk through every day or so to see how the work is shaping up. They say the building cost $2.5 million to build, more than was promised in 1900 when work started. Still, with all the stops, starts and political wrangling, it's a wonder it was ever finished at any price."

His frank disclosure brought more of the Arkansas history I'd studied over the years flowing back across my mind. Governor George Donaghey had led the drive to build the state capitol in which we were standing. The man was, or at least would be, wealthy before the end of his life. The Donaghey Foundation was prominent in the Little Rock of 2011. His name was affixed to an office building in downtown Little Rock, and I knew that proceeds from his foundation trust supported at least some colleges in the state.

"It may cost me the governor's office, I don't know," the articulate man continued. "But regardless, I'm quite proud of this building, which has taken well over a decade to get to its almost finished stage. What do you think of it, Mr., Mr. Kernick wasn't it?"

"Sir, it's just about the finest state capitol building I've ever seen." This was actually, I thought, one of the more truthful statements I'd made since I arrived in the year 1911. The Governor, his fingers laced in the lapels of his suit, beamed with pride, as if I had remarked how handsome were his children.

"Thank you, sir. I'm indeed very proud of this new house of the people. So you are in town for the old soldiers meeting, are you? You're a bit young to have been a part of that unfortunate conflict. Would you perhaps have had a father who fought?" Clearly the man was curious about what would have brought a Texan to his Capitol building.

"No sir, none of that. I just was invited to meet a friend here who lives in the area. It seemed like such an historic occasion, one I didn't

REUNION IN TIME

want to pass up." The answer seemed to satisfy the man, who gave me a rather pensive expression.

"Well, I'm glad you're here, and that you were at least not touched by that tragic chapter in our nation's history. Certainly the aftermath of the war and the reconstruction that followed still to this day leave my state poorer for it. You know, I don't remember the war. I was born before it ended, in 1863 in Louisiana, where I can assure you they are still fighting it, almost literally. This historic reunion is certainly helping out the economy of Little Rock and the state. I'm glad you came. I hope you enjoy my state."

With a parting handshake, George Donaghey moved on down the hallway. He indeed had much to be proud of I thought. as I looked back down the marble stairs and up at the stained glass skylight over my head. Try as I might, I could not recall what the reminder of his life would hold or how long he would live. Just as well I thought, as I hoped the kind man still had many years in front of him.

I pondered how to get to the gallery and, hopefully, above that to see if I could find a way out onto the outside area around the dome, where I knew Dave was slated to die three days hence. I made my way back toward the rotunda, and following my memory turned right to find a staircase leading up to the gallery that overlooked the House chamber.

Stepping into the gallery, I found it still lacked any seats, but offered a view onto the House floor, unimpeded by the plexiglass shield I knew was present in 2011. I walked to the edge to get a birds-eye view onto the House floor, which was very much in session. The debate, a poor term I thought as the outcome was a foregone conclusion, seemed to be the resolution honoring the Confederate veterans.

I was momentarily distracted by a flash to my right, and when I turned toward it, I found a photographer with his tripod holding a large camera angled down at the House floor.

"Damn, another spitter! I have to take it over." And with that exclamation, the man began to reload his camera. Noticing me for the

RAY HANLEY

first time, the photographer started reloading the bulky film plate in the camera. "You said "spitter"? I asked him. His odd statement of consternation piqued my curiosity.

"Damn right, the spitters. Look next to almost every desk, there is a spittoon. Just as I pressed the shutter, at least two of the sons of bitches down there bent over to spit tobacco juice into their spittoons. I could never sell a copy of the "statesmen at work" with a couple of heads hanging over a spitter can."

When I looked down onto the House chamber, it was apparent that the spittoons were standard equipment – almost as would be the laptop computers at the members' desks a century later. "Maybe I could help you with your picture," I offered. "You line up your view finder and get ready. I'll try to give you the go signal when everyone is heads up and not spitting." The rotund little man thanked me and took his position behind his camera. It took several minutes before I could catch a break from some of those below hanging over their spittoon, but finally upon my signal, the large flash reached across the chamber in a second, finding all the men upright.

When I later obtained a copy of the photographer's view looking down into the House chamber I thought he must have been pleased, he avoided a "spitter" in his shutter, all seemed interested in being captured in a more statesman like pose.

"Thank you sir, I don't think I could have done the camera work and spitter watching at the same time. My name is Schrader... got a studio over on Main Street. Don't think I've had the pleasure." I took the man's proffered hand. "Jack Kernick, sir, from Texas...just in town to meet a friend and take in the reunion."

"Great, great! It's going to be quite some shindig. I expect to take, and I hope sell, lots of pictures, especially picture postcards. Tell you what, I do appreciate your help up here, so you drop by my studio while you're in town. I'll give you a copy of the picture you helped me shoot, as well as some others of the reunion doings." In response, I told him I'd be sure to take him up on the offer. Like any traveler, I needed to go home with trip photos, though displaying these might be a challenge.

Bidding my new photographer friend goodbye, I stepped out of the gallery into the narrow hallway, trying again to get my bearings. I was almost run over by a pair of workman coming through with toolboxes and carrying a bundle of ropes. Looking back in the direction the men had come, I saw an unmarked door at the end of the hall that seemed as likely access to the outside of the dome as I'd seen yet. I quickly mounted a long steep stair case to reach the door.

Although shut tightly, the door was not locked and swung open easily. After climbing a narrow set of steps and opening another door I was struck by a combination of a stiff breeze and the glaring May sunshine. I found myself on a curved walkway atop the building, circling the dome. The immediate view was impressive, looking north over the Arkansas River and onto the cliff-top grounds of Fort Roots. To my right, closer in, only blocks from the Capitol, I saw the train station with its imposing tower. Almost as striking were the vast covered structures extending down the tracks from the station. I realized, after a bit of thought, that these were covered loading platforms for passengers in an era where train travel was dominant.

I looked around and above me with my back to the Capitol dome. The walk I was standing on apparently circled the base of the dome which, from where I stood, looked 100 feet tall. I was reminded that the dome would be covered in gold leaf before it was finished. I was familiar with the finished structure as it would appear in the future, gold dome gleaming in the sun. Pulling myself away from the scenic view, I made my way around the walk, coming quickly to the front of the building. A steel ladder was joined to the base of the dome, and with little thought, I started to climb it. "In for a dime, in for a dollar," as an old friend had said often.

Fifteen feet up, I came to the highest flat ledge, the highest perch before the marble dome began to curve inward toward the apparently gold plated point at the peak. I turned back and realized that when the wind hit me that there was no rail and I almost fell forward into what surely would have been my own fatal plunge. Falling instead backwards toward the gently curving base of the last section of the dome, I eased down into a sitting position on the three-foot wide ledge.

I kept my gaze focused downward until the dizziness passed and then I raised my head up and looked straight down what would become Capitol Avenue, leading toward downtown Little Rock. It was a marvelous sight and I guess it would have been even for any of the people who actually belonged in the city of 1911. For me it was perhaps more so because, with a memory of the view almost a century forward in time, I saw a lot that would remain, but so much more that would be long gone or greatly changed in the decades yet to come.

The long sloping street that I knew as Capitol Avenue was in the same spot, leading to Main Street in the distance. However, where office buildings and branch banks would sit in the future, the street instead was lined with large Victorian era homes. A clanging bell, barely reaching my ears, seemed to come from one of the streetcars moving on the twin sets of tracks, with cars going in both directions. A panoramic sweep showed another remarkable difference; the skyscrapers I would know in my own time were absent and instead the city was sprinkled with church steeples rising from among a sea of trees. The spire of the St. Andrews Cathedral was a familiar survivor in my day, but I knew that many of the other steeples I saw rising toward the heavens of 1911 would be long gone before the next century rolled around.

REUNION IN TIME

I sat between the scaffolding that wrapped around the columns on the unfinished doom, looking out over the Little Rock of 1911. I would recall the view looking east toward downtown Little Rock was incredible as I sat at the base of the dome atop the Capitol. 5th Street, which would be Capitol Avenue in my own time, was broad and expansive and heavy with streetcar traffic. I could recognize only one landmark that would still stand in 2011, the towering white building I would know as the Boyle building at the corner of Main. Nobody in 1911 could have imagined the 30 and 40 story high rises that would arise in the future.

As I fixed the location of the tall white Boyle Building, surely a skyscraper of the day, I knew the location of Main Street. The building, though dwarfed by high rise banks a century later, was still part of Main Street in 2011. I knew it stood, a bit shabby and largely vacant, at the corner of Main and Capitol Avenue. Marking a certain location in my line of sight helped me settle my jumbled mind and contemplate my course of action.

It was May 15, 1911 as I sat high above the distant city. This I knew. What I also knew, if the version of events I'd read before leaving the year 2011 was accurate, was that on the night of May 18th, three days hence, my young friend Dave Rawlins would die in a plunge off the top of this building – perhaps from the very spot where I sat, or perhaps down lower on the edge where the ladder rested. How could I prevent this event? I knew it would happen, indeed had happened, or had by 2011, but not yet…….it was all quite confusing.

Hopefully I could locate Dave some time during the next three days, before the events in and on the Capitol would result in his death. My second goal after that would be to deal with the "time bandits" as I had come to think of them, Gabe and Henry. Clearly this had to be "Plan A", but that plan was really thin on details. What about "Plan "B"? I needed to have a fallback strategy.

As I mulled it over, it became obvious that, failing any luck in finding Dave in advance of the night of May 18th, I would have to be here at the Capitol to prevent the series of events that would lead to the deaths of Dave and the night watchman. Could I do this alone, or should I alert the police? I racked my brain for ten minutes and finally rejected that idea. To begin with, I didn't know the time at which the murder would occur. The almost century-old microfilm newspapers had not given a time, only reporting the discovery of the bodies and the crime. If this wasn't enough to dissuade me on that course, I couldn't think of any believable way to explain to the Little Rock police how I knew the crimes would be committed.

My course of action more or less decided for now, I started to ease back onto the narrow steel ladder that would take me down to the curved walkway when I was almost startled into falling off by a shrill shout, "Mister, what the hell are you doing up there?" Grabbing the top of the ladder while trying to will a slowing of my heartbeat, I looked down into the face of a construction worker whose ample girth surely had blocked any view of his shoes for years.

"I'm on my way down. Just hold on," I shouted to the man with his clenched fists on his hips. I dropped the final three feet, bending forward to brace myself, before raising up to meet the man at eye level.

"You don't work here. You don't belong here. What the hell are you doing on top of my building mister?" Forgetting that I surely didn't belong on top of the Capitol building, I cheerfully replied, "Just taking in the scenery, if you please. I believe I've seen enough for today." With that pride-saving response, I moved around the man's enormous girth toward the door that would take me back into the building.

My rooftop acquaintance followed me around, unsure of what to make of my response. "Mister, if you had fallen off the damned dome, you know what a mess you would have made on the new sidewalk down below? It would have taken half a day to shovel you up. You listening to me feller?" In the absence of a reply, he pointed off to the west and stammered, "You crazy maybe? You see that tower out there? That's the State Insane Asylum over there. Maybe that's where you need to be." Still electing not to reply as I made my retreat, I followed his waving hand to see most imposing brick tower in the distance, rising over other buildings. As best I could orient the view, this was the approximate location of the University of Arkansas Medical Center and the State Hospital where indeed "insane" people were treated in my day.

"Thank you sir but I believe I'll pass on that idea." With that I went through the door and closed it, shutting out whatever reply the man might have made. "Insane Asylum" indeed….but if I were to tell anybody, other than the remarkably wise priest, where I'd come from, it's to the Insane Asylum I might well be sent. This troubling vision was in my mind all the way back through the building to the front door.

As I left the Capitol building, a thought struck me, and I extracted the by now well wrinkled photos of Dave and the culprits, Gabe and Henry, from my pocket. Looking back into the rotunda, I saw a guard seated on a stool, smoking a hand rolled cigarette and reading the newspaper. He proved to be quite talkative, and offered the first serious proof I might succeed. I handed him the photos and he toke a battered pair of glasses out of his pocket to get a better look. "Yep, this young one, he came in here yesterday," he said. "I'm sure it was him."

I restrained my excitement when he checked out the other photos of Gabe and Henry, standing before a work table in Charlie's lab. The guard was quicker to reply this time, "Sure, them two was here… been two, maybe three days ago. That one," he said, poking a finger in Henry's face, "The shifty-eyed one…didn't like him a bit…rude, he was." Pausing to scratch his chin, he continued, "Funny thing, you know, I've seen this here picture before. The young feller in your first picture… he showed me this same one of these other two guys you got here. Now ain't that odd. Maybe you can tell me….." Before I heard the last of the questions I would not be able to answer, I bid the man farewell and headed back outside.

Chapter 17

A NICKEL BOUGHT me a seat on one of the trolley cars that was making a return trip back down the street from an area in front of the Capitol. I decided to return to the central business district to look for Dave or failing that, for Gabe and Henry.

The uniformed conductor on the trolley seemed in a jovial mood as I boarded. He was talking to an ancient grey-bearded man dressed in a moth-eaten Confederate uniform. "No sir, you don't have to get off. You can just ride back downtown." I took my seat beside the old man, who had not one, but two canes, leaning for now between one of his legs and the wall of the streetcar.

Raising a wrinkled hand, the old man called out to the conductor's back, "Oh son, not quite downtown…kin ye just let me off at the Freiderica Hotel? I think it's not fer down this here street wes riding on?" The conductor had moved on up to the front of the car, apparently failing to hear the old gent's question, so he turned to me, "Young man, maybe you kin hep me make shure I get off at the Freiderica Hotel, it's on this street I know. I'm pretty tuckered out… need to take me a nap cause I want to go over to Camp Shaver later and see all the boys coming in for the reunion."

I got up and followed the conductor to tell him the man in the back wanted to get off at the Freiderica Hotel. "No problem, sir. It's coming up on the right here in about four more blocks. I stop in front of it anyway."

I returned to my seat and told the old soldier not to worry. He would be able to get off at his hotel. Thanking me, he did what struck me as poignantly odd. He saluted me, saying "Thank you, sir. I'm Col. W.H. Freeburn… served with the 34th Virginia. I surely do thank you." I almost felt obligated to return the salute but restrained the impulse. I listened to his suddenly firmer voice as he gave me his name and rank, a status I was sure he had carried long with pride long after his military career ended.

The streetcar halted in front of the Freiderica Hotel, a new-looking, five story building. The conductor rang the bell, looking back over his shoulder to be sure that the elderly soldier got off at the hotel. However, though he leaned forward, extending both arms over his twin canes Col. Freeburn couldn't rise under his own power. "Son, I find I can't quite pull myself up this here seat, my old war wounds you know."

I was easily able to help the frail man to his feet; he could have weighed little more than 90 pounds. His hesitant shuffle made it clear he would likewise need help to exit the streetcar, so soon, with some effort, both of us were on the sidewalk watching the streetcar clank on toward Main Street in the distance. "Thank you young man, I believe I can navigate now. I'm sorry you missed your trolley." With that he laughed – more like cackled, I guess. "But like I always say, streetcars are like women. Miss one and there sure be another along in a bit." I decided to sit on the bench in front of the hotel and wait to see it that were true, for from my earlier perch atop the Capitol I knew there were indeed plenty of streetcars traversing the wide avenue. Col. Freeburn elected to join me, rather than go into the hotel, he seemed to need to sit with both arms extended, propped up by his canes.

"You know, I'm 87 years-old. This might be my last reunion, but the good Lord has given me a good life and watched over me during the war, even when I was in that Yank prison up on Johnson's Island outside of Sandusky, Ohio. I was wounded bad, you see, at the big battle at Petersburg, Virginny…Beat all, thought I was bullet proof." Pausing to catch his breath, he continued, "Should have been like old Smith Lipscombe…think he was from Texas. Old Smith, see, he was standing in a shell crater at Petersburg when there was an explosion that hurled him high in the air. He landed safe, he said, near a whole different regiment. He rubbed the dust off his carcass and out of his eyes, and asked the commander, "Where in the hell am I?" "With the Alabama troops" came the reply. Cool as a cucumber, Lipscomb asked back, "Might I finish the day fighting with you sir?" Col. Freeburn had obviously told this story many times, but slapped his hand on his knee, dropping one cane, and roared with laughter.

"Well, enough war stories, son. If you would help this old soldier up, I'll go take me a nap and get ready for a big night…got me a lot of visiting and talking to do." I helped the old man up and, once inside the hotel, made sure he got his key from the desk clerk and got on the elevator. As the elevator cage was clanking shut with the old rebel leaning against the back center wall, I was struck by the imagery; I knew the doors on the old man's life on earth were closing on him as well, along with the many memories of battles won and lost from 50 years before.

When I exited the hotel onto Capitol Avenue, with no streetcar in sight, I noticed the Freiderica Drugstore on the side of the hotel and decided it was worth a visit. I was greeted by a pharmacist behind the counter, looking up from his mortar bowl where he was busy compounding something. "Be right with you, sir… just need to finish mixing up this prescription."

I told him I just wanted to sit at a small table in front of the store window for a while, across from the soda fountain. A young "soda jerk" soon brought me a coke float, and the first sip made me realize how thirsty the hot May day had left me. I paid ten cents for the float to quench my thirst and gave some thought to what I'd learned and what I might do next. My spirits and sense of purpose were renewed with the Capitol building guard's confirmation that Dave, Gabe Sexton, and Henry Cabot were indeed here in Little Rock.

Weighing my options, I considered just walking the streets, going in and out of stores and hotels until I sighted any of the three men. It occurred to me there was some risk involved, as I had met Gabe Sexton once at Charlie's farm. He might well recognize me, even see me before I did him. He would have to assume my purpose in traveling to 1911 was not to wish him well.

RAY HANLEY

I noticed a folded newspaper in the window beside my table that turned out to be that days copy of the *Arkansas Gazette*. The Reunion dominated the front page, and I thought that perhaps knowing a bit more about the reunion activities – what was happening and where – might point me to likely places I might find my quarry in the gathering crowds.

The paper was open to the editorial section, and a previous reader had marked a column with a thick pencil, drawing it to my attention. "*The chances are that a piece called Dixie will be heard in Little Rock this week.*" A great tongue and cheek piece of humor I thought, reading on. "*Nothing has so united the North and South as business, intermarriage, and the Spanish American war. The South today is more loyal to the government than any other section of the country, because she has more native-born American citizens in proportion to population, and to these the government must look for aid in the event of foreign wars. Her loyalty was demonstrated in the Spanish American War beyond all question.*" The "native-born" remark puzzled me for a minute, before it came to me that, in 1911, Ellis Island in New York was working overtime to welcome countless thousands of immigrants from Ireland and other countries, not a lot, but some, of whom would have migrated to a rural state like Arkansas.

A chance encounter with a frail old Confederate in need of help off the streetcar put me in front of the Freiderica Hotel and then into the soda fountain and drug store located on the side of the building. I realized that, though considerably expanded, the old hotel was still present in the century removed from which I'd traveled. It would be within the drug store where I'd make a good friend and form an invaluable alliance in the quest for which I'd traveled back a century in time.

REUNION IN TIME

I turned back to the front page to read of a controversy that apparently had been raging for some time, that of how to pay the city's tab for hosting the old rebels. When city fathers had gone to the host city of Macon, Georgia a year ago to woo the UCV reunion, they had promised the veterans would be housed and fed at no cost. Had the attendance been the expected 6,000, the promise might have been easily kept. Now, the day before the reunion officially opened, the city was expected to have twice that number of old soldiers, and the money was not coming in from donations as fast as needed, a part of a story I'd read on old copies of the paper before leaving 2011.

The Attorney General, a man named Hal Norwood, was heading up the fund-raising committee, and he was threatening the Little Rock saloon owners who hadn't anteed up large enough donations. In the article I read, he almost screamed off the page that the saloon keepers, who expected to profit handsomely from the flood of visitors, had only given a "paltry" $600. He was threatening to return the money and seek a city resolution to shutter the bars for the entire three-day event. Apparently the bar keepers thought he was bluffing because they had refused more money.

A more successful fund-raising story was reported from Lonoke, a small farming some 20 miles to the east of Little Rock. The Lonoke Daughters of the Confederacy was awarded a silk Confederate flag in a ceremony the day before after raising $279. In making the presentation, the UCV fund-raising spokesman, a Charles McKee was quoted as saying, *"I am grateful for the honor and privilege to present you with a flag dear to every Southern heart. Many a Confederate flag during the dark days of '61 had been stained with the blood of the South and softened by the tears of weeping mothers and wives."* I almost felt myself tearing up as I read.

In a speech when she accepted the flag, Miss Mattie Trimble, whose name I thought could not have been better coined by Hollywood, said, *"I assure you we will always regard this flag as the most precious of all our sacred possessions. I can't say more, for as you know, when the heart speaks most the lips are dumb."* I tilted my head back, looking up at the pressed tin ceiling and the slowly oscillating ceiling fan, and in my mind imagined how Mattie Trimble had looked and sounded as she gave that speech.

My thoughts were interrupted by a voice from an adjoining table, "Pardon me, sir…didn't mean to disturb you. You seem so lost in thought." Apparently the smartly dressed, handsome man had bumped my table when sliding into his seat. I looked around and noticed for the first time that the soda fountain's compact little dining area had filled up with a lunchtime crowd.

"Quite all right," I assured him. "I was just a bit engrossed in the reunion news. It seems to be a pretty big deal for folks around here." His reply came with a chuckle. "That it is… that it is. By the way, my name is Fred Allsopp. I own this hotel, drug store and eating establishment."

As I took his hand and introduced myself as a doctor who appreciated the role of a pharmacist, the name "Allsopp" resonated with me. For one thing, the name was attached to a major Little Rock City Park in the year 2011. It filled a wooded valley on past the Capitol in an area filled with early 20th century high-end homes.

"I'm here to meet a friend at the reunion," I said, and added, "But I've lost the name of the hotel he is supposed to be staying at. I've checked several hotels that sounded familiar, but no luck so far. I've got his picture here. A friend of mine took it…asked me to give to him when I saw him, saw Dave, that is – my friend." I handed Allsopp the photo I had in my shirt pocket, thinking it worth a chance.

Accepting the proffered photo, and perhaps looking at me only a bit oddly, Mr. Allsopp looked down at Dave's face staring back up out of the black and white photo. "What's this he's standing by?" I looked down at where Allsopp's finger was pointing and my stomach sank. What I'd not noticed before was there was more to the background of the photo than the knotty pine-wall behind Dave. In the corner of the photo, only partly blocked by his jacket, was part of a computer screen, with – if you squinted – the various program icons.

"Uh, I'm not sure. I wasn't there when the photo was taken… maybe a photo frame or something, or perhaps something he was working on. He's a scientist of sorts," which was about the best mix of truth and cover-up lie I could manufacture off the cuff.

"You don't say. You know, I'm a bit of a scientist myself, as well as a businessman. I've been working of late overseeing the installation of a telescope and observatory in the house I've built up in the new Pulaski Heights district." With that surprising bit of back ground, my new friend Fred returned his gaze to Dave's photo. Looking up, he said, "handsome lad, but I've not seen him around the Freiderica or here in the drug store."

He handed back the photo with a mix of curiosity and amusement on his handsome face, and I thought, why not try another tack. "Here are photos of a couple of Dave's friends. I know he was expecting them to be here in town for the reunion. If I could locate them, then perhaps Dave will be with them." I slide the photos of Gabe and Henry across the small round table.

The recognition in the face of this man, whose business it was to remember his hotel visitors, was instant. "They are, or at least were, staying here in my hotel. I saw them only yesterday, I believe, sitting on the bench out front." Looking over my shoulder, he called out, "Hey Matt, come here. Take a look at something for me please, see if we can help out Doctor Kernick a bit."

It was the hotel desk clerk as it turned out, apparently taking a soda break, and he hurried over. He looked at the photos and, without hesitation, said, " a bit rude, crass they both were. I'm glad they're gone…checked out this morning." My rising spirits sank back to earth as Hank handed back the photos.

"Did they say where they were headed by chance?" I hoped the urgency in my voice wasn't evident, as I tried to appear calm.

"Well yes sir, they did…said they were going to take the train over to Hot Springs, guess the noon Iron Mountain…takes about two hours. They said they were likely coming back tomorrow for the reunion doings, but they said, well, uh, it's just…"

"Just what Matt? It's OK. Just tell us what they said, no problem. I'd like to help my friend here find these men." The reassurance his employer offered got the rest of the story out of the blushing young man. "Well sir, they said they was looking to take one of them hot baths and wanted to find a whorehouse…said we just didn't seem to have any here in Little Rock."

Laughing, Allsopp said, "I guess they didn't ask for directions to those down the hill near the depot." He turned back to me, still chuckling, "There you have it Dr. Kernick, they went to Hot Springs looking for a bath and the ladies."

As I processed this latest news, wondering what more I could say, the soda jerk approached our table. "Mr. Allsopp, the city feller brought these by… said expected you wanted to put them in the window, what with all the reunion people coming to town… said you knew the rules."

"Yes, Hank, I was at the Reunion Committee meeting when those were planned. You just put a couple of them in the window there. Make sure they show up real good now." Looking at my puzzlement, Allsopp explained, "These yellow placards with the UCV Reunion logo are supposed to tell the soldiers and the visitors my little eating establishment has taken the pledge not to gouge on prices. Our prices will be the same over the three-day reunion as they were last week or the week before. The Reunion Eating Committee came up with the idea, which I guess is needed. Shameful as it is to say, likely there are some business folks who are greedy enough to gouge the visitors flooding my fair city."

I knew I needed to be moving on and not get too comfortable talking to the interesting Fred Allsopp, but I couldn't resist keeping the conversation going by asking him about his own background and how he came to be in the hotel business. "Well Jack, it's not my first career here, as I was the business manager for the *Arkansas Gazette* for a number of years. I wasn't especially happy with new owners of the newspaper and I decided to build a hotel here." Fred pointed with pride to a framed photo of the hotel under construction on the nearby wall. "The steel frame was raised up and in place in only 18 days."

I checked the clock on the wall and saw it was already 12:30. If Gabe and Henry had followed their intentions, they were now on board the train headed for Hot Springs, which, at least by highway in my time, was an hour to the Southwest. It appeared two of my quarry were to be there, at least for the evening, but Dave was still here in the city that was rapidly swelling to 150,000 people according to the newspaper archives I'd read in 2011. What to do? Whatever the course, I knew I had to get moving.

Bidding farewell to my new friend, I found his firm handshake accompanied by an invitation. "Dr. Kernick, I'm having a dinner party at my home tonight. I know the Mayor and other prominent folks are coming. We're trying to get the UCV leaders to come – at least for a while – just to thank them for picking Little Rock for this shindig. I hope you can come as well. Just take the street car up to Pulaski Heights. The conductor will know where to let you off."

With a promise to attend if I could and a request just to call me Jack, I was soon back on the sidewalk in front of the Freiderica Hotel, as an east-bound streetcar pulled to a clanging stop. I paid my nickel, climbed aboard, and was soon heading back downtown, my indecisive mind torn between two courses of action.

On the one hand, I could continue to walk the streets of Little Rock – now swelling with massive numbers of people arriving– looking for Dave. The "needle-in-a-haystack" analogy seemed to characterize this plan in my mind. Could I find him this way and stop both the robbery of the jewelry store on the night of the 17th, as well as the murders at the State Capitol on the night of the 18th or early morning of the 19th?

On the other-hand, it was a short train ride to Hot Springs where I could search for not one, but two men, in what should be a much less crowded, smaller city. Which direction to take? Regardless, the more logical course seemed to be to return to the St. Edwards rectory and regroup.

I disembarked from the streetcar once it hit Main Street and I'd gone but a couple of blocks toward ninth street where I'd turn left to go towards the rectory, when I noticed Bracy's Hardware. I'd forgotten, in the course of all the twists and turns of the day's events, that I'd planned to buy a gun. Whatever direction I elected to take, buying the gun seemed a comforting next step.

A helpful young clerk, his oiled hair parted neatly in the middle, met me in the hardwood-floored aisle of the hardware store with a squeaky voice, "Yes sir, what can we help you with this fine day?" I suppose he must have been expecting me to ask to look at his selection of hammers and saws, for he seemed a bit surprised when I told him, "I'm in the market to buy a gun...a pistol of some sort. I believe I was told you stock such guns."

He paused to straighten his black bow tie and replied, "Yes sir, we sure do carry guns...have a nice selection we do at that. Just follow me to the back of the store. Threading my way through the crowded aisles, past customers and store employees, I noted the differences between a 1911 hardware store and the "Home Depot" of my day. No slick, colorful packages; no power tools... just racks of hand saws, big heavy wrenches, and bins of nails and screws. I wondered how the young salesman would have reacted to the riding lawnmowers and power tool section at one of the big box superstores of 2011.

In glass cases and wall racks, one back corner of the store displayed enough firepower to outfit an army. If General Lee had access to this stockpile of weaponry, the outcome of Gettysburg would have surely been different.

"Now sir, you said you needed.... was it a shotgun?" asked the young man, as he assumed his best sales position behind the counter. "We have a fine selection...even have some here imported from England, we do."

A shotgun? Now I'd be a sight getting on a train to Hot Springs carrying a shotgun. The image crossing my mind almost made me chuckle. "No son, I think just a reliable pistol is what I need." Looking down into the glass case between us, I asked, "Which of these do you think is best?"

"Well sir, depends on what you want to shoot – just targets, or do you want something with a bit more stopping power?"

"I think something small. I travel a lot, you see, on business. I just want to feel like I'd be able to protect myself. These days you just never know, do you?" The young man digested this, and said "That's the truth sir...a shame, but there's a lot of meanness about, as my grandpa likes to say."

"This here colt might work for you," he told me, as he removed the pistol and laid it on the counter. "We could throw in the holster and a box of bullets for you for I think another three dollars." I wondered idly if, in this era, salespeople like him worked on commission. If so I'd do my part for his paycheck this week. "That looks fine son. Wrap it up."

I looked at the gun, oiled and shiny in the light as it disappeared in the wrapping paper used by the clerk. A gun? What business did a physician like me – a man who'd never fired a shot in anger – have with a gun? The rationalization came to me, wiping away the anxiety with almost eerie ease. I was seeking two men who had, or rather would commit murder and other crimes. Would, not had, based on almost century old history I'd read some three days before, but history not yet occurred….if I thought too much on that, I'd have gone crazy enough to be hauled off to the Insane Asylum I'd seen from the roof of the state capitol.

I paid from the cash in the well-worn wallet and took the gun wrapped in the brown paper. The clerk said, "You know I'm a college graduate…went down to Ouachita Baptist College. That's in Arkadelphia…just working for now in this store cause my uncle, see he owns it. But I'm learning to shoot. Me and my friend Wilbur, we go down to the river at night to shoots rats. I got four last night. I'm really thinking about joining the army, maybe they would let me be one them there snipers, you know, like I read about they had in that war with Spain. But guess I wouldn't see no action…no wars anymore…but sure am getting tired of just clerking in this here store."

It seemed almost like the wound-up young man had put out all that in a single breath. "No wars anymore," he'd said. If I could only tell him that within 6 years, young men like him would be fighting and dying in the trenches of France, battling the Germans in World War I. Instead, of course, I thanked him, took my package, and headed back out on the increasingly more crowded street. Each arriving train was pouring out more Confederate veterans, for there were surely twice as many shuffling down the sidewalks and riding past on streetcars than I'd seen when I first left the rectory early that morning.

RAY HANLEY

Moving on up Main Street and turning left toward St. Edwards, I found the path in front of one store window completely blocked by a crowd, mostly consisting of old men in gray. I squeezed past the back of the group, stepping into the street and narrowly avoiding being nipped by a horse harassed to a parked buggy. My attention was drawn to the window as the crowd parted. I realized I was in front of Cave's Jewelry Store, and dominating the front window was General Lee's sword, its edge catching the light. I stepped up to get a closer look and was again reminded of the story of Lee offering it to General Grant at Appomattox, an offer General Grant refused.

History yet to occur, but recorded on the microfilm of 2011, told me that the sword and the gold and jewels in the store would be taken two nights hence. The burden of pre-knowledge, and the confusion about what to do with that knowledge settled on me hard, but I shook it off and moved on. Indecision was an enemy I had to confront. A quote from Ghandi came to mind, hurled up from the some book stored in my brain: "If you make an attempt, nothing may be accomplished, but if you make no effort, it is certain that nothing will be accomplished." Ghandi? He would be a very young, very unknown man in 1911, living somewhere in British-dominated India.

Feeling a sense of urgency, I hopped on an East-bound street car when I reached the corner of 9th and Main. When I looked down the street from my perch in the front of the car, one more glaring thing not found in 1911 struck me for the first time – traffic lights. Nothing impeded the streetcar, except if it had to slow for a horse- drawn buggy, or to pick up a passenger on one of the marked corners. It was a quick trip, and soon I was stepping off the car at the entrance to the teeming City Park across the street from St. Edwards. It was a sea of canvas tents, with old Confederates mingling with US Army troops in khaki uniforms.

Waiting to cross 9th street in front of me was an stooped, Confederate veteran with a cane, who was aided by a young man, also in a uniform, who had to be 75 years younger than the man he was helping cross the busy street. The young Boy Scout, oblivious to me, spoke loudly to his apparently hearing-impaired charge. "Sir, let's be careful. Cross on my signal. You know a man was runned over last year by a streetcar... squashed his guts out, I hear tell. Well, I didn't see it, but Asher Staples – he's also a Boy Scout – says he did, and my, it was awful." I recalled from studying the old newspaper accounts in 2011, the local boy scouts had been called into service to help the elderly vets get around town.

I was still thinking about the man whose guts were "squashed out" by the street car when I went through the rear door of the rectory. I was greeted by the housekeeper, Mrs. Merkel, "Oh Dr. Kernick, we was getting a mite worried. Father is in the parlor awaiting on you, along with your friend.

Friend? With the exception of the priest, I was at a loss to think who in the Little Rock of 1911 could fit that classification. I stepped into the parlor and saw Father Schultz seated in front of the window, laughing at some remark made by the person facing him in the high-backed, a person whose identity was masked by the back of the chair.

"Ah, Jack, you have returned. We were getting a tad worried about you." The "we" was made clear when Sarah Murphy rose from the chair, turning to wave a hand at me, badly concealed mirth on her face. "Hi Jack, guess this is a bit of a surprise."

Chapter 18

THE YEAR OF our Lord 1911 was indeed a surprise in many ways for a man from a century in the future, but finding the lady from Bigelow in the Father's parlor had to rank near the top, at least so far.

Rolling with the newest development, I recovered my composure and dropped into an empty chair between Father Shultz and Sarah. "Well, yes, it is a bit of a surprise, but not an unpleasant one. How did you know to look for me here?" It seemed an obvious question, as my mind raced ahead evaluating what this newest development meant to my pursuit.

"Well, that's pretty simple. I got the telegram from Father Shultz, and the message that 'my friend arrived safely' pretty much had to refer to you since I'd never had the pleasure of meeting him before today. I had a hankering to see some of the reunion, and I also needed to restock some linens and things for the boarding house. All in all, it seemed a good reason to come to Little Rock, so I got the 10:00 a.m. train this morning and here I am. One of my brothers living over on Cumberland attends St. Edwards, I believe."

Reading my face like an open book, Sarah answered the question I needed to ask, but might not have. "Oh, by the way, don't worry about your jail break in Bigelow. The two pieces of trash that kidnapped me were caught up at Morrilton. They held up some farmer after we left them, took his horses and made it that far until they had to get a doctor to look at the broken leg of the one you put the mule down on. The doc didn't believe their story about how it happened and called the Conway County Sheriff. Turns out he had warrants out on the two of them for other meanness and pegged them for the Bigelow bank robbery."

Showing my obvious relief, I asked, "So that Deputy doesn't still want me, I hope?" This would take one concern off my plate at least, knowing the local police wouldn't be keeping an eye out for me.

Laughing, Sarah said, "Well, he's sure not happy you got out of his jail, and can't figure out how you did it. He isn't going to waste any more effort on it, however. Looks like the Sheriff those two shot will recover over at St. Vincent's. I think you can quit worrying about that score at least." The "at least" seemed to hang in the air, almost inviting further discussion.

Before I could respond, however, Sarah stood up, "If you and Father will excuse me, I think I'll see if I can help Mrs. Merkel in the kitchen. She and Father were kind enough to ask me to have lunch here."

After Sarah left us, Father Schultz smiled and leaning forward, elbows resting on his knees and an expression on his face that telegraphed advice would be forthcoming. "That is a very strong woman there, Dr. Kernick. You seem to have made both a good impression and perhaps an new ally who can help in your quest."

I didn't answer at first, playing over in my mind his remarks. "Does she have any idea who I really am, Father, and where I came from?" Part of me feared she did, but a part of me hoped that was the case.

"No, I don't think she has any idea where you came from. My heavens, I know it myself, but have a hard time accepting it as fact. She does, however, have a driving curiosity along with a quick mind. She also seems to have the heart and soul of a good person whom I am confident God put in your path when you most needed help in Bigelow. I don't believe for a moment it was by chance you traveled back in time almost a century to rescue her on a deserted road in the forest."

Speaking the first thought that came to mind, "The Lord works in mysterious ways, you mean," a reply that brought a pleased smile to the elderly man's wrinkled face.

"Yes, my son. It is surely so. It is for that reason, among others, I believe you need to confide in her. You need another pair of eyes and legs that can navigate this town. I'll help you, of course, but alas, I'm an old man with limitations you see." "Not nearly as many as you let on, Father" was my unspoken reply. I made a decision. "Yes Father, I believe you're right, though she may go flying back to Bigelow after labeling me a mad man."

After lunch, during which the three of us talked of the reunion and other news having nothing to do with a time traveler intent on preventing crimes yet to happen, Mrs. Merkel took her leave early at the urging of Father Shultz. Seeing her broad back go out the back door, I turned by to my companions at the kitchen table, knowing the moment of truth was at hand.

Sensing I knew not how to start, Father Shultz rescued me. "Sarah, our friend Jack here is in a bit of a pickle and needs more help that I can provide." I coughed, perhaps to keep from laughing, perhaps to keep from panicking. "Jack, you see, has come to us on a long journey, one I at first had great trouble believing, as I expect will you at first. Jack, I think it's your turn here."

I looked at Sarah who, to borrow an old expression, was "all ears". She rested her chin atop clasped hands and waited for my explanation. How to start? How to not sound insane, I wondered.

"Oh, shit, uh, sorry…but let me get it over with. Sarah I came here in a time machine from the year 2011. "I am a physician in Little Rock, but I was not even born until 1961. I'm here to….." Her expression stopped my narrative mid- stream. First shock played across here pretty features, and then she let loose a fit of laughter.

"Jack, what in the world have you been drinking? Father, what in the world? You two are playing a real joke on me……", but her declaration seemed to melt as she turned to the priest and sensed that he wasn't having any part of a joke, and that he believed what I'd just said. "Oh my God, you really believe that Jack…? but Father, it can't…just can't be. Can it?" She kept her gaze focused on the priest, somehow knowing she must believe what he pronounced.

Father Schultz didn't let me down. "Sarah, I found Jack in my barn last night, and believe me, my initial reaction was every bit as disbelieving as yours, probably more so because I'd never met the man before. He has, however, convinced me that he did indeed come from the future. He traveled here intent on stopping bad men from doing bad things-from committing murder even. He needs our help – already, of course, has mine. But there is a limit to what one old man can do, you see. I've advised Jack to take you into his confidence, to see how you might be able to help."

That statement did most of the movement toward acceptance, a testament to the remarkable aura the wise Father conveyed. Sarah turned back to me and opened up, "ok, my rational nature still really doubts this story Jack, but on the other hand it's harder to doubt Father Shultz, if he believes you. Let's pretend for now that I believe you, please start at the beginning, and tell me what I can do to help, though I have to tell you I'm having a very hard time believing this."

I spent the next 30 minutes compressing the past few days into what had to sound like a story written for the Twilight Zone. I followed all the way through the events of the morning, my trip to St. Vincent's and the State Capitol, and my time with Fred Allsopp at the Frederica Pharmacy where I'd learned that Gabe and Henry were most likely in Hot Springs. Father Shultz was quiet, nodding here and there, laughing about Congressman Robinson, but watching closely Sarah's reaction to the tale.

Amazingly, Sarah interrupted only a few times. She expressed concern over my near snakebite on the climb up to Foot Roots, but overall she just listened. This, I thought, was a remarkable woman who had not only broken me out of jail but perhaps, just perhaps, did not think me a mad man telling a tale that defied all rational belief.

A silence of undetermined length followed the end of my story of who I was and why I was there in Father Schultz's parlor some 50 years before I was born. The silence was broken by Sarah's decisive comment, "OK, it's almost 1:00 p.m. The trains go to Hot Springs on the hour this week; I saw the posted schedule when I arrived at the depot this morning. If we hurry, we can make the 2 o'clock train and be in Hot Springs by 4:00 at the latest. One of my brothers manages the Arlington Hotel. He can find us rooms for tonight. Let's go."

"She's right Jack," said Father Shultz. If Hot Springs is where those two have gone, it will be easier to find, and hopefully stop them there, than to find them in Little Rock. I think I can get you a ride to the train station. You go pack your grip. Sarah's already got hers by the back door."

By the time I came out of the guest bedroom, Sarah was yanking me toward the front door of the rectory. "Father called from the porch. He has us a lift of some sort."

Indeed, he did find us a ride. Parked in front of the church was a buggy and two-horse team. The driver bent down talking to Father Shultz, who saw us out of the corner of his eye. He motioned us across the lawn and made the introductions. "Jack, Sarah, this is my friend Andrew. He is using this rented rig this week to transport visitors around town. He'll get you two to the depot in time to catch that 2 o'clock train."

In short order, we were seated behind the driver with our bags, and the horses responded to Matthew's gentle whip and voice commands. We pulled away quickly down Sherman Street, and I found that I had to hold on with both hands as the horses picked up their speed around the corner of East Markham, headed for the Union Station several blocks to the west down that avenue.

The buggy only stopped a few times, but for as much as ten minutes we struggled to get through a maze of streetcars, buggies and pedestrians, many in Confederate Gray around the Hotel Marion, the headquarters location for the UCV Reunion. Getting past that my glance up at the Pulaski County Court House clock tower gave us but 25 minutes before the train was supposed to pull out. I could not help but notice the Old State House just beyond the Marion Hotel, it's Greek Revival front dating from 1836. I wondered whether anyone from 1911 would still be alive in 1992 to witness the election-night acceptance speech in front of that building by the Governor of Arkansas, Bill Clinton the night he was elected President of the United States.

When the buggy came to a halt in front of the depot, Andrew refused any payment. "I'm doing this as a favor to Father Shultz. The ticket window is right there in this end of the station. If you hurry, you can still make the train." Once we had our bags on the sidewalk, I looked up at the depot and realized that this building would still be around in 2011, although it would undergo changes over time. The peaked roof certainly did not survive in the 2011 version of what I knew as Union Station, an infrequent stop on the Amtrak line.

We reached the ticket counter just inside the station, winded from the run, and the ticket agent accepted my $6 for two tickets to Hot Springs. It appeared we might have been the last two people to board the train, as its whistle blew to announce its departure and its smokestack billowed up ahead.

The car we picked had no two seats together, and was filled with locals, visitors, and a few old veterans headed for the resort city. Before we had time to settle into separate seats, a rotund man, his buttoned vest threatening to send pearl snaps flying in all directions, stood up. "Here sir, I'll let you sit here with your pretty wife. I'll just move over here next to my partner." This brought a blush to Sarah's pretty cheeks as we slid into our seats, thanking him. He added, "That's quite all right, and by the way, you wouldn't like a real deal on Dr. Hester's genuine elixir, would you? I've got some samples right here in my grip and plenty more back in the baggage car." I politely declined the bargain offer. Neither Sarah nor I commented on the "wife" remark the traveling salesman had made, which was just as well.

Sensing a building battery of questions would be coming from Sarah, I looked out the window as the train pulled out of the station. I could see the dome of the State Capitol topping the hill to my left, reminding me that if I didn't accomplish my mission, it would be a crime scene before the week was out.

The train picked up speed as the conductor came down the aisle collecting tickets. I asked him if the train stopped before reaching Hot Springs. He replied that it stopped at Benton some 20 miles from Little Rock; that would become a bedroom community by my own time when an interstate highway made the commute a few short minutes, depending on traffic.

The passing landscape was a collection of small farms and cut-over logging sites. None of the farm houses I saw from the train window looked like they could have sheltered any but the poorest people. At one point, the train passed through a cotton field, and my attention was drawn to dozens of black people weeding the rows of knee-high cotton plants. I wondered, as I watched them fade from sight, if perhaps I'd gone to public school with the grandchildren of these farm workers, as their descendants became the first members of their families to integrate previously all-white classrooms. As different as the worlds of 1911 and 2011 would be for the relatively affluent aboard the train, the difference paled in comparison for the poor farm workers hoeing cotton in the hot sun.

Sensing my pensive mood, Sarah remained silent, leaning back in her seat. I knew, however, the silence wouldn't last long. I pictured myself in her place, imagining the thoughts and questions that must be racing through her mind. How did she go from a little logging-town boarding house proprietor to sitting on the train with an almost stranger who had traveled back in time from the next century? She must have resolved to believe my mind-boggling story because she leaned close to me and asked, "Tell me, Jack. What are trains like in the year you came from? Do they go faster? Are there more of them?"

Without considering her reaction, I responded, "Well, actually very few people ride trains. Mostly the trains just haul freight. People generally travel by automobile or airplane. The trip from Little Rock to Hot Springs takes about 45 minutes by car on a four-lane highway." At first she seemed to take this in stride. I suppose, once she had accepted the rest of my story on face value, this new information was comparatively easy.

"Airplanes? Fast cars? Jack, tell me again. This isn't some sort of prank? Airplanes? You know, I kept the Little Rock newspaper that had the story of those Wright brothers. I think it was in one of the Carolinas where they flew their airplane. Sam read it until he about wore it out…tells me he plans to fly one someday." Thinking a bit more, she asked, "45 minutes in an automobile? Jack, you can't drive anything much past Benton out of Little Rock today. Those must be some terrific cars in the future." If only she knew, I thought, dismissing the idea of trying to explain an SUV with air conditioning, on- board GPS and DVD movies.

REUNION IN TIME

Sarah remained lost in thought all the way to Benton, where some passengers got off and a few more took their place. The Benton depot was small but busy, with freight wagons lined up waiting for goods to be offloaded from boxcars behind the passenger cars. In little more than 20 minutes, the train was once again rolling toward Hot Springs.

At one point, as the train slowed to cross a trestle bridge in a curve over a creek, I saw two small boys, bare feet dangling in the stream, cane poles extended over the water. One waved, and the locomotive train whistle replied. My mind flashed back to my own childhood when that kid fishing in a creek was often me.

"Hot Springs station in 10 minutes folks," the conductor announced as he moved down the aisle. Acting like a tourist, I began to crane my neck to take in the view. As the train began to slow, I saw a sight that took me back to my own childhood – –the observation tower poking above the trees atop Hot Springs Mountain. My family had often visited relatives living in the city and I'd climbed the open stairs to the top of the observation tower often. As best I could recall, the tower was closed and had actually blown over 30 years or more before the year 2011.

As the train pulled into the Hot Springs depot we could see crowds around the depot but more striking was the rising steam from the hot thermal waters on the other side of the tracks.

The outskirts of Hot Springs provided a stark contrast to the impoverished shacks I'd watched from the train's window earlier in the trip. Rising at various levels, the large homes and hotels came into view along the avenues glimpsed in passing. The brick-lined streets leading toward the train station were filled with activity and vehicles of all types. When the train had pulled into the station, I looked out over a sea of elegant coaches and buggies and an occasional open-topped automobile. I watched as a uniformed black man helped a woman, ankle-length dress covering all but the tips of her feet, into an impressive carriage that had three rows of seats. She settled under a large umbrella mounted on the back of the open coach, intended to shade her from the sun. The gold-lettered placard on the side of the coach read "Park Hotel." I gathered that this was the 1911 version of the airport shuttle bus that would carry passengers to the Hilton or the Hyatt in my day.

I picked up mine and Sarah's bag, and we followed the rest of the passengers disembarking from the train to find ourselves amidst a swirling mass of humanity at the end of the red brick depot. "Sarah, I'm not sure it's going to be any easier to find those two men here than in Little Rock when they return. This is a mob. Maybe we need to take the train back."

"No Jack, not yet anyway. This is a bit deceiving. It's a busy town, but almost all the activity and all the hotels line up and down along two or three avenues. There is Central, Park Avenue and, of course, the Park Hotel is out on Malvern. Oh my, it's grand…has its own park and hundreds of rooms. Most likely, though, the men you're looking for are staying somewhere on Central Avenue. That's the main street. It's where most of the bath houses are located." Sarah had taken charge, pulling me away from the train. "There, let's go. I see the coach from the Arlington. It will take us to the hotel." So I resigned myself to follow her lead, at least for the time being.

The uniformed black driver of the Arlington Hotel coach bowed to Sarah, saying, "welcome back, Mrs. Murphy. Let me take your bag. You don't have a trunk this time?" The man must have been 70 years-old, and he was very good at what he did. Sarah replied, "No Sam, not this time. I think I shall only be at the hotel one night." Turning

REUNION IN TIME

back to me, she continued, "Sam, this is my friend Dr. Kernick. He's also staying at the hotel, if you can transport us both, please."

Eyeing me a bit like a suspicious father sending his daughter off on a dubious date, the old man replied, "for sure, Mrs. Sarah. I's take both of you. Let me have your bag sir." He put both our bags in the back of the coach and assisted Sarah to step up into the red leather-lined seats beneath the umbrella mounted over the back of the vehicle. Then he stepping aside to let me climb aboard. He took his own seat, picked up the reins, and backed up the two-horse team, maneuvering the 15-foot coach out of the crowed area onto the street.

Throughout my childhood and as an adult, I'd visited Hot Springs often, and had studied a good bit of its history. My adult memories – the freshest – were of a town that had long passed its prime, with boarded-up hotels and vacant lots where grand things had once stood. Tourists still came, but more to flock to surrounding lakes than to visit the one bath house still in operation. The sights that surrounded me from my perch on the Arlington Hotel coach were in stark contrast to my recent memories of the resort city that I'd brought back in time with me.

Looking at the street signs, I saw we were preparing to turn the corner off Malvern Avenue onto Central, which in my time was called "Bath House Row." On my right, I saw a wooden structure of multiple spires covering the hillside. Following my gaze, Sarah pointed up, "That's the Army Navy Hospital. My brother took me up there once to visit a friend. There is the grandest walkway behind it. It follows the edge of the mountain all the way up Central behind the bath houses." In my day, the hillside was occupied with a more modern building, which I recalled had been a military hospital, but was later converted into a state rehab facility.

I was drawn to an elegant building on a side street below the hospital. "What's that one?" I asked, pointing to the intricate stone building below the military hospital. "I don't recall. Sam, what is the name of that wonderful building over there? I know it's a bath house, but I can't recall the name." Sarah got his attention as he waited on a streetcar to pass before he turned out onto Central Avenue. "That there is the Imperial Bath House. My nephew, Homer, he works there as an attendant. It's grand, but lordy, it's just for rich folks. He told me a course of baths there costs more than $20. He said some rich man from Chicago gave him a $5 tip last week after taking the baths." I wondered what a "course" was, but before I could ask, Sam whipped the team around the corner and we were going up Central Avenue, another sharp contrast to the one I'd last seen in 2011.

It was hard not to be impressed by the Horse Shoe Bath House we passed on Central Avenue, a Victorian-era structure that I knew would be long gone by 2011, although I could not place exactly what would sit on the spot.

The left side of the street was lined with shops in between small hotels. There was no sign of the vacant lots of my time that had taken the place of buildings burned or torn down. It was an unbroken line of bustling commerce. Sam had to go slow, accommodating two-way streetcar traffic and both horse-drawn carriages and some automobiles that shared the wide avenue. "Look, Jack" Sarah said, "This is where the bath houses start. My, aren't they grand? Look at the windows on that one. It's the Horse Shoe." Indeed, the front windows on the wood-frame building were in the shape of horse shoes.

Most of the bath houses, fronted by trees and a broad walkway, were intricate wooden Victorian era structures. Many had rocking chairs, all occupied, on the porches. The walkway was a promenade of slowly walking men, women and an occasional child. As they strolled, they talked and pointed at various buildings and sights. It was in many ways the grandest sight I'd ever seen, whether in 2011 or 1911. It had an almost museum-painting quality to it, all come to life. A bit of the "life" hit my nostrils about that time; the street's brick pavement was well-seasoned with horse manure, releasing its pungent odor in the hot May sun. Somehow I expected I was the only one to notice.

Turning my head 180 degrees, I marveled at the sight of the grand avenue seated at the base of green mountains rising on both sides of the street. I could not help but wish that more of this grandeur had been saved for people in my time to enjoy. I knew, however, from my own reading and visits to the city that much of its activities had faded away after World War II, as those who drank and bathed in the hot waters, believing in their curative powers, began to die off and as modern medicine began to take the place of the hoped for healings those who drank and bathed in the hot waters longed to receive.

Suddenly, there was an eruption of band music from a Greek revival-style bandstand at the top of a twin pair of steps built into the hill, above the rising steam of a spring. A military band was playing a John Phillip Sousa number, their well-trained notes wafting out over the street. I knew this structure did not survive until my own day, although the steps looked somewhat familiar. I recognized that this area would someday be between the Fordyce Bath House and another I could not remember. The Fordyce, which clearly had not yet been built, would house the visitors center for the National Park Service having jurisdiction over the springs in my own era.

A journey on a steam train and a ride in an elegant coach brought me to the lobby of what might have been the grandest hotel I'd ever seen. The 500-room hotel was destined to be destroyed by fire in the 1920s, to be replaced by a new Arlington

"Jack, look ahead, on the right. That's the Arlington." I following Sarah's pointing hand, expecting to see the Arlington Hotel I'd visited often in my own time. However, it was clearly not the same. This sprawling, Moorish-styled hotel was on the opposite side of Fountain Street from the Arlington I knew. Then I remembered the photos I'd seen on the lobby wall of the Arlington in my time. The original hotel we pulled up in front of would burn down in the 1920s, to be replaced with the one I was familiar with. I stepped out of the coach and helped Sarah alight. I looked down the long verandah fronting Central Avenue and thought, "if only I were on vacation, and not pursuing two criminals."

Chapter 19

ASSURED BY SAM that our bags would be taken to our rooms, Sarah and I entered the hotel, finding the registration desk set under the same arched design that followed the porch out front. Unsure about how to check into a hotel in 1911 (Somehow I was sure an American Express card wouldn't do the trick), I was rescued by Sarah's, "Billy, surprise!" With that a handsome man who had been working on a ledger with his back to us, turned around, his face immediately lighting up. "Sarah, my Lord! Why didn't you call me to tell me you were coming?"

"Oh, you know I don't have a telephone in Bigelow, big brother. That's for you city slickers," came Sarah's laughing retort. "Besides I'm only here over night…uh…trying to help my friend here." In response to her brother's puzzled look, she said, "Billy, meet Dr. Kernick from Texas. Jack, meet my brother Billy. He runs this hotel." Hesitating only briefly, Billy extended his hand, "Welcome to Hot Springs, Dr. Kernick."

I accepted his hand, imagining what he must be thinking about my showing up unannounced at his hotel with his sister. "The pleasure is mine, Billy. Sarah has been most kind to show me around. I'll need a room for tonight if you have one free."

"Yes, we can fix you up with a room, Dr. Kernick," and turning to the desk clerk, he said, "William, please find Dr. Kernick here a nice room please, and have Sam take care of his bags." Any awkwardness about whether Sarah would share my room was resolved when Billy added, "Sarah, you'll stay at our house. Mildred will be really glad to see you. It's been so long." Mildred, a name that I guess had gone out of style by my time, was obviously his wife, Sarah's sister-in-law.

I signed the guest register, watching Sarah out of the corner of my eye pull her brother over to the most ornate grand staircase I'd ever seen. What she was telling him, I could only imagine, but I knew it had to be about me. In my distraction, I didn't hear the clerk the first time. "Sir, here's your room key. You may settle your account when you leave us. The room rate is $6 for a very nice one overlooking Central Avenue." The heavy key was affixed to a round medallion engraved with Arlington Room 412.

Sarah met me as I turned away from the desk, her protective brother maintaining his guard only a few paces away. "I've got to have dinner with Mildred and Billy's kids. They live just a few blocks away on Park Avenue. I'll try to make it back here afterwards to see if you have any information on what you plan to do. Maybe there is something I can do to help. I did find you someone else to help though. I told Billy you were looking for two men, and he offered to lend you Sam. Just show him the pictures. He knows every hotel employee in the city." With that, Sarah waved and followed her brother out the door.

"Sir, Ms. Sarah and Billy says you needs a bit of help." Sam, our livery driver from the depot, had slipped silently up beside me. The man exuded a quite aura of competency that seemed to go with his carefully groomed uniform and wise old eyes.

"Sam, yes, thank you. I do need a bit of help... actually a lot of help." I took the men's photos from my pocket, handed them to him, and watched him study the faces, glancing from one to the other. "I know the men are in the city, though I think only for one night, two at the most. It's very important that I locate them, but I must warn you, they are likely dangerous. I don't need anyone to speak to them. If I can just find out where they are, I'll see to it after that."

He smiled and said, "Sir, I'll make the rounds of the main hotels now... even some of the smaller ones...take me two hours, maybe three. I knows all the housekeepers, and folks like me that makes this town's hotels work. If'n these fellers are in my town, I'll find out where they be at. Yes sir, I will. Why don't you freshen up, have you some dinner, and I'll give you a report… oh, 'bouts 8 o'clock." With those confident words, he took the photos and left.

Grand Stairway in the Rotunda.

As we stood at the registration desk and looked around. it became apparent that the interior of the Arlington was as grand as the exterior that had greeted our arrival.

Assuming my bag had already gone up to my room, I took the elevator to the fourth floor, it's elaborate crafted iron cage operated by yet another polite, uniformed elderly black man who greeted me with a smile and wished me a good day as he slide the handle that opened the doors at my floor. "Next to the last room to the left sir."

My $6 hotel room proved to be grander than some I'd paid $200 a night for in my own time. I unlocked the door to a room with "antique" furniture and deep piled rugs, art work on the walls, and drapes parted to reveal a mountain view across the street. My bag was already placed on a bench at the foot of the bed. I wondered what amenities the room didn't have. A bath room was missing, as was the TV and telephone I would have taken for granted in my own time.

The bathroom was surely down the hall, but a marble washstand was stocked with a bowl and pitcher of water that contained ice.

At a temporary loss for what to do next, I stood in front of the room's wide windows, looking down on a bustling Central Avenue. Streetcars were passing in both directions, and the sidewalks across the street, lined with businesses of every kind, were filled with men in suits, some with derby hats, and women in long dresses – nobody in the shorts and tee shirts that would be standard garb on a warm May day in the Hot Springs of 2011. Looking up and down the avenue, I was amazed anew at the grandeur of this 1911 resort city that would largely vanish well before the time from which I came.

Shaking off my melancholy thoughts, I opted to get out of the hotel and look for dinner somewhere on Central Avenue. I stopped to ask the uniformed staff on duty in the lobby for a recommendation about where to eat, and I was assured that Hot Springs, even New York City, offered no finer dining than could be had in the Arlington Hotel's restaurant. Nevertheless, upon my request to find something outside of the hotel, they finally suggested that I dine at Frisby's, which I was told was south on Central next to the Lyceum Theater.

I stepped off the porch, which had to be 500 feet long, and had to wait to find an opening in the traffic to cross the street. Once on the other side and pointed south, I wished again anew that I could be freed of the burdens of the pursuit for which I'd come. The city was truly fascinating. I walked by places I thought still survived in 2011. One such place was the Ohio Club, a bar with second-floor bay windows and piano music flowing out onto the sidewalk. A major difference that struck me was the absence of gaping holes between buildings for the parking lots of my day. Across the street, the bath houses were very different from the ones in my time that were built, I realized, after these grand, mostly wood-framed Victorian era buildings were razed.

I came finally to the Lyceum Theater, its arched door lit by bulbs, and the adjacent Frisby's Café, packed with diners. An open seat in front of the window seemed empty for the moment. I settled into it and accepted a menu quickly placed in front of me by a polite waiter.

REUNION IN TIME

The meal of broiled fish was excellent and, as I ate, I watched the crowds pass back and forth on the sidewalk outside. I saw one man leaning on a lamp post and smoking an enormous cigar, his head turning to follow the better-looking women as they passed. Some things hadn't changed from this century to the next I guess, though the ankle-length flared dresses left a great deal to the imagination. I wondered idly how the man would react if he were hurled a century ahead to see the shorts and tank tops girls wear on warm days in 2011 Hot Springs. As I concentrated on my meal, an angry shout outside caught my attention, as well as that of the cigar-smoking man I was watching.

"Mister, that's my wife you're leering at. I've a good mind to knock you into the street. I don't know where you came from. We here in Hot Springs don't treat good Christian women that way. Why don't you go over to one of the whore houses. Those women need the money." Apparently the angry man had been walking behind his wife and noticed, as I had, the appreciative gaze the cigar-smoking man had affixed to the backside of the passing woman.

I didn't hear the accused man's response, but from what happened next, I could safely assume it was neither apologetic nor contrite. The aggrieved husband swung a walking stick at the man's head. Saved by quicker reflexes than I would have had, the man ducked and the walking stick splintered against the lamppost. Not waiting for his assailant to recover, the man – cigar still clenched in his mouth – drove a fist into the husband's stomach, knocking him to the ground. He pivoted to walk away, thinking the angry husband was down for the count, only to be grabbed around the knees and pulled down to the sidewalk.

The ensuing fight unfolded like a movie scene, the men being no more than five feet from my face through the thin glass of the window. The ogling man – younger and stronger – quickly gained the upper hand, straddled the other man, and pinned his arms down, apparently not desirous of injuring him and perhaps hoping to tire the fight out of him. I came near losing my dinner when the husband raised his red face up and seized the other man's nose in his teeth, holding on like an angry dog.

Upon the hotel's advice, a short stroll down Central Avenue brought me to Frisby's Café located next to the Lyceum Theater, for which the posters appeared to make it a place for traveling vaudeville shows.

I'm not sure who would have won, but the "bout" was interrupted by the arrival of a very large policeman who didn't waste time evaluating the situation as he struck the man on top across the shoulders with his nightstick. The impact caused the husband beneath to lose his grip on the other man's nose, which by then was gushing blood. The crowd that formed around the scene blocked both my view and my hearing, as they shouted and laughed.

Just as I was turning back to my plate, I recognized a face in the crowd, craning for a look at the melee. In a flash I recognized Gabe Sexton, in need of a shave, but clearly one of the men who had fled Charlie's Arkansas lab in the year 2011. I leaped to my feet, paid the check with a wadded $1 bill from my pocket, and headed for the door, which I found blocked by several customers whose exit was impeded by the events ensuing outside.

I don't know how long it took to push through and get outside. It could have been 5 minutes. However long it took it was too long, for I found only the portly policeman, arms crossed, and the younger man holding a bloodstained handkerchief to his nose. Frantically looking in all directions, I saw no sign of Gabe Sexton. He may or may not have seen or recognized me through the window. He could have gone in either direction, up or down the street. Which way to follow? What was he wearing? I racked my brain, but all I could remember was a man with a bald spot on the back of his head wearing a black coat of some sort.

Knowing one direction was as logical as the other, I opted to head back north toward the Arlington, scanning both sides of the street for a glimpse of the man. Almost every man seemed to be wearing a black coat, strolling along without a care in the world. Gabe Sexton was not among them. He either went the other way or was in one of the shops. For that matter, he could have gotten on a streetcar, or crossed the street into one of the bath houses. But at least I knew he, and presumably Henry Cabot, were in Hot Springs. With that news in mind, I hurried back to the Arlington to find Sam in hopes his network could give me direction on where to look next.

I didn't have to look far, for he greeted me on the hotel porch as I topped the steps. "Dr. Kernick, I was fixin' to head down to Frisby's to look for you. Sir, I believe I knows where them men you's searching for is." Stopping to catch my breath, with hands holding my sides and sweat dripping from my brow, I realized I must appear as rattled as I felt. Sam never let on, only giving me a minute to get myself together. "Them men is stayin' at the Great Northern Hotel. It be on the upper end of Malvern Avenue. The shoeshine boy down there knowed them from the pictures you had… says one of them is mean and nasty, Dr. Kernick." That I knew had to be Henry Cabot. Gabe Sexton was a puzzle I needed to better understand.

I turned to look back down Central in the deepening twilight, and it occurred to me I didn't know how far away the hotel was but, reading my mind, Sam said, "It's not all that fer. I lives down past the depot, off Malvern Avenue… stay with my granddaughter and her husband, I do. I walks it most days… cost a nickel to ride that streetcar, so I only rides it when it be a raining. You can take a street car down there, they runs until 10:00 at least." Thinking a bit more, the old man said, "but Dr. Kernick, what is you goin' to do if you goes down there and finds these men?"

Now that was a good question, I thought almost aloud. It seemed a reasonable first step would be to go up to my room and retrieve my pistol from my luggage. Though breathing a silent prayer I would not need it the gun, I recalled the violence these men were fated – absent my intervention – to commit, and I was soon headed back down the grand staircase with the gun tucked uncomfortably inside the loosest shirt I could find. As I stepped into the lobby, I ran almost headlong into Sarah, who was hurrying in the front door with Sam trailing behind.

"Jack, Sam told me the men are down at a hotel near the depot. What are we going to do? The police could help maybe." I considered this idea and dismissed it quickly. "No, that won't work, Sarah. The police would never believe the truth. Nor can I furnish any proof, for that matter. I'd be more likely to end up in jail than they would, or in the asylum, more likely. I have to deal with this myself, and do it now while I know where they are." With that, I started for the door, hoping she would stay put.

"I'm coming with you, Jack," to which I turned to insist absolutely not. But one glance at Sarah's determined expression told me such a proclamation would fall onto the deafest of ears. Sam met us at the foot of the steps. "Sir, I got one of the hotel's coaches round the corner on Fountain Street. I can drive you down to the Great Northern." He was as good as his word, for within minutes Sarah and I were settled into the back of the coach and waiting at the corner for a slow-moving streetcar to pass.

"Whoa, whoa there," shouted a driver pulling his coach up in front of the hotel a few feet from where we sat. My casual glance gave way to the greatest shock of my life as I saw my daughter, Lydia, who I'd last seen almost a century into the future, bound out of the coach and run up the Arlington steps.

I was climbing out of the back of the coach even as it was moving into the street. Sam turned to see me leap onto the curb and hit the ground running. "Lordy, Lordy, I's goin' to take up drinking again," he exclaimed before Sarah ran after me pleading, "Jack, slow down, what's going on?"

"It's Lydia, Lydia my daughter. She was the woman who bailed out of that coach there, the one who ran into the hotel. She shouldn't be here. I've got to catch up to her." Almost stumbling through the door the doorman opened for me, I entered the grand lobby, Sarah close behind, in time to hear Lydia bark at the startled desk clerk. "Jack Kernick, I have to find Dr. Jack Kernick. He's here in the hotel. Please tell me he's here. It's a matter of life or death."

"Lydia! What in the world are you doing?" My question was cut off when she spun around, a look of panic melting into something resembling relief, then joy as she threw her arms around my neck. "Dad, Dad, I got here in time. You aren't dead, not even shot." The handsome young desk clerk just stared at us, wondering what would come next.

"Dead? Uh…nope, don't think so. I'm…but never mind me, what in the bloody blazes are you doing here? I'll kill Charlie. He promised me… promised me, no matter what, he would not let you come here. Why are you here, and how in the world did you find us?" Then it occurred to me that I needed to introduce Sarah, who was standing discreetly out of the way. "Lydia, this is my friend Sarah." I could almost see the sparks in the air as the two women connected.

"I've heard a good bit about you," Sarah said, extending her hand, which was quickly grasped by my always-nosy daughter, glancing back and forth from me to Sarah faster than my eyes could track. "Hi Sarah, I'm sorry to meet you in the midst of this confusion, but, well, I was afraid I'd be too late. Charlie miscalculated. We missed by a whole day…landed in the back of St. Edwards at 5:00 AM on the 15th. We were trying for the 13th. He, Dad I mean, he was…was… geez…he was killed here on the 15th."

Startled, Sarah's hand flew to her mouth. "'Today is the 15th.'"

It was all becoming more than I could follow, and a glance around the lobby found more people had joined the desk clerk in staring at the drama we must be presenting. "Come on, both of you. Let's go upstairs to my room. Lydia, you've got a lot of explaining to do."

The uniformed elevator attendant whisked us up to the 4th floor, Lydia gripping my hand tightly but in silence until we exited and the door to my hotel room closed us in. "I need a drink, Dad. Do you have any water?" She downed two glasses from the pitcher on the wash stand, after which she collapsed into a chair with her face in her hands, as I paced the room and Sarah sat on the edge of the bed.

Instead of talking, Lydia reached into a pocket of the long dress she wore and pulled out a folded paper. She handed it to me without explanation. "Please don't be angry with me. Just read this and you will know why we had to come." Taking the paper, it finally struck me, "We? You mean Charlie came, too? Where is he?"

"He should be back in 2011 by now, Daddy. He couldn't leave the time machine in the St. Edward's churchyard, not with daylight coming. I was sitting in the swing on the front porch of the rectory when Father Shultz came out to get his newspaper not long after daybreak. The man was wonderful. He just stood on the walk a minute looking at me and then said, 'Hello Lydia, I'm glad to meet you. Please come inside and I'll fix you some breakfast. Dad, he knew who I was."

I couldn't help but smile. Although I didn't recall showing Father Shultz Lydia's picture, which I carried in my wallet, maybe the good Lord just told him who was on his porch in the wee hours of the morning. It somehow seemed to fit the way God would reach out to speak to the kind old Priest.

At this point, I was beginning to wish for something stronger than water to drink as I sat on the window ledge, my back to bustling Central Avenue below, and opened the paper she handed to me. It was a photocopy of the Arkansas Gazette, dated May 20th, 1911. Circled in red on what was folded to page 3 was the headline, "Funeral Mass for Hot Springs Murder Victim held at St. Edwards." The story began with "A mystery from the spa city of Hot Springs remains unsolved, but the body of a visitor, and guest at the Arlington Hotel, to our fair city during this reunion week was laid to rest today in Calvary Cemetery, newsworthy perhaps because of the presence

REUNION IN TIME

of Congressman Robinson. The Congressman – apparently at the behest of the St. Edwards Priest, Father Shultz – provided part of the eulogy about a Texas Doctor named Jack Kernick who cared for an elderly stranger who fell on the sidewalk and broke his arm, comparing him to the biblical good Samaritan. The Congressman's booming voice echoed over the sparsely attended funeral as if he were addressing the entire Congress in Washington."

The mystery of the man's death remains unsolved, but an eyewitness, who the Hot Springs police report only as an unnamed woman, gave the police reason to contact Chief Tom Robinson in Little Rock. The reported theory was that the murder of Dr. Kernick was somehow connected to the rash of violent crimes during the just-concluded Confederate Veterans Reunion. The Texas doctor was slain on the tracks near the Rock Island train station in a confrontation with two as-yet unidentified men."

One of the experiences I knew I'd never forget, whether I made it back to 2011 or died in 1911, was sitting on the Hot Springs hillside on a May night inside a marble bandstand. There was a hot spring bubbling below, and voices of visitors passing by the bath houses drifting up.

I handed the paper to Sarah and watched her start to read. Her breath caught in her throat and she turned to me with a horrified look on her face.

You're not mad, are you Dad? You see why I had to come." Lydia, who I realized had to be exhausted, waited for an answer. "Lydia, Lydia…for crying out loud! Part of me wishes you were back home safe, but I know why you came, and I guess – for now at least – you saved my life. What happened…or rather, what is…or was… or, I guess, didn't happen because you came… is…is…aww, this is crazy! No, I'm not mad at you. It's just been a mind-boggling last few days."

Sarah broke the ensuing silence. Well, I guess I'll be the first to ask. What do we do next?" It was an obvious question, just as mine was the obvious reply. "I'm going to the Great Northern Hotel, but forewarned by what you've told me was supposed to happen. I'll be very careful. I'll just…just….." Before I could finish my train of thought, Lydia was all over me. "No! No, I won't let you. Let's just go home. Let those two stay here. I don't care. Getting yourself killed on the train tracks won't change any history but mine and yours. Please, Dad. Let's just go home."

Sarah chimed in, "Jack, she's right. Let them go. Let's go back to Little Rock and sort it out. You don't need to confront them here in Hot Springs. Once we're back in Little Rock, we can look for your friend Dave again…figure out how to stop his murder and the others." Lydia, in her anticipated grief over my demise had forgotten about her old crush, Dave. "Yes, Dad, please. That's it. Leave them here for now and let's go back to Little Rock to look for Dave."

Stubborn I'd always been and, I guess, stubborn I remained even in 1911, for my reply was, "No, it has to be easier to stop them here and now. I'll just stay away from the train tracks, which is where the newspaper said they shot me. I'll be careful. I've got my own gun." There was nothing I could do, however, to keep both women from following me out of the room and downstairs, both insisting on going with me or changing my mind about going at all.

Sam was sitting on the porch smoking a pipe when we exited the front door, obviously anticipating our return from what his look

REUNION IN TIME

suggested he knew, that I'd been locked in an argument of strategy with two strong-willed women. "Sir, I's figured you'd be back down in a bit. The rig is still hitched up there on the corner, so tell me what you's needing me to do."

"Sam, I still need to go to that hotel." Before he could reply, both Lydia and Sarah informed him they would be going with me. Protest was pointless, I knew. The best I could do was to try to reach a compromise. "Only if you stay in the coach with Sam and don't go into the hotel, understood?" The women looked at each other, understanding arcing in the air between them. "OK, Jack, but let's just go" said Sarah. Within five minutes we were back in the coach at the corner of Central and Fountain where Lydia's surprise arrival cut short my plans an hour before.

Darkness had fallen over the city. Central Avenue, though, was aglow with street lights as people strolled between the restaurants and nightclubs on the side of the street opposite the bath houses, most of which were closed for the day. The one exception may have been the imposing Buckstaff, lit and glowing, with people still going in and out. It occurred to me that of all the bath houses I'd seen, this might be the only one that would still stand in 2011.

Sam slowed the coach and turned back to us, "There up ahead, that be the Great Northern, Mr. Jack. I's goin' to park round on that side. Let's me go in first and see if I kin find Jeter. He's the shoeshine boy that told me them fellers you looking fo' are here. I'll find out and then come back to get you." From the vantage point where Sam parked the coach, I could see the train station no more than two blocks away, lit up with a train slowly starting to move out of the station.

Waiting on Sam to return, a tense and worried Lydia asked, "Dad, what are you going to do? You can't arrest them, and I don't think you can shoot them, can you?" It was a question I'd racked my brain over for the three days I'd been in 1911, and the truth was I didn't know still. "I hope I can reason with them – tell them I know that the police know what they're doing…that they can't escape. If they will return to 2011, maybe we can set it right. If not…well…maybe I will shoot them, knowing what they will do if not stopped."

My speculations and "what ifs" ended with Sam's return. "Mr. Jack them two men be gone. They was on that Little Rock train that pulled out just a few minutes back. Jeter, he tells me they got in some trouble earlier this evening over at Mabel's house with one of her girls. Got threw out. I hear one of them men hit one of the girls. Jeter, he say they packed up not more than half hour ago… He says he seen 'em get on the train, headed fo' Little Rock."

The collective sighs of relief from Lydia and Sarah were as audible as the couch's horse blowing in harness. "Sam, when is the next train going to Little Rock?" The old man, pulling off his hat to run his hand across his wiry grey hair, told me, "Well aint' no more trains tonight. Next one be in the morning…not sure the time, but 'spect bout 8 o'clock. I kin find out fo' you though."

"Thanks, Sam. Yes, please do find out, and I guess take us back to the Arlington for now." Sam climbed back into his seat and turned the coach around to head back north on Central, giving me a glimpse of a familiar landmark on the hill in the distance. The twin white towers of St. Joseph's Catholic Church led me to breath a silent prayer that somehow I could find a successful conclusion to this mission that would bring Lydia, Dave and myself back safely to the Arkansas of 2011.

When we arrived once again on the Arlington porch, Sam told us that the next morning's first train to Little Rock was to pull out at 8:30 a.m. He promised to get us to the station on time. Sarah, sensing that I needed some alone-time with Lydia, left us to go back to her brother's house, courtesy of Sam's couch. She assured us she would meet us in the lobby by 7:30 in the morning for the return train to Little Rock.

The hotel desk clerk rented me the room adjoining mine for Lydia, apparently having been given instructions from Sarah's brother to take care of whatever we needed. The weariness of the long, anxiety filled day was grinding down on me and my intention

REUNION IN TIME

was to go to bed. Lydia, however, had other ideas. "Dad, there's no way I can sleep. Let's take a walk, like we used to do, OK?" It was an invitation that I couldn't refuse, tired or not.

We walked in silence south down Central Avenue past the lit, but closed bath houses. Most were wood-framed structures I knew would be gone long before my time. We stopped at the Horse Shoe Bath House, which Sarah had pointed out that afternoon. Lydia, laughing for the first time since arriving in 1911, walked up on the porch to look through the horse shoe-shaped window that gave the building its signature name. "Twenty-one baths for $12, Dad. That's what the sign at the desk says. I'd sure like to have a least one of them about now."

A bit further down, we came to a walk separating the Maurice and Palace Bath Houses. I realized that I knew this walkway from 2011 when it would pass by the yet unbuilt Fordyce Bath House, the elegant restored building a century in the future that would house the National Park Visitors Center. What would sit on the site of the Maurice, I could not recall, but certainly not the wood-framed building I saw before me. I also realized we were standing below the Greek Revival bandstand that hosted the military band concert I'd heard earlier in the day when Sarah and I were headed to the Arlington.

A hot spring was bubbling up midway up the steps, and a memory came to me that this must be the Maurice Spring. "Lydia, do you remember coming here when you were small?" She smiled and nodded, taking off her shoes to dip her toes into the steaming water, as she would almost a century later when she was a child.

It occurred to me that, while the spring surrounded by rocks at the base of the stone wall would still be in place in 2011, the bandstand above us would be gone. It seemed reachable by steps that ascended from either side of the spring, only to join up above to form an approach to the bandstand. When Lydia put her shoes back, I took her hand. "Come on. Let's climb up."

The bandstand looking out over the bath houses, with the lights of the street carrying only a few feet above the rooftops, seemed an appropriate vantage point to assess where we were and figure out what we should do next. I could hear the hot water softly bubbling up down below from the depths of the earth, just as I guess it had for thousands of years.

Lydia broke the silence, "Dad, I gotta tell you. There have been times since arriving in St. Edwards church yard before daylight this morning that I really thought I was in a dream – one that I couldn't wake up from. I watched you vanish before my eyes in Charlie's lab three days ago, but somehow, it just wasn't real until I was rushing across Little Rock in a horse-drawn cab to catch the train to Hot Springs. Only then did I start to believe this is really possible. I was scared to death I would be too late, that you would already be murdered on the train tracks. Once I determined from Father Shultz I arrived two days later than Charlie intended I really panicked. Now I know this is all real. We're in 1911, chasing two men we know are going to kill people."

"Yes, kiddo. It's as real as life gets. We're sitting here on the side of a mountain more than 70 years before you will even be born. There are two men on a train headed back to Little Rock right now who will kill someone three nights from now that we both care deeply about, unless we stop them. They will also kill a night watchman whose only crime is to get in the way of two men from the 21st century. Somehow we have to stop the murders and any other harm these men will cause. Piece of cake, right?"

"I wish, Dad, but I'm scared. I'd like to just go home, but I know we can't leave Dave to die…not the other man either. We'll just have to figure something out…maybe count on all the prayers Father Shultz is saying for you. He really likes you a lot, you know. When I told him you were killed, or rather that you would be, he made the sign of the cross and prayed aloud that the Lord deliver you. I guess he did, huh Dad?" In the moonlight reflecting into the marble bandstand, I saw her smile, and told myself that maybe, just maybe, this would all work out.

"It was you who saved me, daughter. Perhaps, as they say, "The Lord works in mysterious ways," a thought that flashed me back to the words of the ancient old rebel on the train from Bigelow.

"Dad…uh…tell me about your friend Sarah. You didn't travel back a hundred years to find a girlfriend, did you? I'd hate to have to go home to 2011 and leave you here. She certainly is pretty and seems quite taken with you." I was not at all surprised by this line of questioning, having grown used to my daughter's interest in my love life, or lack of one.

"Not to worry, Lydia. She's just a good friend – as Father Shultz might say, one sent by God when I most needed a friend and ally." While Lydia sat against the stone railing of the bandstand, a full moon rising behind her over the mountains, I told her the story of rescuing Sarah from the bank robbers, and then Sarah more than returning the favor by springing me from the Bigelow jail.

I sensed she wasn't quite convinced that my interest in Sarah wasn't of a more personal nature, so I tried again to relive her mind. "Lydia, I promise you. If we can just do what I came here for, I'll go home with you gladly. Shoot, I've still not given up hope your mother will take me back one day."

Taking my hand to pull me up from the stone bench, Lydia said, "Let's get back to the hotel. It's close to midnight. I've traveled almost a hundred years today. I'm beat and we have a train to catch in the morning."

Fifteen minutes later, we were at the Arlington. Fifteen minutes after that, I was sound asleep, oblivious to having died that day, only to be reborn again because my daughter charged back in time to change my fate.

Chapter 20

SARAH WAS WAITING in the lobby at 6:30 the next morning when Lydia and I came downstairs. She seemed none the worse for the events of the previous evening, greeting us with a smile. "Good morning, you two. Lydia, let's take your father to breakfast. My brother has reserved us a table in the dining room by the window. Sam is already out back, seeing to the coach and the horses. He'll take us to the train station. Train leaves at 8:30."

The dining room of the Arlington where Lydia, Sarah, and I had breakfast was as elegant as the rest of grand hotel.

At Hot Springs' finest hotel, even breakfast entailed being seated by a jacketed waiter, a handsome black man. He quickly served us eggs, bacon and coffee on a table adorned with fresh flowers. Lydia, who always loved eating out, was clearly relishing the experience. "Dad, this is almost as fancy as the Grand Hotel, don't you think?" Indeed it appeared so, as I looked around the room with its fine woodwork and elegant décor. It occurred to me that even as we sat in 1911 Arkansas, upscale diners were likely having breakfast at the Grand Hotel on Mackinaw Island Michigan, for I knew it had been built in the late 1800s.

Outside the windows, Central Avenue was already bustling, streetcars clanging by and occasional open-topped automobile sharing the street with horse-drawn conveyances of all types. I wondered idly how the women I watched crossing the street kept the hems of their long dresses out of the dust and plentiful horse droppings.

"OK, Dad, what's the plan? This is a grand adventure but I'm not sure how much more of 1911 my nerves can take," said Lydia, between forks-full of scrambled eggs. "Well, the first thing we need to do is meet Sam outside," said Sarah. "It's time to get to the train station."

As we stepped out onto the broad hotel verandah, a realization descended on me like a ton of bricks. Had my daughter not talked an old man a century into the future into sending her back to 1911 in a time machine yesterday and an equally elderly Priest had not gotten her on a train to Hot Springs in time, I'd be laid out dead in the local mortuary instead of walking into the sunshine of a new day. Somehow this gave me a sense of peace that no matter what the next few days brought, this whole unbelievable tale could have a happy conclusion.

Lost in our own thoughts, none of us talked, even to Sam, on the ten-minute ride to the depot. At one point, I saw the gleaming steel observation tower atop Hot Springs Mountain through a break in the trees and wished I had no worries. How I would love the chance to climb to the top to see the panoramic view. I envied those people I knew were up there, looking down and commenting on the grand city view.

At the station, I bought our tickets on what was going to be a crowded trip. The platform was jammed with people, including a few old men in tattered Confederate gray. The talk around us was of the UCV reunion, from the frailest old soldier to the young people that in some cases seemed to be their caretakers. I picked up a booklet someone had dropped. Published by the Missouri Pacific Iron Mountain Railroad, it explained at least part of the crowd. The railroad had used the occasion of the reunion to promote the sale of tickets, outlining the attractions of Hot Springs that could be visited enroute to Little Rock.

Once onboard the train, we found it impossible to find three seats together. Sarah insisted Lydia and I take the two together that we did find in the crowded car, but I told them I needed to sit by myself and think about what to do over the next couple of days. I squeezed by an elderly lady who had hobbled down the aisle ahead of us with the aid of a rough hand-carved cane. Sarah and Lydia settled into seats a few rows up from mine and shortly the train, at least our car, was filled to capacity.

As the train began to pull out of the station, a man across the aisle form me pointed to a minaret-like tower a few blocks from the depot. "Now that's surely the tallest thing in town." What is it, do you know?' Although I had no idea, a heavyset man in the seat in front of me rose to answer her question. "That there is the Eastman Hotel…finest in the city…don't care what those folks over at the Arlington say. It's got almost 500 rooms setting in the middle of the grandest gardens you've ever seen outside maybe somewhere in Europe." I'd have to take the man at his word for I knew the hotel was long gone by my own time.

As the train pulled out of Hot Springs, we could not fail to be impressed with the view of the Eastman Hotel, another part of the Victorian era splendor that would be gone by our time.

Seizing more upon a potential business opportunity than just conversing with strangers, the man extended his large doughy hand to me, "Henry Hines is my name. I represent the Arkansas Bank and Trust here in Hot Springs. If you fine folks are needing a bank that ain't ever been robbed, that's the place." Not waiting to see if we might be future bank customers or not, the portly man went on. "You're headed for the reunion, I'll bet. I am, too…expect most folks on this crowded train are likewise. My old daddy, God rest his soul…see he fought in the Civil War, enlisted in '63, wounded in the head at the battle of the Wilderness…wasn't ever himself again after he came home."

Prompted by a mix of curiosity and politeness, I asked him, "Is he going to the reunion with you?"

"No sir, my daddy, see he died in 1885…got to having flashbacks to the war he did, that head wound I guess. Went charging out of the house one cold winter night, just him and Mama home. I was away at college, down in Arkadelphia at Ouachita. Mama tried to find him…they was living on a farm up by Mt. Ida. Said he was yelling about the yanks attacking. "Run for cover," he yelled. My uncles hunted him for two days. Found him finally, froze to death in the middle of the woods."

The train went around a steep curve about that time, propelling the man back into his seat, cutting off any further conversation about his war-damaged father. A woman seated behind me, apparently with good hearing, leaned forward to say, "That's so sad isn't it mister. Did you ever hear such a sad story?" With more humor than the human tragedies warranted, my reply was "Mam, you wouldn't believe the stories I've heard since I arrived here."

I looked forward in the car to where Lydia and Sarah were seated and deeply engrossed in a conversation I suspected resembled that of two women from any era discussing shared concerns about men… and me, in particular.

I wasn't far off, as I would later get the condensed version of the conversation from Lydia when she stretched her legs and wandered back to my seat. Apparently Sarah had asked her whether she had questions she'd been too polite to ask, like why Sarah followed me to Little Rock and took such an interest in my unbelievable situation. Although Lydia was, no doubt, dying to hear the answer, she responded that Sarah didn't owe her any explanation.

Sarah assured her that she really wanted to be friends and help us both face whatever is to come over the next few days. The relayed version verbatim went like this, "I'm a small town widow with a young son, and I'd be lying if I said your Dad wasn't a very interesting, attractive man. In another time…, wait that's almost funny, another time…but I mean I know he's here to on a serious and dangerous mission. I know you two will be going home to your own time when that's accomplished. I have no illusions of romance, although…In normal circumstances, I feel it would be inevitable." I found myself blushing in front of my daughter as she recounted Sarah's words as I, too, had to admit that my attraction to the lovely widow was the strongest I'd felt for any woman in this century or the next. I knew her beautiful face and striking red hair would haunt my dreams.

Apparently convinced that she should downplay her feelings for me, Sarah had assured Lydia that her trip to the reunion was a welcome break in her routine in Bigelow – something along the lines that she didn't get to go to the big city as often as she would have liked. Lydia, for sure, wasn't buying it. Sarah added, "After meeting you, I'd like to have met your mother. She must be proud of you".

Lydia didn't hesitate to brag about her mother. "Oh yes, my Mom, she is pretty amazing, and it was painful to watch her and Dad drift apart in my teens. She's a forensic psychiatrist and spends much of her time with criminals with serious mental health issues – even axe murders and who committed awful crimes. I guess to offset that side of her life, she runs long distance races and does 100-mile bike rides, all things she tried to get Dad to do with her. He wasn't having any of that and, over time, they had less and less in common, well, except for me and my younger sister who recently started college."

Their conversation had ended with Sarah saying "I hope our little talk has helped and we can be friends," and Lydia squeezing her hand to show that all was well.

To change the subject from Sarah, Lydia said, "Dad, I'm taking home a few souvenirs from Hot Springs. Look at these postcards of the city that the Arlington desk clerk gave me." She extracted a thick stack of picture postcards from the handbag loaned to her by Mrs. Merkel. Flipping through the cards, I was reminded anew how much of the grand city would be lost by 2011, almost a century into the future. I also remembered the Little Rock photographer I'd met at the Capitol, who had promised me a set of postcard photos. It occurred to me that if we did succeed in returning to 2011, such images might be the only thing to prove – even to ourselves – we had actually not dreamed this entire thing.

The rocking motion of the train, combined with a lack of sleep in recent nights, lulled me to sleep less than 20 miles out of Hot Springs. I even slept through the brief stop in Benton, Lydia told me later. The stirring of the passengers awoke me as the train pulled into the Little Rock station.

The platform was jammed, for this was the opening day of the reunion. There seemed to be enough old soldiers milling about to restart the war. Lydia tried to tell me something, but her efforts were drowned out by the sound of Dixie played by a band somewhere out of sight, and soon it seemed that every old soldier on the platform had joined in singing with the band.

The three of us hurried through the train station lobby and into the street to hail a horse-drawn carriage. "Where to, folks? Glad you came along. I was getting a might tired of waiting for those old soldiers to finish their singing. Been listening to that dad-blamed song all morning, playing it all over town. Much more of this, and I'll start in with Battle Hymn of the Republic," he spouted nonstop as he turned his horses lead downtown. "Which hotel would you be a needing me to take you to?"

"Actually, sir, we need to go to St. Edwards, please," I said. From the surprised driver came "Ah, Father Shultz's church. Well, that's a first for me…not sure I've ever taken folks off the train who wanted to go straight to church……But, no problem sir. I know exactly where it is."

The carriage driver took us up Victory Street, telling us it was almost impossible to get down East Markham like he normally would go to get on Main Street. "The rebs' reunion headquarters is at the Marion Hotel. A bunch more of them are filling up the Capitol Hotel – guess the "generals" with money. Even the lawn of the old state Capitol next door to the Marion is full of the old guys. I'll have you over to the church pretty quick, though, going this way."

The coach moved quickly, first down Victory Street, then Ninth, and soon we had pulled up in front of St. Edwards. I paid the driver, seeing that he was still clearly puzzled about why we had rushed from the train station to the church, saying only to myself, "friend, if you only knew."

When we reached the church Father Schultz opened the rectory door, relief apparent on his face. "Well, my son, I see my prayers were answered. Your lovely daughter seems to have saved you from harm in Hot Springs." Lydia responded to his kind observation with, "Yes Father, the Lord, he does indeed work in mysterious ways." Amen." Glad to be alive, I added a silent "amen".

When we were all settled in the parlor with glasses of lemonade, I thanked him for taking Lydia in and helping her catch the train to Hot Springs. The priest bowed his head slightly, his hands in a prayerful formation, and said, "The Lord is good, my son, and is, I think, looking upon you with favor."

Lydia opted to take charge at this point. "We need a plan to help the Lord out, stop those bad guys in their tracks, find Dave and head home. My nerves can't take much more of this." Her use of the term "home" puzzled me for a moment before realizing she meant a century in the future.

Father Shultz brought us up to date on Sexton and Cabot. "They're back in Little Rock. I went down to the train station to meet the night train arriving from Hot Springs; I thought you might be on it. It had been delayed for hours below Benton because of some switch malfunction where a load of logs dumped over. I remembered the photographs you showed me, and there they were, leaving the train. They were in a foul mood, arguing with one another."

REUNION IN TIME

Having our undivided attention, the priest paused to sip his lemonade and continued. "I decided to follow them; when they got a coach, I got the one behind them." That tired old movie line from my own time, "Follow that car!" flitted through my mind.

Lydia couldn't contain her excitement. "You know where they are then, Father. That's great! Dad, we can......" The priest, with a pained expression on his face, held up a hand, saying, "No, my child. I'm sorry to say I don't know where they are. My coach was following theirs down Capitol Avenue and I was close enough at one point to listen to them talk, though I couldn't make out the topic."

"We were passing the Gleason Hotel, which had a big crowd in the street. A man ran out to the curb – one of my parishioners – to hail me. He said an old soldier had fallen down the hotel stairs and was seriously injured. He was asking for a priest." Reading the disappointment on our faces, he went on, "I was truly conflicted, but I had no choice. I had to comfort the old gent and give him last rites…to anoint him. He died, I think, more peacefully because he knew I was there to ask the Lord to receive him."

"So we don't know where they went, only that they are back in Little Rock," was my disappointed assessment.

"Well, not quite" came Father Shultz's reply. "I knew you told me they had stayed at the Freiderica Hotel, and it was only a couple blocks from the Gleason. I went down there, talked with young Matt, the clerk. He told me the two men came in, expected to get their room back from the other night, and he explained to them the hotel was full up, there were no rooms. He said they got very angry, but about that time, a policeman came in from the ice cream parlor next door. He suggested they try the Terminal Hotel over by the depot, and they left quietly."

""So there're at the hotel by the depot then?" asked Lydia, her hope restored. "Alas, no," replied Father Schultz. "Matt called the clerk over at the Terminal Hotel for me…asked if the two men were staying there. The answer was 'no'." That hotel was full as well, but they had showed up trying to rent a room. The clerk didn't have a clue where they went after they left."

While we pondered a next step, the rectory telephone rang. Father Shultz got up quickly and spoke into the cone-shaped part on the front of the boxy wood telephone. "Thank you Matt. Thank you very much. I'm not sure what it means, but I'll relay it to Dr. Kernick."

Settling back into his chair, he told us that the call had been from Matt. "He called to tell me Fred Allsopp – he owns the hotel, you know – came back a bit ago from downtown. Said he was in the M.M. Cohn's department store earlier this morning and saw Cabot and Sexton buying things in the men's clothing section. He knew the men looked familiar, but he couldn't figure out why until he got back to the hotel and it came to him. Jack showed him photos of the men yesterday at the drug store soda fountain."

"Fred told Matt to call down here… see if I could get a message to you, Jack.. Funny thing, though, Fred told Matt the fellas were buying uniforms. They both got fitted for new Confederate uniforms. What, pray tell, could they want with rebel clothes? I wonder, but wait. I saw something in today's paper somewhere." He was soon flipping through the morning paper which had been laying on the floor by his chair.

"Ah, here it is…not losing my mind after all, am I?" Father Schultz folded the paper and handed it to me. The illustration of a man in Civil War dress was captioned, "We have in stock for immediate delivery Confederate gray uniforms for veterans and sons of veterans: Prices $9.00, $12.50, and $15.00." "Dad, they're too young to pass as veterans, but could certainly pretend to be sons of veterans," said Lydia. "But what would be the point?"

I didn't try to answer the question, but instead rose from my seat and walked out on the porch. Father Schultz, Sarah and Lydia followed me before the screen door could close. Pointing toward the bustling City Park across the street with the rolled up newspaper, I answered, "They needed the uniforms to move around the camp unnoticed."

"Lord help us all" was my next thought. They will be virtually unnoticed when surrounded by the remains of General Lee's army. What on earth will we do?

Chapter 21

MY INITIAL PLAN was to walk over to the park by myself and see if I could find the two men, hopefully without them seeing me. I rejected Lydia's request to come along and I was crossing Ninth Street within the hour, hoping I could bring the situation to a successful conclusion. It was not to be that easy, which by now should have come as no surprise. From the sidewalk in front of the park, I could see a sea of white-haired, bearded men in gray, many waiting in a long line for a meal. A jumble of voices carried out of the camp, a vocal collage of battle stories long over but retained now as highlights of lives well into their twilight years.

My attempt to enter the park encampment was defeated by three uniformed rebels, none of whom were younger than 80. They had their orders to let no visitors enter until the appointed time.

I was met at the entrance to the camp by three elderly soldiers carrying muskets and blocking the drive. "Halt Sir," commanded the soldier in the center, as the others closed ranks. "The camp is closed until 1:00 this afternoon. No visitors are allowed until after our noon mess."

Not wanting to risk the fate of Yankees the old men might have slain in battle a half century earlier, I reluctantly returned to the rectory across the street. The camp was closed for another hour. I could deal with that, or maybe I just didn't want to dwell too much on the fact I'd been tossed back onto the street by three men well into their 80s.

Lydia and Sarah were waiting on the front porch, having watched my trip over and back from the park entrance. "Ladies, I'm afraid my advance has been repulsed by the Confederate army, at least until 1:00 when the public is allowed to enter the park."

I accepted another glass of lemonade from Father Schultz and sat in the porch swing. "Dad, I think Sarah and I have a better idea for how to find out if the men are in the camp. We know that you've met Gabe Sexton and he would likely recognize you if you run into one another in the camp. He could well panic, or who knows what he would do, especially if he has a gun?"

"Looking at the two women, I should have known what was coming, and Sarah didn't disappoint. "Neither man knows Lydia or me, but we'll recognize them from the photographs you have. There have been lots of women walking through the park during the hours open to the public so we won't stand out. We have a better chance of finding them without alerting them that anyone is even looking for them. I can certainly blend in, and Lydia has the dress Father's housekeeper gave her."

My natural inclination to reject the idea to keep them out of harm's way was defeated quickly by the clear logic of their plan. "OK, I agree….but only to see if they're there. You won't do anything, won't say anything, right? Promise me."

They both nodded almost at the instant the clock in Father Shultz's parlor chimed for 1:00 pm. The camp would be reopening.

There was little choice but to sit on the porch and watch the two women, sharing Sarah's umbrella to fend off the hot sun, head across Ninth Street into the sea of gray uniforms spread across the city park.

The time crawled by as I sat on the rectory porch with Father Shultz, all the while fretting about "what ifs" that might have happened to the women across the street. By 3:00 p.m., I was starting to fear the worst, that the headstrong women had done more than just look for the men. I was on the verge of heading into the park myself when I caught sight of Sarah and Lydia exiting the gate, acknowledging the appreciative glances of rebel attendants with a smile.

I met them at the end of the sidewalk, hopefully appearing calmer than I felt. We didn't speak until we were back on the porch. "Well, we found both of them in the camp," said Sarah. They seem to have been put to work by the mess officers. When we saw them, they were peeling potatoes and cussing a mean streak." Lydia added, "One of them – I think it was Sexton – was complaining to the other one about someone he must have antagonized to get them assigned to kitchen duty."

I let the information sink in for a bit that the men we'd chased back in time were only a few hundred feet away from where I stood. However, any elation I was feeling about our progress was quickly doused with the reality that I had not a clue how I was going to get them out of the army encampment, let alone back to the year 2011. Before I could voice my frustration, a young delivery man walked up to the rectory, bearing a box in his arms. "Uh, excuse me folks. I've got a delivery here from Cohn's for Father Schultz." Before any of us could reply, Father Schultz appeared on the porch. "Ah, there you are, young Joseph. I've not seen you in Sunday Mass of late, but I'm sure I will soon, shan't I? Thank you, though, for being so prompt with that package I'd called Mr. Cohn about a little while ago. I'll take it off your hands."

"Here you go Father, but…uh…geez…I mean, didn't you fight in the Yankee army?" The young man was clearly puzzled as he handed the box to Father Schultz, who smiled and tipped the boy a nickel. My curiosity was rapidly building at that point to match that of the delivery boy.

Father Shultz settled back onto the porch swing and carefully opened the large flat box, unfolding tissue paper covering its contents. I almost laughed out loud when he held up a Confederate uniform coat against his skinny chest and, almost on cue, a band practicing in the park sent out strains of "Dixie" across Ninth Street. He handed me the neatly-folded gray uniform from the box and there was no mystery about his plans for me.

"Oh shit, Dad. This can't mean what I think it means?" Lydia's sometimes unfortunate choice of words stated the obvious. Father Shultz intended for me to enter the park dressed in a Confederate uniform. The priest nodded his assent. "Once we determined where those two were, I called Cohn's to get the uniform. There can't be a much better way to search the park, ask questions, and get close to your two outlaws than this. I'll be the ancient, creaking old rebel and you will pass nicely as my son, a proud member of the Sons of the Confederacy. I had Mrs. Merkel bring me over the old reb uniform that belonged to her daddy. She kept it all these years, and it's a pretty good fit for me. I suggest we get changed. We've got a reunion to attend across the street." With that, he headed into the house to change into his uniform. I had little choice but to do the same.

In the rectory's guest room, I changed into the crisp gray pants and shirt and caught my stark reflection in the mirror of the marble-topped wash stand. My mind called up the sepia toned studio-posed

I'd set a new bar for "what can happen next" in 1911, as I found myself opening a package containing a new Confederate uniform Father Shultz was expecting me to wear.

images I'd seen in books of Civil war soldiers before heading off to the bloody fields of battle. My reflection, however, showed me that I was missing something, and I returned to the package on the bed to uncover the gray, black-billed forage cap. With it firmly jammed on my head, my image in the mirror now looked even more like a page out of the history books. I pushed the oft-repeated dream of my death at Gettysburg back into the depths of my subconscious mind, as I retrieved the pistol I'd bought from beneath my bed and dropped it into the surprisingly deep pocket of the uniform coat before heading out to the porch where Lydia and Sarah waited.

Father Shultz and I almost collided in the parlor on the way to the front door, my reaction to his image brought me up short, as had my own mirrored reflection. His frayed and faded uniform was at least two sizes too big and his body seemed more stooped and frail than it had encased in his black suit and clerical collar. We stared at one another, at first in silence. Then the old Priest began to laugh, softly at first, then with a great guffawing sound. "I'm sorry Jack; it's just that…well, who would believe this? Looking at you, I'm reminded of the rebel prisoners we marched around Little Rock when I wore the Union blue in the capture of this town in 1863."

For my part, my remarkably well-cut uniform, almost sized as if I'd gone to a tailor, could not help but make me smile. "I did a good job guessing your size, it appears," he said. "Mine is a bit large – more to play the part of the frail old soldier, you know." Back on the porch, Lydia just stared, her hand over her mouth, but Sarah smiled. "Jack, you make one handsome soldier."

Seeing no reason to delay, the Father and I headed across the street to the park. I looked back to see Lydia and Sarah standing on the rectory steps – as if watching their men go off to war…with a prayer for their safe return.

The entrance gate to the park was still guarded by three veterans, but none appeared to be the one who denied me admission into the camp earlier in the day. I need not have worried. A surprising crisp salute from Father Shultz, wearing his sergeants stripes, was returned by the guards who moved aside to allow us to enter the bustling acres of massed, old soldiers. Father Shultz, however, lingered to ask, "Say there, comrades…wondering about some directions, if you could point us the way to the mess tents?" It seemed prudent to try to begin our search where Sarah and Lydia had found Sexton and Cabot peeling potatoes. The closest guard, who seemed considerably more elderly and certainly frailer than the priest, was hard of hearing. "Say what? What regiment did I serve with? Proud to tell you, I was with the Little Rock Guard… helped defend this very city, and this old arsenal, though we was overrun by the yanks, sad to say. What unit did you fight with Sarge?"

Father Shultz, whose hearing wasn't in the least impaired, hesitated, then put his cupped hand to his ear, "Uh, what's that you say?" He obviously couldn't admit, "Oh, I was with the 5th Wisconsin regiment of the Union Army who marched into Little Rock in 1863." After all, he was a Priest. Didn't he have to tell the truth?

I guess, though, the Lord has some dispensation to cover such matters of life and death. "Well Private, thank you for asking. I was with the 3rd Alabama, I was…fought at Shiloh, Chickamauga, and Franklin, Tennessee." The old private seemed suitably impressed, "Well you certainly seen more action than I did. I finished out the war a prisoner of them God-damned Yankees. My, my, you say the battle of Franklin. That's where General Cleburne was killed. You know there was an old colored man here this morning, says he was the General's camp boy fore the battle, had him a horseshoe, said it came off the horse General Cleburne was a riding before he was kilted."

I wasn't certain who General Cleburne was, but I did know the county north of Little Rock was named Cleburne, surely for this fallen rebel general.

"Yes Private, I saw General Cleburne the night before the battle at Franklin…fine man, terrible loss to our cause when he was killed." The Priest was raising his voice now, trying to compensate for the old guard's hearing deficit while telling lies that even I almost found believable. This was one Priest who would be overdue for the confessional I told myself with no small amount of amusement, as someone who was considerably overdue for the sacrament himself.

"Tell me, how might we find the mess tent? We are sure looking forward to getting some chow." One of the other guards stepped forward to help, "Sarge, just follow the main road around behind the arsenal.

RAY HANLEY

Take the center path. Look for the flags flying over General Shaver's tent. He's the camp commander, you know. Mess tent's just about 50 feet past the general's headquarters."

We made our way around the arsenal building, familiar to me from 2011. It appeared not to have changed over the years, certainly not at all from the outside. At the rear of the building, as the guard had told us, we came to the wider path leading into the center of the park. Park it may have been, but the term "camp" was certainly a more suitable label today. There had to be hundreds of military-style canvas tents erected in neat rows, interlaced with straight paths. I recalled the microfilmed 1911 newspaper accounts I'd studied in 2011 in Charlie's kitchen. The US Army from Fort Roots had erected 1,300 of the tents which I'd help haul to the park to house the old soldiers, keeping Little Rock's commitment to house them for free, as well as feed them. We could see the stars and bars of the Confederacy flying in the distance, apparently marking the location of the headquarters tent that was our beacon.

The mess tents, behind which we would stumble upon Sexton and Cabot, were just beyond General Shaver's tent. They were some of the 1,300 I'd helped transport in wagons but days earlier.

The path was jammed by shuffling groups of stooped old soldiers headed toward the meal tents. There were also a number of

REUNION IN TIME

women in full-length skirts moving with the traffic as well, as the camp had just opened to the general public. Soldiers and sightseeing visitors formed a human traffic jam.

Without warning, Father Shultz tripped over something and grabbed onto my arm to break his fall somewhat. He still wound up on his knees, and I had to help him back to his feet. He wiped his brow on his sleeve and said, "Sorry Jack, guess I'm not battle ready, am I? Just let me catch my breath and cool off a bit. This heat and this wool uniform are not the best combination." Looking around, I found a vacant bench in front of one of the tents that seemed like the best place to sit.

As we settled down, a young uniformed boy scout materialized from the crowd with a bucket of water and a dipper. "Sir, you look like you could use a drink of water." Father Shultz responded, "Why Joseph, I certainly could my boy." The boy, who must have been all of twelve years-old, recognized the priest and stammered out, "Uh...but...uh Father, I thoughts you was with the Yankees....." Father Shultz held his finger to his lips as he handed back the dipper. "Now Joseph, let's make that our secret. I just knew some of these old soldiers might need a priest, you know, and I couldn't exactly come over here wearing a Yankee blue uniform now, could I?" The boy thought about it and replied, "Well no, Father, I guess you couldn't at that."

The faces of 1911, would be forever engrained in my mind. None were more so than the frail old drummer who seemed to almost stagger beneath the weight of a drum I knew could not be heavy. In the depth of his sunken eyes, I could almost see the memories of battles 50 years before.

While we waited for the Father to rest a bit, the flaps of the tent we sat in front of were thrown back and a photographer emerged to set up his large tripod- mounted

RAY HANLEY

camera in front of the tent. When he was done, he called out, "All right sir, I'm ready when you are."

Responding to the call, an elderly veteran, brushy beard covering his face and neck emerged from the tent, dragging a military drum behind him. The photographer, seeing me sitting idly by, asked, "You there, sir. Might you help Private Thomas here get his drum in place so that I can take his photo? He was fourteen years old at the battle of Shiloh – a regular "little drummer boy" – who led troops onto the field of battle." The former drummer boy had a crutch under one arm and initially looked as if he would have trouble standing for a photo, let alone holding the big drum. However, seeing the camera, the old soldier tossed his crutch aside and pulled himself erect and began to beat a soft tune on the drums.

When the photographer was done, I helped the old drummer onto the bench next to Father Shultz. He took a long breath and said, "Thank you, son. "You look mighty fine in that uniform – just like all them boys that fought the yanks in that peach orchard at Shiloh back in '62

When Father Shultz got his second wind, we resumed our walk toward the dining area in the center of the park, and found our way blocked by a crowd headed in the same direction. However, they parted for a snowy-haired old general, with an escort of officers.

He paused for a moment and bent down to talk to a girl of perhaps five years of age who clutched her mother's hand and a doll against her chest.

Father Shultz commented, "Read all about him in the papers. That would be 'Fighting Bob' Shaver, the Confederate General who now lives over by Mena. He's the commander of this camp; it's named Camp Shaver in his honor. He has quite a war record, if the stories are true. See that white glove? He only wears one to cover a war wound. Hear tell, he never takes it off. The Gazette story reported he had more than one horse shot out from under him at the battle of Shiloh."

While General Shaver resumed his tour of the camp, a bugle call erupted from the dining area. "Chows on. Let's get it before it's all gone," said one old vet on my left. After that, it might as well have been a stampede of elderly buffalos. The rows between the tents filled with old men hurrying toward the commissary area where the food was being served. The stampede abruptly halted when a thundering gunshot stopped the rowdy crowd in its tracks. General Shaver held a smoking pistol in the air and called out, "If I see any more of this pushing and shoving, I'm going to shoot those responsible. I order you to form a single, orderly line for this meal and all others. Conduct yourselves like soldiers of the Confederacy and like the gentlemen you claim to be, or you will answer to me." Like magic, the veterans did as they were told and an orderly line slowly inched forward.

Taking Father Schultz by the arm to present the appearance of a proper escort, I took a place in the line moving toward the mess. I could only hope that when we finally made it to that point, we would find Sexton and Cabot where Lydia and Sarah saw them earlier in the day. What I would do then? I had not a clue.

Watching "fighting Bob", the old Confederate General, I had trouble imagining this now frail man having had two horses shot from beneath him at the battle of Shiloh. However, it became easier to believe after I watched him firing a pistol into the air and lecturing the old rebels in a firm voice on proper decorum at meals.

Chapter 22

WE COULD SEE the stars and bars hanging over the headquarters area next to the mess tent. Father Shultz had noticed the same landmark, which led him to make the sign of the cross and softly utter what I was sure was a prayer.

When we were next in line, we picked up plates and utensils, all of which were embossed "US Army" which could not have gone unnoticed and unremarked on by the old Confederate soldiers. Taking my plate of roast beef, pinto beans and potatoes, I moved on to another table and came face to face with Henry Cabot, serving coffee in large metal mugs from a huge urn. He was unshaven, bleary eyed, but dressed in an obviously new Confederate gray uniform. He never made eye contact, just handed me the coffee mug and accepted another from the Boy Scout pulling the battered tin cups from a burlap bag. At the next table in line, two more boy scouts handed out dishes of some sort of pudding, ladling it from a large bucket with military precision. As the two boys moved apart in the act of handing out the bowls, I saw Gabe Sexton seated on an upturned bucket peeling potatoes, a crude handmade cigarette hanging from his mouth. Father Shultz, at my elbow, nudged me to move on. I'd paused longer than I should have – too long as it turned out.

Sexton's eyes turned toward me, as if he had sensed my fixed stare. His expression left no doubt he had recognized me, the hand-rolled cigarette falling from his lower lip into the bucket of peeled potatoes. Too late. I had no choice but to move on in the serving line. Father Shultz pulled me toward the left between a row of tents.

"Let's circle back around the mess tents. If they try to leave the park, I expect they will go that way, not the direction they saw you going."

Belatedly getting my wits about me, I countered, "No, let's do this. They know me, but can't know you are with me. I'll circle back around the mess tents. You just take your plate and head on back past the serving tables, maybe like you forgot something. I'll be waiting back up the path."

"The best laid plans of mice and men" keep running through my mind, and I mentally tipped my hat to poet Robert Burns for his understanding of the pitfalls of planning ahead. As I carefully stepped over the maze of ropes and stakes behind the tents, the rear flaps of the largest mess tent flew back and out stumbled Gabe and Henry – directly into my path, not two feet away. Their backs were to me and they were arguing. "God Damn it, I know who it was, Henry. It's that Doctor pal of old Rawlins. I've seen him a half dozen times. Shit, what's he doing………?" At that moment, Gabe turned to find himself virtually nose-to-nose with me. "Henry, I do believe you're right. Look here."

"Well, well, Dr. Kernick. Whatever brings you to the year of our Lord, 1911? You're a long ways from home." I swallowed hard when I noticed the large meat cleaver dangling from one hand that he must have picked up in the mess tent.

Such an eloquent question was owed an equally artful reply. "Well Gabe, I've come here after you. Attacking an old friend and fleeing a century back in time to steal, murder, and change the course of history doesn't become you. Your plan here just isn't going work. You may as well come back and face the music."

Both men turned shoulder- to-shoulder, facing Father Schultz and me, taking on identical smirks. Henry, clearly the muscle of the two, spoke first. "Now why would we want to do that Doc? We sorta like it here, with all these old rebs. Though I gotta say you don't look like you belong in that gray suit yourself. Maybe Yankee blue would look better on you. Now, though, the old man here, I bet he sings Dixie in his sleep…ain't that right, Pop?"

I decided to turn my arguments to Gabe Sexton who I knew was a bright educated man whose engineering skills Charlie had greatly valued. "Gabe, I think you are a better man than to be here to harm people or break laws. At this point you have not done anything we can't set straight back in 2011. Will you and Henry come back with me and we will work this all out with Charlie.?" Something told me not to mention Dave because as far as I knew they had no idea he had come to 1911 looking for them.

Gabe, letting out a deep breath while seeming to think about a considered reply said, "Doctor Kernick, I appreciate your logic, I really do and I wish you no harm. I can't go back to 2011 and it has nothing to do with Charlie. I'm really sorry Henry hit him with a board, that should not have happened and I'm glad to hear he is ok. The fact of the matter however is I'm wanted by the FBI and likely other federal agencies for selling some weapon plans. If I go back I'll end up in prison likely for the rest of my life. I'm staying here, and so is Henry."

Father Shultz, erect and almost regal in the old gray uniform, replied, "My son I prefer to pray for your souls and for the protection of those Jack here believes you will harm here in this city."

"My soul?" came the reply from Henry. "You some sort of preacher, old man? I think I like my soul better here in 1911…lots of money to be made, women to chase. Nope, think I'll just stay here. Doc needs to haul his ass back to where he came from – more sick folks there, I'm sure."

Gabe, feeding off his duller partner, finished painting the picture for me that we were in a proverbial "Mexican standoff." "Doctor Kernick you don't seem to be in a position to make us do anything or go anywhere. I suggest you just go back where you came from and take your friend with you."

An impasse indeed. What cards did I have to play? "Gabe, I've read the newspapers from the next few days already." This remark totally baffled Henry, and briefly Gabe, but he caught on quickly. "So that makes you some sort of fortune teller Doc? Maybe you should have also read up on who is going to win the horse races over at Oaklawn before you let old Charlie put you in that time rocket… might have turned a nice profit. Still don't change anything. We are not going back."

"What if I say you either head back to 2011 or I'll talk to the police here in 1911 – tell them you're going to rob a jewelry store?" Both men interrupted me in mid-sentence, Gabe laughing out loud. "The police? What are you going to tell them, Doc? Far as I know, Henry and I haven't broken any laws here. You gonna tell them we all came here in a time machine? Go ahead, tell them that. Henry and I'll be walking around free as a bird, and you and the old man here will be locked up in the loony bin they got out the other side of the state capitol." With that, he jammed the meat clever he had held by his side into a tree and disappeared back through the tent flap, Henry following him with a laugh. I'd forgotten all about the pistol in my jacket pocket, though when I thought about it later, I'm not sure what I'd have done with it in the crowded park to change the outcome of my encounter with the two men.

My temporary inertia was interrupted by Father Shultz's hand on my shoulder. "Well my son, that was not the most productive conversation I've ever had with a couple of louts, but we do know a bit better the challenge we face. Let's leave them for now… go back to the rectory and think about what we can do next." Seeing little other choice, I could only nod, and we were soon making our way out of the park.

Chapter 23

LYDIA AND SARAH were waiting on the porch when we returned, with my hangdog expression telegraphing loud and clear that we had not accomplished our mission in the park. Seated on the porch with a glass of lemonade from the rectory kitchen, the four of us took stock of where things stood and considered our next move. Lydia, always the methodical one, took charge. "Ok, we know where the bad guys are. They know Dad has traveled back here to 1911 to take them back to 2011, but they seem to feel he's no threat…Right so far?" "True, of course" I agreed, "but what's our next option?"

She had a suggestion – more than one actually. "What if we could get them arrested for something they didn't do, something that has nothing to do with where they came from? If they're locked up, they can't hurt anybody."

Seeing that she had our complete attention, she continued. "We know where they are, right? Or, at least, where they were a half hour ago. I'll find a policeman on the street near the park, and I'll tell him…Oh, what…Let's think?" Lydia picked up the thread of the idea from there. "Yes, one of us can tell the cop, uh, policeman we were walking in the neighborhood last night and were attacked, but escaped, from two men." Sarah, getting more excited about the plot, took over. "Yes, yes, that's it! And we will say we were visiting the park this morning and saw the two men who attacked us working around the cook tent."

"No, absolutely not! I won't allow it" was my reaction. As expected, the women stood their ground. "Well then, what's a better idea?" Admittedly, I had no ready answer.

"Uh, I think it may be a moot point, my friends," interrupted Father Schultz. "Look across the street there."

Gabe and Henry were locked in what was obviously a serious argument. They had not, it seemed, observed us sitting in the heavily shaded alcove of the rectory porch. Sexton's angry words traveled clearly through the hot May air. "Look Henry. I don't know and I don't care why the dammed doctor came here. It changes nothing. He can't do anything about us, and so it doesn't make any difference." At that moment, Gabe glanced across the street and he focused on the four of use seated not 40 feet away. I don't know why. It was silly, but I raised my hand in something between a casual wave and a salute.

Henry, seeing the shocked look on his partner's face, slowly turned around and followed the other man's gaze; the look of shock followed by anger did nothing to enhance an already ugly face. Giving him no time to react, Gabe pulled him by the arm and soon the two men were moving rapidly in the direction of downtown and disappeared around the corner of 8th and Sherman, with Henry giving us a middle finger salute as he disappeared from sight.

"Well, well, that was quite rude, I'd say. No fine Southern gentlemen, those two", said Father Shultz. Sarah started to laugh. Lydia followed, and soon all four of us were laughing out loud.

The laughter faded as quickly as it had come, however, leaving Lydia to ask the question we all had to confront. "Well, that was fun…the look on their faces…but what do we do next?"

Chapter 24

WHAT, INDEED, TO do next? I retrieved from my bag something I'd forgotten for a time, a folded envelope upon which, before leaving 2011, I'd made a list of the robberies noted in the old newspaper archives for this week of 1911. I was virtually certainly Gabe and Henry committed, or rather would commit, the murders of Dave and the night watchman at the Capital the night of May 18th. It was now the afternoon of May 16th, and I knew from the same newspaper account that generated my notes; there would be several robberies between now and the night of the 18th. Based on conjecture made by the police to the press in the days after Dave's murder, we though it reasonably likely the men had committed at least some of these crimes as well. There had to be a way to put this information to good use.

I outlined an idea to Father Shultz and the women. "OK, let's see….tonight, if I can read my shorthand, two armed men will rob Forester's restaurant at gunpoint just after 9:00, hitting a waiter in the head with uh, let's see….a beer pitcher, it said. Where's Forester's located, Father"

"It's down from the Hotel Marion in just about the busiest place in town this week, the hotel being the rebel headquarters for the reunion." The old man scratched his chin and then pushed back his snow white hair, clearly deep in thought. "Ah, yes, Jack. I think I see your idea. We somehow intercept the men at one of the earlier robberies this week and put them out of commission before they can kill you friend Dave the night of the 18[th.] Am I following you here?"

"Yes Father, yes. I think that's where I'm going with this but I need to note that I have no way of knowing for certain if it will be Henry and Gabe who rob the eatery, it could as easily be someone else. It's far from the optimum solution, but at best, we get them arrested, and worst, they or someone else gets injured. Credit cards have not been invented yet; so on a packed night like tonight, a bar is going to take in a lot of cash – an attractive target for a bad guy looking for a place to rob." Father Shultz, nodding, asked, "Uh, Jack, what's a credit card?"

We decided that making a call to the police from the rectory phone would invite questions. There would be no caller ID in this era, but rather a local switchboard operator would first talk to Father Shultz in order to put his call through to the police station. Instead, we decided that I would go to the Marion Hotel, which had telephones available. He would go with me to ensure I was allowed access to the phone. The operator would not recognize my voice, as she might well his.

The buggy taking us the Marion had to wait on a street car to pull up in the front of the hotel in the distant right. I was able to recall the implosion of the long shuttered hotel sometime in the early 1980's. In 2011 all in this photo was gone, replaced by a high rise modern hotel and convention center complex.

By way of a streetcar we arrived at the Marion, the entire front of which was draped in banners, Confederate flags, and pictures of Robert E. Lee and his generals. The lobby was jammed, with about half men in business suits and half old vets in Confederate uniforms. We found our passage blocked by a crowd of soldiers, whose attention was fixed on a performance occurring for their benefit on the second floor balcony. An old soldier and two women were singing, their lyrics portraying the one on the left who weighed no more than 90 pounds as the "fattest lassie in Dixieland" and the one on the right as a delicate magnolia blossom, although she looked to tip the scales at over 300 pounds. All seemed to be enjoying the show. A number were either drunk or on their way. "Magnolia blossom, ha!" shouted a fat man in a suit in front of us. "It would take a cotton scale to weigh that one."

"We need to get to the back of the lobby, Jack, to reach the office and the phone," said Father Shultz in my ear. It took effort, but eventually we worked our way around the rowdy crowd and emerged on the other side. Father Shultz was recognized immediately by the young man behind the registration desk. "Ah, Father, good to see you. What brings you to this noisy place with all these hooting rebs?"

"Sean, tis good to see you as well. I've not seen you in Mass lately, have I?" The young man blushed a bit and the priest continued, "Sean, my friend here, Dr. Kernick, has urgent need of a telephone for a private call. I wonder if perhaps you might let him use one of the phones in the office back there?" Seemingly relieved to drop the Mass attendance topic, Sean readily agreed. "of course, Father.... come right around the corner here, through this side door."

He led me into a hall containing several dark wood-paneled offices, while Father Shultz waited outside. He stopped before a frosted glass door reading "Assistant Manager. "Here you go, Dr. Kernick. Just pick up the phone and the operator down the hall will connect you." Seems I had to use the hotel's switchboard. This was getting complicated. I settled back in a chair, looking at a calendar for Western Union on the wall. I picked up the phone and was immediately greeted by a woman's voice, "Hold on please, and shortly the ringing – more like a doorbell buzzer – connected me to the local telephone company switchboard. "To what party may I connect you sir?" Apparently few women made telephone calls. "Uh, the police station please."

After a brief hesitation, the woman replied, "Oh my, the police, what happened?" "Uh, nothing, it's just a personal issue, a relative of mind works there." She had serious "nose trouble" as my grandmother used to say. "Oh, what's his name? You know my nephew works down there. He's the weekend jailer, and you wouldn't believe the tales he tells me at Sunday dinner." I was growing a bit annoyed by now. "Please, it's important. Just put the call through please." The operator got in the last word, "Well, alright sir, but you don't have to be rude."

"Sergeant O'Malley speaking." The booming voice, with its Irish accent, almost scared me into returning the hearing end of the phone apparatus to its cradle. Still, this had to be done. "Yes Sergeant, I can't give you my name, but I wanted to let you know there is going to be a robbery tonight. I, uh, heard two men in the saloon planning it." "A robbery you say? Who might I be speaking to again sir?" Still fighting the temptation to end the call, I instead replied, "Sergeant, I really don't want to get involved. I just want to prevent the robbery and anyone getting hurt. Now please listen and I'll give you a description of the two robbers." I was then able to give him a description of Henry and Gabe, along with the approximate time of the robbery, as best I could deduce from the newspaper account. Not waiting for further argument, I ended the call at that point. We had opted to give the advance alert on the jewelry store robbery rather than the one at the eatery, reasoning that it seemed less likely Sexton and Henry would stoop to that type of robbery.

I'd done my best and could only wait until evening to see if my plan worked. However, as the adage goes, "The best laid plans of mice and men...."

Chapter 25

WE WERE BACK at the rectory in less than 20 minutes, filling in Sarah and Lydia on the trip to the Marion, when there was a pounding on the front door. "Father Shultz, this be Sgt. Brennan. I needs to speak with you." Somehow I knew he wasn't selling tickets to the Policeman's Ball.

The policeman Father Shultz showed into the parlor was well over 6 feet tall and must have weighed 300 pounds, a walking mountain of Irish man. The Priest proceeded with the obligatory introductions and the Sergeant got right to the point, after taxing the durability of a winged-back chair in front of the bay window. "Father, I'm sorry to be disturbing you, but see, we's got a wee bit of a problem. Someone called the station a bit ago, saying that there was going to be a robbery tonight over at Stift's Jewelry store." He paused at that point, seemingly waiting for one of us to explain something. None of us answered and we hoped he wouldn't ask the next question, but we all knew better.

"See Father" the policeman picked back up, "The clerk at the Marion, he says that you, and I think this gentleman here, came to the hotel a bit ago to use the telephone." With our silence unbroken, he continued, "and the telephone switching station operator, Maude, who you knows tells all she hears, says the call about the robbery was put through from the Marion, She listened in, she did. The clerk, he says there was only one person using that phone around the time she put the call through to the police station, and that seems to have been your friend here."

Father Shultz cleared his throat, clearly in an awkward position, for I doubted the Priest would, or could lie blatantly, let alone to a policeman who seemed to have us dead to rights. Lydia rescued us all. She didn't have the Priestly qualms about shading the truth a bit, and had always thought on her feet.

"Officer, I can explain," and I knew she was making it up as she went, having no more clue where she was going than I did. The fact that she was young and very attractive was not lost on the burly policeman. "See I was sitting on the porch swing, uh late, yes late last night. It was dark. These two men...they were walking, yes just walking, uh....down the sidewalk out front. They stopped to talk, and, you know, not knowing I was out there on the porch, see it being dark and all..." Father Shultz, Sarah and I just sat; sharing the rapt attention shown to Lydia by the policeman, who was twirling the ends of his bushy red mustache.

"I could hear what they was saying real good. They said they was planning to rob that jewelry store, and even said about what time they thought would be best. Well, then they went on, but you see, I had to tell my father here about what I heard." The policeman leaned back, his overloaded chair groaning, his arms crossed, clearly weighing the merits of what Lydia had recounted. "Well, I see Missy. That had to have been interesting. But, well, what I don't understands is, why one of you didn't just call the police station or come by to tell us about this. Why did you go to the hotel to make the call and not give your name?"

Sensing Lydia had run the course of fiction on the fly, I started to take over, but Lydia dived back in. "Really officer, that is all my fault. See, we are visiting from out of state...and...well, I argued that question with my father here. See, he was all for just going to the police station, and gee, I guess I should have listened to him, being my daddy and all." She paused to catch her breath, or more likely to think up the rest of the whopper she was telling, intentionally, I was sure, avoiding eye contact with me. "I argued it was best we not get involved, just being here for the reunion, then going right back home to Texas... Doing it the way Daddy did it still got the message to the police, and that's the important thing, isn't it officer?"

The policeman had certainly seen a lot in his chosen line of work, but I expect a very pretty young woman with a glib tongue tied to a rapid fire imagination was not often encountered among the criminal element of Little Rock in his time. He said nothing for a moment, looking from one of us to the other, and finally nodded, "Well, Missy, I guess that does make at least a wee bit of sense.

We will post a man or two to watch that jewelry store tonight at least an hour before midnight and if the blokes do try to rob it, we will nab them." With that, the officer said an extra 'thank you' to Father Shultz and made his exit. I watched him through the parted curtains in the parlor stop at the end of the walk, rub his chin, and glance back at the house. He clearly still had misgivings, but he just couldn't put his finger on what was wrong with Lydia's story or what he could do about it.

I turned back to face our little group and found us all momentarily speechless. Sarah broke the silence with, "Whew, now that was about as much fun as watching the greased pig chase at the Perry County fair" and then she started laughing. "Lydia you were marvelous. You should be on the stage."

Father Shultz was clearly not as pleased, "My, my, may the good Lord not strike me down and take me home. I sat through a fabricated story – told to a policeman no less, and in the parlor of the church's rectory. Still yet, may he forgive me", but after making the sign of the cross, he added, "But Lydia, you did handle yourself marvelously, and though you should let me hear your confession soon, I think we accomplished the mission."

"Uh, I had to break up Lydia's path to an academy award but what can we do tonight to help make sure Sexton and Henry are out of action. And even if they only temporarily would stay in jail, get out, do we still need to figure out how to return them to 2011?" No sooner than the words came out of my mouth did Sarah ask, "Jack, what's the academy that gives awards?"

The second response came from Father Shultz, "Which academy might give an award, might you mean Mount Saint Mary's? That's a girl's school here in the city." Silent film was only then emerging and

I'd made reference to Hollywood, but then I could have added that Lydia was actually a graduate of Mount St. Mary's Academy which was still in business as an all girl's Catholic school in 2011.

"No Father, sorry, just an expression from my own time. We just need to think about what to do, if anything tonight." The first priority is to get Cabot and Sexton at least off the street so that we can prevent the rest of the crimes, especially shooting Dave. The best of all outcomes of course is to somehow force them to return to the year 2011, to get them out of this time where we know nothing good will occur from changes they make."

Father Shultz was on his feet pacing the floor between all of us and seeking to solve our dilemma. "Well Jack, the first goal, getting them off the street, likely locked up seems possible, even likely if the police apprehend them robbing the jewelry store. I don't see how though you can get your hands on them and convince them to return with you in one of the time machines." The old man paused, his hand clasping the bridge of his nose in thought, adding, "Unless of course they decide their fate is worse here than back in 2011."

Father Shultz, of course, hit the nail on the head, but how to accomplish this was still a mystery Still, I reasoned, we had made progress. We had found the men and had alerted the police to their plan to rob the jewelry store, giving at least odds of changing the course of the next few days in which Dave was to be murdered.

Chapter 26

WITH LITTLE CHOICE but to await the outcome of the promised police stakeout of the jewelry store, we turned our discussion to how to best spend the afternoon. Lydia said, "Look, I think we have done all we could do for now. Let's spend the afternoon walking around the city. I want to see it anyway... soak up a bit of the history before we hopefully resolve everything and go back home... or back to our own time, with Dave in tow. Besides, we might get lucky and just bump into him on the street and a lot of things would be easier then."

As the cuckoo clock on the rectory wall struck 4:00 PM, Sarah, Lydia and I started out for Main Street a few blocks away with a parting "God go with you" from Father Shultz. We went north on Sherman Street in the direction of what would be the River Market District, housing my condominium in 2011. Along the street, which I'd first seen from atop Gabe's freight wagon earlier in the week, the sidewalk followed the brick-lined street that was busy with buggy and wagon traffic. The worst job in Little Rock that hot humid day was surely that of the elderly black man pushing a cart and shoveling up horse manure as he went along.

At 5th Street we turned west and, a few blocks later, we were looking up and down Main Street. I'd been in 1911 for some four days now and in Little Rock for the past two, but the sights and sounds of the now-jammed street I'd walked so often decades removed was truly amazing. Street cars were moving in close lines both ways; we could see at least a dozen from where we stood, all packed with people. Each trolley car was driven by a uniformed man standing in the front and carried passengers that were a mix of old men in Confederate gray, young women in long dresses, and children, all clearly enjoying the day and the scenes around them. Reunion decorations were everywhere – banners spanning the streets and storefronts adorned with Confederate flags and pictures of Robert E. Lee.

Crossing the street, I looked up at an 11-story building at 5th and Main which I knew as the Boyle Building in my own time. However, the painted sign on the window said "State National Bank". Our arrival in front of the building found the sidewalk blocked by a photographer with a large camera set up on an expansive tripod. It was pointed at three vets standing together at 'parade rest'. About the time the photographer pulled his cable shutter release, a loud "boom" erupted in the street just behind the three old soldiers. An open-topped automobile had backfired, its retort echoing like a cannon shot, prompting the man in the middle to bound forward screaming, "Run boys, the Yankees are a shelling us agin." He knocked over the photographer and his tripod and the camera crashed into the street, as the old soldier bounded around the far corner, still yelling about the yanks.

I helped the photographer up off the sidewalk, ignoring his curses, while the old vet's two companions tried to make amends. "Mr., please don't blame poor Lester. See he ain't been quite right in the head since the battle up at Pea Ridge." The poor photographer's camera, its lens shattered, would not soon be right as well.

The excitement of the photographer's mishap behind us, Lydia and I walked west on Capitol Avenue, the dome of the distant Capitol building looming in the distance. Crossing Center Street two blocks down, we stopped to watch an elderly, snow-thatched black man pushing a high-back wicker wheelchair off the curb, its occupant being an equally aged, but much frailer, white man whose long white beard covered the front of his gray uniform. The wheelchair apparently hit an uneven paving brick in the street and before we could react, the chair tipped over on its side, spilling the geriatric rebel onto to the street. Lydia and I raced to his side and lifted him up before his ancient companion could even right the wheelchair.

Turning the corner onto Main Street, we encountered a crowd in front of a store window. The attraction was an automated diorama of a Union and Confederate soldier warmly greeting each other.

REUNION IN TIME

"It's OK. I'm fine. Don't worry Rosco…you too ladies, nor you sir. I was hurt worse by that Yankee cannon shot at Jenkins Ferry for sure," he told me as I grasped his elbow to ease him back into the chair. Only then did I notice the man was missing one leg, the left uniform pants leg being an empty sleeve. I had a grip on the other arm which felt like a broom stick, small and boney. "Thank you folks, said Rosco. I just don't know how that happened. You know, I's been with the Major Sam here since da war . I was his servant in the camps when he was fighting. Stayed with him after he freed me…worked on his farm down near Camden since the war ended." With a wave of his gnarled hand, Roscoe pushed the old soldier's chair on toward Main Street.

Ten minutes later found us nearing the Freiderica Hotel where I'd visited earlier in the week with Fred Allsopp, the owner. I suggested to Lydia that we stop for an ice cream soda at the Frederica pharmacies soda fountain to combat the heat of this Arkansas May day. The invention of air conditionings was still decades away, but when we stepped into the tiled drug store and soda fountain, it felt like the temperature dropped 20 degrees. Hank, the soda jerk, was still on duty, speaking politely to me but momentarily losing his tongue when he tried to stammer a like greeting to Lydia.

"Hello Hank, I'd like you to meet my daughter, Lydia. She is, uh…also in town for the reunion. We both could use one of those coke floats you know how to whip up." Maybe it was Lydia's smile but the poor kid dropped the first glass onto the tiled floor, shattering it. While he was trying to recover from his mishap, apologizing to Lydia, I heard a booming voice behind us, "Well, Dr. Kernick, you must really like Hank's sodas." Turning, I was greeted by the kindly face of Fred Allsopp, the proprietor of the hotel and fountain.

"Well, ain't that the truth Fred, but let me introduce you to my daughter Lydia and our friend Sarah. They…uh…joined me on short notice to take in the reunion." Lydia, turning away from poor young Hank's bumbling misfortune, greeted the hotel proprietor with poise I know she didn't inherit from me. "Mr. Allsopp, I've heard about your delightful place here and I just insisted my father bring me in here to cool off. We just don't have a place like this in Little…un…Texas." Well, she was almost truthful. In the Little Rock of 2011, there was certainly nothing like this soda fountain of 1911.

"Well, delighted to meet you Miss. I'm sure you will enjoy our fair, albeit crowded city. Why don't you and your father join me at a table over by the window. Hank will bring your drinks." We were soon seated by the large window, as a crowded streetcar jammed with old vets went clanging by toward Main Street.

No sooner had I settled into the wire-backed seat than young Hank, still red faced, was placing the frosty coke floats on the table. "Thank you, Hank. This looks yummy,", said Lydia, easing the young man's fluster noticeably. Fred Allsopp stiffled a chuckle as Hank returned to the counter. "That boy, he's like my own son, but he sure gets tongue tied around a pretty girl." Taking a sip of his own coke float he told us, "the lad is going to Draughon's Business school over on Center Street. Thinks he might like to learn the hotel trade. Haven't told him yet, but I plan to move him out of here, let him help run the hotel part of this business here."

"How old is Hank, Mr. Allsopp?" asked Lydia, never shy about asking questions for which she might have a motive in mind. "Well my dear, I believe he would be 22 years old…lives with his mother over on Scott Street. She's a widow woman. Her husband, he was some sort of engineer…caught the yellow fever down in Panama where he was working on Roosevelt's big canal. He never recovered, died a few weeks after getting back home. Poor Hank, the couple's only child, was only about 14 and still in school. He tried to drop out to get a job, but his momma wouldn't have it." I could tell by her expressive face that this tale of hardship served to deepen Lydia's curiosity, in the young man polishing glasses behind the counter who had been born almost a century before her.

"Well Dr. Kernick, did you find the friend you were looking for, the one whose picture you showed me? I'm glad you stopped in because Hank swears the fellow walked past the hotel this morning. He said he was walking fast, but Hank – see he's good with faces

– swears he got a good look at him when he stopped to look through this window. He said he was walking toward the new Capitol building up the hill yonder."

Lydia sat upright in her chair. "Well, that's good news. At least I know for sure he made it here OK, but we still haven't been able to locate him, the town is so crowded, "I replied, hoping to sound reasonably casual, though the I felt anything but casual with the affirmation that Dave could be within a few blocks of where we sat. "He isn't at the Hotel Marion, nor at the Gleason, and of course not here at your hotel. We have just about given up the prospect of finding him unless by accident at some of the reunion doings." Pinching his lip in thought, Allsopp replied, "Well on a normal day this town has about 45,000 folks, but the Mayor tells me the total this week is well over 100,000 – maybe 150,000 or more. It's a bit of a needle in the haystack."

Allsopp seemed thoughtful for a moment and then his face brightened. "Now here's an idea. The three of you should come to the Confederate Ball tonight. I've got some extra tickets. It starts at 7:00 over at the auditorium... going to be some stem-winding speeches and some dancing." Glancing across the room toward the soda fountain, a new inspiration struck our host's face. "Now that's another idea... young Hank there... see, he needs to get out more, see some folks, dance with the girls. Maybe... uh... well, if it's OK with you Lydia............?" Lydia, always quick to put people at ease, replied, "Well of course. That's a great idea. Why I'll just ask him to go with me...uh...I mean, with us."

"OK look, I've got a big automobile. Why don't I pick you three up, and Hank as well, say about 6:30? Which hotel? Oh wait, you said you were staying with Father Shultz up at St. Edwards, right? Let's invite the Father to come as well; some of those old soldiers may have some confessing to do." Thinking about the jewelry store robbery that was to occur at midnight, I made a decision. "That would be perfect. Yes, 6:30 would be perfect."

I turned to confirm with Lydia, only to find myself preparing to speak to her empty chair. She was leaning over the soda fountain. "Hi Hank, would you please... uh ...do me a big favor. See I don't know anybody in this town, and we now have tickets to the Confederate ball tonight that officially opens the reunion. Would you mind escorting me? Mr. Allsopp says he can pick us all up in his automobile." After a surprisingly brief stammer, Hank said, "Wow... uh yes. I mean, gee, that would be swell." He then dropped the glass he had been polishing, and we left hoping broken glassware didn't come out of his salary.

Out on the sidewalk beneath the hot sun, I checked my pocket watch to find it was almost 5:00 and turned to Lydia attempting to contain the lopsided grin I knew so well. "Well you must be pleased with yourself. You gave that poor boy in there near heart failure. No telling how many glasses he will break before the ball tonight."

"Aw Dad, lighten up. I felt sort of sorry for the guy, listening to the story of how he lost his father and all. Besides, he is kind of cute and we have the evening to kill anyway. The jewelry store robbery isn't set to come off until midnight, based on the newspaper article we saw before we left 2011. I'm guessing you want to be somewhere in the vicinity when the police arrest them in the act, don't you?"

"Well, I guess that makes sense. Heck, maybe Dave will be at the ball. And you are right. I'd like to know Sexton and Cabot are out of commission tonight, and hopefully stopped from hurting anyone." Lydia, nodding, came back with the obvious issue I'd had on my mind but avoided. "We'll be changing history though, right? I mean, by having the police there to stop the robbery when they were not there as it actually happened, right? Is that a problem? I mean the guard won't be killed if the police are there? That's a good thing." Indeed, I had to agree, yet I felt an uncertain, unspoken unease at the reality of changing history. Lydia read my mind. "Look Dad, yes, interrupting the crime is changing history, but remember in the original history there was no robbery or murder. They would not have occurred had those two not stolen one of Charlie's time machines to come here in the first place...right?" That was indeed right to a point, but if they were arrested I'm not sure how I'd get them back to 2011.

Chapter 27

AFTER A RIDE on a crowded streetcar we arrived back at the St. Edwards rectory in time to wash up and brief Father Shultz on the plans for the evening. I relayed to Father Shultz his invite to the Confederate Ball , assuring Allsopp's influence would gain us all admission to the gala affair. Father Shultz, the former Union soldier, provided what I assumed was a bit of comedy. "Well Fred that sounds like a right entertaining evening, but tell me, do you and I have to wear those Rebel uniforms to this shindig?" Lydia laughed, Sarah saluted and I ignored all three.

A bit after 6:00 Fred Allsopp pulled up in front of the rectory in an open topped automobile that looked a block long. To my surprise, when he stepped out of the car onto the walk he was decked out in Confederate gray, wearing the insignias of a Major. Seeing the look on my face he only laughed, "OK, maybe it's a bit much, but it belonged to my old daddy, it's a bit moth eaten, but it likely will never be worn again."

"Looks fine to me" and turning to the rest of my group, "you know of course Father Shultz and you met our friend Sarah this afternoon who is from Bigelow. I hoped you would have space for all of us?" "Not a problem Jack, I think my Confederate Major's rank here should get us all in down at the auditorium." While "Major" Allsopp turned the crank on the front of the big car Lydia, Sarah and Father Shultz climbed into the back seat, while I eased into the fine leather passenger seat. Thrown forward and back as Allsopp pulled away from the curb I was reminded once more that seatbelts were decades away.

RAY HANLEY

Within 10 minutes the we were rolling- up Markham crossing first Main, then Broadway where I saw for the first time the City Hall building, remarkably like it appeared in 2011 but with a dome atop the roof, a feature I had never seen. Fred Allsopp pulled up in front of the building next to City Hall which I gathered was the auditorium where the reunion ball was to be held. "Just get out here folks, and I'll ease my machine town the street a bit and park way from the horses and streetcars, hate to have it kicked by a horse or scrapped by a trolley."

On our way to the City Auditorium we passed the City Hall, decked out in Confederate banners. The building still served in 2011 but without the distinctive dome. I'd been into the building often on business and recalled the plaque reading it had been built in 1906, but five years before the reunion.

I alighted, helping down first Lydia, then Sarah and finally Father Schultz, dressed in black, wearing his clerical collar. Upon turning back toward the auditorium I was struck by the Spanish design, almost looking like the front of the Texas Alamo, it was a building clearly long gone before my own time of 2011.

The exterior of the City Auditorium, next to the City Hall, which was hosting the Confederate ball had to have been inspired by someone with an Alamo fascination.

Confederate banners adorned the building, as well as I'd noticed the City Hall next door, the stars and bars as well as huge portraits of Robert E Lee and other generals whose countenances looked familiar. Standing under one of the general's banners, holding his hat, was young Hank from the pharmacy, looking as nervous as must have one of General Lee's troops awaiting the first cannon volley.

Before we had found the path to the front entrance Fred Allsopp had joined us, as had the nervous Hank, to whom Lydia presented her arm. I was glad the boy didn't have any glassware to drop. A band's rendition of Dixie was wafting out the open doors onto the sidewalk, prompting two cigar smoking old soldiers to burst into singing the lines, one of them waving a small Confederate flag.

We were greeted at the door by a pair of young women, dressed in floor length, flared skirts, apparently the events greeting party. Jack handed one of the ladies our tickets and we entered the huge open building which was filled with the din of hundreds of voices, muted only slightly by the band playing across the room. Draped from the ceiling I saw what was surely the largest Confederate flag in Arkansas, along with more portraits of young, dashing soldiers.

Turning to see where my party was I caught sight of Lydia leading poor hapless Hank toward the end of the building where a waltz like dance was starting up. A bit mesmerized I stood watching the dance floor, finally noticing Sarah watching me from the side, a bemused look on her face. Lydia almost dragged the young man onto the floor, leading him to what I recognized as Suwannee River, the poor kid as stiff as a store window mannequin. Hank was out of his league, for as I started to turn away an old soldier who had to be at least 80 years old cut in, sweeping Lydia away across the floor with the grace I'd thought impossible. The other dancers on the floor moved outward, giving them room, struck I guess by the elegant old soldier paired with the striking young woman being led like Fred Astaire and Ginger Allen in the decades yet born. It was a sight that would forever burn in my memory.

I didn't have a chance to monitor the dance long as Sarah stepped in front of me saying, "Come on solider, dance with the lady". The next few minutes were as close as we had come physically since that fateful day I found her tied to tree in the woods. For those few minutes I paused in my worries about how we were going to accomplish what we came back 100 years to do.

My worries were briefly set aside by bit of historical observation from Sarah I wouldn't want to dwell on long.

Wow, quite a couple there", Sarah's observation beside me bringing me back to focus. "Indeed, like nothing I've ever seen." about the only truthful observation that came to mind. On my other side stood Father Schultz, who had in his hand a cup of some drink, and he had commentary of his own. "Jack, best keep an eye on that old gray coot out there, you know there are old reb's around that have married ladies as young as Lydia there. Guessing you don't want an old Reb as a son-n-law whose 30 years your elder." I couldn't help it, I just starting laughing.

As the dance was ending, and Lydia was collecting hapless young Hank, the music was dying down and the attention was switching toward a stage in the center of the ballroom. Caught in the flow of the crowd my little group was soon in the front row as speakers started to line up for the podium beneath a massive Confederate flag. A large man, bald head gleaming, stepped up the center stage, shuffling his speech papers. Father Shultz had eased in beside me and filled me on the speaker's identity, whose introduction I'd not heard over the strains of Dixie.

The inside of the City Auditorium proved almost as crowded as the Little Rock streets as the packed throngs cheered the tales of valor about the Confederacy.

"That's Daniel Jones, was Governor of Arkansas a few years back, and if I recall correctly, the last Governor that actually fought in the war. He's been out of office for ten years or so, but when he was campaigning much was made out the fact he had been shot through the chest on a battlefield in Mississippi early in the war, was taken prisoner, either escaped or was exchanged, and then he went back to war. Should be a stem winder of speech."

"Fergit Hell" was a comic license tag I remembered from my childhood, bearing the image of an old rebel waving the Confederate flag, an image evoked by the opening salvo from the former Governor Jones. He seemed to still be angry at the Yankees for shooting him a half century earlier. Without the aid of any microphones, which I guess had not yet been invented, his voice boomed over the 2,000 or so gathered in the overheated ballroom. "NEVER let it be said that your fathers fought for what they believed to be right; rather that they knew was right. Nor NEVER say that the cause was lost. It was the Civil War that made possible our present Union; without the

RAY HANLEY

war our existing scheme of things could not have been. We fought for the Constitution and now we have a Union I'm proud of, but which I was not proud of before the war." I recall the exact wording in that I tore the text of the speech out of the *Arkansas Gazette* the next morning, though it didn't make a lot of sense when I heard it or the times I've reread it since.

With Governor Jones still pounding the podium I drifted off the side of the ballroom looking for something cool to drink in the hot, humid crowd. Reaching a table with a large punch ball staffed by young women in antebellum type dresses my thirst was soon quenched. Toward the end of the room I came upon a reunion host committee table that had been erected by what a banner said was the Robert C. Newton Camp of the UVC. Asking a gray veteran manning the table, "Who was Mr. Newton?" drew a shocked look of "I can't believe you don't know" followed by an excited "Son, you need a good history lesson"…and need or not I got one.

The photo is of the reception desk at the Confederate Ball. I learned all about Robert C. Newton, whose name appears on the wall.

According to my new friend, Little Rock was expecting an invasion of the Union Army in 1862 when most of the able bodied fighting men had been sent East to the major battles of the war. Robert Newton, a Confederate Colonel in charge of defending the city hatched a plan to have hundreds of local women write fictitious letters to their men folk fighting in the East, saying that thousands of Texan Confederates were pouring into Little Rock to replace the men who had been dispatched to the Eastern battlefronts, and that the city was well defended. Newton then arranged for a courier to "lose" the mail bag somewhere near Union lines in Tennessee. Once the Union commander, General Steele, who was preparing the Union invasion out of Missouri got that word he backed off, fearing the city was too strong to be taken." Giving his accounting its due reverence, I asked, "Is Mr. Newton here at the reunion, I'd really like to meet him?"

Shaking his head the old soldier replied, "No, sadly the good Lord done took Col. Newton to his reward some years back. He was some kind of hero though, was another year before the damn Yankees got up their nerve to march into Little Rock. We gave old General Steel his comeuppance though when they marched out of Little Rock in 1864 trying to take our new capitol down at old Washington. I was there with General Kirby when we whupped his arse at Jenkins Ferry."

Still thinking about Col. Newton's great deception I moved back toward the center of the ballroom where the next speaker was proclaiming the glories of Arkansas and the lost cause. The Commander of the Sons of Confederate Veterans, a uniformed gent named Henry Hartzog was proclaiming "Arkansas is great place to live in and also to die in. Because it's so close to Heaven the transition is much less abrupt." The boast brought loud applause and some shouts of "Amen." I made a mental note to remember that line after I returned to 2011, stopping to breathe a silent prayer that I and Lydia would indeed make that return.

"Dad, Dad....I saw him!" With that, Lydia was behind me, dragging me toward the door. "I was dancing with Hank, and I caught just a glimpse of Dave over his shoulder. He was over by the front door, but, before I could get through the crowd, he had vanished.

I couldn't see if he came inside or it he went out into the street. I just couldn't." Looking around, I found a chair shoved in next to a supporting column and climbed onto it to better scan the room. From my vantage point some three feet above the crowd, I did a slow 360-degree scan as the band struck up a loud, and slightly off key rendition of Dixie. It was hopeless. If Dave was in this mass of humanity, I could not locate him.

Climbing down, I almost knocked over Father Shultz who had reached up a helping hand. "Jack, I saw him too. I know it was him. He was by the front door. I was calling his name, trying to reach him through the crowd, but he left the building. I looked for him on the porch, the sidewalk, but he just disappeared."

"Well, at least we now know beyond any doubt that Dave is actually here in Little Rock. We just have to find him within the next 48 hours to prevent his death on the night of May 18th." My resolute logic seemed to have the desired calming effect, which coincided with Jack Allsopp's arrival and enthusiastic, "Wow! Wasn't this quite an evening? Those speeches were just amazing. Listen, I know Father Shultz here is pretty tuckered out. I can drive you back to the rectory when you are ready."

Father Shultz turned down his kind offer, saying. "Jack, I have had about enough of the crowd and noise here, but what I really need now is just some air. Let's let our friend Mr. Allsopp enjoy some more of this party and we can walk at least part way back... take the trolley car after we get down to Main." Lydia agreed, "That's a great idea, Dad. Let's get out for some air. It's almost 10:00." Her pointed look served as a reminder that the robbery of the jewelry store – according to the newspaper account we read in 2011 – would occur at midnight.

Sarah had been standing behind us during that conversation and stepped in at that point. "Jack, count me in, I could use a good walk and some fresh air after this crowded place."

Once out on the street, standing on the corner of Markham and Broadway, streetcars clanging by even at this hour, Lydia, Father

Shultz and I reconnoitered to plan our next moves. "its 10:00, two hours before the robbery Dad", Lydia bringing us into focus. "What's the plan?" Indeed I wondered? "OK, let's just head on toward Main, Cave's Jewelry is at 6th & Main, we will just hang back a block from there. If the policeman kept his promise they will have the store staked out, and we should see Sexton and Cabot taken into custody where they can't hurt Dave or anyone else. We can figure out the next step after that." I seemed like a sound plan, only later would I be reminded of the adage, "the plans of mice and men....".

A crowd was gathered near the corner of Markham and Main as we passed the Marion and Capitol Hotels, all clustered around a performance on the sidewalk. A man, uniformed in the garb of what might have been a movie count had seated upon his knee what would have been less than described in my own time as politically incorrect, a midget. While I was trying to make heads or tails out of what it was about Lydia picked up a flyer from the sidewalk that showed the larger man holding the tiny one out in the palm of his hand. "Benefit U.C.V. THE FAMOUS LITTLE RUSSIAN PRINCE". The flyer went on to proclaim that Prince Nicholai was "no larger than a three month old baby" being 32 years old and weighing only 16 and ½ pounds. The crowd was putting money into a hat passed around, I gathered for a show just concluded.

As we tried to move around the crowd to move up Main Street a man in a long trench coat leaped forward and grabbed the tiny Prince. Jamming him under his coat he spun around and pushed back through the crowd, intent on escaping with his tiny captive. As he bolted in front of me, without thinking, I reached out and snatched him by his long hair, pulling him to an abrupt halt. As his arms flew up in reflex reaching for my hand gripping his greasy mane Nicholai slid from beneath the long coat, landing on his tiny rear end and quickly bounding to his feet turning to shake a minute fist at his would be kidnapper, shouting what must have been expletives in what I supposed must be Russian.

A policeman appeared from behind me, reaching around to take a firm hold on the frustrated kidnapper, "Well, well Dr. Kernick, you seem to be everywhere you do. Let me take this bugger off ye hands there." It was the same Irish policeman who had visited us at the rectory earlier in the day, intent on knowing details of my phone call made at the Marion Hotel. Noticing Father Schultz, the officer, changed persona quickly, "Oh, hi there Father, guess these folks are still with you?" Taking the policeman's beefy hand in his own the Priest confirmed, "Indeed they are Officer Brennan. We will just move along and get out of your way, but I have not seen you in Mass of late?" The inquiry seemed to have what I expect was the intended purpose, causing a loss of interest in Lydia and myself. "Ah, Father, that is so, but you see, I have been every Sunday at St. Andrews I have."

Freed from the attention of the law once more we moved onto the corner where Father Shultz realized we were intent on waiting near the site of the foreordained midnight jewelry store robbery. Saying a quick prayer and offering a blessing the kind, wise old priest boarded a streetcar that would take him up to Ninth & Maine where he could get another car east to the rectory.

Glad to leave the kidnapping scene behind, and avoid any more notice, we started up Main Street, intent on getting closer to Caves Jewelry. We had just reached the window of Gann's store, with its hand clasping Reb and Yank window figures in the 200 block when what sounded like shots rang out up the street, followed by shouting and then more shots. It took almost ten minutes to move a block up the street after the crowds on the sidewalks were jammed to a halt, even the streetcars that had been moving up and down Main Street had stopped in their tracks.

"Someone done robbed Stifts" echoed over the heads of the throng from a voice moving through the crowd, a portly man who soon broke through moving by us. Finding me unavoidably blocking his path I was able to ask him to explain what I thought I'd heard him shouting. "Yep, two men done robbed the jewelry store, hit the old night watchman to they did over the head. Worst part though the bastards stole General Lee's sword right out of the window they busted through." With that bad news the man hurled his sweating bulk around me and moved on down the street.

Lydia was pressed to the wall by the throng unable to move ahead by I assumed the police. The look on her face told me she had reached the same conclusion as had I, one she voiced before I could. "Dad, they robbed the store two hours earlier than they were supposed to didn't they?" Before I could answer her familiar voice in its Irish brogue sounded nearby, "Any of you folks see two men running away, likely with a gun? Them that robbed the store up there are loose somewhere here, we can't chase them unless we know which way it is they went.? Turning, using his height to see over the crowd Officer Brennan spotted Lydia and I in front of Gann's store window.

"Well, Doctor Kernick, you seem to be a turning up everywhere I goes this week." It was ironic. Search as we might, we could not find Dave Rawlins, but we kept bumping into the Irish policeman. "Well, your robbers did bust into the jewelry store. They just did it almost 3 hours earlier than you thought you heard them say they would, Missy. They whacked the old night watchman pretty hard over the head, they did. We be trying to get an ambulance to take him over to St. Vincent's. They stole General Lee's sword, to boot. My Captain, he will be all over me 'cause of that." Turning back to me, a frown on his face, "Now tell me, Doctor Kernick, is you and the young lady real sure you don't know more about this here mess than you be saying?"

Stalling for time, I replied, "Not really officer, just what we told you today after Lydia overheard them talking about robbing the store." The policeman clearly thought I was holding something back, but he decided to let it go for the time being. Looking at Lydia, I knew we had the same question. What did it mean that the jewelry store robbery had occurred at least hours earlier than we knew it had from what we had read in the newspaper archives before leaving 2011?

The crowds were starting to thin out as we moved South on Main Street and we soon availed ourselves of a bench on the corner of 4th & Main to sort out what to do next. As had often been the case in her young life Lydia was ahead of me in sorting out the time paradox. "OK, here's how I see it…we did change history when you told Sexton and Cabot this afternoon that you knew they planned to rob the store tonight. They clearly had planned to do it at midnight, knew that's what we expected, what we had read in the papers in 2011. They just moved up the time a couple hours, right?"

Thinking for a moment I replied, "yes, they moved it up to a time they had given no thought to earlier, to a time they felt was safe." My obvious next thoughts out loud came quickly. "Do we know then if they will change the timing, even the actions, we know from 2011 they took, or will take?" Lydia digested the thinking quickly, "you mean like the violence at the State Capitol two nights hence, right?" "Yes, that and I guess anything else they will do, even things we don't know about", my reply I knew Lydia's mind had already captured ahead of me.

Solving the paradox question before I could even reply to it in my mind Lydia offered up an analysis I could find no fault with. "No Dad, because they likely don't know yet what they will do, where they will be over the next couple of days. The incidents at the state capitol, that we read in the old papers, didn't seem pre-planned, and as to other things though, I wonder....?" Reading her face I knew more was going to pour out of her thoughts. "Geez, Dad, it's a mess, we may have changed events anyway. See, we don't know everything they did, or rather will do over next few days, only what we guessed at in the old papers." I had a second thought, cursing myself under my breath. "They changed the time of the robbery tonight because of what we said to them this afternoon, trying to scare them. They have to wonder if we have called the police, right?" Giving me only time to nod she continued. "They may well then change their pattern of movement, behavior....they may not go to the places, in the direction, at the same times.....that they would have went otherwise."

"Which means, well damn, what does it mean?" was all I could think of, but more of the logic percolated up from my frazzled brain. "It means we have no idea what the two will do, if they will even come to the Capital building two nights from now, if Dave will be there, what, if anything will happen to the guard."

"Exactly" was Lydia's short conclusion. "So we should keep looking for Dave and the two SOBs over the next two days, and if we have not found them, then we must be at the Capitol the night of the 18th." I could only agree, for I had not a clue what else to do. We decided for now to take the street car at 5th and Main back towards Sherman, where we could make the short walk to St. Edwards.

Chapter 28

OUR EVENING WAS not destined to end so easily and quickly as a ride back to the rectory and a comfortable bed. Within seconds of boarding the streetcar, we realized, that while in deep discussion on the theory of time paradox we had gotten on a west bound streetcar going not in the direction of St. Edwards but rather toward the new State Capitol building. "It's OK, Dad. Hey, I haven't seen the Capitol yet, well not in almost a century anyway." I could not help but smile at my "the glass is always half full" daughter. Sarah chimed in, "Count me in, I've not seen the Capitol since it was completed myself."

Even at the late hour the trolley car was crowded, mostly with old soldiers seemingly intent on wringing out what would be the last adventure of their eight decades or so of life. A trio of the old rebels burst into a very off key version of Dixie, made even more off key I thought by the flask from which the old men were trading sips. In mid verse one of the singers, who might have been pushing 90, stopped singing and got down on bended knee in front of Lydia, removing his forage cap. "Young lady, you are about the prettiest thing I've seen her in Little Rock. Marry me won't you? I've got a plantation and a big house back in Alabama, it could all be yours…why even my Confederate pension." Lydia was torn between laughing and embarrassment. She countered with taking my arm and saying, "Sir, that is a most attractive offering, but you see, I'm already taken."

As the unsuccessful suitor's companions were dragging him back into his seat the trolley car ground to an abrupt halt. Looking out the window I noticed that we were facing a three story brick building that my pharmacist friend Fred Allsopp had told me earlier was the

Peabody School at the corner of Gaines and 5th Avenue, the same spot Father Schultz had told us of administering the last rites. From my memory of 2011 I knew it as the site of the Federal Building, perhaps the ugliest building in the city.

"Someone get a doctor, please, we need a doctor", the shouted plea of an old man on the sidewalk, his back to a crowd in front of the school building from which lights blazed. Before I could react, Lydia was up, pulling me by the hand, pushing to get by the old soldier who had only minutes before proposed marriage, "Sorry gentlemen, but my Dad here is a Doctor, and there seems to be need of one if we could just get off here."

Once on the crowded sidewalk Lydia, still in command, said loudly…"Who needs the doctor, we have one here." The reply seemed to come simultaneously from several old Confederates, "its Jeb, he's fallen out the window, he's hurt real bad." Several of the old troopers cleared a path for us and we found ourselves kneeling next to an old veteran lying on the sidewalk in front of the school, below a large window up above. Equally old soldiers seem to fill each open window, gazing down below.

A glance showed the poor old man was badly injured, frothy blood bubbled from his toothless mouth, running down his ancient face, his breath coming only in labored gasps. An old soldier, holding the injured comrades head cradled on a folded gray jacket, tears streaming down his face, pleaded with us, "Doc, I shure hope you can hep Jeb here, he was a leaning out the winder up there, waving at some of the boys hanging out of one of the trolley cars, and he just tumbled out, hit the sidewalk here."

Lydia was holding the injured old man's hand while Sarah was cradling his head in both her hands. "Lord, Lordy, It's an angel I be seeing coming to fetch me home." His voice rose in excitement, looking into Lydia's tear-streaked face. "And I see Elizabeth, and I see John. I see the boys who died at Antietam. I see…they are all waiting for me on that river, and I see…I see Jesus. His arms are open and I see….". With a final gasp, arms uplifted the old man's body shuddered and he breathed his last.

Finding no pulse on the old soldier's neck, I could only deliver the truth to the by now dozen old soldiers crowded around us. "I'm sorry, but he's gone." Rising up, only then did I notice the poor old rebel only had one arm, his left sleeve lay flat on the unforgiving cement.

"Aw Doc, ye did your best we know," came a gravely comment from an old veteran behind me. While it was true that nothing could have saved the badly injured man, I had the same sense of failure I had felt when I practiced medicine and lost a patient. The ever present reminder of mortality had always been a sobering, reflective event for me. All I could say was, "I'm sorry, so sorry I could not help him."

"Hit's alright. We understand, Doc" came the voice behind me again, as I felt a thin bony hand clasp my shoulder. "See old Jeb, he always said any time he had after Gettysburg was nothing but a gift from the good Lord – that he should have died at Gettysburg. He was part of Pickett's charge, lost an arm from his wounds, but most of the men who made that charge with him died that day." Another old soldier stepped forward to say, "Doc, thanks for trying to help. We will tend to old Jeb here. You and the ladies can go on your way." The crowded trolley car was still waiting behind us, so we accepted that offer and were soon back aboard.

Lydia was uncharacteristically silent, a tear running down her face. "Dad, I never saw anyone die before. The light, it just slipped away in his eyes. It's so bizarre, I watched the poor old man die and a part of me knows he was born at least 150 years before I was. It's just, just so....." It was a sentence she couldn't finish and one I wouldn't even try to complete for her as the streetcar began its journey toward the illuminated State Capitol topping the horizon at the end of the tracks.

The streetcar made the circle at the head of the avenue and stopped to allow us, as well as most of the old soldiers aboard, to climb out of the car into a circle of light cast by the illuminated Capitol dome. Looking up, I recalled an observation I'd once heard a northern tourist express about the grand building in my own day,

"What's a magnificent building like this doing in a poor state like Arkansas?" Standing there looking up at the partially finished dome past the statute of the Confederate soldier, I shared that memory with Lydia and Sarah. Lydia was still lost in thought about the man who had died holding her hand a few minutes earlier.

We made our way up the walk, pausing beneath the soldier's statute, his raised battle flag seemingly posed for a charge down the hill, the taller bronze angel looming above him. I told Lydia about my visit to the site two days earlier and the banter I'd overheard between two old soldiers about which of them had been the model for the robust young rebel in bronze that we stood beneath. She smiled and took my arm, saying, "It could have as easily been that poor old man at the Peabody school. He would have been about my age when he went to war."

We climbed the Capitol steps to the top, stopping to sit on the wall to the right of the great bronze doors. The view back towards Main Street, still brightly lit, was, I thought, many times more interesting that the bland line of tall featureless buildings that occupied the same view in the year 2011. "This is really awesome," said Lydia, "and you know, no matter what happens over the next couple of days, I'll never forget this."

Sitting side by side, having the top of the steps to ourselves with the milling old veterans on the lawn below, we took the opportunity to try to formulate a plan or, at least, to understand our options. "OK, Dad, first let's think about the time paradox. It's hard to realize. I'm just starting to figure this out...but whatever will happen this week...tomorrow, the day after...it's already happened for Charlie sitting in his lab in 2011. He knows, has to know, whether or not we found Dave, prevented his murder, or even if we made it back to 2011, right? Whatever we changed by being here, it's just part of history now, something Charlie may have read in the old newspapers, right?"

I picked up the thread of logic, "That makes sense, I think, but a part of it is what separates what happened after we left 2011 and what happened after Dave, Cabot and Sexton left to come here.

Before we left 2011, the newspaper microfilms recounted that Dave had been murdered. If we prevent that and then return, it didn't happen, right? If it didn't happen, how will Charlie know, had we not traveled here to change the course of events?" This seemed a puzzle without answer, leaving Lydia to draw the inevitably conclusion, "Well Dad, I guess we will just find out the answer to that part of the paradox when we get back to 2011. No point in wasting energy on it here."

Thinking ahead though, she added, "Well, you know, until I came to Hot Springs from 2011, history relates that you were murdered in 1911, but I was somehow still born in 1989, and that means, uh, it means….?" I picked up the thread, "It means that – in the final version of history, the one unchanged in the end – I wasn't murdered, we made it back to our own time, I still met your mother before you were born….and, and….oh, never mind, you are right, we will understand when we get back."

Seeing the approaching streetcar coming up the hill from downtown, we climbed back down the steps toward the pickup point on the circle. When we reached the Confederate soldier statute in the center of the walkway we had to detour slightly around three old gray uniformed veterans gazing up into the face of the bronze young rebel, as they passed a flask between them. "Yep, that shure looks like me at Helena when I charged the Yankees." Taking his own turn at the flask, one of the others retorted, "Now was that before or after you got shot in the ass, Billy?" The third man laughed, "let's go round back of him and see if that part looks like him. Then we kin know for sure." The three of the good natured old men shared a laugh at that suggestion.

We boarded the streetcar after the arriving passengers exited, finding seats in the front of the car just behind the driver. We sat ,not trying to talk above the clanging of the trolley, and watched the passing streetlights illuminate within a radius glimpses – almost ghostlike – of gray-clad men in the twilight of their lives. In the silence, my mind alternated between trying to figure out what to do next and searching for answers to the time travel paradox issues Lydia had addressed.

We exited the streetcar at Capitol and Main before it turned north on Main, intent on walking at least up to the crossing of Ninth Street, which would take us back to the St. Edwards rectory. We were crossing 7th Street, and had just reached the curb where a small grocery store stood on the corner when I was pushed forward roughly by a hard round object in the center of my back. "You just couldn't let things alone, could you Doc?" Without turning, I knew the voice was that of Henry Cabot and it was the barrel of a gun that was jammed into my spine. Looking back at the reflection in the grocery store window, I could see both Henry Cabot and Gabe Sexton, who grabbed Lydia by the arm. We found ourselves roughly shoved into the alcove of the grocery stores entrance, which left us hidden from any but a direct view.

"Gabe, way I see it, we have a problem in need of a solution. These three are the only people in 1911 who know what we look like or where we came from," was Henry's chilling observation. Gabe's silence reflected that he had not considered that possibility, but was thinking it over now. Wanting to help him make a decision more in mine, Lydia's and Sarah's interest, I pointed out what should have been obvious, "Gun shots will sound like a cannon on this street at this hour, and I expect there are more policemen out on patrol than usual. What say we talk this over a bit guys, before anybody gets hurt.?"

Henry's response was only to press his pistol harder into my spine. "A tad late for that, Doc. See we already whacked the watchman down at the jewelry store, so don't look like we have a lot to lose by getting rid of the only people who know us by sight." While I weighed my chances of being able to turn and strike him before a bullet shattered my back, Gabe Sexton, an educated and I hoped reasonable man, offered, "Henry, the doc's right about one thing. Gunshots likely would bring the cops. We need to work this out some other way."

Henry was not to be persuaded so easily and I feared the more reasonable Gabe had lost control over his volatile companion. "We still got that sword from the jewelry store. Let's just run them through with that…be nice and quiet." An image of the three of us being dispatched by Robert E. Lee's sword in a city filled with remnants of the Confederate army sprang into my mind.

"Hold it right there, you hombre, or it'll be you who goes to meet his maker. I've got a gun barrel pointed at your head which will go off in about 3 seconds if you don't drop that pistol." The reflections in the glass of the jewelry store window to my right showed an elderly, but proudly erect, Confederate in uniform, who had eased up behind Cabot and Sexton unnoticed. "Mister, you in the front and the pretty ladies, I was coming up the street around the corner, overheard these outlaw's threats, and by gawd if I didn't see a chance to get some action again."

Gabe dropped General Lee's sword, which fell clattering to the walk of the sheltered alcove of the stores interest, a positive event. Positive though only until the clattering of the sword on the marble entry of the store caused our elderly rescuer to back up a step in surprise. It was then that Sexton must have seen that the old rebel had not a gun pressed in Cabot's back, but rather a walking cane. With this revelation, he turned toward the old man, cursing loudly.

With reflexes that greatly belied his age, our elderly rescuer swung his cane in an upward arc, striking Cabot's gun hand from below and sweeping his hand upward. The gun went off, reverberating like a cannon in the enclosed alcove of the store. Simultaneously I heard Lydia scream in apparent pain to my right, but before I could respond I found myself shoved hard in the back toward the locked glass door of the store. When I struck the glass it shattered, a shard ripping the sleeve of my suit coat as I slid into a pile of broken glass on the entryway tile.

Before I could pull myself up and around I found myself being helped up by the old rebel, joined it seemed by several of his equally uniformed companions. Pushing the old man aside, more roughly than I could have thought possible, had I been thinking, I could only remember Lydia's anguished cry when the gun had gone off. I was greeted by the sight of her, sitting with her back to the wall, holding a bloodied arm, clearly in shock and in pain.

"Lydia…my God, how badly…" Sarah was already on her knees beside her, ripping open the sleeve on her dress to show the wound.

My training as a physician registered that it was not a life-threatening wound, but rather a ragged groove in in the flesh of her arm where the likely ricocheted bullet had luckily missed the bone. "Here, son. Use this, offered one of the rebels, holding out a white handkerchief. It's OK. I patched up a lot worse than that at the battle of Franklin, Tennessee." "I shoulda ducked, Dad." Lydia's attempt at humor recalled the line Ronald Reagan had used when shot by an attempted assassin in 1981. Wrapping the handkerchief around the wounded arm seemed to staunch the flow of blood pretty quickly, but I knew she would need more treatment that I could render here. I stood quickly, looking around. "Where are they…the two men who did this?"

"Last I seen them, son, they was hightailing it South down the sidewalk , but the one…see, he dropped his gun." "But, he still had that sword when they ran off." I dismissed quickly the temptation to tell him that sword, had belonged to Robert E. Lee. Turning to the grouped old rebels I decided to add the rest of the story. "Fellows, I hate to tell you this but that wasn't just any sword they ran off with. That was Robert E. Lee's sword they stole from the jewelry store window down the street." The taking up of breath in the group might as well have been synchronized. One of them hollered, "Come on boys let's try to catch those bastards and get General Lee's sword back" With that the dispersed in at least three directions. Something told me Gabe and Henry were not in danger of being apprehended by the old soldiers.

Turning back to Lydia, knowing she was going to at least need stitches, I was brought up short by a familiar, booming voice behind me. "Move aside, out of the way, if you would". As I turned, I was greeted by the familiar splotched red face of police sergeant Brennan. Stopping short, looking down and he said, "Mary, Joseph and Jesus….it be you again, Dr. Kernick. You just can't stay out of trouble." He stopped short on the lecture when he saw me trying to clean and wrap Lydia's arm in the handkerchief .

The Policeman stepped to the curb and quickly flagged down a passing buggy to take us to St. Vincent's Infirmary where we'd been earlier with the soldier who broke his arm on the steps of the Masonic Lodge. As we were pulling away from the curb, Sergeant

Brennan climbed aboard with the driver, telling me in a stern voice, "Dr. Kernick, you and I are going to have to us a talk at the hospital after we get your girl fixed up." It was not a discussion I was looking forward to while fending off Lydia's protest that a trip to the hospital wasn't necessary, that I could just bandage the "scratch" back at the rectory.

At St. Vincent's a nurse allowed me to use supplies to clean and bandage Lydia's arm. I found no bullet fragments, but cleaned the wound. "I'll give you some antibiotics after we get back to the rectory. I brought a supply with me." A voice behind me said, "anti what, Doctor?" It was the by-then rather nosy nurse, whose bat-like hearing prompted a question that reminded me penicillin and other antibiotic medicines had not yet been discovered. The nurse's question was easier to deflect, however than those of policeman Brennan, who waited in the hallway.

"Now, Dr. Kernick, I'm a patient man I am, but I got to tell you, I need to know what the bloody hell happened tonight. I've had a jewelry store robbed, Robert E. Lee's sword stolen, an old man hit over the head who is already in a hospital bed upstairs, and you seem to be in the middle of it." Collecting my thoughts, and deciding that half the truth at least was required, I spun the tale as best I thought I could get away with.

"Sergeant, it was the two men we reported this afternoon, who were near the rectory. We overheard them planning to rob the jewelry store. You know, we reported that." Almost before I could finish, however, he fired back, "Yes, that be true, but see Dr. Kernick, you told us they was going to rob that store at midnight. They did it before 10:00 tonight. That's a fact, but I wonder as well, how is it you suppose these same two men were trying to shoot you just up the street a bit later?"

Would he believe coincidence I wondered? One glance at his scowling face told me decidedly no. "Well Sergeant, I can only surmise that they recognized us from this afternoon and realized we might be the only ones who knew them by sight...who could connect them to the robbery." It was a bit lame, but it's all I could make up in the late, weary night. The Sergeant clearly thought there was more, but he didn't know what or how to probe further. "Well Doc.... we shall see. You just don't go leaving town. I'm glad your daughter is going to be OK." He strode off and Lydia moved up behind me to ask me to take her back to the rectory.

We walked to Ninth Street and found the trolley cars still running both directions on the busy route and, with but a five-minute wait, we were aboard rumbling toward St. Edwards. Lydia, in pain but without complaint, leaned her head on my shoulder, seemingly lulled to sleep by the clanking noise of the iron wheels on the track. She woke with a start when the street car halted on the corner between the City Park and St. Edwards and grimaced in pain as I helped her up and off the car. Her spirits and sense of humor seemed unabated, however. "Dad, what else can happen? I've traveled a century back in time, saved your life, been shot, and I'm sleeping in a church rectory." What could I say?

The rectory door was unlocked and the living room dark, but the glow from the kitchen was soon partially blocked by Father Shultz's shadow. "Jack, my son, what happened this evening?" They waited until I'd gotten a glass of water from the kitchen to give Lydia the antibiotic tablets I'd brought from 2011and Sarah took over and helped her into the guest bedroom . She was fast asleep when I looked into the room, her bandaged arm atop the sheets.

Later, seated in the kitchen with Father Schultz, Sarah and I filled him in on our tumultuous evening over a glass of wine. "What on earth do we do next?" he asked. A sleepless hour later in the early hours of May 17, 1911, I still had no plan other than hope that the light of a new day would bring some inspiration.

Chapter 29

I AWOKE BEFORE 7 AM the next morning to the smell of frying bacon coming from the kitchen and the banter of Father Shultz and the housekeeper Mrs. Merkel, who I found at the stove after visiting the small bathroom at the rear of the rectory. "Well, good morning to you, Dr. Kernick You sit down here with Father and I'll put your breakfast on the table. After looking in on Lydia and finding her still sound asleep, I sat down to a heaping plate of eggs, bacon and biscuits. I listened to Father Shultz read aloud some of the highlights from the morning paper. It went without saying that there would be no discussion about the challenges before us in the presence of Mrs. Merkel. She assumed Lydia was just sleeping a bit late, and we didn't say anything about her being shot last night.

Sarah was soon seated at the table, a tired expression on her face. "Jack, you look a bit rough this morning." I could only groan a bit and agree. She told me she was overdue to pay a visit to her brother who lived a few blocks away and would get that out of the way during the morning.

I sought to fill the silence after Sarah departed, and to perhaps clear my head, by reading the *Arkansas Gazette* spread out on the table. It was on the tip of my tongue to tell Father Shultz that the oldest paper west of the Mississippi would go out of business toward the end of the current century. Mrs. Merkel's hovering presence – keeping my coffee cup filled – helped stifle that temptation. I was struck, however, by the almost unreconstructed adages in the paper, one which had been lifted from the *Atlanta Constitution*. *"The South owes much to the Confederate soldier for what he did for the country from*

1865 to 1911. The Confederate soldier in every community is strenuous for law, for order, for decency in living and for good citizenship, and from now until the last one of them passes away, the Confederate soldiers will be a benefit to the young men of the South…Fifty years ago these veterans, now gathering, in the buoyancy of youth, were marching throughout this land. Then they were boys: now the burden of the years is on them. Time, who is ever old, but never grows weak, may crush their bodies back into the earth from whence they came, but their knightly souls will never die and the record they made time will never efface from the scrolls of Fame Impermeable." I could not help but be struck by this poignant essay and what it said about the still open book on a conflict over less than 50 years.

    Father Shultz, sitting across the table with reading glasses balanced on his nose, was focused on another part of the paper, startling me when he said, "Well, I just don't think I will ever understand some of my Protestant colleagues in the ministry. This story lifted part of a sermon from last Sunday by William Du Hamel. He's the Pastor over at St. Paul's Episcopal, and he seems to be missing some history lessons. Listen to this sermon: *"If there had been no Civil War, there would be no reunions nor remembrances of the deeds of heroism, and no precious history to teach our children that instills patriotic devotion, without which our nation would die."* Father Shultz shook his head, paused for a sip of coffee, and then started up again. "It gets worse. Listen to this, Jack. *"Moral reforms should not be attempted by fanatical appeals to passion, nor by deceit, nor force. Fire-eating abolitionists, attempted raids and the underground Rail Road were responsible for all the horror and suffering of the Civil War….Again though the Confederacy lost, yet it is victorious in this, that until the thrilling record is forgotten, no section of the country will attempt to dominate another portion---the price paid by the North was too great. Every man ought to thank God that we are united and cemented stronger together than we could have been without the War."* Throwing the paper down in some disgust, the Priest proclaimed, "Dab blamit! Doesn't he understand the "moral reforms" he talks about was freeing millions from the bondage of slavery and that it was the South that fired the first shots in South Carolina?"

Mrs. Merkel left the house to tend to the chickens in the back yard of the rectory leaving me free to comment on the quoted Episcopal pastor's tirade. "Father, your point is well taken, but I'm drawn more to the Reverend's last points about the Civil War making the country more united. I guess I have the advantage of hindsight on this issue because – looking in the rearview mirror of the history I've studied – there were two world wars in which a very United States, North and South, rose up to defeat far greater tyranny than can ever be imagined here in 1911." I left it at that, leaving my knowledge that it was a "United" United States that helped defeat the evils of Nazi Germany and the ruthless actions of Imperial Japan unsaid.

Putting aside our newspapers, we picked up again on the more immediate problems at hand, those being what to do next to find Dave Rawlins, stop two criminals from the next century murdering Dave and another man – in other words, accomplish the mission I'd traveled back in time to attempt. Before we could discuss it, however, I was interrupted by a hand on my shoulder and the words of my daughter, "Good morning, Dad. Father, I may have been shot, but I'm ready to eat", with which she slid into a chair with a plate already in hand, her other hand still in a sling.

"My child, I'm surprised to see you out of bed. You had quite a night," Father Shultz perhaps understating last night's events. "I'm fine really. It was just a scratch. I'm ready to with whatever we plan to do next." Her voice broke a bit after that declaration. "Then, I…I just want to go home." A single tear ran down her face, and then she regained her composure.

I sensed it was my role to lay out some semblance of a plan. "It's the morning of May 17th. The town is packed, according to the paper, and there may be 100,000 or more visitors here. We know that the big finale parade is tomorrow, the 18th, and that Dave will be shot by Sexton or Cabot, tomorrow night at the Capitol, if we don't stop it." We considered our options in silence as the history foretold – but yet to occur – visualized in our minds.

"I think for today there is nothing we can do but perhaps make the rounds of Camp Shaver across the street, showing the photos of Dave, Sexton and Cabot…then go down town, hit a few saloons, hotels. If I can find Dave, we will have accomplished enough, as I hope to take care of him. If I can find Sexton and Cabot, or even one of them, then odds are we can alter the course of the events that are otherwise supposed to happen at the Capitol tomorrow night."

It didn't take Lydia's quick mind long to speak the obvious, "Dad, it's a good plan, but what do we do if we can't find any of the three of them?" My slightly slower mind formulated what could be the only "Plan B". "If that's where we find ourselves by late tomorrow afternoon, then I have to be at the Capitol tomorrow night."

Chapter 30

WHILE LYDIA HELPED Mrs. Merkel with the breakfast dishes, despite her bandaged arm, Father Shultz and I went out on the rectory porch to continue the strategy session out of Lydia's earshot. Outside in the bright sunlight and Arkansas humidity the task seemed a bit more daunting that it had at the table earlier in the comfortable rectory. "Father, I can't make the mistake we made last night, assuming the original time frames would hold only to find the jewelry store robbery occurred two hours or more early." The Priest considered my problem and, not surprisingly, asked, "what can I do to help you?" After the unexpected violence of the preceding evening, I wanted no one else in harm's way, except – unavoidably – myself. "If you could just stay here with Lydia, Father. That would be, I think, the most help to me."

Before the Priest could reply, however, Lydia's voice came through the front door, followed rapidly by the rest of her. "No way Pop. Two eyes…two heads are better than one. And besides, the dirty bastards who shot me. I want to see this thing through with you." Lydia slid into the porch swing across from me, winching only slightly when she moved her bandaged arm, the sling now gone. I knew I should protest but didn't seem to have the energy., Instead, I asked her, "How's your arm? How much pain"?

"I slept like a log, Dad, and it really only hurts if I press on it or bump on something. I'm fine. I really am, and we have a lot to do if we're going to save Dave and do what we have to do to go home." "Dad, I really want to go home, back to 2011."

REUNION IN TIME

Seeing both her determination and her fragility, I sketched out our situation. "OK, we know what happens, or at least what is supposed to happen, at the Capitol late tomorrow night. We also know that the events of last night occurred earlier in the evening than was reported in the old newspaper accounts we read before leaving 2011, right?" "Right Dad, and of course, unlike the old newspaper stories, I got shot in the revised story." Seeing me flinch, she changed the subject, "Let's start with a stroll through the old soldier's camp across the street there."

I decided the best way to blend in was to don the Confederate uniform Father Schultz had obtained earlier. Maybe passing as the son of an old reb would give me more access. Lydia looked the part of a young woman in the year 1911, as we set out, the long dress belonging to Sarah, and a bonnet she had borrowed from Mrs. Merkel helping her to blend in with the other ladies we could see streaming into Camp Shaver to mingle with the old vets. Myself, I could only imagine my old med school colleagues' reaction to seeing me as a "Johnny Reb".

As in our past visit to the Camp, we were greeted by a pair of soldiers, beards hiding much of their chests, standing "guard" at the entrance. Their attention was so much focused on Lydia that it crossed my mind I could have been disguised as Ulysses S. Grant and they wouldn't have noticed. Once we were through the gate, I overheard one say to the other, "Sam, you forgot to salute that young fellow I uniform. He was wearing Sergeant's stripes."

Lydia put her good arm through mine as we weaved our way down the crowded drive into the sea of tents and crowd of visitors. The morning paper had said the camp was temporary home to 10,000 old vets. I had no trouble believing that... as the odds of my finding Dave or the two outlaws seemed to shrink. Still, it was surprisingly easy to get caught up in the spectacle we were witnessing. The expression on Lydia's face suggesting she was feeling the same.

"Pardon me, sir." A grizzled old soldier's hand on my arm brought me to a halt. Holding a tattered bible, he introduced himself as J.A. Templeton of Texas. He asked if we perhaps knew the whereabouts of another veteran, E.E. Caldwell, whose name, he pointed out, was inscribed in the front of the bible. He told us he had picked up the bible on the battle field at Peach Tree Creek, Georgia in 1864, and he hoped to reunite it after almost fifty years with its owner, if he still lived. He handed the bible to Lydia, whose interest seemed happily apparent to old gent, and she sat down on a bench and soon began to read aloud.

"This is amazing, Dad. Listen to what is written in the front. The bible seems to have been a gift from the sister of a young man named E.E. Caldwell who was headed off to the war." She read aloud: "The Gift of a sister to her brother going to war. Read a portion of this holy book every day. Don't forget the prayer our mother taught us. Fear and trust in God, obey your officers, be true to your country. You have a sister's prayer. Shelby County, Alabama, April 1864." While imaging the sister's hand as she penned the message, Lydia turned another page and found a passage apparently written by young Caldwell. "If I ever fall on the battlefield among the glorious dead, I want my Bible to accompany me to my grave."

Taking the bible back, Mr. Templeton advised he was headed down to the headquarters tent, hoping that he could find locate the bible's owner in the reunion registration records. Looking at Lydia I could see she had the same thought, an almost certainty that E.E. Caldwell had died on the battlefield upon which his Bible was found. We wished Mr. Templeton well and watched him shuffle off down the crowded path toward the distant headquarters tent, over which we could see the Confederate flag high upon a pole.

Clearly the Bible story had touched her deeply, but Lydia composed herself and we moved deeper into the park and the tattered remains of the Confederate army. I scanned the faces on either side of us, and those approaching. Trying not to be too obvious. I knew there was virtually no chance Cabot and Sexton would return to the park where I'd encountered them earlier, but there was still the chance Dave Rawlins was somewhere amid the crowd milling about. With Dave's help, we would have a better chance to take control of Cabot and Sexton, if we could find them again.

We took a smaller path that branched off the main walk that bisected the park and found ourselves in a cluster of circled tents. In front of each were frail veterans, some with crutches, and one with an eye patch who actually saluted my Sgt. stripes. Their collective attention was taken by an equally elderly woman, assisted by a pair of younger women who were displaying a battle flag of some sort on a rack erected in the center of the circle. We stopped and watched what was clearly some sort of appeal or presentation just underway. It would prove to be, like the story of the Bible, one of the events we would never forget.

The elderly, but erect, strong-voiced woman in front of the showcased flag was Mrs. Frank Anthony from Virginia. The flag had belonged to a regiment from Louisiana called the Cheneyville Rifles. Mrs. Anthony related a story handed down by someone who had picked up the flag from a battlefield near the end of the war. She said that the flag, white on one side, blue on the other, and embossed with 11 stars, had been made from the wedding dress of the wife of the regiment's commander. Pointing to an inscription on the flag reading "For God and Country," the woman explained the flag had been given to her late husband years ago and she was at the reunion in hopes of returning it to any remnants of the Cheneyville Rifles who might be in attendance.

Moving on, and stopping beneath one of the massive oak trees that lined the pathways in the park to collect our thoughts Lydia said what was indisputable. "Dad, you know I never thought too much about history. You know, science and math were my things, but I gotta tell you, what we have seen and heard this morning is as moving and thought provoking as anything I think I've ever heard or seen. That Bible, that flag, geez….I mean, the woman's wedding dress sewn into a battle flag. Nobody in our own time has any idea what motivated these people who fought and died a century before us. I mean, you know, if anyone ever mentioned the Civil War, all I thought about was the South had slaves, the North didn't want them to have slaves, and they fought a war to free the slaves. It's just wasn't that simple was it, Dad?"

All I could say was, "no, it's anything but simple honey… anything but." We had wandered into the middle of the encampment, just following the paths, watching faces, and picking up snippets of conversation amidst the laughter and backslapping of the old soldiers. I was starting, however, to feel building frustration that we had come no closer to solving the problems that had hurled us back in time. However, we turned a corner and found ourselves in front of Camp Shaver's headquarters tent. There was a sea of flags flying overhead, beneath which a line of tables were staffed by a mix of old soldiers, young women, and even a few uniformed boy scouts.

Our arrival saw the Camp's commander, "fighting Bob" Shaver, emerging from the tent, assisted on one side by a uniformed boy scout and the other by an old veteran. He greeted a stout woman wearing in her own Confederate uniform, topped by a campaign-style hat and set off by the largest belt I'd ever seen on a woman. I would have guessed her to be in her 70s at least, but she had a proud, straight-backed stance as she reached out with both hands to clasp the extended hand of General Shaver. With the exception of a gray skirt and the belt buckle, her uniform matched those of the men.

"Dad, I didn't think there were lady commanders. Who is that woman I wonder?" A man behind us answered Lydia's question. "Lassie, that lady is Miss Mary Hall from Georgia. Her brother was wearing that belt she has on when he was killed by Yankees at the battle of Murfreesboro, Tennessee in 1863. She never forgave the North and after the war refused to take the oath to the Union. That belt she has on… them are gold buttons – 11 of them, one for each state in the Confederacy." We watched Miss Hall shake hands with General Shaver, and a woman accompanying the man who had filled in the old lady's story added, with tears in her eyes, "Miss Mary served as a nurse during the war. I know she closed the glazed eyes of many young men who gave their all to the cause. She is also the official historian of the Southern Confederate Memorial Association. She is just a saint."

Lydia and I were about to move on when it occurred to me the couple so generous with Miss Mary's history might recognize Dave's photo and possibly recall seeing him. They gladly looked at the sepia-toned photo I'd brought back in time, cropped to show just his face. The husband, whom his wife called J.D., quickly said, "nope, can't say that I've seen this young man." The wife looked longer but her reply was the same. I next showed them the photos of Sexton and Stephen. The reaction was almost immediate.

"I hope, sir, these ruffians are not family or friends of yours." I assured them, "by no means. It's just that they may have information to help me find our friend." The wife, who was named Beatrice, took over. "We met these men on the train coming from Hot Springs. This one tried to steal my purse when we were getting off the train. I showed them, though. I hit him with my parasol. I did…walloped both of them and didn't let go of my purse." Not surprisingly she was pointing at Henry Cabot's photo. The husband, J.D., trying without success to contain his laughter, added, "yes sir, last we seen of these two, they were running up the hill from the Little Rock depot as fast as they could go. We found a policeman at the station pretty quick, but there was such a mob around, it was hard to even move. Weren't nothing he could do about catching them."

Pulling my pocket watch out, I realized it was past noon and I could tell Lydia was fading on me, wincing a bit when I asked how her arm was doing. I decided to head back to the rectory, and though frustrated by being no closer to accomplishing our mission, we headed for the gate on Ninth Street. All three elderly sentries saluted my Sgt. stripes this time, and I responded in kind.

Chapter 31

WHEN WE ARRIVED back at the rectory, Father Shultz was sitting in the swing on the porch, his bible on his lap, glasses perched on the end of his nose. He knew from my expression that we had nothing to show for our morning. Lydia, however, attempting to lighten my mood, spent the better part of a half hour, around a pitcher of lemonade, telling the priest about the lost battlefield bible, the wedding dress Cheney Rifles battle flag, and all the other things we had seen in Camp Shaver. It was left to me to add the part about the aborted purse snatching, at the point of an umbrella, with Sexton and Cabot. Father Shultz seemed to enjoy the image that evoked. After the chuckle he wondered out loud, "I expect they are out of money and maybe can't afford a hotel. They may be just out in the city now for lack of anywhere else to stay."

The out of money issue might well be correct, for even if they had jewels taken from the store the night before converting it to cash would take time.

After a late lunch prepared by Mrs. Merkel I made a decision on what to do for the afternoon. My observation that Lydia was not feeling well was confirmed when she accepted my suggestion she stay behind while I went out into the crowed town in the hopes of seeing Dave. There just wasn't anything else I could think of that had any more chance to succeed for the balance of the day. Father Shultz however offered what I had to agree was the best idea. "Jack, you can walk all over this town but it would take you a couple of days and you would only see the people to your right or left on crowded walks.

REUNION IN TIME

Why don't you instead spend at least part of the afternoon riding the streetcars? You would have an elevated vantage point, you can cover all the major city streets, and pretty well see out in the open." I could not fault the logic of that plan as the heat of an Arkansas May day radiated just off the rectories porch.

A half hour later, having changed out of my Confederate uniform, I had caught the trolley car in front of Camp Shaver and was headed toward Main Street and Ninth, packed with a mix of old rebels and other visitors. The sidewalks passing by out the open windows of the trolleys were lined with strollers but I tried to watch both sides of the street, but in the crowded car found it anything but easy. I was reconsidering the reconnaissance value of riding the trolley car by the time it stopped at Main Street to let some passengers off and others on. I opted to disembark and try a stroll down Main Street which was surely carried the most concentrated crowd that afternoon.

I was standing on the corner of 9th & Main, inclined to go north toward the river and most of the hotels when I heard a name behind me that resonated back into my own distant past, or distant future as it was. "Ollie, I told you it was too hot and crowded to bring Wallace out here." I turned around to see a man who must have been in his early 30s, beside a heavy set woman a bit younger who holding by the hand a boy of perhaps two years of age. The realization of who this family was arced through me like a bolt of lightning. Yet, what were the odds of such a meeting, surely it was just a random, though bizarre, coincidence of names, not who I knew with the same names.

I guess I was starring, for the husband looked at me and said, "Sir, do we know you?" He extended a work-harden hand and jolted me out of any idea of mistaken identity. "I'm Robert Kernick and this is my wife Ollie, and this is our son Wallace. We came up on the train from Malvern this morning." Taking his offered hand I stumbled through giving him my own name, knowing after it was too late I should have used a made-up name. "Kernick you say, same as us, well I'll be."

Turning to his wife, he said, "Ollie, can you believe that, this man's name in Kernick, why we might be related." When I released his hand I felt a tug on the knee of my pants. Looking down I found the young boy was reaching up with his hand, imitating his father. I took the small hand and was captivated by the intensity of the boys blue eyes looking up at me.

"Time paradox" should have raced through my mine like a runaway freight train but all I could think of holding the child's hand was that, as unbelievable as it was, I was shaking hands with my own father who was only two years old. Kneeling down on his eye level when he didn't want to release my hand, the family history raced through my addled brain. My father had been born in 1909 to my grandparents Robert and Ollie Kernick who lived in Malvern, Arkansas about 40 miles Southwest of Little Rock. I'd grown up in the small town, my grandfather had died when I was about nine years old, my grandmother standing before me as a woman in her twenties had died before my 30th birthday, and she must have been in her eighties at the time. My father, whose two year old eyes locked on me, would die from tobacco induced cancer more than thirty years before the year 2011 I'd traveled from only days earlier.

The almost trance-like state induced from meeting my two-year old father was abruptly shattered by an almost foghorn blast behind me. My senses returning I looked around to find Joe T. Robinson, the Congressman, waving a leather clad ham of a hand, from behind the wheel of his large opened topped automobile. "Doctor Kernick, we meet again, how you enjoying the big doings?" A high pitched wail at my feet came up as my toddler father crying loudly from being startled by the proximity of horn blast from the Congressman's automobile.

"Oh, my, sorry, didn't mean to startle your young friend Doctor Kernick, just thought you might like a lift, I'd headed over to Allsopp's soda fountain, get out of this heat for a bit with something cool to drink. Climb in, and why don't you bring your friends there with us?" A bit slow on the uptake, I realized finally he was referring to my grandparents and my father, my father the toddler. Looking back at my grandparents, a bizarre term I realized for a couple younger than I was, I told them, "Yes, why don't you come with my friend and I?"

Ollie, my Grandmother was staring at the massive automobile, her mouth a bit agape, one hand against a cheek, when the first words came out in response to the invitation. "Robert and I, we never have rode in one of those automobile contraptions. There are only two in Malvern, both belong to doctors." Looking to her husband she said, "Robert, I'm not sure this is a very good idea, why little Wallace is plumb terrified." Actually the toddler had calmed down and was pointing at the car with a stubby finger, with what looked like a real smile on his face.

My grandfather, who I could only vaguely remember as a very old man, looked over from his height of some six feet, standing a head taller than his short, and rather rotund, wife with a look of a man trying to make a decision to be brave in front of his family. "Why yes Ollie, I think it's a fine idea, I've wanted to ride in one of these contraptions ever since Doc McCray pulled up in our front yard in his shiny auto back when Wallace was sick." With that he scooped up his son in one arm and reached for his wife's reluctant hand starting toward the car. To help their confidence I held open the door to the Locomobile.

Grandmother Ollie however was not convinced, holding her bulk firmly on the sidewalk she tried a new line of resistance. "Robert, we just met this man five minutes ago on the street, and Lordy, you don't know who this man is driving this here machine, he could be, well he could be..............". Grandfather Robert though would not be denied, "Dab blamit Ollie, I know who he is, seen his picture in the *Daily Record* back home, why this is the Congressman Robinson."

Her resistance to the adventure abated, my grandmother allowed her husband to help her into the back of the car, handing her his son, my father, before slowly sliding into the leather seat beside the two of them. Looking first to his right, then left and eventually all around him my young Grandfather was soon beaming, perhaps in part because of the crowd of sidewalk spectators taking in the Congressman's huge vehicle. I climbed into the front seat with the Congressman and we pulled away from the curb in a jackrabbit start. My young grandparents were holding onto the sides of the doors with both hands, perhaps too scared to speak, young Wallace was laughing with abandon like a child on a carnival ride.

My mind, a maze of conflicting emotions roaring through it, screamed again "Time paradox". My grandparents and my toddler age father were taking their first automobile ride only because of a chance meeting with me on the sidewalk. What if the Congressman lost control of his massive automobile? What if my father was killed and never grew up? Would I be born? It did seem a possible scenario in the event of a fatal car wreck.

Congressman Robinson hurtled the Locomobile on down Ninth Street and made the turn on to Gaines Street pulling up in front of the Freiderica Hotel. Ollie and Robert, or my grandparents as I tried to dislodge from my mind least I blurt out something, had relaxed their grips on the car door. From little Wallace came "More, more, go more". Ollie shushed the child and said only, "Well Robert that was an experience but I want out of this contraption right now, right now Robert, right this minute." I got the decided impression that Robert may have been more than a bit henpecked or maybe her first car ride had been a little much for my grandmother.

The Congressman was the first out of his car, reaching back to lift Wallace out, the toddler still pointing toward the steering wheel, squealing "more, more, ride more". My Grandfather eased out with the caution of the old man I would know him to be 50 years in the future, reaching back to help his wife whose girth proved a challenge to pull out of the backseat of the large, but two door automobile. Finally on the sidewalk, bracing herself on the side of the car to smooth her dress, she admonished her husband, "Robert, that's all the automobile riding I intend to do, we will walk or ride the trolley from now on." His response was only a muted, "Yes, Ollie, whatever you say Ollie." My inclination to feel sorry for him was quickly brushed aside when he winked at me and smiled.

It crossed my mind to excuse myself over some manufactured appointment or errand but instead I found myself following my young grandparents and two-year old father into the drug store and soda fountain, while Congressman Robinson held open the door.

REUNION IN TIME

Young Hank was behind the soda fountain counter polishing glasses when he saw us, his face lighting up, at least until he realized Lydia wasn't with us. "Dr. Kernick, it is good to see you again sir, and how is, is uh, I mean, I hope Lydia is well today, I don't see her....." Seeking to put the boy at ease I told him, "Hank, she is fine, just stayed behind at the rectory to rest a bit." If I'd told the boy she was actually nursing a gunshot wound he would have probably dropped every glass in the place.

We took up seats around a table by the window facing out onto Capitol Avenue, Robert pulling a chair out for his wife, young Wallace opting to stand up in his round bottomed, wire backed chair. Hank materialized quickly with his order pad and a stubby pencil posed to take our order. Congressman Robinson seized the role of host, making sure Ollie ordered her vanilla milkshake first, with an ice cream cone for Wallace. The Congressman, my Grandfather and I settled on just a cold Coca Cola. With my mind blaring in my head about the danger of "time paradoxes" I was rescued from a possible miscue by the Congressman who with the skill of the master politician sought to draw out the young family to talk about themselves.

I sat there in what I hope was somewhat disguised rapt fascination as my grandfather told us he was 30 years old, having been born in Malvern, Arkansas, and working for the Iron Mountain and Missouri Pacific Railroad for the past eight years. Ollie followed with even more history that I'd never heard growing up, telling the Congressman she had come from Georgia as a child of two in a covered wagon in 1884 to settle on a farm outside of the then new railroad town of Malvern. Young Wallace had been born almost two years earlier, the couple's only child. He would be in his 50's when I was born which made it all the harder to comprehend the current situation if I were to think too hard about it. I knew my grandparents would have three more who I realized were my then unborn uncles and an aunt.

My Grandfather Robert went into some detail telling us that his father, my great grandfather whom I'd never met was a Confederate veteran who had fought at the battle of Shiloh, Tennessee among others. He had died of a heart attack behind his team of mules some five years earlier on his Malvern farm. Robert had come to the reunion in some hopes of meeting some survivors of his regiment. "You know since I work for the railroad we get to ride free, if'in we had to buy tickets would have cost us $2 for a ticket to come up here from Malvern."

Sipping my coke, listening to the information drawn out of potential voters by the Congressman the only descriptive term that made any sense was "surreal". I was learning a lot of history on my grandparents, a young couple thinking I was but a cordial stranger of a chance meeting earlier in the morning while at the same time I knew much of their future, how many children they were yet to have, even the names, where they would live and even when they would die. The tension of the conflicting emotions began to build up rapidly within my head.

As the conversation lulled I shifted my attention to Wallace, or as I tried not to visualize, my two-year old father. He had vanilla ice cream all over his face and the napkin his mother had tucked under his chin. Looking intently at me, his blue eyes twinkling, he laughed and tried to hand me the remains of his ice cream cone.

Sensing that if I stayed any longer the conversation from my grandparents would shift to questions about me and I knew I was not in the frame of mind to tell enough lies to stay out of trouble. "Robert, Ollie, it was a pleasure to meet you, but I've got business I must attend to. Congressman, thanks so much for the ride and the coca cola, it hit the spot." Waving at the four of them I was soon headed out the door. Glancing back through the large plate glass window at their table once I was out of the sidewalk I watched Wallace stand up on his seat and wave at me with a sticky hand. As I turned away to head down the street the thought tumbling from my jumbled mind was "Lydia will never believe this."

Chapter 32

MOVING QUICKLY TO get out of sight, if not memory, of the soda fountain conversation I stopped briefly across the street from the Peabody School building where Lydia had comforted the dying old Confederate who had fallen to the sidewalk from the second story window. Looking down Capitol Avenue first west toward the State Capitol looming at the end of the street and then east toward the skyline of Main Street which I decided was my best destination. If by chance, with odds so high as to be so incalculable I could not even guess, I'd met my grandparents and father 50 years before I was born then surely I could find Dave Rawlins somewhere in this crowded city.

On impulse, rather than head directly toward the crowded Main Street, I decided to take a round-about path and walked north once I reached Center Street toward the tower of the Pulaski County Court House. I knew from there I could next pass through the crowds around the Hotel Marion, the headquarters of the reunion. Approaching the court house I noticed a crowd assembled to listen to somebody on the lawn and emerging from the crowd I was greeted by the last image I would have expected. An elderly, bordering on ancient, black man was standing on the lawn, dressed in a tattered Confederate uniform adorned in ribbons and medals. It was his surprisingly booming voice that had the attention of the crowd.

I asked a man to my left who the elderly gentleman was and why was he, of all people, wearing a Confederate uniform. The short portly man was quick to address my curiosity. "Damnest thing mister, see there is honest-to-God a second reunion here in town.

The elderly black preacher told his heart-rending life story that began with slavery. In three lifetimes I could never forget looking into the eyes of this man nor the saga of his life he shared on a bench with me as scores of former soldiers passed before us.

It's the Negro Body Servants, the coloreds, mostly slaves, that traveled with the Confederate Generals – you know, like old Stonewall Jackson – tending to their needs and helping around camp. This one here, he's a just warming up his speech. Sure the old coot can't read, but he can talk up a storm."

Indeed the elderly man could offer almost a sermon, more than just a speech. "We are gathered here today to give thanks to the good people of the city for their kind treatment toward the Negro veterans…..we have met with many reunions but we would like to say the Lord lives in Little Rock. For according to God's word, we must say where there is good enacted God is in it. So for this cause we believe that the Lord lives near Little Rock. If I were permitted to do so I would change the name of Little Rock to "Little Rock Paradise," or I would call it the "Paradisical City." "I have been almost persuaded to say, like old St. Peter of old, "Let us build here three tabernacles in Little Rock and stay here."

The old man finished speaking, looked heavenward, and I noticed then a tattered bible in one hand. With a parting "amen" he stepped down from the grassy embankment by the City Hall steps, putting his eyes toward the ground, as if embarrassed or more likely a reaction from a lifetime need to be humble around white people. I grasped his hand, which felt like leather encased twigs, telling him "Thank you sir, I enjoyed listening to you. I'm Jack Kernick, it's a pleasure to meet you." The deep set eyes peered intently at me from out of a deeply furrowed face, amazed I guess that a white man had reached for his hand.

Recovering himself, overcoming perhaps a lifetime of submissive conditioning the man gathered his voice saying, "well thanks you suh, I'm Rev. C.W. Perry. I'm the Chieftain of the Colored Veterans. I'm pleased to make your acquaintance, yes suh, I surely is." I found myself matching Rev. Perry's halting steps as we moved down the sidewalk away from the crowd in front of the court house. We came to the corner of what I knew to be Spring and Markham, across the street from the Old State House, waiting for a chance to cross the busy street, myself perhaps unconsciously keeping pace with my new elderly friend.

RAY HANLEY

Classic Entrance, Old State Capitol, Built in 1832, Little Rock, Ark.

The grand Greek Revival-styled old building that I sat in front of to talk to the ancient former slave Rev. Perry had been the State Capitol until the year before when the move started to the new one. In 2011 the building was a museum that had served as the backdrop to secession in 1861 as well as Bill Clinton's acceptance of his election as President in 1992.

REUNION IN TIME

At the wrought iron fences gate onto the Old State House grounds, what I knew until just recently to be the State Capitol building, Rev. Perry told me, "Mr. Kernick, if you will pardon me, I needs to sit a spell, this heat and dat speechifying is hard on an old man like me. You know I's was 94 my last birthday, least if my age is right on what my momma told me back on the plantation." With that he dropped onto a bench, and I settled down beside him under the shade of a massive tree. Looking up I caught the stare, and almost glare, of two passing women in long dress, one of them uttering, "look at the man sitting with that old nigger, he must be a Yankee."

With nothing else on my schedule that seemed helpful to my challenges I opted to sit in silence for a bit there in the shade with a man who I knew had been born a slave sometime before 1820 based on his age. After seemingly getting his second wind, leaning forward on a cane while seated a respectful two feet from me he began to talk. "You know suh, this is I think the number eleven of these reunions I's been to, last year was in Mobile, that's over in Alabama. I'm afraid this may be my last one."

Without thinking I guess I introduced myself as Jack Kernick, a physician from Texas, and for some reason I seemed to trail the conversation off without trying to explain why I was in Little Rock, or rather the lies I'd been telling for the past three days. Looking to my right I found myself captivated by the deepest, darkest eyes sunk deep into the wrinkled folds of the almost century old former slave. His seemingly casual gaze intensified as he looked back into my own eyes and he began to tell me his story.

"I was birthed down in Louisiana on a Cane River plantation, near as I could ever knows, around the year of the Lord 1817. Never know'd my old daddy, as way my mother explained it to me he was sold off to a slave trader headed for New Awlin's before I was a year old. My Momma, she cooked in the master's big kitchen, took care of his children's. I's was always playing with the white children's when I was little, swimming in the river, and chasing alligators, fishing. I was happy, at least until I was bout 8 years, then I had to go to work in the fields , a mostly hoeing and a picking cotton."

The old man seemed to run down, to almost fall asleep I thought for a minute. I'd noticed a group of children outside the iron gate of the old capitol selling lemonade when we came in, and decided both my new friend and I needed a drink in the heat. Returning to our shared bench the ancient man hesitantly accepted the cup of lukewarm liquid I handed him, looking first side to side as if to see if anyone was watching a white man serve a black one. "Thanks you sir, I shore was getting thirsty", and after drinking down the contents of the paper cup he picked back up on his story.

"I's learned to read and write at night in our shack on the plantation, even thoughs it was agin the law to teach Negro's to read or write. My Momma, she made me learn, but told me I wasn't never to tell anybody I'd learned. She told me she had learned from my daddy after they was married, that he had learned from his Momma when he was little just like she was a teaching me. I learned quick, and even could read the old New Orleans's newspapers Momma would sneak out of the trash from up at the mansion."

When I was bout 16 years old my Momma, she got with a baby, and after that things just was never good for us again. Fore the baby was born, I's come in from the fields one night and Momma, she was gone, even her clothes be gone. I's looked everywhere on the plantation for her and finally one old Mammy, she tells me, "Boy, your Momma, she gone ands she not coming back. Was the master up at the big house that put that baby in her belly. His wife, she found out, and oh Lawd, was she mad. Hear tell she was chasing him all over that big old house with a fireplace poker she was. She made the master sell your Momma, she done been taken over to Mississippi somewhere today." "I's never saw my Momma again Mr. Jack, I just never did."

I found, in listening to this ancient man pour out in a sometimes halting, but surprisingly strong voice, an incredible life story, I could only listen, there seemed nothing appropriate to say, but only to give him respect of allowing him to share his history.

"I was a slave on that Cane River plantation for more than the first forty years of my life Mr. Jack, I picked cotton, I must have picked ten tons of that cotton in my life time, I butchered hogs in the fall, skinned alligators out of the river, cut cypress in the fall that we would ship up river after making lumber. I even married a good woman, a slave like me who worked in the fields. Zeede gave me 12 children, all born slaves like me and their Momma.

The master, he fell into hard times after a couple bad years on the cotton crop, turned mean and things got bad on the plantation. He started selling off slaves, sold nine of my children, guess the youngest bout 10, oldest about 24, oh Lord did it hurt to see them taken away in a wagon, had to chain up Moses, my oldest, he couldn't stand sight of his Momma a crying and trying to chase that wagon down the driveway headed for the Red River boat that was taking the sold off slaves down to the market in New Orleans. My wife, Zeede, she never got over that, just curled up and died, expect of a broken heart, a few months later. No way I could work in the fields and care for the three little chilren's left, and the Master, he said they were too little to work, and one day I came in from working in his sawmill, and theys was all gone, just gone. I's found out later he sold them to a passing slave trader for $10 a piece." "if all that weren't bad enough the master, he up and sold my oldest Moses."

Sitting on the bench in the May heat, watching on occasion the disapproving glances of people strolling by, seeing in some disbelief a white man seated with a black one, I could almost forget about my own troubles and challenges, which seemed almost trivial compared to life as told by the old man seated beside me. I continued to find myself without anything to say but it seemed unnecessary as the old man picked back up his story for me.

"I couldn't, wouldn't work no more for the master after that. I tried to run away, thinking maybe, somewhere I could find my childrens…even steal them back…maybe run away to the north where there weren't no slaves. I got as far as Baton Rouge when the slave catcher's caught me for the reward my master was paying. I didn't go back to his plantation though. He had me sold in the New Orlean's slave market. Guess this was a two or three years afore the wah started. I was taken in chains to a plantation in Mississippi and that's where I was when the rebs started the wah over there in South Carolina, afiring on that fort."

"My new master, he was not a bad man…didn't whip his slaves, made sure we all had enough food, even let us have a church. That was when I was saved by Jesus and when I started preaching the gospel on Sundays for the rest of the slaves. The master, he know'd I could read, but he didn't care… even gave me some old books and newspapers, he did. After Mississippi left to join the rebel states the master he got made a General and raised a local company of soldiers to go fight the Yankee's. When they marched off to war the master, he took me with him to help him around the camps. I was with him for four terrible years, one battle after the other, the things I seen, oh Lord Mr. Jack you just don't know how terrible war is."

"My master, he was wounded at the battle of Shiloh up in Tennessee, guess was in 62, lost a hand he did, bullet in a charge on his horse nearly cut off his hand at the wrist. I was with him in the hospital tent, holding him down while the doctors cut off what was left of his hand with a saw and wrapped up the stump. Oh Lord, did he scream, I tried to keep a rag in his mouth, keep him from biting off his tongue. After that the other officers, they had me and the other slaves digging graves and picking up bodies after that first day's battle. Ifs I lives to be a hundred I's will never forget that, heads blown off, legs gone, men still dying a holding in their insides where they'd been shot."

"The master, he kept fighting after Shiloh, let the stump of his hand heal up, just kept it covered and he went on fighting that awful war. I was still taking care of him when the war ended. The Yankees had won and I seen in an old Cincinnati newspaper that Abe Lincoln, he had done freed the slaves. I didn't have no place else to go, so I went back to plantation in Mississippi and worked for the same old master for a little pay till he died."

"Miracle of God, praise Jesus, cause few years after da wah ended and the master died, somehow my son, Moses showed up one day at the door of my shack. I'd not seen my oldest child since he was sold off by the Master in Louisiana. Moses, he had been living up north for years, had run away before the wah', living in Ohio, had done become a lawyer. Somebody passing through the plantation had met my boy in Memphis, told him where I was living, he come to get me. I've lived in his basement up in Cincinnati for many years now, got to watch my grandchildren's grow up. I's also got to come to these reunions which has been real important to me Mr. Jack."

    I found myself at a loss for words as the old man finished his life story, not sure what to say, not sure there was anything important enough to say after all I'd heard. Lost in the conflicting emotions of thought I was staring toward the iron gate at the end of the brick walk leading onto the street as a photographer trundled by with a camera and large tripod over his shoulder. The thought that scene triggered could be best described as visceral, how could I have been so stupid. How could both Lydia and I miss so obvious a lead.

Chapter 33

SITTING THERE ON that bench with the elderly former slave my mind flashed back with almost week old crystal clarity to the unfolding revelations around Charlie Rawlins table. In the newspaper microfilm account detailing Dave's death, still more than 24 hours away in my current world, the story had made reference to a studio posed photograph of him taken sometime in the two or three days before his murder. It was only through this that his remains had been matched up with the image on the front page that told Charlie his fate almost a century, or days, later depending on one's point of view. I even recalled the unusual name of the photography studio, "Stonecipher". How I could not have connected the now obvious logic before now was simply maddening. I had to find that studio, I had to see if Dave's photo was there, if it had been picked up, if the studio had any idea where he might be lodging even.

With what I hoped was the due deference to which the elderly Reverend was due I stood up, shook his hand, and wished him well on the rest of his visit. He in turn held on to my hand, and staring deeply from beneath his wrinkled brow simply told me, "you's go with God Mr. Jack, I pray's that you will slay the demon's that I know are a troubling your soul."

Once out on to Markham Street a glance to the East found that the photographer I'd spied earlier had not gone far for his tripod borne camera was showing above the heads of the throngs crowding the sidewalk. By the time I caught up with the camera and it's operator he was in the process of setting up near the entrance to the

REUNION IN TIME

reunions Hotel Marion headquarters. I felt both a sense of jubilation, tempered by renewed self-directed fury at my own stupidity, I saw at a glance "Stonecipher" painted in neat white letters on the side of the cameras tripod.

After assuring the young man I had no need of my own portrait he told me the studio of his employer was located at the end of the 900 block of Main Street. I realized it was but a couple of blocks beyond the store alcove where Lydia had been wounded. It would however take me more than a half hour to make my way over the nine blocks of humanity jammed sidewalks. Old men in Confederate gray simply didn't move fast, especially those lost in animated conversation with equally elderly comrades or in some cases talking seemingly to themselves. I tried to walk in the street, avoiding the sidewalks but a near miss of a foot by one of the streetcars, which were passing two abreast in opposite directions, quickly showed the error of that alternative.

As crowded as were the sidewalks getting there I found the entrance to Stonecipher's studio equally jammed by old soldiers and other visitors either waiting to be photographed or trying to purchase scores of picture postcards coming out of the back of the business to stock a display rack on the sidewalk. Sliding inside, around an immense woman holding the arm of an old soldier weighing I was sure a hundred pounds less, I saw a wall of studio posed photographs displayed in rows. At first glance the photos all blurred together, but in one of those "Eureka I found it" moments my eyes came to rest on the image of Confederate clad Dave Rawlins staring back at me.

I was standing in front of the display, by then holding Dave's photo in my hand, when the young ladies voice behind me said, "Sir, what can we do to help you?". Collecting my thoughts my, hopefully calm, reply was that I had come to meet my friend who was to pick up his photo for which I was holding. "I guess he hasn't been here yet, has he?" The look on the young clerk's face told me I probably wasn't going to like the answer.

"Well sir, odd that you should ask about that young man. See, he has already been here, but he didn't want his picture, never came back for it." Somehow I knew there was more to the story, at least I hoped this trail had not come up as empty as had all the others. "You see, he came in here this morning, he did…just today, I'm sure, though maybe it was yesterday. No, wait, I'm sure it was this morning. He was standing here like you was a while ago, just looking at the pictures, like he was looking for his own, but since we hadn't taken it yet, I guess he couldn't have been looking for it, now could he?" The fuse on my impatience must have been noticeably burning down which seemed to help the young lady get to the point of her story.

"I don't know what got into me mister, but your friend, he was just, well, I'm sorry, this is, well, a bit embarrassing, but he was a real find looking young man. I talked him into letting me take his portrait but he has never come back to pick it up."

Before I could make my way out the crowded door of the studio I heard a voice behind me, followed by a grip on my elbow. "Wait a second fella, your friend, he was in here, not 15 minutes ago." Turning around I found myself meeting the intense gaze of a tall, thin man with a bushy mustache wearing an apron stained with what I assumed where photographic chemicals. "I know that picture of him was still here, but my daughter, Emily, she was in the back studio taking portraits when he came in a few minutes ago. She forgot she made two copies of his picture I guess." 15 minutes ago? My mind screamed that he had to be close, but Mr. Stonecipher was still talking.

"Your young friend there, see he came in showing the pictures someone else had taken of two men he was trying to find, thought they might have come in here. I told him the two men had not been here as far as I knew. I gave him his own photo, though to tell you the truth, he didn't even look at it, just gave me the two bits and off he went, you couldn't have missed him by more than I'd say 10, 15 minutes. We still have that one on the rack because my daughter made two copies for some reason."

I rushed outside, once more squeezing around the very large lady who was apparently planning to have her photo made with the shrunken little man she seemed to be holding up. The empty buggy parked at the curb seemed a ready- made vantage point and upon climbing into it I found I could see over, and in some cases, see into, the crowds on both sides of the street. Hanging onto my perch by one edge of the black canvas top of the buggy I methodically started scanning the two blocks I had some vantage point on, first the nearest one, and then a block down toward the center of town.

At the same time a booming voice below me shouted out, "Hey bub, that's my buggy you are standing on, why look at the dirt on the seat, you get down from….", at that same moment the crowd I was gazing into a half block away parted, and I saw Dave leaning against the same lamp post by which I'd met my young parents earlier in the day. He seemed to be showing something, the photos of Sexton and Stephen perhaps, to a man. Resisting the urge to yell over the crowds spanning the block, I instead decided to climb out of the buggy with a plan to race down the street to catch Joe.

There was to be no mad sprint down the block to reunite with Dave Rawlins. As I turned to climb down the buggies owner reached up to pull on the hem of my pants, still irate over his seat cushions. My balance faltered and I found myself tumbling head first toward the side walk at what felt like a most alarming velocity. As fate would have it I hit first not the sidewalk but rather the ample bosom of the large woman who had been pulling along her aged and frail old Confederate husband when I had exited the photographer's studio minutes before. The lady screamed loudly but had the girth to stay on her feet and I more or less careened off, striking the back of my head against the spokes on one of the buggy wheels. Like the cartoons I had grown up with, I literally saw stars before my eyes as I completed the fall to curb.

It could have been an hour but I'm sure no more than five minutes before I regained my equilibrium and soon my feet with the help of the profusely apologizing owner of the buggy I'd invaded for an observation perch. A touch to the back of my head found a bump, and pain to the touch, but thankfully no blood or oozing brains. I would visualize only later that perhaps my life had been saved by colliding with an ample woman's chest, that dying from a fall onto a 1911 sidewalk would have not been the noble fate to end the chapter of my time on earth.

Clearing my head almost on the run I soon found myself on the crowded corner of Ninth & Main at the lamppost where I'd spotted Dave from atop the buggy seat before my ungraceful tumble. There was no sign of him, not even from the vantage point I gained by pulling myself up some three feet onto the lamp post to scan the crowded streets and sidewalks in all directions. I'd come close, so maddeningly close to perhaps bringing this bizarre saga towards a close.

Lacking any better idea I moved on down Main Street toward its most crowded point, the intersection with Capitol Avenue in the hopes that Dave had moved the same way, stopping to ask about the photos of Cabot and Sexton as surely he would be doing. When I reached the intersection I crossed the street and slowly moved back up the four blocks toward the Ninth Street crossing, pausing to look through store windows. It was fruitless and I knew with reasonable certainty Dave had moved in another direction from the point I'd got the glimpse of him before my tumble off the buggy.

After a fruitless circling of a several block radius, with my head starting to pound, I found myself seated outside the Freiderica Hotel and soda fountain on 5th Street, at a loss of what to do next. Feeling a tap on my shoulder I looked up to see a smiling Fred Allsopp with an icy coke float in his extended hand. "Dr. Kernick my friend, I saw you taking your rest out here, and I had Hank whip this up for you. I must say, you look like you just fought the battle of Gettysburg." Realizing that with sweat running down my face, and staining my now scuffed and dirty cloths, I felt a bit like the truth of my friend's observation.

"Just keep your seat Dr. Kernick, I've got to take care of old lady Worthen inside, she is picking up her husband's laxative that I've got to mix up in the back. Lord, every week she comes in for that stuff. I'm sure the poor man spends more time in the outhouse than in the big house. But truth be told, if I had to listen to that woman much I'd move to the crapper myself." With that commentary my friend left me in the shade of his hotel's awning with my coke float.

Sitting there trying to collect my thoughts my attention was drawn to two elderly gray clad veterans across the street, on the lawn of the Peabody School, the window from which another old soldier had fallen to his death the night before. They seemed to be entertaining a small crowd gathered on the sidewalk by swapping artificial legs back and forth between them. In my fatigue and frustration, I was having trouble seeing the entertainment value in this show when Fred Allsopp rejoined me on the bench.

"Those two have been at that show all morning Dr. Kernick, swapping those cork legs back and forth, back and forth. I walked over there earlier, just to try to figure out the story. Both of those old rebs, they each lost the same leg at Gettysburg, both of them, same leg blown off just below the knee. They are from Georgia somewhere, both came with same identical cork leg." With a bit of hesitation he added, "and I think the fruit jar of moonshine they were passing back and forth earlier, along with those legs, help them find the humor in the show."

The entertainment value was lost on me, though perhaps a few nips at the moonshine would have helped that, as well as my general disposition, maybe even the throbbing ache in the back of my head where it had collided with the spokes on the buggy wheel earlier in the day. Perhaps to lift my mood my friend had yet another favor to extend to me. "Dr. Kernick, you know this reunion, its big finale tomorrow is a parade, expect the biggest that town has ever seen. They say there may be 50,000 people or more out to watch these old rebs parade, bands, horses, and I don't know what all. Since I donated a fair amount to the reunion fund I've been given some seats on the reviewing stand they are putting up over at 5th and Main."

Shaking myself out of the fog of frustration I accepted my friend's parade route invitation, unable to think of anything else helpful to completing my mission. "That is very kind of you, I'm sure Lydia will enjoy the parade, we will be there, and if it's ok bring Father Shultz?" My friend slapped me on the back and said, "that's great, parade starts at 10:00, and by all means bring Father Shultz and you friend Sarah I met the other day if she is still in town. Now, if you will excuse me that was old Mrs. Zwadski that just went in the store here, know she is looking for medicine again for that always constipated husband of hers." Despite my worry and fatigue that comment struck me as funny as I told my friend I'd see him at the parade.

I walked back up to Main Street in the afternoon heat, maneuvering to avoid the crowds moving both ways on the sidewalks, staying focused on watching faces lest I luck upon Dave. At Main I debated catching a streetcar but all that rumbled past were full to overflowing, with old soldiers hanging out the open doors and even windows singing Dixie. I continued to walk on up 5th Street which I knew was slated to be renamed Capitol Avenue well before my own lifetime, at least that is my original lifetime into which I'd been born.

A block east of Main I stopped in front of a building that I'd not noticed before but which was immediately familiar. It was marked as the YMCA, but I realized that in my own time, in 2011, it was the offices of the *Arkansas Democrat-Gazette.* The building was a beehive of swirling activity, most of it of old soldiers, moving in and out, occupying the steps, some even leaning out the open windows. I prayed silently none would fall from those perches, the last thing I wanted to do was try to comfort another broken elderly warriors dying moments on the sidewalk.

As I was about to turn to resume my intended walk back to the rectory I felt a tug on the back of my pants leg. Turning and looking down I found looking up the emerald green eyes of a girl of perhaps four. "Mister, I'm Emma, and I'm here with my daddy and my grandpa over there, see he was a soldier in the war." I looked up in time to greet the outstretched hand of a man of about 30. "Sir I'm sorry, Emma here is a bit forward, she has never met a stranger, I'm sorry she bothered you."

Accepting the young man's hand, I replied, "I was not the least bothered. She is a very pretty little girl, and I have two of my own, though not so little anymore. I'm Jack Kernick, by the way. Pleased to meet you." Releasing my hand the young man seemed a bit distracted, "I'm Spencer Hines, I just lost track of Emma for a bit, trying to help my father over here on the bench."

Looking over the young Spencer's shoulder I saw an aged vet man holding his wrist in obvious pain, a partially unfurled Confederate battle flag standing up at the end of the bench, one corner of the faded red banner draped over is gray uniformed shoulder. Stating the obvious, I said, "Your father seems in pain, is there any way I can help? I'm a physician by the way." The young man, his daughter and I moved without further debate over to where the old soldier sat gripping his wrist, his face showing obvious pain.

Spencer felt obligated to explain the injury, reaching down to clasp his elderly father's uniformed shoulder. "This flag is one he carried into the battle of Franklin Tennessee in 1864. He was standing up there in the door, trying to show some of the men how he charged across the battlefield waving the colors. He hit his hand or wrist on the stonework up there. If you could take a look at him I'd be most appreciative Doctor."

An examination of the old man's proffered wrist found nothing broken. "It looks to me like there are just abrasions on the back of his hand and wrist, nothing appears to be broken. The wound does need to be cleaned and bandaged." Looking up into the old man's face I saw the light of relief from my prognosis and immediately was greeted with gravelly voiced gratitude.

"Thank you doc, I tried to tell Spencer here I'd be OK. Weren't nothing compared to what I went through in the war. You know I was charging the yanks fortifications alongside General Patrick Cleburne at Franklin. Helped him up after his first horse was shot out from under him I did. Was helping him back onto another horse with bullets whizzing by like they was hornets." The old man paused a bit, clinching the wrist of his injured hand before he continued. "When I was helping him up on that horse that I guess someone else had been shot out of the saddle on, and before Cleburne could get mounted a cannonball hit the horse, blew clear through his hindquarters, nearly took my head off. I had blood and horse guts all over me I did."

I vaguely recalled my Civil war history and General Cleburne for whom I thought the county in which the resort town of Heber

Springs sat had been named. My history lesson wasn't over yet from the old soldier who seemed to have temporarily forgotten about his painful hand. "Well, General Cleburne, he told me, "Never mind private, I think losing two horses are quite enough for one battle. He pulled out his sword and he charged off toward the dug in Yankees, with the rest of us trailing behind. I saw him hit and fall just in front of me, lordy lordy, the men, they were dropping all around me as I knelt down by the General, but he was already dead, shot through the heart he was."

With my history lesson concluded and my patient clearly on the path to recovery, I said my farewells and resumed my trek toward the rectory. I knew the images however of General Cleburne's death on the battlefield would be with me for a long time however. When I looked back from the corner the old rebel was resting the butt of the staff of his tattered flag on his bench and was looking up at its tattered furls, perhaps transported in his mind back to the horrors of a Tennessee battlefield.

The rest of my return trip to the rectory went quickly on the crowded streets and sidewalks but my mood was darkened by the fact that more than a half-days effort had produced but a distant, fleeting sight of Dave Rawlins and nothing of the two men I had come ever more to despise, Sexton and Cabot, for the grief they had caused. I was jarred a bit out of my thoughts upon turning onto the walk of the rectory when I saw Father Shultz, Sarah and Lydia on the porch seemingly entertaining two grey bearded elderly men, one dressed in a faded Confederate uniform, with a pitcher of lemonade.

"Dad…there you are. We were about to dispatch Will and Gus here to look for you," was my greeting from Lydia, who seemed to be enjoying herself without concern for her injured arm. Father Shultz, standing at the top of the steps, joined in the welcome back and introduced me to our guests. "Jack, glad to see you back, let me introduce you to Gus and Will Thompson here." The old soldiers, one of which appeared to be in his eighties, the other a bit younger, stood to shake my hand.

REUNION IN TIME

Once I was seated with my own glass of lemonade Father Shultz and Lydia filled me in on how they came to be sharing the porch with a remnant of General Lee's tattered army. "Dad, it's just fascinating. See, Gus and Will are brothers who have not seen each other in 50 years, not until today." The older of the vets, who I learned was Gus, put his hand on his brother's shoulder and offered me the story which was indeed amazing.

"Yes sir Dr. Kernick, it's a miracle from the Lord, it truly is. See, Will and I were both living at home in Atlanta when the war broke out, I was 22, and he was only 6 years old. I enlisted and went off to fight, never seen Will again until today. When old Sherman and the Yankees were closing in on Atlanta in 1864 Will got put into a wagon train of emigrants headed to Texas. By the time I returned to Atlanta after Lee surrendered it was nothing but burned out rubble, Yanks had burned it all. For all I knew Will and all my family were dead."

The younger man, Will, dressed in a black suit, picked up the rest of the story. "Our mother died on the way to Texas, and I was raised by a farmer and his family there. I never knew if Gus had survived the war or not. I came to the reunion here in Little Rock on a train from my farm near Waco, just in hopes of finding someone who knew anything about Gus. At the camp over in park I found the tents for the Georgia regiments, looked at the roster and praise the Lord, there in his own handwriting was the name Gus Thompson, 4th Georgia Calvary."

Father Schultz wrapped up the story to explain how the men came to be on his porch. "Will and Gus came to Mass this morning, to offer a prayer of thanks for their reunion. When I met them afterwards I invited them over here today because I thought Lydia would enjoy meeting them and well, because, maybe, just maybe they could help, them having been in the camp over there for the past couple of days."

Lydia, the brother's reunion tale told, looked at me with an expression that imparted a question not spoken but clear enough, Had I learned anything today while out in the city? "No, I'm afraid I accomplished nothing for my time today. I caught a glimpse of Dave from about three blocks away but could not catch up to him and not a clue on Sexton and Cabot." Looking back at Father Shultz, I waited for him to explain how he thought these two elderly brothers could help.

"Jack, I took the liberty of telling Gus and Will here you needed to find Dave and maybe the two men who were intending to, well to do him harm. Showed them the photographs of all three you left here. Turns out they have seen all three."

Gus, waiting until the priest finished, picked up the rest of the story. "Dr. Kernick, it's true, Will and I, we done seen all three of them fellers. See, our Georgia boys, our regiment is in the first group of tents you comes to when you enter the park. Will and I was sitting on bench there by the path a getting caught up, and Lordy 50 years, it takes a heap of catching up, when the young man I now know is Dave stopped by to show us some photographs of the two other men, those Father Shultz tells us is out to do folks harm. We hadn't seen them, not yet that is, and we told your friend Dave that. Right polite young man he was."

Will stepped in to take over from his older brother, "Yes sir, that's right, we didn't recognize the two men in the photographs, not then that is. But see, later that evening we was visiting over with some of the veterans from Texas and Arkansas, near the mess tent, which is over close to General Shaver's headquarters. There was a poker game going behind one of the tents where we heard some angry folks yelling about someone a cheating." Somehow I knew who the cheaters would turn out to be as Will continued the telling of the account.

"Gus and I walked over to where the yelling and card playing was happening. Sure as I'm sitting here drinking lemonade there they was, them two men your young friend Dave was looking for. Same men Father Shultz showed us pictures of they was. The two was being accused of cheating by the Texas veterans they had been playing poker with, was cards and money spilled on the ground and I tell you, one of those old soldiers had drawn a Bowie knife, a threatening to carve the gizzards out of those two cheaters. The two them, they just threw down their cards and ran, one of them tripped over a tree root though before he got very far. Then, and it was a sight to see, one of the old veterans, he whopped the man, the one you called Cabot, over head with his cane. Last we seen of him he was crawling, trying to get up, headed after the other man."

Leaning back against the porch post I came rapidly to the conclusion that I voiced, "Well, as interesting as that is we still don't know where the two of them are or more importantly where Dave Rawlins is." Reading the faces around the porch it was clear there was consensus on that point.

Chapter 34

I SAT ON the porch for perhaps an hour after Will and Gus left us to return to the camp across the street, lost in thought until I realized Lydia had taken her seat beside me on the swing. "Ok Pop, penny for your thoughts, or make that a Confederate dollar. Sarah is in the kitchen, starting supper for us, Mrs. Merkel is off this evening." As she often could, my daughter brought me out of my funk and gave me the opening to think out loud about a problem at hand.

I filled Lydia in on my trip around town earlier in the day, even the meeting with the elderly black veteran while leaving out some of the sadder episodes about losing his children to the slave trade. That I'd save until the day we returned to 2011. I also elected to save the story of my grandparents and two year old father for a later telling as well. "This reunion ends tomorrow with what is supposed to be the largest parade in the state's history according to what the papers say. Fred Allsopp has offered us all seats on the bleachers at 5th & Main, I told him we would be there." Lydia processed this information with the intense look that told me she was thinking about how this could help us solve our dilemmas.

Later that evening, as the sun was starting to sit, over a dinner of fried chicken and wine of undetermined vintage I recapped my day for the benefit of Sarah and Father Schultz, adding a bit to what I'd already told Lydia earlier. Maybe it was the effects of the wine, or maybe just fatigue, but I relayed the entire story of the elderly black veteran including how his family was scattered by the practices of slavery. The tears on the faces of both the women, as well as the

"May the Lord bless their souls" from Father Shultz came as no surprise. To lighten the mood I proceeded next to tell them of meeting my grandparents and two year old father.

Lydia, as well as Sarah and Father Shultz greeted the story of my family with dead panned expressions, at least at first. Lydia then started to laugh, which prompted the other two listeners to turn to her with a puzzled look that said, "why is this funny?". Lydia, gaining her composure, said "I sorry guys, it's just, just funny to think about Dad sitting in that drug store watching his two year old father with ice cream all over his face." Thinking further and without the mirth, "but Dad, I also know the issue of time paradox had to weigh heavily on you, I'm sorry for laughing." She kept laughing however. There really wasn't much else to say after that.

As Lydia and Sarah were clearing the table I heard the kitchen door at the rear of the house open and close. Realizing everyone I thought was in the house was in my line of sight already I turned toward the door. My surprise may have topped anything I'd experienced since I left the year 2011.

Chapter 35

LYDIA DROPPED A plate to shatter on the floor in front of the sink and I guess I just stood there for a minute in open mouthed loss for words. Standing in front of us was Charlie Rawlins, wearing the ragged reproduction Confederate uniform we had seen him in upon our arrival at his laboratory a century removed from where we now all stood. Charlie broke the silence, "I know this is a shock, but Lord I'm an old man and the trip was a shock to my old carcass, and I gotta sit down." By the time he fell into a chair at the kitchen table he had our undivided attention.

While Lydia sat a glass of wine in front of Charlie I opened the discussion with the most obvious of questions. "Charlie, what in the world are you doing here?"

He snaked a surprisingly frail hand inside his Confederate grey jacket and emerged, in almost slow motion, with what turned out to be a folded Xerox of a newspaper. Charlie slid the paper aside, even I recognized the type face and date as 1911. Beneath the newspaper copy were pages apparently torn from a history book.

The headlines were as large as anything I'd ever seen, even on Sept 11, 2001 with the bombing of the World Trade Towers. "NEW STATE CAPITOL VIRTUALLY DESTROYED IN TERRIFIC BLAST" The special edition of the *Arkansas Democrat* was dated May 19, 1911. The math was quick, even for my rattled brain, the paper was dated the day after tomorrow.

While I was starting on the newspaper story Lydia had taken the pages ripped from what turned out to be an Arkansas History book. Reading quickly, she looked up to say, "Dad, I hate to tell you

REUNION IN TIME

but according to this book I think you, Dave and I all died the night of May 18, which is tomorrow night, when the capitol building exploded." We both stopped reading at the same time, looked first at each other, then at Charlie.

Charlie realized he had our undivided attention, not only mine and Lydia's but Father Shultz and Sarah's as well. "You understand now why I came. Landed the time machine I'm afraid in your garden out back Father, afraid you may be short some tomatoes." With all of us still transfixed, before we could start reading again, Charlie continued to lay out what we could not yet begun to comprehend.

"It's about gold, at least a thousand pounds of gold, which was stored in the basement of the Capitol. Cabot and Sexton, couple of locals were there to steal the gold. That's why they were at the Capitol, that's why I can only guess that in the version of history you came to change, Dave had followed the two and died himself in a plunge from the dome."

Lydia, always faster, asked the obvious question only starting to form in my mind. "Uncle Charlie, I don't understand. In the old newspapers we read before you sent Dad back here to 1911 there was no story in the papers about any explosion, nothing like that." Another thought occurred to me as well. "Charlie, in our time, at least the 2011 I left, the Capitol building was standing, just as it had been built almost a century earlier and it had a gold dome."

Charlie was ready for the questions, having clearly had time to think through what now made no sense to us. "You, we changed history, more than once I believe. It's simple… well no, I guess none of this is simple – even to me." It sure wasn't to me, that was for sure.

"In the original time, the events of this week, before I built the time machines that Cabot and Sexton stole, there was no explosion and of course no murder of Dave. You and Lydia were never here, never met Sarah or Father Shultz. The old rebels had their reunion and went home. End of story. As to the absence of a gold dome in 2011, I have not had time to think that one through."

"Sexton and Cabot came back to 1911 and committed crimes which Dave and I discovered. Dave came here after the two of them.

RAY HANLEY

He was murdered, according to the old newspaper accounts. I called you, you traveled back a century to find Dave, and Lydia followed later to stop your murder in Hot Springs." He paused to collect his thoughts and to take a sip of wine, and then picked up what was like a classroom lecture of the old professor that he was.

"What I don't know, but can deduce, is something in the past days caused Cabot and Sexton to alter their plans, to somehow change something, maybe as simple as the time they went to the Capitol even. You in turn, from having read the altered version of history in 2011, knew they would be at the Capitol building tomorrow night. The fact that you were here, and knew of their whereabouts in advance from the old newspaper accounts, somehow factors into the next big change in the timeline, in what became the alternative history of the explosion that brought down the Capitol building. It was done, by the way with, dynamite that was stored behind the building near the railroad tracks. It belonged to a railroad construction company."

When Charlie stopped talking to take another sip of his wine I picked up the newspaper copy and resuming reading, conscious of Lydia reading over one shoulder, Sarah the other. In the few days I'd been in the year 1911, I had learned that the use of photos in newspapers of the era was rare, but the events at the Capitol had prompted an exception. Beneath a banner headline spanning the page was a photo of the front of the State Capitol building, or rather what remained of it. The wings were intact but the center dome, from which I'd had the bird's eye view earlier in the week was gone. It had collapsed into the middle of the building, a huge pile of broken stone and concrete.

The newspaper story was focused on the explosion, but was short on the who and why. "Shock hangs over Little Rock today, greater surely than even when the capital city was captured by Union troops in 1863. Our states grand capitol building, modeled after the one in our nation's Capital of Washington DC lays in ruins this morning. A massive explosion last night around midnight brought down the great dome which lies today but shattered rubble.

Great mystery remains about who committed this sacrilege. What is known is at least three lives were lost, as there battered bodies were extracted near the entrance of the building by Little Rock fireman moving debris to make a path into the shattered building. Governor Donaghey, accompanied by Little Rock hotel owner Fred Allsopp, was on the scene early this morning when the fireman uncovered the three bodies. Our reporters on the scene overheard Mr. Allsopp identify the dead as a visiting Texas physician Jack Kernick and his daughter Lydia. The third man known killed in the explosion was thought by Mr. Allsopp to be a friend of Dr. Kernick's named David Rawlins, although the condition of the body was said to have left some doubt." An alteration in history had Dave dying not from a plunge from atop the building, but from being caught beneath the falling stone in the aftermath of an explosion.

While the women and I had been reading the newspaper copy Father Shultz had been reading the pages Charlie had apparently detached from an Arkansas history book. "I think this fills in a lot of details, it's a history written and updated long after the what happened, that is, what is supposed to happen tomorrow night. The Capitol building was destroyed and rebuilt, but not until three years later when the state found the money." Before we could ask the obvious question the Priest added "and the gold was never found and hence the dome was never gilded with any gold leaf."

We were all lost in a bit of silent shock and perhaps reflection for a time after reading the accounts of our death and the destruction of the Capitol that was slated to occur in just a bit over 24 hours. We of course had to change history again, something we seemingly had already done more times than I could almost count. It was becoming hard to realize what was the original, pre-time travel, course of events.

Regaining my confidence, said. "OK, here's the plan. In the morning we will accept Fred Allsopp's invitation to join him in the parade route bleachers at 5th & Main. We should have the best view of the crowds and everyone marching. Who knows, we might get lucky, see Dave marching by, get him, and go back home to 2011."

What I left unsaid was that scenario would leave Sexton and Cabot behind in 1911 to blow up the Capitol or otherwise wreak havoc.

By 11:00 we had all turned in for the night. I gave Charlie my guest room while Sarah and Lydia shared the other spare room, and I took a not too uncomfortable cot on the rectory's back porch. For me, it was a restless night, the dream of dying on a Civil War battlefield returning once I finally did get to sleep. I was awakened by the "revile" of Father Shultz's rooster in the chicken house not more than 20 feet behind the porch upon which I'd tried to sleep.

Once fully awake I was struck by the smell of frying bacon and biscuits coming from the kitchen where Sarah and Lydia were already preparing to put breakfast on the table. They both put on a smile when I entered the kitchen but the strain we all felt was obvious on their faces. The most relaxed was likely Father Shultz who raised his head over the *Arkansas Gazette* to offer me a hale "Morning Jack, how'd you sleep?" and answered the question himself, "not so good I see".

Picking up the front of the paper the Priest laid down I was greeted by a banner headline about the grand parade finale of the UVC reunion set to kick off at 10 AM. The paper was filled with praise for the old soldiers and with congratulations on the way Little Rock had played host to old rebels. My attention was drawn to another paper however, the Xerox of the next day's newspaper with its banner headline about our deaths and the destruction of the Capitol. I offered a silent prayer that the headlines would never need to be set to type, that the next day would bring instead perhaps little more than the news of a successful reunion of old Confederate soldiers.

Chapter 36

BY 8:30 WE had gathered on the porch in attire that, a week earlier, I'd have laughed at any suggestion of such dress. Lydia and Sarah were garbed in almost floor length dresses' from Sarah's trunk, Father Shultz in his black shirt and clerical collar. Having faced the choice of either the by now ragged clothes given me back in Bigelow by Sarah or my reproduction Confederate uniform I finally opted to attend the parade dressed as a Confederate sergeant.

Lydia came up in front of me, straightened my collar, gave me a hug and a bit choked "It's going to all work out Dad." I had no choice but to tell her "I know it will" whether or I not I was ready to believe such a declaration.

The trip downtown was quick, we seemed a bit behind the crowds who lacked a reserved viewing station that Fred Allsopp had arranged for us. Charlie was getting his first real look at 1911 sights, his head almost on a swivel. After catching the streetcar beside St. Edwards it was a short ride to the intersection of Ninth and Main where we disembarked amidst what I knew from having read the old microfilm newspaper accounts was the largest crowd in Arkansas history, well over 100,000 people.

It took us almost 20 minutes to make our way the four blocks North to where we knew the reviewing stand sat at 5th and Main. People were lined six deep on the sidewalks, some in the back had built up almost bleachers to stand on, using wooded boxes and even sawhorses with lumber planks for a perch. Looking up it was apparent that every window was filled with spectators and even roof tops were lined with people awaiting the parade of the old rebel soldiers.

We paused at the corner on 6th street, only a block from the reviewing stand, temporarily halted by the packed sidewalks. A block North we found the sidewalks already jammed well in advance of the parade's start.

It was less than twenty minutes before the announced start of the parade by the time we faced the reviewing stand and saw Fred Allsopp waving to us with his reserved seating near the top of the bleachers sat in the eastern part of 5th Street, or what I'd known as Capitol Avenue in 2011, with a distant view of the State Capitol doom. With a few acrobatic maneuvers to help Father Schultz we were soon seated with what surely was the finest view in town of the coming march of General Lee's remaining army. Looking over the crowd, many waving the Confederate stars and bars I almost forgot for a minute the gravity of our intentions, to try to find a way to keep from the Capitol building exploding and our dying in the process during the forthcoming night.

By the time we were seated, Fred Allsopp was handing us bottles of beer that had been handed up from below the bleachers, and the hands were all I could see of the server. I introduced Charlie as a newly arrived friend from Texas. It was only 10 AM, but the temperature had to be in the 80s and the wool uniform I was wearing made it feel more like 100 degrees. I gladly accepted

REUNION IN TIME

and downed the offered beer. Lydia and Sarah chose cokes instead from the unseen assistants below.

I was scanning the crowd lining the street, hanging from windows and adorning rooftops, in hopes of perhaps catching sight of Dave, Sexton or Cabot when I heard the first sounds of Dixie wafting up the street from what had to be the lead of the coming parade which I knew had started from the Old State House next to the Hotel Marion, some 10 blocks away. Picking up on the festival mood soon much of the crowd was also singing the fabled tune as the head of the parade came into sight lead by a marching band from Henderson College which I knew was located at Arkadelphia, in southwest Arkansas.

"You know they say this parade will take two hours to pass any given point", Jack's voice bring my concentration of my more immediate surroundings in the bleachers back into focus. Thinking about that, in a less than politically correct reply, I answered, "well I guess it takes that long for 12,000 old men to march by." There turned out to more than just the old soldiers.

Interspersed among the bands were former Confederate soldiers, some afoot, others riding in open-topped automobiles and buggies. Early in the parade, a mounted group of old soldiers passed carrying a banner denoting that they were the remnants of Nathan Bedford Forrest's famed Confederate Calvary. I'd not realized how many dignitaries, including Governor Donaghey were below me in the reviewing stand until the mounted troopers turned in unison to salute in our direction

Sandwiched between the mounted surviving members of the fabled Nathan Bedford Forrest's cavalry were two well-appointed young women.

As well intentioned as had been my plan to continually scan the crowds for signs of Dave or the two bad guys, I found drawn to the moving history in the parade that was passing below me on Main Street. I watched an elderly black man I'd helped earlier in the week pushing along the route the stooped gray clad veteran in high backed wicker wheelchair, struck by the irony and wondering what tied the two men who had seen likely almost a century of life together.

A large open topped automobile slid by between a marching band and a group of mounted old confederates. Seated high in the back, waving to the crowds was Mary Hall, her belt buckles representing the 11 Confederate states catching the bright May sun as she turned from one side of Main Street to the other. I recalled what I'd been told when we saw her in the old soldiers' encampment earlier in the week, how she had "closed the eyes of many a dying solider" on the battlefield. Where I'd come from a century hence, the Civil War was largely faded images in the history books, but how vivid the images of battles fought five decades earlier had to be ingrained in this extraordinary woman's mind.

The parade ground to a halt at one point when a mule drawing a wagon upon which the Queen of the Confederate Ball and her court sat decided to just stop. The lead mule pulling the wagon had simply decided he was through marching and refused to go. A burly policeman materialized, first pulling on the reins, and finally swatting the beast on the flank with his nightstick. Nothing worked, and shouts from impatient parade watchers shouted things like "build a fire under him". The matches were not needed in the end when the policeman thought to take the mule by the ears and twist hard, finally motivating the stubborn animal to resume pulling the Queen and her entourage.

My attention on the parade had drifted as I had instead been drawn to watching people on the rooftops across the street, a couple of which I noticed drinking from a paper wrapped bag while waving a Confederate flag. My attention was drawn back to the street level of the parade by a collective gasp from people surrounding me in the bleachers. Looking down at a group of marching old soldiers I could see that one of them, bearing a drum had fallen in the street, halting the parade.

REUNION IN TIME

The postcard image was apparently taken from a rooftop looking down upon the early part of the parade. The reviewing stand where we sat was out of the camera's lens across the street from the building with the striped banner. The May heat was stifling, how the old rebs marched in those wool uniforms I could only imagine. In my time of 2011 almost all the buildings seen in that image would be gone.

RAY HANLEY

Lydia, reaching for my arm, exalted me to go to his rescue with "Dad, please see if you can help." I made my way down the end of the bleachers and then onto the street amidst the frail old men huddled around their fallen companion. "I'm a doctor. Please let me through. Let me see if I can help." That was enough to open up the circle of aged soldiers.

The prostrate old man's arm still wrapped around his drum, his head resting on the knee of a companion, waved his other had at me weakly. I recognized the grizzled old soldier as the "drummer boy of 61" we had seen in the City Park encampment two days earlier, a veteran of the battle of Shiloh.

In response to my questions about where he hurt, he raised his bearded face to just mouth in gasping breath, "I'm OK, doc I'm OK. Just let me finish this march or die trying. I got to keep going." My limited observation suggested the old man had simply became overheated and fatigued, but I didn't see how he could possibly get back on his feet and march for another hour or more, something I think his companions realized. They helped in to his feet and removed him to the alcove of the bank building on the corner that to me, in my time, would be the Boyle Building.

Once I turned away from my attempt to help the old drummer I found myself confronted with the challenge of crossing the street back to the viewing stand and General Lee's army, or what was left of it, was a flowing obstacle. I found myself looking up at the passing mounted troopers of General Forrest's cavalry, which had apparently been delayed by the collapsing old drummer. From where I looked up the mounted men, gray beards flying along with their tattered battle banners were well above my head. One of the men looked down and smartly saluted, why to me I could not fathom until I realized I was wearing also Confederate gray.

REUNION IN TIME

After tending to the fallen old Confederate soldier who had collapsed in the heat, I found I had to navigate through the remnants of famed Calvary leader Nathan Bedford Forrest's mounted troops.

Awaiting a break in the flow of the parade, the tune of Dixie coming from bands I could not see, I looked up at the reviewing stand across the street and saw Lydia waving to me. As I waved back my attention was drawn to movement atop the building behind the stands and starring back at me, perhaps as amazed as was I, was Cabot and Sexton. By the time I found a break between a group of marching Elks Club members and the marching band of Hendrix College the two men had vanished.

The automobile was still new in 1911 with horses and buggies still outnumbering the horseless carriages. Still from our viewing stand we witnessed a half dozen autos like this one.

Once across the street instead of heading back up to my seat I veered left to go around the corner of the building. Seeing my change in direction, and knowing there had to be an urgent reason, Sarah and Lydia were quickly at sidewalk level catching me as I headed down 5th Street to get to the alley that I knew would run behind the building, just as it still would in my own time a century later.

REUNION IN TIME

I had sat and watched thousands of old Confederates ride and walk by, knowing all were at least in their 80's. I wondered almost aloud what their collective memories could paint into history, having survived a war 50 years ago, going on to live five decades, fathering children, earning a living but surely never forgetting the fiercest battles ever seen on American soil.

Slowing long enough to explain who I'd seen I asked, or rather ordered, the women not to follow me as I headed into the alley. I might as well have been trying to reason with one of the parade mules for both women followed me down the deeply shaded alley littered with trash. It was probably a life-saving decision on their part for I heard "Look out Dad", and when I turned I found Henry Cabot leaping from a loading dock door with an axe, swinging it toward my head. I ducked and stumbled into a rolling heap on the ground, through a pile of what appeared to be discarded scraps from a café located on the Main Street side of the building. The axe came down less than six inches from my face, splitting the rind of a watermelon instead of my head, as Cabot clearly intended.

"Damn it Doctor Kernick. You are really starting to piss me off and it's time to……." The last of his oath trailing off as Lydia hit Cabot across the back with a jagged two-by-four she had picked up. As I was attempting to get to my feet, Lydia slammed him again across the side of the face and a stream of blood flew through the air. Cabot took off running down the alley toward Sexton once he regained his feet. I staggered to my feet, not realizing I now had the axe that had almost killed me in one hand. and we watched Cabot meet Sexton at the exit to the alley, and they disappeared to the east away from the parade route.

Assuring both Lydia and Sarah I was OK I noticed the board Lydia was still holding in both hands was dripping blood. Reaching out to take it from her still firm grasp I noticed several large nails protruding from one end, explaining the blood that had come flying from Cabot's face when Lydia struck the second blow. She wrapped her arms around me, now starting to cry, as I dropped the axe with a "Thanks slugger, I think you hit a home run."

It was hard not to be frustrated in that, once again, we had encountered the criminals who started this whole episode in 2011, but had failed to bring an end to the still unsuccessful mission. On the bright side, I told myself at least I wasn't lying in the alley trash with my head cleaved by an axe. Somehow I knew I was running out of the proverbial "nine lives". For one thing, with both Lydia and now Charlie here in 1911, there was nobody left in 2011 to read another microfilmed account of my demise and mount yet another time travel rescue.

By the time we made our way around the corner back to the reviewing stand, Father Shultz was clearly worried, and grew more so when he saw my pants ripped at the knee, and my uniform stained from my fall into a pile of garbage in the alley. Assuring him I was OK, we dropped back into our seats, me on one side of him, Lydia on the other. She leaned into his ear and quickly filled him in on the events of the past few minutes, causing him to shake his head but offer the sign of the cross for my life once again being spared, in his mind clearly by the divine hand of God.

I realized now that the parade had reversed directions and was passing in the opposite direction, heading north on Main instead of South. Seeing my obvious confusion Father Shultz leaned close and told me, "They turned around at the City Park camp, the parade is marching back to the Old State Capitol, and those old rebs are in a marching mood I guess." I wondered fleetingly about the fate of the old drummer to whose aid I'd gone before my near fatal encounter with Cabot in the alley.

The last of the parade was starting to pass the reviewing stand, its marching ranks reduced finally to the stragglers, those old men who just would not quit despite their frailty and the heat of a hot Arkansas May day. I watched a group of uniformed Boy Scouts, probably in the age range of 12 to 14 years old move into the flow of the old men, some of whom appeared ready to drop. Some old men got the aid of one scout, the frailest one on either side, helping them continue the march north. By my calculation it was another seven or eight blocks back to the Old State House where the parade would end.

Perhaps to show respect, perhaps to encourage the old men, the remaining crowd took up the tune of the long departed bands and started a rendition of Dixie. I noticed Governor Donaghey rise to his feet below me, singing and applauding at the same time. What appeared to be the last in the long gray line of General Lee's army, a lone struggling veteran, propped up on one side by a Boy Scout, was passing the reviewing stand and raised his hand into a smart salute to Governor Donaghey. With that he shuffled on, the young boy still holding him up. I could not help but think I was watching a part of history march off into eternity. I recalled an editorial in one of the papers I'd read in Bigelow about the old soldiers passing over the last hill to *"sleep in the peace that passeth every understanding."* I hoped this old man, and all those that had passed before him found that peace, hoping at the same time I could as well find the peace of successfully righting the wrongs I'd traveled back a century to fix and to return to my own time and place.

With the parade clearly over we assembled back on the now much less crowded sidewalk to begin the trip back to the rectory. What we would do next I had no idea but the destruction of the State Capitol building, and our deaths if we followed the latest version of history by appearing there was less than 12 hours away.

Chapter 37

IT WAS ALMOST 2:00 before we left the streetcar between St. Edwards and the City Park encampment. Looking across I could see the tan uniformed soldiers from Fort Roots mixing with the old Confederates, I guess helping them pack up before the tents were taken down. I could not help the fleeting thought that if only Lydia and I could pack up and head "home", a thought I by necessity of a mission yet fulfilled pushed aside. None of our little group was talking as we headed up the walk onto the porch of the rectory.

It must have been 90 degrees and close to that in the shade of the rectory porch. Not wanting to face the confined inside of the house I dropped onto the porch swing and in I guess symbolic support Sarah, Lydia, Father Shultz and Charlie found their own seats among the chairs on the porch. Lydia put to words what we all had to be thinking, "What next guys?"

"Well" I opened up, "It seems we start with what we know will happen tonight and that's the explosion that brings down the center of the Capitol building and kills us....but I trust we can at least change that latter event." I got no immediate reply, but one look told me the wheels in Lydia's blonde head were spinning with possible scenarios. "OK Lydia, you clearly have some ideas here?"

For someone supposedly destined to be crushed beneath tons of marble in a few hours, my daughter smiled before opening up. "We know what was supposed to happen tonight based on the newspaper microfilms Charlie brought last night from 2011. Still, it wouldn't be the first time the history of this 1911 week has changed from what it was before, as well as after, we left 2011 and arrived here. How do we know that the run-in with Cabot and Sexton this morning, something that never happened in the original time stream, doesn't' change what they do tonight?"

In view of the puzzled faces around me it clearly fell to me to pick up Lydia's thread of thought. "No, I think regardless the encounter this morning the direction of events, from the old newspapers we read in Charlie's lab, where Dave died in a fall from the dome, …everything has pointed at the State Capitol building this evening. As Lydia started to rebut me I headed her off, "Yes, yes, I know the explosion at the Capitol was a change from the original time path we first read about but I think, somehow, we influenced that, made them change their plans, do something more dramatic because they knew we came here after them.

Charlie, who had been quiet but attentive stepped in at that point. "I think you're right, Jack. Because they know you came after them, something that didn't originally happen, they decided to go for broke, do something dramatic, maybe with an idea of a big score and a return to 2011 or some other time before you did something to interfere with their criminal endeavors here in 1911. Maybe, just maybe, the plan to blow up the Capitol was about creating so much chaos that the police, even with your possible help in identifying them, wouldn't be able to catch up with them and the stolen gold." Listening I concurred he had a point, that it would take law enforcement several days to clear the tons of collapsed marble from the Capitol ruins before they would realize the stored gold was no longer in the vault.

Listening to Charlie, it occurred to me that to date here in 1911, despite more than one encounter, I'd given Cabot and Sexton little to worry about, having failed at every turn to stop them. Suppressing my frustration, I asked Father Shultz, "Do you by chance have a Little Rock map here?"

A few minutes later we were gathered around a tattered city map spread across the rectory dining table. With a stubby pencil I pointed out the State Capitol building location, which at the time of the map had, based on the wording, been the state's prison. Seeing my pencil hesitant in confusion Father Shultz stepped in, "Jack, this map is about 10 years old, at the time construction of the capitol was just underway, the site was still occupied by the old buildings of the state prison. Some of it dated from the Civil War."

Looking to the west end of the map where I knew the Capitol building stood I could see the railroad tracks snaking behind where the building sat. I'd of course seen more than once the front of the building and it's still rough front lawn that looked out toward downtown. I'd had a view to the west before I'd been run off my perch just below the rooftop dome. I just could not recall what the terrain behind the building looked like. With only a vague shape of a plan emerging in my head I asked Father Shultz to fill me in on the gap in my geography knowledge.

"Yes Jack, I've had a passing look at the area a few times. Best view is from the streetcar heading up to Pulaski Heights, it passes right over the tracks that run behind the Capitol, good view of the hill behind the building that slopes down the hill toward the tracks. The area looks pretty wooded and overgrown, at least from the trolley." The priest stood back and stoking his chin, "What are you thinking Jack?"

With everyone looking at me when I looked up at the map it was apparent that everyone expected me to have a plan, regardless my bungled past efforts at bring this bizarre tale to a peaceful conclusion. I sensed that we had but one more chance to finish the job.

Looking at the intense faces around the table I took a deep breath and pointed to railroad line below the back of the Capitol building. "They will use this approach tonight. They won't use the front. If it's like the last few nights, even with the reunion ended, there will be lots of people milling around the front lawn." I could see the doubt and questions forming, especially on Lydia's face.

"Dad, this is all too dangerous. Lets' just anonymously tip off the police that a robbery is going to occur, that they will have dynamite and then the police are there, arrest the guys, game over, we go home safe." I had to admit to myself for a few seconds that, at least in a common sense normal world that made sense. Hurled back a century in time though that really didn't work and I had to explain why and at the same time sell my own strategy.

As I picked up a pencil and a pad I gently started to rebut my daughter's appeal, despite it's on the surface logic. "If the police are there and arrest Cabot and Sexton this alters the events of the evening as occurred in the most recent occurrence of events we read about in the newspaper Charlie brought back. Maybe the Capitol isn't blowup, with us inside it." Pausing for a thought collecting breath my initial analysis was met with Lydia's "I like that outcome."

Shaking my head I continued. "However, that doesn't solve the problem of still having two very intelligent, dangerous men left here in 1911 with a century worth of "I know what happens" about future events, with the ability to alter those events in who knows what manner." Lydia was at a loss for words, as was Sarah but Charlie trained scientific mind was racing. "Jack's right, we can't allow the two men to remain here." Not surprisingly he raised his head to add, "And I don't think bringing in the police helps us save Dave before he dies or otherwise disappears here in 1911."

Anticipating the "how" questions on the tip of the groups tongue I scribbled something on the pad and handed it to Father Shultz. "Call the drug store and tell them your doctor wrote you a prescription for this. See if they will compound it and deliver it here this afternoon." Charlie leaned over to read the note in the Priests' hand, remarking, "Well that would certainly put a man down for several hours."

Deciding it was best to get everything laid out before anymore arguments opened up, I next turned to Father Shultz. "Father, we have two time machines parked in your barn we are going to need to transport to the vicinity of the Capitol." We had discovered the morning after Charlie's arrival he had, addition to the machine he came in, sent back the second machine, albeit unmanned so that we had both available.

Thinking but a few seconds Father Shultz replied, "I can call Gus who you met the night you arrived here atop his freight wagon loaded with army tents. He already has some wagons waiting over at the park across the street that will be used to start hauling the tents back to Fort Roots tomorrow. I saw him at a distance when we got off the streetcar when we were returning from the parade." It belatedly occurred to him to ask, "Why do we need a wagon?"

I was gathering my thoughts to lay out my entire plan but in watching Charlie call up a slightly grim smile I could tell he might have already jumped ahead to the end game. "It might work Jack, but you are going to need a couple of syringes." Everyone but my own head seemed to swing in his direction with that statement.

"That's right Charlie. Father Shultz when you call the drug store tell them you will have the, uh, medicine, I wrote down picked up. I'll go myself just to explain in case the druggist has any questions. For that matter let's use Fred Allsopp's pharmacy up at Freiderica's, he will trust me and compound it as written. Now, as for the syringe, there is a feed store I think over on Markham isn't there? I'm sure they will have a large syringe used by farmers for livestock. Lydia, you go get two of those while I go get the compounded medicine."

The expressions around the table were getting even more confused when Charlie stood up, paced a minute and then explained. "What Jack has in mind, and fill in what I miss Jack, is that we will use a freight wagon tonight to haul the two time machines up somewhere in the vicinity of the Capitol tonight." Looking at me and seeing no dispute he continued. "We will then intercept Cabot and Sexton on the slope behind the Capitol tonight, I expect at gunpoint, and drug them into quick unconsciousness with a shot of the powerful sedative Jack scribbled on that notepad." Pausing to gather his thoughts, "Right so far, Jack?"

Upon my nod, Charlie continued to lay out my own plan more methodically than it had emerged in my addled mind. "The time machines each transport two people and we will load one drugged bad guy into each with one of us in the front seat to return the machine to 2011. Once there we will decide how best to send them to where justice can best be served." Looking at me, he added, "that it so far Jack?"

While I nodded Lydia beat everyone to a most obvious question. "OK guys, I follow this to a point. We capture the bad guys, dope them up, and two of us drag their butts back to 2011. I get that, not that it's easy, but I follow it so far. But, and it's a big but, that leaves one of the three of us here in 1911 with both time machines back in 2011..well, two of us, assuming we find Dave. Not to add leaving two of us here in no telling what kind of mess after our escapade to the Capitol tonight which may or may not explode." She added before anyone could respond, "Not to mention the plan needs to be to take four of us back to 2011, as we surely plan to find Dave somewhere tonight around the Capitol. The three of us, plus Dave, plus bad guys make six for only four seats."

I looked at Charlie for support because Lydia had outrun my plan. I just had not gotten that far. The ability for one of the two who take Sexton and Cabot back to 2011, to be able to target a return to retrieve the third, and hopefully fourth with Dave, was indeed a challenge. I recalled the process of getting here was not an exact science, either in hitting the planned location or the desired time. The landing could miss by at least days and by miles.

Charlie thought this through quickly and offered back a plan – risky but without a viable alternative that I could see. "Assuming we subdue and drug Sexton and Cabot and find Dave, then the two of them go back, one in a machine with you, one with Lydia." What could go wrong there? A question fraught with so many possibilities, I could have laughed out loud if not feeling a mounting life or death pressure bearing down. "I will stay here, with Dave I hope, and you send one machine back to us, I guess to the rectory."

One concern I thought obvious jumped to the top of my mental "what if" list. "Charlie, how can we know both machines will return to 2011, at the same time, at the same location? What if mine lands, say in 2011 but Lydia's hits another year, a different time, date in 2011?" The image of her landing in the middle of a highway in an unpredictable year with a drugged felon buckled into the back seat of a machine resembling a rocket was so unnerving as to make me rethink the whole scheme.

Charlie seemed not at all concerned on that point. "Once the machine has occupied a particular location, it's ingrained in the software – not just the place, but the time it originally left 2011. It's a bit hit or miss the first time a new date and location is transmitted, just as it was in coming to 1911, but the return coordinates, date, time and location are captured from the point of origin."

While I was mentally processing Charlie's reassurances, Sarah, who had listened in silence for the preceding half hour asked a question that, for a supporting player to be left a century in the past, was a logical thought. "Does that mean, Charlie, that, from 2011, you could as easily return to this time and place?"

Charlie, answering as a scientist, and not a man reading a woman's deeper meaning, quickly replied. "Yes, for sure, that is the way the software works. It captures the exact amount of energy and the celestial positioning to return a machine to any place it went before. The garden behind the rectory here or that barn in the woods Jack first appeared in." I tried not to look at Sarah and get away from this line of scientific probing. The fact that she was an attractive and appealing woman had been apparent since I rescued her from the bank robbers. I was still however a century from home and my world.

On that note we ended the conversation before the scenarios got so as to paralyze us all with indecision. For better or worse the plan was set. Lydia headed off to the feed store to obtain the syringes and I went to catch the streetcar to make the trip to the Frederica drug store.

Chapter 38

FRED ALLSOPP WAS behind the counter of the pharmacy when I walked into the store, his back to me reading something. Upon hearing the bell clang with the opening of the door he turned to greet me. "Ah Jack, there you are, come to claim the potion Father Shultz phoned me about. I must say Jack, I realize you are a physician but this concoction is a puzzle, unless of course you need to put a mule down for a six hour nap maybe." I was clearly invited to elaborate but nothing plausible came to mind other than the literal truth. Telling this wise, kind man who had befriended Lydia and I at multiple turns that we intended to subdue two felons from a hundred years in the future didn't seem like an option but then making up a lie seemed equally out of the question.

Without probing further Fred put a small bag on the counter containing the drugs Father Shultz had asked him to compound. "Thanks, I appreciate the help" was about all I thought an honorable reply would stand.

We chatted a bit about the reunion and parade, I thanked him for his hospitality and accepted his wishes for a safe journey after telling him Lydia and I were likely heading home. Whether he believed that meant a return to Texas was a question left unasked and unanswered between two men who had become friends over the past few days. I clasped his proffered hand firmly and the look in his eyes conveyed the likelihood we would never meet again.

When I stepped out of the drug store onto Capitol Avenue I could not help but glance to the left up the hill where the afternoon blazing sun was beaming off the Capitol dome. It seemed likely that, whatever it was to be, my fate was likely to be played in within the next few hours under or around that looming marble dome.

When the sun arose in the morning would the dome still be here and would I still be here to know?

Lydia and I arrived back on the sidewalk in front of the rectory at almost the same time, my coming from trolley car stop to the south, she coming from the north where she had visited the feed store. She held up a paper bag and I did the same to signal we had both accomplished our mission. "Pop, I don't know about you but my nerves won't take too much more of this. I just want it over with and I want to go home."

Taking the bag I put an arm around her slim shoulders, "me and you both kiddo, me an you both" was the most honest refrain I'd likely given in a very long time.

"Any problems getting the syringes", a question that seemed unnecessary but one that might distract her from worries. "Nope, it was easy, the clerk seemed a little surprised but he actually laughed and asked if I was putting an elephant down for a nap."

I managed to not laugh but had to smile at the relayed version of the conversation. "The needles are a bit large, I will adjust the dose of the drug, but if we are lucky enough to get close enough for the injection I want to make sure we have the best chance to make it work.

By 6:00 Sarah and Lydia had prepared a full dinner of roast chicken and vegetables, laid out on the dining room table. Gathered around the table an awkward silence enveloped the group. Without anyone needing to say it we all knew that after tonight odds were high we would never again be together. Whether or not we succeeded in accomplishing the capture of Cabot and Sexton and returned to 2011 or if something more ominous occurred, things were coming to a rapid impact of events.

Sarah broke the silence, "Father Schultz, I think a special blessing over this meal is called for, don't you?"

"Sarah I could not agree more" and with that Father Schultz reached for Sarah's hand on one side and Lydia's on the other. As on cue Charlie, and I joined the circle of hands that formed a ring around the table. "Dear Lord, you know the hearts of men no manner the century in which they spend their allotted time on earth. We know that you have a plan for all of us, that you care deeply and hear the prayers of those gathered around this table tonight. Please bless this meal and give us the strength and wisdom to the things that must be done this evening. In the name of the Father, the Son and the Holy Spirit, amen." The sign of the cross and the echoing 'amens' reverberated around the table.

After Sarah and Lydia had cleared the supper dishes away I spread once more the tattered Little Rock city map of Father Schultz's across the table. Rubbing my eyes to try to focus I was struck by how dark it seemed to have grown outside the kitchen window, part of my puzzlement answers by a loud clap of thunder that seemed to roll through the house. I walked to the front screen door in time to watch the large rain drops begin to pelt the cobble stoned street in front of the rectory. If the rain kept up it could complicate the plans for the evening but it occurred to me I had even less control of the weather than I'd had of the series of events that had occurred in the year 1911.

As I was turning away from the door the first of what would be two freight wagons pulled up in front of the curb at the end of the rectory's walk. I recognized Gus, but not the black man driving the second wagon. Charlie move around me and went out to the porch to greet Gus and to direct him to pull the wagons around the corner and into the alley that ran behind the rectory's back yard, telling him we would meet him there. Seeing my puzzled expression Father Shultz told me, "While you and Lydia were out Sarah and I have covered the machines with canvas, got them both wrapped with rope. Gus won't ask questions."

That had to be enough assurance for me, at least for the moment. I followed Father Shultz around the side of the house, through his garden gate and helped him open a larger gate that opened up to the alley just as Gus pulled up the first freight wagon. Hoisting his bulk down from his high seat Gus was about to ask what he was supposed to be hauling when he saw the canvas wrapped missile shaped bundles pointing at him from the opened door of Father Shultz's small barn. Cleary the burly man had questions but looking first at the elderly priest and then at me he only turned back to his helper, "Jonah, here's what we need to haul for Father." The black man I now knew as Jonah moved closer as Father Shultz held a lantern above his head illuminating the canvas packages. "I sees, um, Mr. Gus, but I's wonders how heavy is them things?"

Charlie was in the yard with us by then and he sought to relive the concern about the weight of the time machines. "Two men can lift the machines into the wagon. The plastic, aluminum and the electronic components aren't heavy" I'd not given that issue much thought until now but moved to help Gus with the tail end of the first machine, just behind the canopied cockpit, while Jonah with some testing probes for a grip picked up the slopped front end. With surprising ease we were able to slide the machine into the first wagon leaving enough room to close the large gate at the end of the wagon. They had to wonder what they had just loaded but neither raised a question.

Once done it was apparent that the high sides of the large wagon would completely conceal the machine. The process of loading the remaining time machine into the second wagon went as easily. When the work was done Father Shultz took Gus aside closer to the back door of the rectory and engaged a conversation I could not overhear.

I was left with Charlie and Jonah, the latter whose curiosity got the best of him. "I's glad to help you folks and always glad to work for Gus, he always pays me and Lordy, with 11 childens still counting on me I's need tha work. I's got to say though, this is right strange Father, these canvas things, they shaped like some kind of boat. They be's boats Father?' The patient Priest stepping forward to put his hand on the wheel of one wagon answered in a kind tone, "Well Jonah I think that is a good guess, these are, in a way, certainly boats for a very long trip."

As had been prearranged I climbed up on the seat with Gus who would be driving the lead wagon. Lydia elected to ride nestled behind the high wagon seat in the corner of the bed of the huge wagon where one of the time machines rested, while Sarah assumed a similar seat in the other wagon.

The wagons rolled down Ninth Street, the iron wheels clattering on the brick pavement, crossing Main Street headed west toward the area of the Capitol building. The streets were almost deserted even though the hour was just passing eight o'clock. Most of the old soldiers had headed home in the afternoon by train and I guessed the local citizens were turned in early recovering from the biggest event to hit Little Rock since the Union army marched into town in 1863. The silence was broken as we rolled through The intersection of Ninth and Broadway with a booming voice out of the fog. "Dr. Kernick, is that you? Well yes, as sure as I'm not Saint Patrick it is. What brings you out for a wagon ride this evening?"

Before even catching sight of the policeman under the cone of light from the gas streetlight I knew we had again encountered Sergeant Brennan. Gus, respectful of the policeman, pulled up the reins and brought the team of mules to a halt.

The burly Irish policeman stepped to the edge of the curb and looking up at us on the elevated seat gave a short laugh, but not necessarily of amusement. "Every time I've met up with you Dr. Kernick there seems to be a spot of trouble either just happening or about to happen. It's a nice quite evening and most of the old rebels have of gone home, I do hope there's not something about to create any work for this officer of the law."

I returned the cops laugh with one of my own, that I hoped wasn't too forced. If he only knew that, at least in a version of time, the dome of the State Capitol building a few blocks away was but a couple of hours from being destroyed by dynamite. "No trouble with us Officer Brennan. Gus here stopped by the rectory to see Father Shultz on his way to make a delivery. He offered to give myself and my friend Charlie on the second wagon a last tour of Little Rock at night. I expect we are headed home tomorrow. It's been quite a week." Surely no bigger understatement had ever been spoken.

REUNION IN TIME

I later found this photo of Sgt. Brennan, one of the two Irish Little Rock policemen we encountered too often, in an old city police souvenir book.

With a start it occurred to me the policeman might well step up and inspect our cargo, something for which there would be no plausible explanation. Instead the man tipped his nightstick against his helmet and directed some advice to the silent, but surely concerned, man seated beside me holding the reins. "Gus, you be careful tonight, I swear, everywhere the good doctor goes there seems to be trouble left behind." Gus replied back with what to me seemed a bit of a forced laugh, "I appreciate that advice Sergeant, I surely do". I heard an audible sigh of relief from the wagon bed just behind me from Lydia as the big wagon rolled on up Ninth street, the second wagon trailing behind.

At State Street Gus slowed to turn the lead wagon right and two blocks down to make a left onto 7th street, the second wagon followed us closely. Shortly we could see the Capitol dome, still lit against the gathering darkness by which I confirmed with my pocket watch had passed 8:00. As we moved past the Capitol heading toward a likely point of entry just west of and behind the building I could see groups of the old Confederates still milling around in the front of the building, perhaps with nowhere else to go with the City Park camp taken down, until there was an available train home.

The wagons moved slightly downhill on 7th street after passing the Capitol and shortly Gus pulled the team up to a halt, with the second wagon doing the same behind us. I realized everyone was looking at me for the next step, one I thought I could best think through with my feet on the ground and soon everyone but Gus climbed off the wagons and followed my lead to gather in the shadows of the trees. Turning to Father Shultz I voiced the first order of the evening . "Father, we need to see if we can talk Gus and into leaving the wagons with us here somewhere for at least the next two or three hours. We really don't want him here if we pull all this off and are able to send us and the machines back to 2011." Father Shultz bowed his head in thought for a moment and then took me aside to whisper a possible solution to the posed dilemma.

After I paid Gus generously, and with a little bonus, handed almost slight of hand to Jonah, the first logistical challenge of the night was met with Gus's intent to go have a beer at one of the taverns that operated down the hill upon which the Capital sat near the train station.

Jonah simply followed Gus's instructions to leave us with the wagons and to come back in about three hours to help return the wagons to Gus's stables across the river. As I watched the men's backs disappear into what was becoming a misty evening, with a growing hint of rain, I paused to consider the next step in a plan that now seemed more challenging in enveloping darkness that it had under the lights of Father Shultz's dining room.

I realized that Charlie, Father Shultz, and the women were all waiting for me to make the call as to what we would do next. With a mental picture of the city map in my head I realized that the train tracks were just down 7th street some 50 yards past the alley in which the two wagons were concealed. "OK, here's the way we will do this. Charlie and I will move on down the hill here on 7th to the tracks, then north up the tracks to where we can approach the Capitol from below." Lydia, predictably, had other ideas. "Dad, you and Charlie need help, there will be at least two, if not more armed men trying to pull off the theft of the gold, not to mention the dynamite. You need me there." I mustered the firmest "NO" I could pull up, even if I did see my daughters point.

Before Charlie and I left I did remember to pull the pistol from beneath the wagon seat, where I'd placed it wrapped in a pillowcase, before we left the rectory. Moving down the hill on 7ths Street, a dirt track at this point, I felt only slightly like a World War II movie character with the pistol in my hand. As we reached the train tracks to turn north the first drops of rain began to fall, with lightening not far behind illuminating the Capitol dome just before we disappeared between the hewn rock walls of the railway cut. I paused to make sure Charlie was behind me, realizing he was indeed and moving with surprising agility, perhaps driven by goals of the evening, not the least of which was trying to recover his son before the murder we had read about before leaving 2011. I breathed a silent prayer and moved on into the dark and rain.

Chapter 39

THE PELTING RAIN and booming thunder likely prevented an early failure to our mission. Walking carefully, stepping from cross tie to cross tie to avoid the uneven footing of the crushed rock of the rail bed, I was startled to hear voices ahead. Holding up a hand to caution Charlie, I flattened myself against the rock hewn wall. Charlie quickly and silently followed my example just as the light of what I guessed was a lantern from above the track grade cut illuminated a section of the track no more than twenty feet ahead of us.

" Dammed, it would raining. I swear nothing goes right, working with those two. As soon as this is done and we get our share of the gold, I don't want to lay eyes on Sexton and Cabot agin, no sir I don't." I knew I'd never heard that voice before, just as I knew the same about the one that came in reply, from a man standing on the tracks under the umbrella of the lantern piercing the building rain storm. "Dobbins, I hear you on that, but if we can get out of this thing as rich as was promised us, it will be worth it. Now toss down the rest of them ropes, that rope ladder as well. The engineer Sexton and Cabot paid, or at least promised to pay, is supposed to stop the train so that just about here will be the boxcar with the unlocked door. All we need to do is lower the gold down into that boxcar and then roll out of this dammed town."

I realized that we must have arrived at the point some two hundred or so yards behind the Capitol at the bottom of the ravine through which the twin track tracks passed. Presumably the train the two men, who had obviously joined Cabot and Sexton, referred

REUNION IN TIME

to was one that would be leaving Union Station, not more than 500 yards away, headed south. I'd worried earlier about how we would locate the approach behind the Capitol but much seemed solved. I hoped it was a sign that our odds of success were looking up that we had found the point of approach.

We waited some 10 minutes once the men's voices and the light of their lantern moved away from the below ground level track grade upon which we perched. Intent on next moving toward the Capitol, pistol in back of my pants, I'd just put my foot into the rope ladder that would give us access to the top of the grade cut and I hoped a clear line of sight to the Capitol when the voice came out of the darkness a few feet further down the tracks. What came just before the voice however was something likely not seen in the year of 1911, a flashlight beam aimed at my face. "It's amazing, you meet the most interesting folks in 1911, how you doing Jack?"

Nothing should have surprised me after the last few days but having Dave Rawlins voice greet me out of the dark and rain might have been the second biggest shock since I left 2011, after only Lydia appearing in Hot Springs.

As I stepped back down onto the track grade, Dave lowered the light and stepped forward to grasp my arm. "I don't know how you got here or what you are doing, but I suspect it's about what I'm trying to do, which is stop those bastards who whacked Dad over the head and fled here to create mischief. I'm really glad to see you. How was Dad? I'm sure he sent you back here looking for me."

Before I could answer Charlie moved out of the darkness behind me and answered himself, "Well your old father is fine, considering all that has happened over the last few days". With that he stepped forward and embraced his son, trying with little success to contain his emotions. "Dad, what in the hell are you doing here?"

Looking over his Dad at me, "Jack, what in name of ....", but Charlie cut him off. "Don't start on Jack, he came back alone to try to save you from being murdered but then, well he was murdered and then, well then Lydia insisted on coming back to stop that and then, and then, well the Capitol blew up and well..."

The rain had abated for at least a time and clearly all needed a bit of time to recover from the shock on the reunification before we climbed out of the rail bed to confront whatever awaited us up the hill. Dave opted to go first to fill us in on his time in 1911. "I landed 8 days before the reunion started, on May 8th, a couple days off, you may remember Dad we tried for a May 10 entrance. I actually landed in the middle of the night down by the river landing. There was no place to leave or hide the machine so I hit the button to return it to your lab. It came back?" Charlie nodded and replied, "yes it reappeared a few hours after you vanished.

Dave picked back up his portion of the account, "The landing wasn't a problem though I had a bit of a headache from the transit process. The rest of the story is pretty simple, I've been moving around town for the past ten days trying to catch up to Cabot and Sexton. I only caught a glimpse of them once, they were on the roof at 5th and Main during the parade this morning. I was a block away and couldn't move in the crowd. As to tonight, well we knew from the first newspaper accounts we read in 2011 both men would appear here at the Capitol tonight. I came into the rail bed cut a few hundred feet back to the north, I started near the train station."

With Charlie sometimes chiming in I filled Dave in on the events, at least the major ones, of my time in 1911, including the times Lydia and I nearly caught up with him. There was an ominous silence when I relayed to Dave that, in one time event he had been murdered and plunged from atop the Capitol building. The mood changed after Dave laughed softly when I mentioned Lydia seeing him at the door of the Confederate ball. "Yes, I stopped at the door, the place was jammed, I just couldn't see Cabot and Sexton being part of such a festive, crowded affair."

After the mutual catching up the discussion turned to where we took things from here. Only then did I mention the Capitol being destroyed and Lydia, he and I dying, which brought Dave up short with "My God, tell me she won't be anywhere near the Capitol building tonight, no matter what happens." While I was giving assurances that she would remain with the time machines and wagons I tried not to dwell on the fact that my daughter didn't always follow orders.

After some debate back and forth on options, we concluded that if possible we would not enter the Capitol building but instead would position ourselves somewhere along the path between the back of the Capitol lawn and the top of the rail cut above our heads. We would try to accost Sexton and Cabot, sedate them if possible with the hypodermics Charlie had in a bag under his arm. With Dave's unexpected appearance the extra set of strong hands should make getting the hopefully unconscious men back to the time machines easier. Mentally calculating the numbers of people against the four seats in the machines was an issue but one I'd deal with when we had to do so. With that much of a decision made I quickly went up the rope ladder with Dave following right behind me, reaching back to help Charlie.

It occurred to me, as I'm sure it did to Charlie and Dave, that we would have had a hard time getting out of the rail cut without the providential presence of the rope ladder dangling next to heavy ropes by which the bad guys planned to move their stolen gold down to the tracks.

At the top of the approximately 20foot rail bed cut through the rocks we moved rapidly into the clumps of brush beside the worn trail. Looking up the hill we could see the Capitol dome, lit from the front with a ghostly glow that wrapped partly around the dome to profile the entire thing against the sky. By that time the rain had started to fall again, heavy clouds darkening the path, giving us view on the ground of only a few feet. A blazing flash of lightning illuminated the path however almost all the way up the hill across the rough lawn to the back steps of the Capitol. It looked like the landscaping in the back was still much more a work in progress than it was in the front of the building.

In an evening of surprises one more spring up beside me when Dave Rawlins pulled from a bag slung over his shoulder an odd bulky pair of binoculars. Seeing my surprise he laughed, "Ok, I brought a flashlight from 2011, I'm no historical purist. I also brought these night vision googles." From my work with the Little Rock SWAT team, not to mention James Bond movies, I knew these goggles could virtually see in the dark by capturing ambient light, displaying the landscape in a ghostly green glow.

While Dave was working on the night vision goggles I noticed for the first time the path up the hill seemed to be through a field of old broken brick walls at varied heights from just piles of brick to head high. I reached out to my left and touched one low wall which toppled over upon contact making me jump. Father Shultz answered the unspoken question for me. "All this land where the Capitol has been built used to be the state prison, from the time of the Civil War. The front part where the Capitol sets is all gone but a lot of the ruins are still down here on the slope until the landscaping gets back here."

Dave soon had the night vision goggles fitted to his face and powered up. Using the goggles and binoculars he soon was studying the back entrance to the Capitol located at the top of the steps. Without the aid of the technology Charlie and I could see little beyond the buildings dome. There was no mistaking however that Dave had seen something when he muttered, "I'm be dammed, shit, I don't believe this. Jack, Sexton just came onto the back steps and he has a red headed woman all trussed up in rope." A sick feeling went through the pit of my stomach as I asked Dave to let me see the night vision goggles.

It took a minute to adjust the goggles and focus my line of sight toward the back entrance of the Capitol but once I did my worst fears were confirmed and then quickly compounded. Gabe Sexton was in the process of tying Sarah Murphy to one of the portico columns near the back entrance of the Capitol. While I was attempting to process this new development into the already uncertain next steps things got worse, much worse. Henry Cabot came into view pushing Lydia, her hands bound behind her back. He proceeded to tie her to a column on the opposite side of the steps from the one Sarah was tied against. I turned back to Charlie and Dave, my head about to explode with the pressure. "They have Sarah and Lydia up there, both tied now to columns at the rear of the building."

Dave's reaction was almost visceral. He wanted to charge up the path and rescue the women. I didn't even know if he was armed, and thus wasn't certain if I had the only gun between us. I should have known better as I watched him pull from his bag a very lethal looking pistol. Still we knew Sexton and Cabot had at least two accomplices, and for all we knew more than that. "No, we can't do that. If bullets start flying, there's too much of a chance Sarah or Lydia will get hit. We have to take another approach." To complicate things even more, the rain picked up and the wind began to roar while lighting ripped across the sky.

We decided to move on up the path to a point where it broke on onto the lower part of the still rough beginning of the Capitol lawn, pausing beside a large pile of muddy earth, the end of what seemed to be a large open ditch. A section of the old prison brick structure gave us some stability to stop to take another look at the situation at the back entrance of the building, now a perhaps 50 yards closer. Dave strapped on the night goggles and didn't take long to assess the situation. "The women are still tied to the columns; no one else is visible." Any thought about what to do with this information faded immediately with the sound of voices and people approaching behind us.

We pulled down behind the low brick wall just in time to see two men, I thought the ones who had put down the rope ladder earlier, emerge from what looked like a side path. They were pulling, with some difficulty, on the wet ground a cart with several wooden cases stack on it, partly covered by a tarp. The sound of the voices soon confirmed the men's identity. "Damn, those sons of bitches are crazy. There must be a better way to get the gold out of the basement than to use this load of dynamite. Why's there's enough here to blow the damn building into pieces."

The other man was quick to explain why the excessive dynamite, "Well the way I heard it Sexton figured that if the whole building comes down it will take days at least before the police dig it out enough to know the gold is gone."

The oaths got worse when the cart bogged down. The thought that crossed my mind then was that we were hidden only twenty feet away from a cart full of dynamite and lightning bolts were filling the sky.

Looking over at Dave I could read his mind, he was on the verge of moving over the mound of muddy earth to take the two men out. I reached over to taken hold of his arm and leaning close whispered "one stray shot and that dynamite won't leave enough of any of us to identify. Let's wait for now." Reluctantly Dave moved back down and we resumed our watchful deliberation.

The two men solved their problem by a decision to lighten the cart's load. "Hell, there's more dynamite here than they need if it's just to blow open the vault holding the gold. Help me take a box or two off this damn cart, we can come back for it if Sexton insists he needs it." Their load lightened the men were soon moving on up the hill with half the dynamite, the balance left beside the path in front of a long, large pile of dirt we would later find sat along the edge of a deep ditch. During their labors, I had not observed any guns. As far as I could tell, the men were unarmed. I could see that Dave was thinking the same thing. With the men now some 100 feet away, he whispered, "Lets even the odds a little bit, Jack." Before I could agree he was moving silently up the hill, crouched low.

It wasn't to be, out of the darkness ahead of the two men with the cart came voices belonging to at least two more men. "Dammit you two, where you been, Sexton sent us to look for you. He's got the night watchman tied up and is ready to set off some dynamite to open the gold vault. He also wants all this extra dynamite up there because I think he wants to bring down the entire place to cover the theft of the gold until we are long out of Arkansas." Dave had flattened himself onto the ground, and I followed the same course of action, hoping Charlie was still well behind us. With the added muscle the cart of dynamite, minus what the men had set aside, went on up the hill toward the capital at a considerably more rapid pace.

The bad guy's plans seem to be moving a lot better than mine and we now knew their ranks numbered at least six. Even more challenging was the fact Lydia and Sarah were tied to the columns of a massive marble building that was set to implode within the next hour or so. The original plan to avoid the Capitol building in favor of waylaying the men on the path to the train tracks clearly wasn't going to work anymore. I turned to Dave to speak the obvious but he was ahead of me. "We have to get the women away from that building Jack." By the time he turned back to Charlie it was clear his mind was racing ahead of mine. "Dad, you wait here out of sight behind the dynamite boxes, we have to move fast."

Dave slipped the night vision goggles onto his face and motioned silently for me to follow him up the hill toward the Capitol looming in the stormy sky. The building was not as well lit at the back as I knew from experience it was from the front, a small advantage we would need to approach undetected. The still new building lacked any of the shrubbery and trees its grounds would have a century later. To add to the odds against us the back lawn seemed to be riddled with holes, ditches and remnants of the old brick prison, reminding me of a shell pocked battlefield that stood between us and our objectives.

As we neared the Capitol though, and I followed Dave into a ditch less than 100 feet from the Capitols back entrance my hopes began to rise. Dave peered over the lip of the ditch with the aid of the night vision goggles. "So far so good Jack. It's just the women still tied to the columns…nobody else in sight. I guess they're all busy with the gold in the basement. Jack, you got a knife?" I didn't, but the boy scout "be prepared" had two and he handed me a pocketknife. "I'll move to the right and come up beside the porch side where Lydia is tied. You go left for the red-headed lady. Let's cut them loose and move back down the hill."

I only slipped back once coming out the ditch but managed to go face first into the mud before regaining my footing and my momentum toward the Capitol. Staying out of any line of sight of the wide steps that led up to the back entrance I quickly arrived at the back corner of the building and using its foundation was able to slide quickly to the dark corner where the steps joined the main building. In a brilliant flash of lighting I saw Sarah in profile lashed to the column. As if on cue. just as I climbed over the block foundation of the lower steps to start up toward Sarah, I saw Dave doing the same across the 30-foot span of steps on the other side.

I'm not sure who saw us first, but Sarah was the first to speak. "Jack, your finding me tied up is getting to be a habit, but I am surely glad to be rescued again. Please hurry." I was behind her, starting to slice the ropes that bound her wrists to the column when I heard booted steps on the marble not far from the Capitol doors, one of which had been propped open. I quickly moved back away from Sarah into the shadows of a recess to the left of the large doors.

Glancing over at Lydia, I could see she was still tied to the column opposite the one to which Sarah was still bound. Dave was nowhere to be seen. Presumably he had heard the approaching steps.

The man who emerged was cursing under his breath at Sexton and Cabot, unaware that Dave and I were on the steps. He veered toward Lydia's side of the portico and, for the first time, I noticed there were at least two boxes of the dynamite from the cart that had come up the hill earlier sitting behind her. "Hey you pretty thing, I may make some time for you before this is done tonight. You just stick around." Struck by his own humor, he began to laugh. The laughter halted abruptly with a soft thud that sounded a bit like a ripe melon being dropped. Dave Rawlins had stepped out of the shadows and struck the man in the back of the head with the butt of a pistol. He caught him before he fell, When I stepped forward to resume cutting the ropes binding Sarah, Dave dropped the man, either dead or certainly unconscious, off the end of the steps, at least 15 feet above ground, into the corner where the base of the marble steps adjoined the Capitol building.

Before I finished freeing Sarah, Lydia started to cross the porch toward me, but Dave grabbed her arm and pulled her aside to keep her out of the path of light coming from the partially open entrance to the Capitol. She spun around instead and threw her arms around Dave, perhaps I told myself because he was closer than her father, and I could hear her louder than the whisper I'd have advised, "Dave, it's about time you showed up. Dad and I have been through half the Confederate army this week, trying to find you." She was frightened but not panicked.

Sarah, rubbed the circulation back into her wrists and, instead of a hug, offered the beginning of a feeble apology. "Sorry Jack, Lydia and I just wanted to help. We left Father Shultz with the wagons, and we thought we could just stay near the building, in case, you know, you had trouble, but one of the bastards caught us. He had a gun, and...." I knew we didn't have time to talk about judgment calls with at least five more men inside the building. "OK, let's just get you and Lydia off this porch." I pointed down to the ground to get Dave's attention. He nodded and we took our respective charges down the outside edges of the marble steps, meeting in the darkness outside the reach of the Capitol lights spilling only partway down the steps from the partially open door.

Lydia threw her arms around me, and offered a version of Sarah's apology for complicating the plan we had laid out earlier. I didn't care at that point. She was no longer tied to a building that might collapse into rubble within the next few minutes. Dave took the time to check on the man he'd hit and dumped off the steps.

"He's alive, at least for now, but he won't be much use to Sexton and Cabot any time soon." It seemed up to me to make the call as to what we did next. "Let's get away from the building and back down the hill to Charlie. We know they will have to come down to the railroad tracks and likely soon."

Dave looked back up the steps and then ran back up, staying on the darker path on the outside edge. He grabbed first one, and then the second, case of dynamite and handed them down to me. After he leaped back down, he said, "Let's move the boxes over there in the dark corner with the unconscious thug. Two less boxes of dynamite might change some of the events the guys inside have planned." I agreed with his logic. I knew that there was at least some dynamite already inside the building, but the missing two cases might at least make it harder to bring down the entire dome of the capitol. Whatever else the evening had yet to unfold, it looked like we had at least altered the last chapter of history we had read about in the old newspapers Charlie brought back from 2011.

Going down the muddy slope seemed to take forever but it was probably little more than 5 minutes before we reached Charlie's position who had moved behind the two cases of dynamite on the path.

Staying here in the open with two cases of dynamite didn't seem like the best idea with lightening flashing across the sky, so we ran across the path and dropped down between two large berms of wet earth. Stepping to the top of one I could see each separated the path from a deep ditch in which had been laid a drain pipe not yet covered over.

The rain, which had slackened, began to pick up again and a new round of lightning lit up the Southwestern sky. Looking around, I decided a position behind the earthen berm to the south in a darker spot beneath a large tree offered the best shelter. "Let's get away from the dynamite," I said, motioning toward the shadow of the large tree beyond the six-foot-high pile of earth. Lydia and Charlie both slipped several times, climbing over the berm, but we were all soon huddled down below the heaped earth which I realized was supported by a weathered brick wall offering some shelter from the rain.

Shouts rolled down the hill from the Capitol. "Johnson, you worthless bastard. Where'd you go and where'd you leave the dynamite?" While the rest of us could see little, Dave had the night vision goggles engaged and filled us in. "Sexton is out on the porch and isn't a happy camper. I guess the guy I dumped off the steps is named Johnson and Sexton has no idea he is laying just below him in the dark with the dynamite. Maybe he will drop a match and save us a lot of trouble." Sexton apparently gave up in disgust, waiting for Johnson to respond and disappeared back insight the Capitol, shutting off the light streaming out the doors as he apparently closed them behind him.

I figured we had at best minutes before the men inside the building started down the hill toward the tracks with the gold, no doubt carrying guns. Our only advantage would be the element of surprise. I was trying to decide what to do with Lydia and Sarah when a rumbling boom came from up the hill. I knew it wasn't thunder and Dave confirmed the obvious.

"They just blew open the vault in the basement to get to the gold. The doors are open again. There's smoke coming out… and one, two, and let's see, four men outside by the columns. Looks like they're waiting for the smoke to clear." "Hopefully that's all the dynamite, counting what we hid and what's left down here. They can't bring down the building dome and we, for sure, are not inside under it, so I guess we changed history one more time."

We of course were still stuck a century in the past, but one thing at a time. I felt entitled to take at least a deep breath over escaping being squashed by tons of falling marble Capitol dome. During what I knew would be a brief respite, I turned to Lydia and started to insist she and Sarah return to Father Shultz, who I hoped was still waiting with the freight wagons and the two time machines. They listened, and despite a protest that they could help be of help, both agreed to head back. There seemed no need to use the steep rail bed, so I pointed straight through the fairly open trees behind us. "Seventy yards or so and you will come to 7th street. Just turn right down the hill and you will come to the alleyway where Father Shultz will be with the wagons."

Dave, Charlie and I watched in silence as the two women moved into the trees, stopping briefly to wave before being enveloped into dark, wet night. With feelings of both relief with apprehension. I turned back to Dave, whose attention was still fixed on Capitol through the night goggles. "The smoke must have cleared. All four of them went back inside, there has to be one more still inside. I don't think it will be long now. They can't take a chance the explosion didn't draw any attention." Dave powered off the goggles to save the batteries and we both settled down to wait.

Chapter 40

I CAUGHT THE first glimpse of light as both the back doors of the Capitol were pulled open and reached out to touch Dave's arm, "Looks like they are coming."

I reached for the old pistol in my belt, hoping it wasn't clogged with any of the mud we had been sliding around in for what seemed like hours. Not surprisingly, Dave reached into his bag of tricks and pulled out what looked like a Colt revolver. Only Charlie wasn't armed. He sat against the tree below our elevated position atop the earthen beam, his arms crossed, his hands within the canvas windbreaker. The humidity had to have been at least 80 percent, and I realized my much older friend must be exhausted. Dave seemed intent on checking his pistol. so I reached over him to pick up the night vision goggles.

Once the goggles were fitted and engaged, I turned my attention to the distant back entrance to the Capitol building. Before the last of five men closed the large bronze doors, shutting off the most of the light, I could see four of the men starting down the steps bearing some sort of wooden platform on wheels. The weight under which the men were obviously straining had to be the gold, in at least two crates, removed from the vault of the Capitol basement. It was going to take them a few minutes to navigate the muddy downhill slope to reach our position, but I knew we didn't have long. I could see that four of the men were carrying, more than rolling, the gold cart, almost like pallbearers at a funeral. There was a second cart load waiting at the top of the steps, which the men brought down once the first was settled at the bottom of the steps.

"Ok guys, let's get ready. It won't be long now." I leaned back against the wet earth and felt something hard jab me in the back and reached by in reflex to pull at the object. Looking down and what rolled down the muddy slope at the water gathered around my feet I let out an involuntary gasp as the empty eye sockets of a skull leered back up at me. I'd startled Dave but he seemed un-phased by the disembodied skull at my feet. "Oh that, it's from a prison graveyard. I was scouting up here yesterday while men were working on removing the old brick walls. They were finding convicts buried in places apparently nobody knew had been used for a cemetery back here. The prison dated from the Civil War."

A quick look up the hill showed the four men were only about 100 yards away, moving slowing toward us, weighed down by the stolen gold. They had apparently given up trying to find the missing man whom Dave had dropped into the dark corner beside the steps. I was turning back towards Dave and Charlie to caution them when I saw Dave pick up the old skull, eerily white with the rain having washed the mud off. "Dave what the...?." Before I could continue, Dave climbed back over the sheltering embankment and carefully positioned the grinning skull atop one of the dynamite boxes located on the far side of the path next to the long ditch we had observed earlier. This was the path down which the four gold robbers must soon pass. I used the night vision goggles to look back up the hill as Dave scampered back to our hidden position.

I was pretty much in a state of confusion about what the prank with the skull was intended to do but not so Charlie. "Son, I'm guessing you had some reason for putting that convict's head out there. Enlighten us, please."

Dave didn't waste words. "We have to stop them here, before they meet any train and likely allies with the gold. The boney old head down there should leave them confused and make them stop a spell." It was hard to argue with his reasoning, but as I watched a brilliant lightening flash showcase the skull atop the wooden crate some 30 feet away, I was really starting to question the whole plan I'd put into place even if the odds were starting to look better for us.

We didn't have long to wait, though just as I refocused the night vision goggles on the five men and their cart of gold drawing closer, my field of vision went from ghostly green to black. The batteries in the goggles had died, the charge they had carried back a century finally exhausted. "Lights out guys, no more juice in the glasses," I explained, which brought a muttered curse from Dave along with "so much for that Eveready bunny."

I had experienced more violence in the past few days of 1911 than I had ever imagined, but what transpired in the minutes that followed would live in my dreams for the rest of my life. The darkness was almost total, except during the flashes of lightening that seemed to come at one-minute intervals. We knew robbers had arrived, lit in the glow of a lantern one carried, when a loud "Holy shit" split the darkness. "Cabot, there's a…a goddamned head sitting here on top of the dynamite." We hunkered down lower behind the berm, peering through an inverted "v" I'd carved out at the top. The next flash of lightening showed at least four men gathered in front of the boxes. Clearly at least some of them were rattled.

Henry Cabot, though, wasn't going to let an old skull interfere with his dreams of wealth and who knew what else, for he stepped in to reassert control. "Shut up you fool. Let me think here a minute." Cabot leaned down close to the dynamite box and the skull with a kerosene lantern aloft to reveal his face in the glow. I watched with a sickening feeling as he slowly turned his gaze in our direction, realizing that he saw Dave's tracks in the mud leading to our hiding place. After that, all hell broke loose.

Without another word Dave fired a pistol shot that shattered the glass globe of the lantern Cabot was holding. At least three of the five men must have quickly pulled their own guns for a barrage of bullets were almost immediately hitting the top of the berm and whizzing over our heads. There seemed little alternative to pulling my own pistol out of my belt and soon I was helping Dave return fire in the direction of the men.

The presence of a case of dynamite in the center of the trail must have not factored into our adrenalin driven responses but as it turned out none of our bullets hit the crate.

REUNION IN TIME

Two of the men had scampered over the edge of ditch on the opposite side of the trail and were using the mounded earth between the dynamite and the ditch as cover to return a cascade of bullets. The other three men were down in the mud around the dynamite crate which they had to know was the most perilous spot but they had little options. A new source of light became quickly apparent, the flaming contents of the shattered lantern which were burning atop and around the dynamite crate. I pulled both Dave and Charlie down as far as I could behind the berm while the three men continued firing their pistols from some 40 feet away. "Cover your ears NOW" was all the advice I had time to give before the flaming kerosene ignited the case of dynamite.

The explosion left us all deafened temporarily, but one of a few distractions as mud, earth and what I later realized were body parts, rained down in the brilliant glow of the explosion that lit the night. It was at least five minutes, though it felt like an hour, before any of us could move as the rain picked up to a driving torrent. Charlie was the last to be fully alert and moving and by then I'd already crawled over the thick earthen berm that had saved our life. The scene before us on the path, or where the path used to be, was illuminated by Dave's flashlight behind me. Where the dynamite had sat was a gaping hole and I saw not sign of the men who had been shooting at us. I knew their remains were likely scattered into the tree tops and for many yards around us. The fate of the two others who had been firing a volley of pistol shots at us took only a bit longer to determine.

As best as we could reconstruct things in the fading light of Dave's flashlight the two men had literally been buried by the explosion which had collapsed the deep ditch in which they had taken shelter. The swath of the ditch where they had taken refuge was filled in, almost as neatly as it done by a bulldozer. There was no trace of the men and as Dave first observed, "Where's the gold?" There was no trace of it either. It mattered not at that point. "We have to get away from here" I told my still shell shocked friends. "The explosion is going to draw the police and no telling who else." We were soon moving rapidly back, via a climb down the railroad bed cut and then south on the tracks to where I hoped Lydia, Sarah and Father Shultz still waited with the wagons and time machines.

We were just emerging from the railroad cut nearing Seventh Street below the Capitol when we heard the clanging of what I suspected were fire bells with likely the fire-fighting equipped wagons racing toward the site of the explosion that had to have been heard over much of the city. The sound was a minor distraction however when we were greeted by a frantic Lydia and Sarah. "Dad, what happened? The explosion, the..., aw geez, you all are Ok?" She was crying when she threw her arms around us.

Taking perhaps two minutes or less to assure Lydia, Sarah and Father Shultz we were OK I left it to Charlie to fill in the details, motioning instead for Dave to help me at the two parked wagons. It was time to go home and I knew time was something we didn't have much of to make an exit. It took perhaps five minutes at most to get the concealment tarps off both time machines and I saw no need to remove them from the wagon beds in order to use them. I turned back to the women and Father Shultz huddled under a large tree, noticing at the same time Sarah begin to move off to the side looking back toward the city and I guess the rectory where I realized she knew she would be returning with Father Shultz but not with Lydia and me.

There wasn't much time but I knew something had to be said and I ran across the open space to try to make some effort at the inevitable closure. "Sarah, I wish I knew what, well if..." She stepped up and took my hands in what could almost be just a sisterly gesture telling me with a quivering voice, "Jack, it's ok, you have to go home and I have to go back home, to Sam. I'll miss you like I can't begin to describe, you and Lydia both but you have to go, go now please." With that she moved further away, putting her back against a tree.

Father Shultz had retreated beneath a large tree away from the wagons, clearly prepared to let us leave without fanfare. I walked over to him, gave him a hug and said, "Father, I cannot thank you enough for all you have done for me and for Lydia. We may not meet again, at least in this world, but we will never forget you." The elderly, now appearing almost frail, Priest said, "You are a good man

Jack, go with God and my prayers for a successful conclusion of this remarkable series of events that I will never forget." With a parting glance, I moved back to the wagons and the time machine.

Dave already had Charlie strapped into one machine and Lydia was strapping down her own self in the second device. There was nothing to do or say but follow their example and I climbed into the wagon and then into the front of the machine in which Lydia occupied the back seat in the missile shaped invention that had so impacted ours, and other lives, over the past few days. Looking at the wagon ahead I could see Dave's outline as he joined his father in the second machine. I leaned slightly forward and flipped the power switch and then the dial to what I knew was the return location to Charlie's lab and the year 2011.

I caught just a glimpse of Father Shultz and Sarah beneath the tree, Sarah with an upraised hand of farewell and quite clearly the priest making the sign of the cross on our behalf. With a start I saw just beyond the two of them coming at a run Police Sargent Brennan yelling something like wait, stop…and then silence. The image was gone a blur as the machine moved first through white light and then a period of darkness.

Chapter 41

THE SUN WAS shining and the steam was rising from what had been an early morning June thunderstorm as Lydia and I stood in Calvary Cemetery, the official Catholic Cemetery of Little Rock since the1800's. We had been back in the year 2011 for two weeks by that time and already the faces and events of our few days in 1911 seemed like an occurrence of literally a century removed rather than of a mere two weeks. Yet the small granite stone partially sunken in the ground before us brought the memories of a battered traveler found in the back yard of a church rectory rushing back into my mind.

Lydia read aloud the words etched in the mossy greren stone, "Ft. Adolphus Schultz born Bermin, Germany 1843 Died Little Rock, Arkansas 1919." Knelling to touch the etched Cross on the stone she added, "He was a lovely, kind man Dad, it's enough to make me want to start going to church again." Helping her back to her feet I could only add, "I think that would really please him Lydia if he is somehow watching over us."

While pondering that thinking from my always surprising daughter my attention was caught by an upright, but leaning, marble stone in an adjoining plot. "Robert C. Newton, Confederate States of America, 1840-1887. I could not help but think, "Captain Newton, I feel as if we have met", recalling the history lesson I was given at the Confederate ball about his ruse that delayed the Yankee invasion of Little Rock for a year.

We were walking back the truck when Lydia asked me a question I wasn't really ready to deal with. "Dad, you want to know what happened to Sarah don't you? We could drive over to Bigelow and...". Taking her hand I said with perhaps more conviction than I felt, "No, I think not, I'd rather trust that she lived a long happy life, that Sam grew up to do great things and that all was right with their world in the decades after we saw them that night in 1911." Maybe I'd change my mind later, but I thought I'd stick with that decision.

The fate of most of the rest of the people we had left two weeks earlier, or almost a century ago in reality, would remain a mystery. Lydia did however do an intertent search on Fred Allsopp and found he lead a long, interesting life after 1911. He later founded a book store on Main Street, Allsopp and Chappell and lived until 1946. Other mysteries remained however that I was intent on trying to resolve. In the days after we returned Lydia, Dave, Charlie and I pulled up the microfiche newspaper stories from the weeks following that May 18th 1911 night at the Capitol. The theft of the gold and the explosion on the slope behind the building was well covered but key questions went without answers. The injured man Dave had unceremoniously deposited in the darkened corner of the steps had been found the next morning but was said to have had a head injury that prevented him from being able to offer the police any details of the evening's events.

Some shattered human remains had been found down the hill, even in the trees, which had of course been the result of the explosion but the names identified two as Jack Hoskins and Ralph Whipple, both of which were well known to law enforcement and I knew they were the two men who had been in front of the dynamite crates. There was however no mention of Gabe Sexton or Henry Cabot, it was if they had never been present. As to the stolen gold, it vanished according to press accounts. A review of two history books spared us anymore eyestrain from the old newspaper archives. The missing gold was never found and the state could not afford to replace it, and hence the Capitol dome remained without a gold sheathing in the 2011 to which we had returned.

As we talked through the events of that May night in1911 and reviewed the press clips available in 2011 we came to the only possible explanation about the gold, and presumably the men, including

Henry Cabot, who were never found. The gold and the remains of the men had to be buried still beneath the now nicely landscaped slope behind the State Capital. The large berm of earth behind which they had taken shelter was at the lip of a deep, wide ditch and the explosion had apparently pushed the berm of dirt into the hole atop Sexton and Cabot.

Knowing this we could have elected to let the men and the gold rest in peace. This wasn't in any of our makeup's, certainly not mine. We spent an evening over beer and pizza and determined an approach to accomplish the mission of finding we hoped the gold not seen for a century.

We were pulling out of Calvary Cemetery into what had to have evolved from country side to a less than attractive urban intercity neighborhood since the day of Father Shultz's funeral. Lydia brought me back to rest of the business of the day with, "What exactly did the Governor say again when you told him he needed to have a big hole dug on the back Capitol lawn.?" For the first time in a hundred years, or I guess two weeks in reality, I laughed. I'd known Mike Beebe for a quarter of a century, long before he became the state's Governor so getting him on the phone a few nights earlier at the Governor's mansion wasn't hard.

"I told him some scattered research I'd pieced together had led me to believe the lost gold intended for the Capitol dome was buried behind the building and that I thought I could pinpoint the location with the right equipment." He laughed, and said, "Damn Doc, you ain't been drinking have you?" We are meeting Charlie and Dave behind the Capitol at noon, the digging should start about 1:00."

When we pulled into a parking spot behind Capitol I saw Dave and Charlie sitting on the back steps we had watched a crowd of bad guys move down with a fortune in stolen gold only two weeks before. As Lydia climbed out of the truck she looked up, taking my arm, and speaking almost to herself. "That's the one I was tied to while they were working on the dynamite inside Dad", and the involuntary shudder moved from her quickly to my own battered but healing body. Putting that aside we moved on to greet our two fellow time travelers who seemed to be in the best of moods, all smiles in fact.

"Hey, Jack, ready to dig for treasure?", was the greeting from Dave. "I've walked down the slope there and I think I know pretty close where that dynamite went off. If the gold is there though there won't be a lot of guess work. The geological survey folks have brought over humdinger of a metal detector, got it mounted on the rear of that little tractor down there next to the big backhoe."

I was looking down the green grassy center lawn surrounded by buildings that had been erected decades after the events of that 1911 stormy night when I heard the familiar booming voice behind me and a firm hand clasping my shoulder. "Doc, you right sure you weren't drinking the other night? I'm going to look a little foolish if all we dig up today is a pile of rocks. The reporters are on their way, word got out somehow. My press guy tried to explain we had big plumbing issue to dig up, but you know those nosy reporters ain't buying it."

"Governor, if we don't find anything but rocks I'll fill the hole back in with a shovel", which was a firmer vow in reply to the states chief executive than I felt in my heart of hearts. Still, the more I'd thought about what could have happened to the gold over the past few days I was ever more certain that it was buried under the well maintained sod on the slope below us. One way or the other we'd soon know. Turning away from the Governor I realized we might know very soon as the small tractor was already slowly moving over the center of the slope pulling the large metal detector behind it. As if drawn by the tractor we all, including the Governor, and behind him a group of a dozen reporters, starting moving down the hill.

We'd been standing under a nearby oak tree watching the search for less than 10 minutes when the driver of the tractor yelled, "Got something on the screen and the signal is screaming in my ear piece." As if on que all us, including the press, moved out next to the tractor and met a geologist coming from the other side of the lawn. The man climbed up on the platform holding the mounted detector and looked down at I guess a computer screen. "Man, something is metal down about six feet and whatever it is it's big."

With that declaration he planted a bright orange flag and signaled for the backhoe operator who had been patiently waiting in the shade. Caution took hold of my emotions, after all there used to be a Civil War era prison on this site and I remembered the brick walls and debris from that 1911 night when bullets were flying. Still, I couldn't contain my excitement any more than could Lydia who was hanging onto Dave Rawlins arm as if an anchor to keep her from sailing off.

    The big backhoe took huge bites out of the ground, slowing just long enough to swing its arm to the side and drop the load across a hastily erected orange security tape the workers had circled the excavation site with. The operator of the machine had studied the metal detectors captured image before starting and seemed to have a good idea how wide and deep he intended to dig.

    He initially dug down only about four feet to open up roughly a square about ten feet by ten feet and then he began to dig deeper into the center. We were all sweating in the June heat but I may have been sweating as much from the apprehension as I watched the Governor peering toward the center of the hole, looking like something out of GQ, having not even loosened his tie. Looking over at me he laughed, "We can find you a shovel Doc, figure would take you about a week to fill this hole back in."

    I needn't have worried about shovel handle induced blisters. A gasp went through the circled crowd when the third load of dumped dirt from the center of the hold delivered a grinning skull peering from the dirt and rocks. It took only an instant longer for the blazing sun to be reflected off a gold bar partially exposed next to the skull. I was totally oblivious by then to the TV news cameras rolling on all sides of the excavation. A State Policeman, from I guess the Governor's security detail, stepped over the security banner at that point bringing the work of the backhoe to a halt. From there the trooper moved over to confer with the Governor and I was sure the human remains had changed the way the rest of the hole was going to be dug.

    My assumption was confirmed as the Governor walked over to pull me aside. "Doc, the trooper says since that skull turned up we have a potential crime scene and the rest of the digging is going to have to be done more careful with shovels and hand tools." I understood and concurred as additional state troopers appeared trying to get the press to move back toward the Capitol building, with only limited success and the cameras kept rolling and a couple of the newspaper reporters tried to shout questions to Governor and even to me. The security tape was expanded considerably which helped push the crowd further back while a crew from somewhere appeared wearing coveralls and carrying shovels.

The digging lasted the rest of the day and into the night with portable spotlights being employed. Lydia, Dave, Charlie and I had stayed for the entire process, retreating into the Capitol on occasion for a drink or to visit the facilities. The Governor had moved onto other appointments but rejoined us at around 8:00 that night. The press never left, their numbers only grew. From somewhere a film crew for CNN and one from FOX news appeared. I later learned both were in town for some event at the Clinton Library. It was clear that the ratings would be high as I surveyed to results of the careful digging and sifting of soil that had gone on for almost eight hours but which seemed to be coming to an end.

What we witnessed, and what I guessed TV viewers around the world were seeing, was the macabre display of two broken skeletons spread out on tarps. I knew the old bones had to be what remained Sexton and Cabot. In stark contrast and adding greatly to the fascination I knew the story was going to draw, the Governor, coming up behind me, slapping me on the back said, "Damn Doc, you were right. I'm getting ready to have a press conference up on the steps, and I've got to thank you."

I was about to turn away when Lydia grabbed my arm, "Look Dad, next to the second skeleton, it's a sword, I bet it's....." I finished the sentence for her, "Yes, I bet that's General Robert E. Lee's sword." Stolen from the display window of a Main Street jewelry store almost a century ago the sword had found its way back along with the bones of the man who had stolen it. I thought we had all had enough excitement for one night, enough for a lifetime for that matter, and I talked every one into going home, we decided to read about the Governor's remarks in the morning paper.

Postscript

A WEEK AFTER the unearthing of the gold and the skeletons, we were gathered for dinner at Bosco's on President Clinton Avenue, seated out on the balcony overlooking the river. Lydia, Dave, Charlie and I had gathered to pay what I thought of as a final tribute to the adventure of multiple lifetimes and to people like Father Shultz, Sarah and all the others we had met a century before. We also had a bit of literal fortune to celebrate. The recovered gold had a reported value of some $60,000 in 1911. It's value, however, in 2011 was almost $1,800 an ounce, with a total value of well over $7 million. We discussed why Sexton and Cabot took such chances for "only" $60,000 before conjecturing they would have carried forward the gold in time to capture a more modern selling price. Through some arcane law, the Governor and the Attorney General had determined I was to get a reward of a $1 million dollars for recovery of the publicly-owned gold. I'd divided it into equal shares between the four of us. This windfall enabled Lydia not worry about finding a job for a while.

The medical examiner's evaluation of the unearthed skeletons was in the news the previous day. He had determined the bones had been in the ground for around 100 years, yet two of them were found to have indications of modern dental work. How they – with their modern fillings - came to be buried with gold stolen in 1911 was a mystery that we agreed was going to take more than even Sherlock Holmes could solve. We certainly had no intention of shedding light on that mystery.

As to the gold, it was deemed much too valuable to apply to the Capitol dome, as had been the intention in 1911. Instead the Governor decided to invest the proceeds into a college fund to recruit physicians willing to work in rural areas of Arkansas upon graduation. I had made that suggestion, but advised Governor Beebe to take all the credit, leaving me out of the announcement. It did, indeed, make for great press.

Lydia had opened an envelope and was passing around postcards she had obtained a century earlier, which led to a bit of discussion about what we had seen that wasn't around today. Lydia stopped a comment I was about to make in midstream, "Hey Dad, you could write a book about our adventure and use these postcards to illustrate it." My delayed retort was, "only if we call it fiction, so that I don't get committed to the state hospital." A book? I didn't think so… at least at the time…but years later, I changed my mine.

At that point I reached into my pocket and pulled out a folded envelope, cleared faded and fragile with time which bore in neat ink script, "to only be opened by Dr. Jack Kernick". Opening it and removing a hand written letter on faded paper I explained, "This was written by Father Shultz on May 28, 1911, ten days after we returned to 2011. It was enclosed inside a larger envelope he had left in care of St. Edwards with instructions to hold in the church until May 28, 2011 when it was to be delivered to Dr. Jack Kernick of Little Rock." Apparently each successive Pastor after Father Shultz had let the envelope lay in the rectory without yielding to curiosity to break the wax seal. "A young Priest handed me this letter at Mass the other day, just saying this is for you, Dr. Kernick".

I read the letter aloud: "My dear friend Jack, I trust this note will find its way into your hands, as I've entrusted it to the Priests who will come after me for the next century. I wasn't sure, but expected that you saw policeman Brennan heading your way when you and the others disappeared that night. We had quite the conversation with him when he demanded to know what happened to you, how you disappeared, and what role you might have played in the explosions over at the Capitol. What could I say? I just said you and Lydia had gone home and there wasn't really much more I could add. He clearly wasn't going to arrest an old Priest, and I think he knew nobody would believe he had watched all of you disappear in a blinding white light like the Protestant rapture."

"You will, I'm sure, have read the old newspaper accounts upon returning to your time and realized the extent of the confusion about what happened. The gold was not found, but I surmised it was buried by the explosion and I chose to keep that to myself and allow you to decide how to handle that in your own 2011. The police found the ropes and ladder leading down to the railroad tracks and made the assumption the gold was carried away by train. The train was stopped and searched somewhere close to Pine Bluff but all they found was an unlocked boxcar. After you and the others left, it began to rain and poured all night. This seemed to wash a lot of loose dirt and mud into the trench, and I guess it sealed up the gold chests to the point where the muddy ground was pretty much leveled by daylight when the police began to go over the scene. And Jack, honestly, the idea of a bunch of politicians gold plating a building just seemed like a bad use of wealth in a poor state like Arkansas. If you have not already done so, my guess is you will determine where the gold went and make the right decisions. God Bless you, Lydia and your friends when you read this. May we all meet again in Heaven."

After we drank a toast to Father Shultz in the silence of our collected thoughts, Lydia asked me. "Dad, knowing everything you know now, would you do it again? If you could, would you let Charlie send you back ever again?" I guess my answer was not forthcoming so she added, "Do you think about even now going back to 1911?" Rather than answer, I turned my chair a bit and stared out at the Arkansas River, the same river I'd crossed less than 30 days before on a hot 1911 night, seated on a wagon bearing tents intended to shelter the remnants of the Confederate army... I was going to have to think about the question for a while – maybe a long while.